WILLIAM WILDE
AND THE
SONS OF DECEIT

THE CHRONICLES OF
WILLIAM WILDE

DAVIS ASHURA

DuSum Publishing, LLC

To my sons once again, although thankfully, they aren't deceitful. They're merely unusual and nerdy.

ACKNOWLEDGMENTS

I have many people I need to thank for this book. It starts with my family, who continue to give me the time to write. Even more amazing, a few of them want to become creators of their own stories.

There's also my office staff. They put up with my pesky habits and behavior. They don't even mind much when I make a note of any funny or odd utterances that they make.

There are the friends I've made in the Terrible Ten, the terriblest Slack group out there. In the group, I have to thank the inestimable Phil Tucker for inviting me into the group. Then there's also Bryce O'Connor and Dyrk Ashton. You guys don't know how much spending DragonCon with you meant to me. To say it was life changing and maybe even life saving isn't an exaggeration.

I can't forget my writing group, the CVAKWG (Catawba Valley Ass-Kicking Writer's Group). We've been stumbling by for the past ten years now, solving the worlds problems and doing everything but talk about our writing. But that's ok. It's more fun that way.

I can't forget my editors, Diann Read and Tom Burkhalter. The two of you helped take a rough piece of work and helped me make it so much better than it ever could have been.

THE PILGRIMAGE SO FAR

William Wilde and the Necrosed

In the winter of his junior year of high school, William Wilde is orphaned by what's thought to be a simple car accident on an ice-slick road in Ohio. The truth, however, is far different. His family—his parents and his brother—are murdered by Kohl Obsidian. The creature is a necrosed, an undead, shambling monster akin to a zombie who seeks and destroys anyone who possess magic. William is one such individual, although he doesn't know it. In addition, his magic is unprimed and quiescent, and as a result, Kohl lets the boy live. The necrosed reasons that he can consume William once his magic awakens. However, Kohl uses his own dark magic to change William, making him sturdier and stronger but also more prone to anger.

William recalls none of this. His memory of the accident is absent. All he knows is that his parents and his brother are both dead. He has a choice now, and rather than move in with distant aunts of uncles, William chooses to remain in his hometown of Cincinnati, Ohio. He

1

moves in with his best friend, Jason Jacobs, and Jason's grandfather, Mr. Zeus, and life eventually continues.

However, life changes for everyone on the first day of William's senior year of high school at St. Francis, He meets a new girl then, Serena Paradiso. She's beautiful and mysterious, and most exciting of all, she seems to enjoy William's company. She is accepted by all of William's friends, including Daniel Karllson and Lien Sun, a Chinese foreign exchange student who lives with Daniel's family. But Serena has secrets. She has been set to spy on William and his friends. She knows that William possesses magic, and she is expected to help steal him or it. She answers to Adam Paradiso, a man who she introduces as her father, but who is actually her Isha, the person tasked with completing her training. Serena is on her pilgrimage from the island of Sinskrill, and William is her final test to see her rise to the rank of mahavan, a Sinskrill master.

William, Jason, and the others, including Mr. Zeus, are unaware of Serena's actual motivations and take her into their homes and hearts. This causes Serena a great deal of doubt and remorse. She enjoys the company of William and his friends, their banter, and their obvious friendship and love for one another. She wishes she didn't have to deceive them. Her home of Sinskrill is a hard place, and this is the first time she's ever experienced such interactions. However, her path is set. She has to complete her pilgrimage. If not, her younger sister, Selene, might pay the price for her failure.

As the late summer turns to fall, the school year progresses and William is confronted by his long-time nemesis, Jake Ridley, a bully and a popular boy at school. Their disagreement results in Jake's suspension from the football team for a number of games. The team goes on to lose those games, and William is blamed for the losses. Desperate to make amends, he and Jason join the football team, and William manages to salvage the season. As a result, he and Jake reach a détente. However, William's passion and fury during the times he played also reawakens Kohl Obsidian, who had resumed his slumber after murdering William's parents and brother. The necrosed sets off to hunt William down.

After the football season, Mr. Zeus explains the truth to William.

He explains that he and Jason are *asrasins*. They can master *asra*—magic—that they are from Arylyn, a hidden paradise. They explain that William has magic, and they were sent to test him, to see if he's worthy of joining their island. Daniel, Lien, and Daniel's parents are also magi and accompanied Mr. Zeus and Jason for the same purpose. Mr. Zeus and Jason also explain about the ongoing war between magi and mahavans, between Arylyn and Sinskrill. *Asrasins* from Arylyn are known as magi while those from Sinskrill are called mahavans.

It is much to take in, and William is furious that he was lied to and astonished to learn that he's an *asrasin*, someone who can master *asra*—magic. He eventually forgives Mr. Zeus and the others for their deceit, accepting their need for secrecy. In addition, he understands that more will be revealed during the Christmas holidays at a *saha'asra*—a place of magic—in West Virginia, a wild meadow in the woods.

However, shortly after their arrival to the *saha'asra*, Kohl Obsidian, who had been tracking William, attacks. Mr. Zeus, Daniel, and Lien escape to Arylyn by means of an anchor line.

William, Jason, and Serena are unable to follow and flee from Kohl, barely escaping the necrosed's claws. William is confronted with further hard truths. His magic has awakened, and he can no longer stay for long in the Far Beyond, the world beyond the borders of Arylyn and Sinskrill. In addition, during the attack in West Virginia, Kohl Obsidian touched William. He can sense the presence of the necrosed. The creature has also touched Serena.

William, Jason, and Serena drive to Cincinnati, seeking to regroup and flee farther from Kohl. Serena, maintaining the web of lies that she's a simple high school senior rather than a denizen of Sinskrill, is forced to go with them since Kohl has touched her as well. She pretends fury at the events that have occurred and all the times William didn't tell her about magic. She claims William lied to her.

As they prepare to leave Cincinnati, Kohl attacks once again. This time his presence is witnessed by Jake Ridley and his friends, late at night in a darkened park. William, Jason, and Serena battle him and manage to escape once again. They drive into the night, putting miles between themselves and the necrosed.

However, Kohl can also travel by anchor lines, the mystical links

3

that connect various *saha'asras*. He's able to transport himself instantly from one part of the world to another. As a result, they have to avoid the anchor lines, including any that might transport them to Arylyn and safety.

William comes up with the bright idea of joining a circus, *Wizard Bill's Wandering Wonders*, to hide from Kohl Obsidian. The necrosed doesn't like large animals, and *Wizard Bill's* has plenty of them, including elephants and bears. During their time in the circus, Serena forgives William for lying to her. They grow closer, but all the while, it is Serena who is lying. Remorse rises within her at what she's doing to William.

Their time in the circus introduces them to Elaina Sinith, a young woman who states that she's a witch from a village called Sand. She claims that William's brother, Landon, is still alive and seems to sense the truth about Serena. William and the others are discomfited by her presence.

They eventually leave the circus in Arizona. This had always been their intention, to journey to a *saha'asra* that contains an anchor line connected to Arylyn. During the long drive to the *saha'asra*, they encounter a kitten named Aia. She can speak to them telepathically, a talent Jason has never known anyone to possess. Neither has Serena.

They bring the kitten along since she states that 'the Shining Man' placed her in their path in order to help them with their task. She also claims they'll have help defeating Kohl.

They eventually reach the *saha'asra*, and Kohl is waiting for them. He's tracked their movements through the connection he has with William and Serena. A battle ensues, and during the heart of it, a man steps through the anchor line.

It is Landon Wilde, William's brother. During the long ago attack on William's family, Kohl shredded Landon's memories, his sense of self, replacing them somewhat with who the necrosed had once been, a holder named Pilot Vent. The necrosed was certain Landon would die shortly thereafter. Instead, Landon somehow lived through the torment. His sense of self fuses with that of Pilot and a new being arises: Landon Vent, the first holder in generations, and the only being who can kill a necrosed. The battle resumes, and William and

4

Landon, working together finally manage to kill Kohl with strange lightning that pours off William's hands.

After the battle's conclusion, Mr. Zeus arrives through the anchor line. William has a choice of whether to go to Arylyn now or wait a little longer. He chooses the latter. He wants to finish high school first.

~

William Wilde and the Stolen Life

William and his friends have returned to St. Francis after the terrifying events of the Christmas holidays. They return more sober and with a greater sense of age in comparison to their fellow students. Right before the beginning of the school day, they meet with Jake Ridley and several of his friends in the parking lot, including Sonya Bowyer and Steve Aldo. William has long had a crush on Sonya, but those feelings wasted away when Serena entered his life.

All seems normal. Jake and his friends appear to have no recollection of Kohl Obsidian. Jason tells William why. Mr. Zeus visited everyone who'd seen Kohl Obsidian and placed a weave, a magical spell, on them that obscured their remembrances of that night. However, Jake *does* remember, and he knows that everyone else doesn't. He stares after William and his friends and wonders who or what they really are.

The school year progresses, and Jake remains cordial, although he shocks William with his knowledge of *Lord of the Rings*. Later, some of the seniors are tasked with cleaning a church in Over-the-Rhine, Cincinnati's ghetto, as part of a field trip. Within the parish hall, they catch sight of Jessira, a tall, blonde freshman they'd met at the beginning of the school year. With her is an Indian-appearing young man who moves with the deadly grace of a leopard. His name is Rukh

Shektan. The two freshmen are striking in attitude, seemingly years older and more mature than even the seniors.

Weeks later, William comes across information about what might have happened to him in the *saha'asra* in West Virginia. Ever since Kohl's attack, William has come to the realization that he's now far faster and stronger than anyone he knows. He learns that Kohl's blood might have mingled with his own during that battle. It would explain the changes in him. He also learns that if Kohl's blood did infect him, his fate might be to either die, be transformed into a necrosed, or have unspecified changes occur to him.

Worse, Jake confronts him, explaining that he knows the truth about the night when Kohl attacked everyone in the park. Jake demands answers, and William reluctantly agrees to bring him to Mr. Zeus. Events continue to accelerate. Jason also discovers the truth about the blood of a necrosed, and he and Mr. Zeus test William. They find him clear of corruption, but Kohl's blood *has* changed him. Thankfully, though, the only changes are the ones William already knows: he's stronger and faster than most everyone else.

During all of this, Serena continues to struggle with her deception toward William and his friends. However, she doesn't know what else to do. While telling Mr. Zeus the truth might earn her safety on Arylyn, what of her sister, Selene? Her life might be forfeit if Serena makes such an attempt. Isha demands that Serena learn just what kind of *asrasin* William might become. They suspect he might have it in him to become a *raha'asra*, a powerful, rare person who can create *lorasra*, the magical essence *asrasins* require to keep themselves alive as well as the means by which they create their weaves and braids.

Isha's suspicions prove correct, and Serena discovers something else: Jake is also a potential *raha'asra*. It is an amazing find, one that will grant both her and Isha great success in Serena's bishan pilgrimage. Isha is overjoyed and plans how to steal the two young *raha'asras* to Sinskrill.

Jake has dinner with Mr. Zeus, William, and Jason and is told the truth about *asrasins* and Arylyn. He takes the information well but needs time to figure out what to do with it. After the evening meal, Jake's car won't start, and William offers to take him home. On the way, Serena, Isha, and mahavans from Sinskrill attack and capture them. They whisk them away to Sinskrill by anchor line.

Sinskrill exists in the Norwegian Sea, a stony island held tight in the iron-fisted rule of the Servitor, Serena's true father. Serena is greeted warmly on her return to the mahavan island while William and Jake glare daggers at her. Hate for her has rightfully spawned in both their hearts. In addition, it seems that Adam Paradiso is actually Serena's paternal uncle, the Servitor's true brother.

William and Jake are given tasks to perform upon their arrival to Sinskrill. They work as farmers, something akin to drones, the peasants who make up most of Sinskrill's population. They will only be accorded greater rights and status if they master their *asra*.

Their instructor in this is Fiona Applefield, Sinskrill's only *raha'asra* and a hard-hearted women of limited patience. She torments rather than teaches. Her brutish techniques almost result in William's and Jake's death at the claws and teeth of the unformed. Like necrosed, elves, and dwarves, unformed are woven, creatures of magic. In this case, the unformed are wild, untamed, intelligent beings who can take on the shape of any animal. They have long been a source of danger upon Sinskrill.

Weeks pass, and Serena accepts William's and Jake's hate for her, but she still deeply regrets what's happened to them. She seeks a way to help them. The easiest is protecting them, something she can only do if she attains higher rank within the mahavan community. She cultivates allies in Brandon Thrum and Evelyn Mason, two young, ambitious mahavans. In addition, Serena speaks to Travail, a troll— also a woven—trapped on Sinskrill to take on the task of instructing William and Jake. He agrees.

Events come to a boil when William and Jake are involved in a fight with a drone supervisor by the name of Justin Finch. On Sinskrill it is a grave sin for someone of lower rank to strike someone of higher rank but matters in this case are confusing. William and Jake are akin to drones but also potential *raha'asras*. A compromise is reached. Justin is removed from his role as a supervisor, but Jake is lashed, a terrible punishment.

The punishment is thankfully interrupted by Travail who has

claimed William and Jake as his students. As such, he states that only he has the right to mete out justice to them. Nevertheless, Jake is gravely wounded by the lashing.

Meanwhile, on Arylyn, Mr. Zeus and Jason search for how to save William and Jake. They understand that Serena and her so-called father were agents of Sinskrill and that she helped kidnap the young men. However, no magi has ever discovered the location of the mahavan home island, just as no mahavan has ever discovered Arylyn. Mr. Zeus has a plan, though. He long ago gave William a *nomasra*, an object imbued with *lorasra*. This particular *nomasra* is basically a magical beacon, and Mr. Zeus might be able to track William down with it. In addition, there are two new members of the Arylyn community: Rukh and Jessira. They are bizarre to Jason since they both seem to have taken to swords and fighting like an eagle takes to the skies.

On Sinskrill, Travail begins instructing William and Jake, after the latter has healed from his injuries. He is a gentle and wise instructor, and they quickly learn to trust him.

Serena visits them now and then. She does so under the orders of the Servitor and reports back on William and Jake's progress. In addition, she also harbors a dream to escape Sinskrill. The island was never the home of her heart, but she now sees a way out. She can sail away on her dhow, *Blue Sky Dreams*, and carry with her Selene, Jake, and William. However, they can't simply sail into the say with no place of safety awaiting them. As *asrasins* none of them can long live in the Far Beyond. They need to get to Arylyn. Serena reasons that William can likely contact Mr. Zeus through a dream, a means of communications amongst *asrasins* who are either family or very close. *Blue Sky Dreams* can get them free of Sinskrill, and Mr. Zeus can bring them the rest of the way o Arylyn.

William and Jake know nothing of her plan and tolerate her presence. However, they make no effort to hide their hatred for her whenever she visits them at Travail's field. William's feelings for her begin to change, though, when Serena asks him to help her restore *Blue Sky Dreams*, which has fallen into disrepair. He does so and ends up meeting Selene, Serena's little sister. Selene is a young girl of around ten and innocent, and William now understands why Serena did as she did. While he can't bring himself to forgive her, he at least understands her motivations. He also picks up on Serena's hints of escaping from Sinskrill. Later on, Jake meets Selene, too, and is also made aware of Serena's plans. His raw hatred toward Serena softens as well.

Other secrets are revealed to William and Jake. They learn that Fiona's grim, unforgiving persona had all been a ruse. Fiona hates Sinskrill. She'd been kidnapped to the island decades earlier and also trained by Travail. She has witnessed her children die, some of them horrifically, and the only light in her life is Serena and Selene, her true grand-daughters, although they are initially unaware of their familial ties with her. She and Travail had conceived a plan to have William and Jake placed in his care. It's where they will be safest. She is a much more caring individual now, and the change in her behavior is remarkable.

William and Jake come to care for Fiona. However, while she wishes she could come with them and flee Sinskrill, she cannot. She wears a *nomasra* necklace that only the Servitor can remove. It will sever her head if she ever leaves Sinskrill. Travail can't leave either. He has a deep terror of the ocean and would likely tear *Blue Sky Dreams* apart if he were in it on the sea.

On Arylyn, Mr. Zeus gains a sense of Sinskrill's location and convinces the Village Council to let him lead a rescue attempt. They'll travel by anchor line to the Faroe Islands, and from there, journey to Sinskrill by ship. With him will go Jason, Daniel, a magus named Julius, and Rukh and Jessira. The latter, despite their youth—they're still nominally freshmen—are revealed to be husband and wife and have matured rapidly. They now have the appearance of folk in their mid-twenties and proven themselves superlative warriors.

Mr. Zeus and William have also been able to share dreams. Both are aware of the others plans and work to co-ordinate their actions.

On Sinskrill, Serena is led by Selene to grasp hold of Shet's Spear. When she does so, her Spirit is transported to the mythical world of Seminal. There, she is confronted by Lord Shet, the god of all mahavans. He is tied to a mountain with chains thick as an oak and black as his heart. From him billows a river of *lorasra* that somehow crosses the vastness between worlds. He is the true reason for Sinskrill's depth of *lorasra*. In addition, Shet promises to break the chains that bind him, enslave Seminal, and then come for Earth. He pronounces five years as the time for when he will arrive on Earth, his home.

Serena escapes back to Sinskrill, shaken and horrified. In addition, she is later attacked by an unformed bear, but William manages to save her. He burns the creature with a bright weave of Fire. Serena later learns that her father is also an unformed, and so is Adam Paradiso, her once-Isha.

It is enough to spark terror in Serena's heart. She and the others have to go. They flee, but their plan is found out. Isha confronts Serena before she can escape the Servitor's Palace, but Fiona knocks him unconscious. Serena then races away with Selene to where *Blue Sky Dreams* is moored. They escape Sinskrill, fighting their way to freedom.

By now, Mr. Zeus, Jason, and the others have arrived by yacht on Sinskrill. They originally land on the island but are discovered by unformed, who apparently serve the Servitor. Rukh and Jessira prove their worth by protecting the small band of would-be rescuers. After their detection by the unformed, Mr. Zeus' group re-embarks upon their ship and plan their next more.

It is then that Mr. Zeus realizes the *nomasra* he gave William is moving rapidly. He realizes that William is upon a boat, and they set themselves to intercept.

But they aren't the only ones. The Servitor in his flagship, *Demolition*, also gives chase. William and Jake use *raha'asra* weaves that can empty *lorasra* from parts of a *saha'asra*. The braids slow *Demolition*, allowing William and his friends to join with Mr. Zeus on his ship.

The Servitor doesn't give up, though, and a battle ensues. Once again, Rukh and Jessira prove their worth, arrowing a number of mahavans and putting them out of the fray. They also display unusual talents, ones no one has ever seen. They form shields and hurl balls of fire. However, it is William who overcomes the Servitor's final attack. The mahavans are forced to retreat, and William and the others celebrate their freedom.

They return to Arylyn, and there, weeks after their escape, William tells Serena of his plans for the future. His feelings toward her remain cool, but he also recognizes that Serena needs a purpose. William asks her to join him in his: he intends on returning to Sinskrill and rescuing Travail and Fiona.

～

W*illiam Wilde and the Unusual Suspects*

While William is determined to return to Sinskrill and save Travail and Fiona, he and Jake continue to struggle with the horror of their lives on Sinskrill. It is understandable and while Mr. Zeus has helped alleviate some of their terrible memories, nightmares still haunt them.

One thing that helps is that the two of them maintain the running ritual that Travail had instilled in them. Joining them are Jason and Daniel, both of who are stunned by the changes in William's strength and stamina.

In addition, they are also expected to attend classes and learn about Arylyn's history and culture. Joining them is Serena, and Jason occasionally acts as their instructor. During one lesson, they learn about Lord Shet's great enemies: Shokan, the Lord of the Sword, and his wife, Sira, the Lady of Fire. Legend states that they killed Shet and were instrumental in the founding of Arylyn. Serena doesn't believe the story because she's met Shet. She knows that mahavan god lives and that he's coming back in five years. Her statement is met with disbelief and derision by Jason, but William and Jake think otherwise. They believe Serena.

However, belief doesn't equal trust. William and Jake have learned to accept Serena's actions, but they remain cool and distant with her. Cruel even, but Serena handles their barbs with mahavan-coolness. She lets nothing touch her heart, telling herself it's a stone. It's a lie, and she knows it.

Seeking to find a place of belonging, although she would never put it that way, Serena seeks out Lien and learns to play enrune, Arylyn's national sport. While Lien isn't exactly friendly, she does offer Serena a small olive branch. It's the first time she's found acceptance on Arylyn.

However, before she can take part in any games, another task is set before her, William, and Jake. They must travel the island and meet with the Memories of the two races that once shared Arylyn with the *asrasins*: the elves and dwarves. It's the magi pilgrimage, and William and Serena travel together under the guidance of Daniel's mother, Trase.

William meets the Elven Memory and discovers something of the history of that fallen woven race. No elves remain on Earth. Next, he meets the Dwarven Memory, which exists within the dead dwarven village of Meldencreche, in the heart of Mount Madhava, the tallest mountain on Arylyn. The dwarves possess a peace that extends to any who linger near them. They also honor humans exuberantly. William finds himself melancholy upon leaving Meldencreche.

Meeting him to bring him home is Serena. Trase Karllson was called away to another task. William and Serena argue, but in the end, she apologizes for what she did. She never had before, and it thaws some of William's feelings toward her. It's an important step for them, and them both seem to understand it.

Once they return to Lilith, the only village on Arylyn, they have a few weeks before they must resume their work since Jake is yet to finish his pilgrimage. During this restful time, they learn to surf, Serena under the tutelage of Jean-Paul Gascon, a flamboyant Frenchman, and William under Jason's instruction. In addition, Serena learns to play enrune, which she loves.

William and Jake's training resumes, and they take instruction from Arylyn's two *raha'asras*, both of who are elderly: Sioned O'Sullivan and Afa Simon. They take a liking to both of them, and Jake quickly learns to use his abilities, forming braids easily. William, though, struggles. He cannot master the simplest of weaves.

During all this, Selene, the young girl William and Jake have come to think as a little sister, struggles to fit in to Arylyn. She is unable to make friends, but eventually she finds her way. One afternoon,

William picks her up from school and drops her off with Serena. It's another small moment of peace between the two of them.

While William continues to struggle with his mastery of *asra*, he hasn't forgotten about Travail and Fiona. He also grows increasingly sure that Seminal is real, that Shet is real, and that he's coming. He devises a means to test some ideas that might put flesh on his notions. It will require visiting a *saha'asra* linked to Sinskrill, and Mr. Zeus eventually agrees to let him do so. However, he'll take to come up with a competent group to accompany him.

First on William's list is Rukh and Jessira. Serena accompanies him when he asks them. They readily agree, and a large group, including William, Rukh, Jessira, Daniel, Jason, and Mr. Zeus make the journey. They travel to a *saha'asra* in Australia where William's theory is proven correct. It isn't definitive proof of Seminal, but it is a strong hint. However, shortly after arrive, mahavans attack. Rukh and Jessira single handedly defeat them. The Servitor arrives, and they flee before him, barely escaping with their lives.

They return to Arylyn, and life progresses. William, who was useless in the fight since he can't form any braids on command, is eventually sent to learn from Ward Silver. He makes immediate progress and is overjoyed. Serena takes up farming with Sile Troy. She learned gardening from her deceased birth mother, and something about the soil, growth, and life calls to her soul. She loves it. Jake wants to master a weave that will allow him to go home and see his family.

They each manage to achieve these small victories. In addition, William spends more time with Serena when she teaches him to sail his newly built dhow, *Blue Sky Dreamer*. He finally forgives her, and they develop a fragile friendship that slowly deepens.

All of them continue to learn to fight and prepare for the assault on Sinskrill. Their desires gain a new urgency when Serena receives a dream from Adam Paradiso, her Isha. In it, he tells her Seminal and Shet. Both are real, and the mahavan god will return to Earth as he'd promised Serena, four years hence.

They manage to convince the Village Council of the rightness of their actions and their plan and earn their blessing.

It will be a difficult undertaking. Traveling to Sinskrill will be William, Serena, Rukh, Jessira, Mr. Zeus, and Julius O'Brien, the same magus who helped in the rescue of William and Jake. And journeying to Australia are Jake, Jason, Daniel, Lien, and Daniel's parents.

A near disaster occurs when Mr. Zeus and Fiona are captured on the cusp of freedom. However, Rukh and Jessira free them. During all this, William and Serena link up with Travail, and the seven of them attempt to flee through Sinskrill's anchor line. The Servitor, the only one who can open it, does so when Jake's group enters the *saha'asra* in Australia that's linked to Sinskrill.

The battle is fierce, and in the end Fiona and Travail manage to escape from Sinskrill. It almost costs Jake his life. He takes a thrust through the heart, courtesy of Adam Paradiso, who is now the Secondus, likely the next Servitor upon his brother's death.

Jake barely survives, only doing so thanks to the actions of Jessira and Rukh. Again, the two possess skills no one else does. They have a weave, a Healing, that manages to keep Jake alive.

The Healing also allows Jake to see part of their lives. Later, after he recovers somewhat, he asks Rukh and Jessira about the visions he saw. In them, he saw Rukh and Jessira held in adulation and standing on the hills of different world.

Rukh finally agrees to tell William, Jake, and Serena about his and Jessira's past, about their previous lives on a world called Arisa.

However, all is not well because the Servitor is determined to have his revenge upon Arylyn. Twice the magi have stolen what he considers his property, and they must pay. And they will because the Servitor has discovered Arylyn's location.

CHAPTER 1: RECOVERED CHOICES

S*eptember 1989*

Serena Paradiso paused to take a breather from tilling Sile's garden. She glared balefully all about her. The blazing hot, humid day and backbreaking labor had her heart drumming rapidly, and she gulped in deep lungfuls of air. Perspiration beaded uncomfortably on her forehead, dripping down her face, shoulders, and chest. The sweat soaked her shirt, and she fanned herself, trying to cool off. She hated this kind of weather. It always left her sapped of energy.

She cast her view west again, checking the time. The sun hung a few fingers' width above the horizon. Twilight approached, and with it relief from this heat.

Thank God.

A stray breeze stirred Serena's hair then, curling it about her face and obscuring her vision. She cleared it off but an instant later it happened again. This time Serena leaned her hoe against her hip, pulled out an elastic band from her pants pocket, and tied her hair off into a ponytail. She also gave her back a muscle-easing arch before resuming tilling the soil.

She had agreed to tend Sile's garden while he did the harder work of planting the fields, and Ms. Sioned had decided to help her out. Serena was grateful for the old *raha'asra's* assistance. Sile's garden was huge. It was an acre of rectangular dirt framed by several rows of bricks, which usually contained tomatoes and other vegetables that Sile shared with anyone who asked and took hours of hard labor to ready for the next round of plantings.

As Serena tilled, she glanced at Ms. Sioned, who worked in silence with her head bent and a thoughtful frown on her face. The other woman acted as if something troubled her, and Serena wondered why. It wasn't like Ms. Sioned to carry such a burden of worry. More commonly the small, white-haired woman had features that held a gentle, generous smile.

But not today.

Serena studied Ms. Sioned a moment longer. She remembered how kind the sweet, old lady had been to her after her arrival to Arylyn. She'd had faith in Serena, trusting her words to be true when few others did. Ms. Sioned never lifted her eyes from her work. She hadn't done so the entire afternoon. In fact, thus far, she and Serena hadn't shared more than a few words.

What's bothering her?

Serena shook off her thoughts and returned to tilling. Minutes later her attention wandered again when the singing of Jennifer Troy, Sile's wife, carried on a stray breeze. Jennifer sang a lively song about summer, sunshine, and waves, and Serena smiled. Sile's wife had a lovely voice.

She was also an excellent baker, and the scent of fresh-made bread wafted from the white, clapboard farmhouse standing on a nearby rise. The aroma was carried on the same stray breeze as Jennifer's singing. Serena's stomach growled. She not only needed a break from the heat, she also needed food. But her hunger would have to wait. Only a little bit longer and they'd have the garden finished.

Serena never broke off her hoeing and actually found herself working in time to Jennifer's singing, cutting through the detritus, digging into the dirt, and levelling it out.

Eventually, her mind moved away from thoughts of fatigue and hunger and drifted to other, more important matters, such as going sailing tonight with William.

"You seem pleased," Ms. Sioned said in her Irish lilt.

Serena's eyes widened in surprise.

"You were humming," the other woman explained. "You only do so when you're happy."

Serena smiled, a true expression of her feelings rather than the feigned emotions she'd often used in the past to accomplish her purposes. Part of her mahavan training. Nowadays Serena was glad of the more natural reaction.

"I *am* happy," Serena replied, explaining the plan about sailing with William.

Ms. Sioned nodded. "I'm glad the two of you are spending so much time together."

Serena maintained a nonchalant air even as suspicion swept over her. While Ms. Sioned's words indicated approval, her posture and visage spoke differently. They told of something negative, but Serena wasn't entirely sure what. She decided to take a direct approach to find out. "Does it bother you that William and I spend so much time together? I know you advised against it before we saved Fiona and Travail, but what about now?"

Ms. Sioned ceased her tilling and muttered something unintelligible before bracing the hoe's blade on the dark soil. She rested her hands upon the tool's knobby handle and smiled wanly. "There is no hiding my emotions from you, is there, dear?"

Serena dipped her head in silent acknowledgement, and her wariness rose further. Whatever Ms. Sioned wanted to say, Serena realized she wouldn't like it. Maybe that was why the other woman had remained so unaccountably quiet and unhappy throughout the afternoon.

"I have worries about you and William," Ms. Sioned began. She hesitated. Her lips twisted, and she conveyed the impression of searching for the right words.

17

Serena remained quiet while waiting for Ms. Sioned to explain herself.

When the old *raha'asra* finally spoke, she surprised Serena with a question. "What do you know about this Lord Shet?"

Serena frowned, unsure as to the purpose of Ms. Sioned's query. "He is the god of the mahavans. Their rightful lord. The Servitor rules Sinskrill in Shet's name."

"And Shet will one day return to claim what is his?"

After silently reflecting upon the question Serena held back a scowl. She now had a sense of the nature of Ms. Sioned's inquiry. The old woman wanted to know if Serena truly believed in something few others did, something others called a fable or the fear-induced belief in a being who didn't exist. Most thought Shet a myth, but Serena knew different. She knew the truth. She'd seen Shet, imprisoned on a high mountain on the equally mythic but nonetheless real world of Seminal. Smoky, black chains had bound the god, but even chained his power had dwarfed anything she could have imagined.

"I've already explained my beliefs to the Village Council," Serena said, careful to keep her voice even and unruffled.

"I've heard this," Ms. Sioned replied. "Does William share your beliefs?"

Serena nodded, and confusion added to her irritation. "Of course."

Ms. Sioned bent her gaze and stared at the ground. "Of course," she repeated softly, seeming to have a silent conversation with herself before shaking her head and lifting her gaze.

"What is it?" Serena asked with a frown, already tired of this guessing game. "What do you really want to say?"

Ms. Sioned sighed. "I know you wish to pursue a more personal relationship with William but is that really what's best if you have to prepare for the return of an evil god?"

Serena's face went drone-blank while fury coursed through her. She now understood the *real* reason for Ms. Sioned's questions. "You still think I'll hurt William?"

Ms. Sioned startled, and some of Serena's rage faltered. "Of course not," the old *raha'asra* said, sounding scandalized.

Serena's fury ebbed further.

"I worry for *you*," Ms. Sioned said. "Not *him*."

"Me?" Surprise eroded the last of Serena's anger.

Ms. Sioned chuckled. "I think in the coming months you'll be pushed to your limits. You'll have to work every bit as hard as William, maybe harder, and as new as you are to emotional truth, to allowing yourself to acknowledge and accept your feelings, I worry about what that might mean for you." She wavered. "You might lose focus, something I don't think you can afford."

Serena didn't reply at once. Instead, she gazed past Ms. Sioned, toward the ocean where the first edge of the sun touched the horizon, and pondered the other woman's words. *Could it be true? Could I lose myself to passions? Become sappy and silly?*

After a little more thought, Serena realized the answer might be 'yes,' which was something she couldn't allow. She eyed Ms. Sioned and noticed an anticipatory cast to the other woman's visage.

Upon seeing it, suspicion rose once more to the forefront of Serena's mind. *Or maybe this was all something Ms. Sioned had planned because she'll never trust me to not hurt her precious William.* Serena's face hardened.

Upon seeing it Ms. Sioned's features became sad. "This truly isn't about William," she said. "This is about you. Many of us understand how much you were willing to sacrifice in order to save Fiona and Travail. You've earned your place here and the respect of your neighbors and fellow magi." Ms. Sioned leaned forward, bringing greater emphasis to her words. "You are a woman of worth and a woman worth loving. Never doubt that I know it."

Serena blinked at Ms. Sioned's passion, and the last of her suspicions drained away. "What do you counsel?" she asked after a moment.

"Work hard, dedicate your life to what must be done. At least, until it is done. Let nothing distract you, or you will surely fail."

Serena forced herself examine Ms. Sioned's advice even though the heart of her fought against it like a hooked fish. *When do I get to choose happiness over labor?* However, a part of her—a large part—was secretly relieved. She wouldn't have to risk her heart, leave it exposed to hurt. In the end, Ms. Sioned's advice gave her the excuse to hide away from the dangers of love, and she knew it.

~

A glorious sunrise bathed Fiona Applefield in its lambent warmth, and she threw her head back and laughed. For most of her life—the first nineteen in England and the last fifty-six in Sinskrill —the sun had been a longed-for but rarely-seen visitor. Now she saw it every day, along with a myriad other wonders she still struggled to believe possible. Carved terraces, fantastical cliffs, arching bridges and rainbows, and an ocean canvas painted in blue hues she never could have imagined.

Arylyn.

"You like it here," Travail noted with a smile.

Fiona viewed the troll's towering form. He paced slowly beside her, muscles rippling beneath short, black fur that covered the entirety of his being except for his coarsely featured face. There, a braided goatee softened his spade-like jaw, and white, iris-less eyes peered from beneath beetled brows. His attire consisted of a simple loincloth and a strip of leather to tie back his long, black braids.

"How can I not?" Fiona asked. "It's beautiful in ways I never expected to experience." She spoke the truth, but her words weren't the entirety of how she perceived Arylyn. Those other opinions were ones she preferred not to voice. Or perhaps she simply didn't want to acknowledge them. They seemed too much like a betrayal of everything Serena, William, and Jake had sacrificed to free her from Sinskrill.

She and Travail pressed on, bypassing a large puddle deposited by last night's rain in a shallow hollow of Sita's Song. The gray-stoned road put the misnamed Great Way of Sinskrill to shame. No grass or vegetation marred Sita's Song, and it ran relatively smooth and unrutted from the enrune fields west of Clifftop, across Lakshman's Bow—a cunningly crafted bridge with flagstones forming the yin and yang—and through Janaki Valley where she and Travail had decided to go hiking. From there, Sita's Song transitioned into a simple gravel trail that ended at the foot of Mount Madhava.

"Arylyn is beautiful," Travail agreed with a grave nod, "but I sense disquiet in your tone."

Fiona cursed the troll's perception. Somehow, he could always sense what she preferred not to say aloud.

Travail faced her. "Am I incorrect?"

Fiona took a moment to gather her thoughts. As she considered what words to speak, she gazed at Janaki Valley, at the green fields of barley and corn, at the whispering sheaves of wheat, and the rolling hills decorated with orchards and vineyards. Here, River Namaste gurgled sedately, still a few miles from the rush of waterfalls where it would cascade down Lilith's cliffs. Fiona caught sight of Sile Troy, the farmer to whom Serena was apprenticed, and waved to him. He dipped his head in acknowledgment before returning to his inspection of knee-high stalks of corn.

"You are delaying," Travail chided.

He was right, but Fiona wouldn't be rushed. She more tightly gripped the walking cane she didn't really need but liked to have with her, a habit from Sinskrill where a stick served as protection. "I don't dislike it, but it seems . . ." She struggled with her phrasing.

"Soft?"

Fiona flashed Travail an expression of gratitude. As he so often did, he'd managed to give voice to her thoughts in a more accurate fashion than she could. "Yes," she agreed. "Soft. The people here have no notion of struggle or hard work. Everything comes easy, and they don't know how comfortable their lives truly are."

Travail grunted in response, neither agreeing nor disagreeing, and they continued in silence.

Minutes later, the quiet was broken when a pair of shoeless boys, wearing pants hacked off at the knees, sprinted past them. No doubt the two were headed for Lake Bindu, a place where one of the many streams feeding River Namaste opened into a sheltered cove. It was also a great site for swimming.

"A regular pair of Tom Sawyers, those two," Fiona noted. She couldn't hold back a smile as the rambling youths ran on, uncaring and happy. Their excited shouts could be heard even after they crested a hill and were lost to view.

Travail smiled as well.

They proceeded onward. A mile later, they passed a vineyard where workers harvested plump, purple grapes and tossed them into woven baskets.

"Hello, there," a stout man in overalls called out. He wore a wide-brimmed hat. "Wonderful day to be out, isn't it?"

"Yes, it is," Fiona replied, with a gladness that surprised her.

She and Travail shared a few more words with the farmer before leaving the man to his work. They pressed forward on Sita's Song, and a few minutes later the troll cleared his throat.

"What is it?" Fiona asked.

"You speak of these people with quiet contempt, and yet perhaps you misjudge them."

Fiona frowned. "How do you mean?"

"When first I came here, they beheld me as an oddity, always staring and pointing. Now they accept me as a member of Arylyn. No one even notices me anymore."

Fiona laughed. "Yes, they do. They're just too polite to point and stare at you like they used to."

"Perhaps," Travail agreed with a warm chuckle, "but isn't politeness another word for civility?"

Fiona shrugged. "I never liked your word games. Say more clearly what you mean."

"Consider your situation and perhaps you'll understand why I think you misjudge them when you consider them soft or self-centered."

Fiona snorted. "I never liked your riddles, either."

Travail came to halt. "How did you arrive here?"

Fiona took a moment to collect her thoughts. She recalled the terrible battle by the anchor line in Sinskrill, and the more terrible sight of Jake's grievous wound. "I came here because a number of magi fought to save me from Sinskrill."

"Then perhaps they're not as selfish and self-satisfied as you think," Travail noted. "Even now, many of them prepare and train for the final assault on Sinskrill. They're willing to sacrifice themselves based upon the words of Serena and Selene, children of Sinskrill."

"A fool's mission," Fiona said. "No one can defeat Shet."

Travail shrugged. "Perhaps. But the attempt is worth the effort. Rather than hide amongst the peace and comfort of their wonderful lives, these people give. They don't lack empathy."

"I never said they lacked empathy," Fiona protested.

"You implied it."

"I . . ." Fiona closed her mouth when she realized Travail was correct. Her thoughts eventually settled on a nettlesome question "Do you think I'm trying to find fault with the people here?"

"I think your time in Sinskrill made you skeptical of the notions of peace, charity, and goodness. You long for it like a flower longing for the sun and yet are afraid to embrace it too completely because you fear the warmth will burn you up."

Fiona frowned as she considered the terrible notion. *Has my time on Sinskrill poisoned me to the possibility of happiness?*

~

Jake Ridley had the front porch of Mr. Zeus' house to himself as he stared at Lilith Bay. The sun had yet to fully set, but it was close, and a few, stray bands of orange light were all that remained of the day as inky blackness slowly curtained the rest of the sky. In the last hour, a trade wind had kicked up, and it brought much-needed relief from the day's heat and humidity. The fall of night and the billowing breeze also brought out the bats, and they wheeled in the sky, twisting and twirling in weird patterns.

In some ways, their movements reminded Jake of a great running back juking a defender out of his shoes.

The thought had Jake scowling. If not for the damn mahavans and their damn island, he'd probably be out on a football field right now, playing for the Fighting Irish and trying to put down one of those very same running backs. Instead, he was stuck here. Frustration bubbled, and Jake took a heavy breath. As soon as he did, a surge of pain spasmed from a two-inch band on his chest, the place where

Adam Paradiso, Serena's uncle, had stabbed him. His breathing quickly became ragged.

The hurt caused his anger to fade, and Jake took a more careful inhalation. He paused, holding his breath when he met resistance, but after an instant he drew in more air, pushing past the pain. He couldn't let the soreness slow him down forever. His chest twinged as he breathed more deeply, and the burning ache soon transitioned to one that was sharp. Jake didn't let up. He went further, pressing for his limit. Seconds later he reached it and was forced to exhale slowly.

Damn Adam Paradiso. The man had stabbed Jake straight through the chest a few months back in Australia. It had occurred during the rescue of Travail and Fiona, toward the battle's end, and Jake would have died if Jessira and Rukh hadn't been there. They'd saved him, using a type of braid no one else knew about. They called it a Healing, and Jake had seen it used a few other times. It basically manifested like lightning, pouring out of Rukh or Jessira's hands, which they sent into the other person.

It also hurt like hell. Every person Jake had seen who received a Healing went into spasms when the lightning entered them. It was like they were having a seizure. His own Healings hadn't been any different, except for one. In his, a temporary connection to Rukh and Jessira had been made, a linkage that opened a part of their histories to him. Jake still had trouble believing it was true. Rukh and Jessira were from somewhere else, a world called Arisa, and in this other place, they had been all-but worshiped. Jake had seen the crowds bow to them.

Were the visions real?

Jake suspected they were, but neither Jessira nor Rukh liked talking about it. They always changed the subject whenever Jake asked.

His musings broke off when the front door opened and William Wilde, Jason Jacobs, and Mr. Zeus—the other three men with whom Jake shared the house—stepped outside.

"Hey," Jake said.

Jason lifted his nose and pretended to sniff the air. "Any one smell smoke?" he asked, sounding worried. Although originally from

Louisiana, Jason could have passed for a native born magus with his odd mix of blond, California-surfer good looks and dark skin. He used to smile more though, been more easy-going. The battle in Australia had changed him, made him more intense, private. It was good to see him happy.

Mr. Zeus—also known as Odysseus Louis Crane III—darted his head about in concern at Jason's question and inhaled deeply. The old man's face broke into an expression of confusion. "I don't smell anything."

Jason frowned severely. "You sure? I swear I smell smoke."

Jake rolled his eyes, knowing where the comment was leading, and sure enough Jason didn't let him down.

"It's coming from Jake," Jason said. "Fumes are pouring off his head. I think he's been thinking again." Jason cocked his head. "I think I can even hear broken gears grinding in that noggin of his."

Jake smirked. "At least I've got a brain. Whenever you try to think, all that empty space you've got trapped between your ears sucks in air like a vacuum. It sounds like a teakettle about to explode."

William chuckled, and Jake shifted his gaze to the utterly unre- markable young man of average height and build who had become his best friend. It was strange how life worked. Hidden beneath William's ordinariness was the nerd Jake had tormented for most of their lives. Then wild circumstances had thrown them together, and they'd bonded over their shared misery

"Ha, ha," Jason said, not sounding amused.

Jake leaned against the porch railing, smug and happy that he'd won this round against Jason.

William kept chuckling, and Jason addressed him. "Don't encourage him. You remember how cocky he was before all this?"

William's brow furrowed. "Sure, but how does that have anything to do with what he just said to you?"

Mr. Zeus harrumphed around the stem of his pipe and aromatic, blue-gray smoke drifted about him. The old man bore an uncanny resemblance to Merlin or Gandalf or any wise, old wizard from myth. "I, for one, think Jake could use some of his old self-confidence back." He stroked his long, lustrous, white beard. His incongruous blue eyes

—strangely young where the rest of him was old—held grave concern. "After everything he's been through, a little cockiness might be a good thing."

Jake nodded agreement. Too much of his self-assurance had eroded away since he'd been kidnapped to Sinskrill. He sometimes— oftentimes—regarded himself as a shell of the person he'd once been. He was tired of it. *Weak.* Jumping at shadows like a scared, little rat. Having people shove swords into him. He was sick of being on the losing end of an ass-whooping.

While he didn't necessarily want to go back to being the person William and Jason had loathed, he could use some of his old fire and arrogance. There were times he missed his old self.

"I like him like this," Jason said to Mr. Zeus.

"I'm standing right here," Jake said in irritation.

"That's my cue," William said, pushing off the porch railing. "I don't need to hear the two of you bicker."

"Where are you going?" Jake asked.

William grinned shamelessly. "I'm supposed to take Serena sailing tonight on *Blue Sky Dreamers.*" He sounded entirely too pleased about the prospect.

Jake mentally shook his head. He liked Serena well enough. He'd even forgiven her for kidnapping him and William into slavery, but dating her . . . He shivered at the thought. No thanks. Despite how pretty as she was, he'd only trust Serena so far.

William was apparently a lot braver. Or dumber. Or more stricken with hormones. Maybe all three.

"Be careful," Jake said to William. He knew the advice sounded weird the moment the words left his mouth.

William obviously thought the same thing because he frowned in confusion. "Careful of what?"

"Nothing," Jake said. He'd dug a hole for himself by saying something stupid, and the best way to keep it from getting bigger was to stop digging. "Have a good time."

"Will do," William said, smiling again like a sappy idiot. He stepped off the porch and went whistling away into the night.

Jake rolled his eyes. *Moron.*

Jason moved to stand next to him. "I'm worried about him."

"You mean about that goofy grin he gets whenever he talks about Serena?" Jake asked.

Jason nodded. He pressed his lips together, clearly bothered by something.

"You don't trust her?" Jake guessed. It had taken him months to learn to trust Serena, and maybe Jason never had.

"I trust her," Jason said. "It's just . . ." He trailed off, and Jake waited for him to finish his thought. "I don't know if the two of them belong together."

Jake had no idea what Jason was talking about. William and Serena had been through so much together, so many bad memories, betrayals —all on Serena's part—but in the end, they'd come out the other side as the closest of friends. If anyone belonged together it was them. Still, a romantic togetherness was a big 'if' as far as Jake was concerned.

"I think I get what you mean," Jake said to Jason.

Mr. Zeus made a strangling noise. "I swear on all that's holy, you two are worse than any group of girls. Will the two of you *please* stop gossiping?" He glowered from one of them to the other before stomping inside.

Jake flicked a glance Jason's way, and they shared a shrug, watching and waiting for the front door to close so they could resume their conversation.

"It's not only about trusting Serena," Jason said. "It's about what the two of them want. William, that gigantic doofus, reminds me of someone planning his honeymoon. But what about Serena? She's impossible to read. What if all she wants is to be friends?"

Jake grimaced at the thought. If true, William's heart would be crushed.

CHAPTER 2: FRUSTRATED HOPES

S eptember 1989

T he lonely cry of a petrel echoed through the jungle as William walked beside Serena toward Lilith Bay. He'd stopped by her cottage, wanting to pick her up for a late night sail on *Blue Sky Dreamers,* his dhow. Unfortunately, Serena had begged off, claiming fatigue after working at Sile Troy's farm, and instead, had suggested a walk.

While disappointed by her response—William had really been looking forward to going sailing with her—he'd readily agreed to the evening stroll. Any alone-time with Serena was fine with him. After a year of doing nothing but train so he could help save Travail and Fiona, he and Serena could finally figure out where they stood. William wanted to know. Most of the time, they had nothing more than the light-hearted, easy-going banter of good friends. Other occasions, it felt like there might be more to it than just that.

Then again, there were moments like now when Serena was as distant and unreachable as a glacier. It left William wondering about her. Even after all the hours they'd spent together, Serena could still be hard to figure out. She remained as mysterious and unknowable as the first time they'd met, and he worried she always would be. Her hidden depths sparked bouts of uncertainty within him, leaving him unsettled as to how he truly felt about her.

They exited the jungle's gloom and entered the relative brightness of Lilith Beach. The full moon had already risen, and its illumination glistened off the waves and the golden sands while soft lights glowed from many of the windows and porches of the homes lining Lilith's lovely terraces above. In addition, a cool trade wind persisted, and it blessed them with relief after the jungle's mugginess. William sighed.

Serena noticed his reaction and graced him with a smile. Despite his inability to see her features clearly, William thought her beautiful. She'd always been exotic and lovely to him, with dusky features, midnight-black hair, and dark eyes to match.

"I thought you liked it hot," she said.

William smiled in response. "Hot, yes. Stifling, no."

"Or maybe you're just hard to please." Under the moon's bright light, it was easy to make out the teasing glint in Serena's eyes.

William hated losing at anything, and for whatever reason, letting Serena get away with making fun of him counted as a contest. "You want to head back to your cottage?" he asked. "We can take a stroll through the jungle on the other side of it." He guessed Serena would say 'no' since she hated sweating, finding it unbecoming.

She didn't let him down, casting him a crooked grin. "Well played, sir." She doffed an imaginary hat.

William grinned in triumph and they continued on, cutting across the sands of Lilith Bay. A mile later they reached the Guanyin, a silvery-metal bridge that spanned River Namaste where the waters gathered at the base of Lilith's cliffs. From there, they rumbled through a canyon leading to the ocean.

"Jake's getting his groove back," William said as they crossed the bridge.

"What?" Serena asked, sounding distracted.

William glanced her way and noticed her stiff, fearful posture as she stared at the statues lining the dark, river canyon. William smiled.

Serena always did that. The statues made her nervous, and even with her mahavan training, she couldn't entirely mask her reaction.

"I said Jake has a third nipple," William said. "It looks like a toe."

Serena's gaze finally focused on him, and he could see her mentally replaying his last words. Her eyes widened in shock. "What?"

William laughed.

Serena's face scrunched. "What's so funny? And what's this about Jake having a third nipple?"

William laughed harder.

Serena put up with his humor for a few seconds, but apparently she had enough when William laughed a little too long. She sent a sharp elbow into his ribs.

He grimaced. "What was that for?" He rubbed at his aching ribs. Serena was a strong woman.

"For not answering my question."

"Sorry," William said, although he really wasn't. "I just think it's funny how much those statues scare you."

"I can't help it," Serena muttered. "They're creepy."

"Sure they are, but I'd have figured you'd have gotten used to them by now."

"Well, I haven't," Serena said. "And was there anything about Jake you *did* want to tell me?"

"He's getting his groove back," William repeated.

"What does that mean?"

"His self-confidence," William explained. "I'm glad, but I also hope he doesn't go back to being the same jackass he used to be."

"You really think that's possible?"

William shook his head. "No. But I'm going to pretend it is so I can remind him about it." He grinned in anticipation. "I'll want to do that early and often."

"Why?" Serena asked, clearly perplexed.

William's grin faded. "Because it'll piss him off," he replied, perplexed himself by her confusion. Making fun of their friends was what guys liked to do more than almost anything.

Serena shook her head in clear disappointment. "Boys," she said, her tone making the word sound like a curse.

"Girls," William mimicked in the same tone.

Serena rolled her eyes, and they pressed on in silence through a half-mile path through the rocks and boulders at the base of Lilith's Cliffs. While they continued on their way, William found himself surprised by Serena's easy admission of a weakness, her fear of the statues along the river canyon. There had been a time when getting her to admit to anything other than perfection was impossible.

Eventually, they reached Cliff Spirit's Main Stairs.

"I'm sorry we couldn't go sailing," Serena said as they ascended toward Clifftop.

William shrugged, doing his best to hide his lingering disappointment. "Don't worry about it. I'm sure there will be lots of other times we can go."

"Are you sure?" Serena asked. "You know about Shet. He's coming, and we won't have time for much of anything when that happens."

William sighed. "I'm trying not to think about him."

"You'll have to," Serena said, her jaw briefly clenching. "Saving Fiona and Travail was only the beginning of our troubles. All of us have to be ready for him."

William had no reply. He understood what she was saying and largely agreed with her. Still, couldn't he forget about his troubles every once in a while? They climbed the Main Stairs, and William caught Serena eyeing him askance. He frowned, unsure as to the strange turn in their conversation, but he had a suspicion. "Why are you bringing this up now?" he asked.

"Because your training isn't done yet. Neither is mine."

Suspicion crystalized to certainty. *She wants friendship and nothing more*. It was the real reason she'd cancelled their late-night sail. William's face unconsciously took on the flat affect of a drone while he tried to hide his hurt. An evening full of promise suddenly tasted like ash. "I see."

Serena stopped and pulled him around. "No, you don't," she said. "I love spending time with you, and in another life that would be enough. But we can't afford that. Not when we have all these responsibilities. They take precedence over our wants and desires."

William stared at her, hope and disappointment warring within him. It didn't entirely sound like a breakup. Serena had acknowledged that something might actually exist between them, which maybe was better than nothing.

"If that's what you want," he said, trying to ignore the discouragement roiling his stomach.

Serena's face held fleeting sorrow. It occurred and vanished so quickly that William wasn't sure he saw it. The rest of their stroll passed in silence.

～

William breathed slowly and steadily as he jogged behind Travail. His breath frosted, but his hemp pants and full-sleeved cotton shirt kept him warm as he and Jake followed the troll on a slender trail—Firedeep Gorge—one made for goats, that wended through the pine forest covering Arylyn's rolling heights. Rather than their usual morning exercise of a light jog followed by lifting heavy logs up and down a hill past Linchpin Knoll, today Travail had chosen to take them on a long run.

The forest here was beautiful, cool and dry, and it was easy to keep on running. Beams of sunshine shone through breaks in the canopy and illuminated the forest floor like floodlights. Wild jasmine grew in clumps, and their sweet perfume mixed with the sharp tang of pine and the loamy odor of mold and wet clay. William noticed the remnants of the overnight precipitation in the form of raindrops beading on leaf and bough. They trickled intermittently onto William's head or down the back of his neck. He ignored the momentary discomfort as he followed Travail.

They dashed along the trail, through clouds of gnats, gauzy spiderwebs, and brushed against wet leaves or splashed through small puddles. Thankfully, the chilly water couldn't penetrate William's rugged boots.

On they ran, and while they did, William kept an ear out for Jake, who struggled to keep up, huffing and wheezing since his chest still bothered him.

Fragging Adam Paradiso. William silently vowed to pay the man back for everything he'd done to him and Jake.

William momentarily slowed when a squirrel darted across his path. The little creature clambered up a nearby tree and chittered at him from the safety of a high branch. William smiled at the animal but never let off the pace. A hundred yards later, they broke through the tree line and entered a meadow. Bright sunshine warmed the wildflower field, but a stirring breeze kept the area much cooler than Arylyn's lower reaches, especially when a colony of clouds, some of them pregnant with a promise of a downpour, drifted across the sky and obscured the sun.

Travail signaled for a halt, and William pulled up, glancing about.

The meadow reminded him of the first *saha'asra* he'd ever encountered, a forest field in West Virginia. However, the clouds, the threatening rain, and the cold, gusting wind reminded him of Sinskrill in summer. At the best of times the mahavan island was icy and uninviting.

Jake finally caught up to them, and he stumbled to a halt. He bent over, braced his hands on his knees, and continued to pant.

William went to check on him. "You all right?"

"Give me a sec," Jake gasped. "I'll be fine." His sandy-brown hair lay plastered on his scalp, and his wiry arms and legs quivered with obvious fatigue. He'd once been thickly built, but since his injury in Australia and being laid up for weeks on end, he'd lost a lot of muscle. Of course, being Jake, he was determined to gain it all back as fast as possible.

William shook his head. Jake always worked harder than anyone he knew, pushing past pain and common sense. "You sure you're all right?"

"I'm fine," Jake insisted, but the tremor in his legs told another story. He was gassed and needed a rest.

William silently passed him a canteen of water.

Travail turned his white, iris-less eyes upon them and dipped his horned head in acknowledgement toward Jake. "You've progressed far," he intoned in his deep voice.

William switched his gaze back to Travail and had to crane his head to meet the troll's eyes. The troll towered ten feet tall and could move with an agility that shouldn't have been possible given his half-ton, thickly-muscled frame.

"We will walk the rest of the way home," Travail added.

"I can run," Jake insisted.

"No, you can't," Travail said. His stony face, with its jutting jaw covered by a braided goatee and craggy brow, showed no sign of bending, and after a few seconds, Jake relented.

William exhaled a breath he hadn't realized he'd been holding. Jake needed protection from his own hard-headed courage.

Travail led them across the field where they picked up the trail again. "We should reach the middle part of Janaki Valley a few miles west of here."

"We can jog some of it, if you like," Jake offered in a hopeful tone.

Travail gave him a hard stare but said nothing, and Jake settled down again, muttering under his breath.

After that they progressed quietly through the forest, and William thought again about last night's talk with Serena. She'd basically given him the *'Let's be friends'* speech, but she'd also spoken about how she wished they could spend more time together.

But which one is it? He wished he knew, and he shook his head in frustration.

Travail must have picked up on his irritation. "What troubles you?"

"Nothing," William replied, not wanting to talk about it.

"He and Serena had an argument last night," Jake not-so-helpfully supplied.

"Jackass!" William glared at him. "That was supposed to be a private conversation."

"Sorry," Jake said.

"Is this true?" Travail asked.

William continued to glare at Jake. "Yes, it's true. Jake's a jackass."

"Hey!" Jake protested. "Ease off. I listened to you bitch and moan about Serena all night long last night after you got home. Maybe Travail can tell you what to do."

William's irritation simmered down. "It wasn't all night," he said.

"It was for a few minutes at most, and I didn't bitch and moan. I was annoyed is all."

"And now?" Travail asked.

William sighed. "Now I'm resigned," he said. "Anything between me and Serena will have to wait until our work with Shet is done. At least that's what she says."

Travail made a rumbling sound. "Rukh Shektan often talks about work, duty, and dedication as if they were the summit of his life's purpose."

"Isn't that a good thing?" Jake asked.

Travail tilted his head in consideration, taking time to collect his thoughts. "It is a good thing," he replied, "but not when taken to extremes, such as when it forbids that which makes life worth living, things like love, family, friends, and joy."

"Rukh isn't like that," Jake said in immediate protest.

William wasn't surprised by Jake's defense of Rukh. His friend had a large case of hero-worship when it came to Rukh and Jessira. And if William was being honest, he did, too.

"I don't think so, either," Travail said to Jake, his tone mollifying. "At least not entirely, but there is definitely a large portion of Rukh's and Jessira's personas that remind me of a diamond-hard edge of dedication. I doubt they'll let anything or anyone get in the way of what they think is their life's purpose."

"No, they won't," William agreed.

Travail faced him, and once more he found himself the focus of the troll's attention. "You're certain you feel nothing but resignation for your situation with Serena?"

William closed his eyes and pinched the bridge of his nose. He wished they could move on from talking about Serena. "Yes, I'm certain. It's fine." He caught Jake eyeing him skeptically. "Seriously, it's no big deal," he added in a pointed tone.

He almost believed his own words.

CHAPTER 3: PLANS OF DECEIT

November *1989*

SINSKRILL

Unaccustomed nervousness made Adam Paradiso's hands tremble as he eyed Shet's Spear, which currently rested in his brother's thick hands. The weapon was shod with steel on one end and from the other rose a leaf-shaped blade the color of coal. A straight bar of ivory-colored wood formed the shaft, and it glowed with whorling designs, red-rimmed like the flickering the embers of a fire.

The constantly shifting patterns had Adam's heart thudding, racing and palpating like that of a stallion fleeing a lion. His reaction made no sense. After all, Adam was a big man, large-boned and powerful, menacing when he wished it, and possessing an intellect that had seen him rise to power here on Sinskrill. He was the

Secondus to his brother Axel, the Servitor, and he answered to no one but Axel, an equally large man with similar heavy-set, dark-skinned features but with a full, thick beard in place of Adam's sculpted goatee.

As Adam studied the Spear, he knew what icy sensation gripped his heart: terror. But he couldn't admit to such a weakness, not on Sinskrill where any perceived vulnerability would be quickly exploited. Instead, he had to maintain a mask of simple curiosity or sneering disregard.

"Take it," Axel ordered.

Adam stepped forward and reached out to receive the Spear, but at the last moment he hesitated. A fresh surge of fear coursed through his veins and held him frozen. He knew what would occur when he touched the Spear, when his fingers closed upon it and he sourced his *lorethasra*. He knew where he would go.

Seminal. The realm of myths and magic. The abode of Lord Shet.

Adam tried to maintain his mask of haughty derision, to hide any sense of his disquiet, but a single drop of perspiration betrayed him. It slid as a thin line down his forehead, circling around the orbit of his left eye before dribbling into his goatee.

Axel noticed, a simple flick of his eyes and a furrowing of his brows. "Take the Spear," his brother ordered anew. "Shet desires your presence. Do not disappoint him." Axel leaned in close and hissed, "Or me."

Despite the coolness of Shet's Throne Hall, Adam broke out in fresh perspiration. Thankfully, no one else was present to witness his humiliating loss of control. No one else but the six-armed monstrosity that towered behind the throne at the far end of the Hall. Adam studied the figure, the statue of their god Shet. Within its three right hands it grasped a khopesh, a mace, and the Book of the Dead while the left ones held a bow, a spear, and the Knife of Woe. It was the statue's features, though, that gave Adam the greatest pause. The jaws of a crocodile crowned Shet's head, while an arrogant sneer—one uncannily mimicked by his brother—curled its mouth. *You mortal fools*, the sneer seemed to say. *You will bow or be burned.*

Adam mentally sighed, unable to delay the inevitable. He grasped the Spear and sourced his *lorethasra*. As soon as he did, a rainbow bridge—or a road, perhaps—opened within his mind. It stretched into an all-consuming darkness.

With a sound like a rushing river in flood, Adam's Spirit set forth upon the rainbow bridge. He'd made this journey on several previous occasions, but those prior excursions did nothing to prepare him for what was to come. Sound and sight faded, and he found himself encased in a black tunnel. His travel surged, gaining speed, covering an incomprehensibly vast distance. A tearing sensation ripped at him, an impression that his core, his soul maybe, frayed. Emptiness tore at his heart, but on he raced, pulled forward by a tide like gravity. Colors faded to bleak, black night. Silence reigned. The darkness never ended, and it encroached upon Adam's mind, threatening to devour his sense of self.

At his breaking point, the travel ended with a jarring halt.

Adam floated in the clouds, high above a foreign realm. *Seminal.* Nearby, a red dragon soared above a world infested by living nightmares: solitary necrosed, wild tribes of constantly shifting unformed, and elegant vampires who held court in dark, unlovely castles. He viewed a rugged range of strangely shaped hills that held the aspect of broken teeth and contained broken palaces on their slopes. There he found armies of ghouls stirring restlessly under the earth, hidden inside dead cities as they waited for the living to provide them sustenance . . . and entertainment.

Adam silently snarled. He hated this place.

An instant later, fear replaced loathing when a voice whispered to him on the wind.

"Come to me, child," the voice urged. "I sense your presence."

Adam knew who spoke to him—*Shet*—and he focused his mind upon a distant range of dagger-sharp, snow-capped mountains. His Spirit sped there, to where desolation and fear roiled off the peaks, dripping like poison into valleys filled with inky menace, places where the sunlight grew strangely dim as it reached the ground. As before when he'd visited this terrifying range, one mountain loomed above all the others, and there he found his destination. On a jutting ledge, wide and deep enough to support all of Village White Sun, brooded a newly-hewn palace built of black stone. It hunkered like a poisonous mushroom, seeming to consume all light. It swallowed sunshine like a snake would its prey.

Adam's heart shriveled.

As he approached the citadel, features became evident. First and foremost was the titanic figure seated in a high courtyard upon a raised throne made from the jaws of a dragon. Lord Shet. His sense of power dwarfed all around him: the throne, the palace, the very mountain range. All shrank to the size of midgets in Shet's presence.

Adam descended and settled his Spirit-self upon the ground in front of Sinskrill's god. He bowed and did his best to control the fear burbling in his mind.

Shet wore a partial, bone-white mask, one meant to hide the gnarled burns marring his features on the right side of his face. It moved with the motions of his features. Shet gestured and bid Adam stand. "Arise, child, and be welcome." Shet's voice rang deep and melodic, and when he smiled, his unruined eye shone falsely warm and fatherly.

Adam wasn't deceived. Shet was cruel and despotic, and the truth of his essence was most clearly reflected by the masked desecration ruining the right side of his face, a true reflection of his nature.

"What news do you bring from Sinskrill?" Shet asked.

Adam cleared his throat. "In the months since Arylyn's attack . . ."

"An attack made possible by your own slovenly lack of preparation," Shet chided in the warm voice of a father instructing his errant child.

Adam dipped his head in acknowledgment. "Yes, my lord, but we've taken steps to earn revenge upon your enemies." Adam spoke in what he hoped was a firm tone, one without the slightest hint of quaver. "We've rebuilt the ranks of the mahavans by enacting your instructions. The Spear restores those who were previously drones."

"Your training of these once-drones consists of . . ." Shet trailed off.

"No different than what we've always done," Adam replied. "The drones are hardened and tempered in the Crucible. They're made strong, or they're broken."

"And if broken, I expect they're reforged." Shet's words were a statement rather than a question.

Adam nodded. "If they fail again, we strip them a second time, and the pain of the second such punishment is far worse than the original such judgment. It acts as an excellent means of concentrating their minds. We then restore and reforge them a second time, giving them a third attempt to achieve the rank of mahavan."

"The failure rate?"

"Less than five percent," Adam answered, "and those who fail twice are decimated, one in ten are hurled from the Judging Line atop the Servitor's Palace." Adam managed a faint grin, a forced sentiment of pleasure that he didn't feel. Terror filled him whenever he spoke to Lord Shet. "None survive the fall from those heights."

"Well done," Shet said. He smiled, a grin that carried across his features, including the mask covering the right side of his face. The resulting image was hideous, reminding Adam of a snake in the midst of shedding its skin.

"What of your plans for Arylyn?" Shet asked. "How do you intend to attack the island of my enemies?"

"By stealth and cunning," Adam said. "We will send scouting teams to learn all we can about Arylyn. And when the time is right, we will pay them back for what they did to us." Adam's features hardened, and his eyes grew flat with anger. This time the expression truly reflected his sentiments. The magi had spat in the face of Sinskrill's mahavans, defeated them, humiliated them. Such a challenge could not go unanswered.

"The World Killers?" Shet's face grew guarded, as it always did whenever he spoke of those two, the strange magi who moved like the wind and struck like a storm of swords, they who had defeated the Servitor.

"We haven't discovered any sign of their presence."

"You will," Shet said, his words sounding like a dire promise. "You may return to Sinskrill."

Adam bowed low and prepared to ascend. In that instant, he noticed a white-cloaked knight approaching the Lord. The man moved in a vaguely familiar fashion, smooth and languid as a cat, yet precise as a raptor. He briefly wondered who it might be before he departed.

~

SEMINAL

S het snorted in derision as soon as the pathetic mahavan departed. Adam Paradiso had tried his best to maintain a semblance of dignity, but in this, he'd failed utterly. In fact, during their brief conversation, the man had almost wet himself in terror, trembling like a broken cur.

Of course, Adam hadn't realized it. He likely thought he'd acquitted himself well, that he'd managed to maintain his facade with no one aware of his terror.

Fool.

Shet saw through all lies, and before his sight all truths were made manifest. The lord of Seminal smiled in grim humor as he imagined Adam's incredulity when the god finished wrecking the magi and then turned about and broke the mahavans.

A white-cloaked knight interrupted Shet's reflections. The figure, a human, strode toward the throne, proud and strong. Shet eyed the man, studied his tall, lean form, the way he paced like a panther, and approved of the manner in which he groomed his black hair, keeping it martial-short. He also noticed the man's unusual skin color, tea touched with cream, and equally unusual, how the knight's dark eyes held no fear. Instead, arrogance filled the man's features even as he dropped to a knee.

Shet remained impassive, waiting for the knight to speak.

The warrior served an elf princess of poor repute. In the three centuries of her life, she'd steadfastly refused all offers of marriage, going so far as to withdraw from her mother's court. This human was said to be her only companion, and with her elf magic, she had made him puissant.

Two traitors to their kind. How delicious.

Of course, the knight's power could have been tenfold greater if not for the Orbs of Peace. Millennia ago, the glowing crystal globes had been forged and scattered throughout Seminal. They were meant to prevent humans from fully accessing their *lorethasra* and deny the rise of another god like Shet. The other races had thought the Orbs would keep them safe.

All they had done was ensure Seminal's eventual enslavement.

Shet gestured for the knight to rise, and the human did as commanded, but he also rested a hand on his sword. The god straightened slightly. He feared nothing, but sometimes this man could put him off balance. He moved too gracefully, too much like Shokan.

Shet mentally sneered at the notion. *Shokan is dead.* A notion flitted across his mind: he couldn't recall his great enemy's features, the same with Sira, the Lady of Fire. *It was of no consequence.*

"We have found one of the Orbs," the man said.

Shet's heart stirred with excitement, and he shifted on his throne, leaning forward. "You have the Orb with you?"

The knight reached into his cloak, into a *null pocket*—a voided area meant to secrete prized possessions. From it, he withdrew a crystal the size of a skull. It glowed, a coruscating wash of blue and green in endless conflict. "One down, my lord . . ."

". . . and six to go," Shet finished. He reached for the Orb and caressed it. He sensed the weaves billowing off of it, the ones that essentially stripped all humans upon conception and kept them weak.

It also sapped Shet's strength, and that would not do.

The god crushed the Orb, and for an instant, he thought he saw relief pass across the human's otherwise impassive face. Shet mentally shrugged. If not for the fact that they pursued the same ambition, he would have long since done away with the knight and his elf princess.

"Find the rest of the Orbs and bring them to me," Shet ordered.

"As you command, my lord." The human slowly backed away, his posture properly bent in obeisance before he reached the proscribed twenty feet. There, he straightened, turned on a heel, and stalked away, moving like a lion in the long grass.

After the knight departed, Shet's mind returned to Earth. More work was needed to herald his arrival. After breaking the chains that had once shackled him to this mountain, this place where he strove to remake his nation of domination, Shet had reached out to the many beings who naturally inclined toward his mastery.

They had answered and bowed to his rising power.

Except on Earth.

The god had never directed his call there, and it was time to correct that oversight. Shet sent a summons to his minions on that faraway world. Minutes passed, and eventually he grunted in satisfaction when he felt the stirring of those born to serve him.

A thought came to him then, and he smiled. He included one final command to his servants. It wasn't likely to prove fruitful, but luck favored those who forced any opportunity.

Let mahavan and magi battle one another with firewagers. They could bring glorious ruin upon one another. The traitors.

~

SINSKRILL

A dam inhaled great gulps of air after exiting the anchor line to Seminal. Sweat poured down his face, and hunger gnawed his insides. He held onto the Spear even as he collapsed to a knee. Traveling to Seminal always left him weak and feeble as wet clay, and he needed a moment to collect himself.

While waiting to recover, he stared around the Throne Hall.

He and Axel were still alone. The light from an early afternoon sun glinted off a forest of gold-enameled columns that led from the double-doors at the Hall's entrance to the Servitor's Chair set at the second step of a tall dais, atop which rested the empty throne of their Lord. The titanic statue of Shet's warrior persona loomed over it all.

Adam blinked as a flash momentarily blinded him, sunlight bleeding through the stained-glass windows lining the room and forming part of the vaulted, ribbed ceiling. There up above, images depicted Shet in various poses of humility: providing shelter from a storm, battling ignorance with the long-lost Book of Binding, or shepherding humanity to a brighter future.

All of them were lies.

Shet was unfettered power made flesh, with no thought or ambition but to acquire ever more. He could never be allowed on Earth.

The last of the journey's lassitude left Adam, and he strengthened his knees, levering himself upright. He allowed Axel to gently pull the Spear from his lax fingers.

"How did it go?" his brother asked as he strode to the Servitor's Chair, seated himself, and laid the Spear across his knees.

Adam inhaled a settling breath. "It went as expected."

Axel leaned back in his chair. "Tell me everything."

Adam did as bade and spoke of all he had seen.

"The lord still supports us?" the Servitor asked.

"I believe he does," Adam said. "Yet it is hard to be sure. Every historical account indicates how much he hates failure, and we failed him when Arylyn attacked."

Axel's jaw briefly clenched. "We can still make amends for that unfortunate incident."

His brother was a fool if he believed it, and Adam kept from rolling his eyes by the barest of margins.

Thankfully, Axel didn't notice his scorn. "We will bury the magi," the Servitor said.

Adam merely nodded agreement, remaining quiet while a long-considered thought circled to the forefront of his mind. As always, he hesitated to speak it.

Axel saw. "What is it?"

Still Adam paused. He knew his thoughts were blasphemous, but at this point, weren't all options on the table, even the profane? "What if we ally with Arylyn?" he asked. "Perhaps together we could learn how to seal the anchor line between Seminal and Earth."

Axel's gaze sharpened. "To what end?"

"To prevent the death of our kind," Adam said. "I don't trust Shet."

"Neither do I," Axel mused with a frown. His gaze grew distant, as if he was lost in thought and hope burgeoned with Adam.

Perhaps Axel will let go of this terrible plan of attacking Arylyn. Doing so would only weaken both islands. Deal with Shet first, and then crush the magi.

"Arylyn has always been and will always be our enemy," Axel said, dashing Adam's hopes. "They invaded our island and attacked us. We won't go to them on bended knee. We are not 'kindred covens' as the witches might reckon matters."

"But when Shet returns to our world, I fear he'll treat us as kindred covens and kill us both."

"A possibility," the Servitor admitted. "But just as possibly, we'll earn the Lord's favor and evade his judgment." The Servitor spun the Spear and rapped its steel-shod heel on the white-marble floor as he rose to his feet. "The decision is made."

Adam mentally grated against the Servitor's decision, but he also knew better than to argue. The matter had been settled. He bowed low. "As you say, my liege."

CHAPTER 4: EVIL AWAKENS

N*ovember 1989*

SOMEWHERE UNKNOWN

Sapient Dormant, the Overward of the necrosed, heard a strange, commanding call. The signal reached across the firmaments like a plucked, stretched, threadbare tendon, a chord that penetrated the large cave that Sapient had made his own. The ancient necrosed shifted, dimly recognizing the great mind who had sent the call.

Can it be?

Again the chord was plucked, but the sound didn't ring in Sapient's low-set ears. Rather, it echoed in his corrupted heart, tolling low and dull like the shutting of a coffin. It set the ruined organ to beating more quickly, and Sapient's pus-like blood oozed sluggishly through his body. The call sounded again, and this time the Overward's lungs inhaled the cave's dank air. His blood further thinned, and the sound of dripping water penetrated his hearing.

Sapient opened his eyes. He lay upon a bed of broken bones—the remains of the many victims of his malice—and his joints creaked and cracked, sounding like distant rockslides as he sat up and stared about.

To any but a holder or a dwarf, the cave would have seemed pitch-black. Not so to Sapient. His onyx eyes, reflective despite the gloom, could see all. The cave he'd made his own stretched twenty yards from a boulder-strewn, choked off entrance to his bed of bones and the crumbled back wall. Spiny stalactites aimed like daggers from the ceiling toward a clear stream that held scuttling, blind crabs. The water flowed near the foot of his bed. A thin seam of gold spread root-like through the black rock that formed the walls, glistening in the occasional flash of light that breached the cave's entrance.

Again came the call, pulsing like a beacon, and once more Sapient's heart answered, skipping a step as it beat harder and faster.

An old memory stirred within the necrosed's mind, but it didn't surface as he tried to fathom who might have dared intrude on his sleep. He inhaled deeply, and his nose flared like filters as he slipped out his dark tongue, which was made black against his albino-white skin and pale lips. He tasted the air.

Nothing.

He waited minutes.

Still nothing.

Fatigue pressed upon him, and he lay down again, resting on his bed of bones and closing his eyes.

The call sounded once more.

This time Sapient's gaze snapped to the ceiling. He recognized the one who had signaled him. *Lord Shet.*

The call, both order and vow, told Sapient that the anchor line would soon open and the god of the necrosed, the one who'd created them and saved them from destruction, would stride across the land. Shet, who had given them a purpose, a plan, and a promise.

Sapient shivered in anticipation, and his lean form quivered. He ran a four-fingered, rotting hand over his bald pâte and considered how best to answer the Lord's summons.

Sapient lay unmoving for hours as he pondered his next step. He'd only recently arisen, and his thoughts, thick as gelatin, took time to clear and grow lucid. Eventually, he had a notion of what to do and he sat upright.

His joints creaked again, shoulders, wrists, back, knees, and hands. He stretched his long limbs, yawning as he clawed his way upright to his spindly eight-foot height. While most of his necrosed brethren chose bulk to aid their strength, Sapient had always chosen speed. He wasn't as strong as the others—Kohl Obsidian, for instance—but his speed was unmatched. When it came to battle, speed evaded power and quickness destroyed slow strength.

Sapient's mind further clarified and he wondered how much time had passed since he'd last roused. It was likely a century or more, given his hunger. And feeding would prove difficult with all the *asrasins*—including the mahavans—hidden away on their cursed islands.

The Overward's mouth curled. *Traitors.* Their weakness had led to Shet's defeat. The same weakness that somehow failed to humble them. Far from it, in fact. The Servitors of Sinskrill actually believed they could compel Sapient's service, that he'd willingly bent his knees to their reign.

Prideful idiots.

Sapient had lied when he'd made obeisance to the Servitor's Chair. He'd only done what was needed to earn their trust, all to further his Lord's ultimate aim.

"Vengeance shall be mine," Shet had said the last time Sapient had spoken to the Master. "Against all *asrasins.*"

And so it will be, Sapient thought.

But first, he required sustenance. A witch or warlock would do. Even an unformed. Whatever being he came across. Then he would gather his brethren and storm Sinskrill.

Sapient nodded to himself. The other necrosed would argue. They fought against one another as much as they did the rest of the world. It was in their nature since none of them remembered Shet and his glory. None of them remembered their god's promise to lift the curse laid upon them by Shokan, to restore them to life, to free them from the bondage of undying death.

∾

ARYLYN

William Wilde stared off in the distance and imagined how to make his Fire burn hotter. If he added a thread of Air to coil around . . .

He started when Serena gave him a gentle shove, and he glanced her way in confusion. "What?"

She shook her head. "I've been trying to get your attention for the past five minutes," she said. "What do you plan on doing for New Year's Eve?"

William blinked in uncertainty. His mind had been elsewhere, and he hadn't heard her question at first.

Serena rolled her eyes, her demeanor clearly one of annoyance.

William shifted beneath her gaze. "Sorry. I was thinking about—"

"Training for Shet and Seminal?"

William eyes narrowed. "You were the one who said we needed to focus on him," he said to her. "We aren't done with him yet, remember?"

Serena had spoken to him about it a few months ago, about how they had to stop Shet from entering their world before anything else could happen, including between them. And with every passing day, William's worries about the god of the mahavans increased. *How will we stop Shet?*

"I know, and I agree," Serena said, interrupting his worries, "but don't you think you should live some? Enjoy the beautiful day and the people you're with." She gestured about them.

The late-day sun shot bars of golden light through bands of cumulus clouds, lighting parts of the Village Green, the heart of Lilith and the only village upon Arylyn. Nearby, a jazz band played a languid tune from within the centrally-placed gazebo, and the perfumed scent of gardenias drifted on the breeze as a small crowd gathered to listen to the music. Beyond the gazebo, William caught sight of Selene and her friends, no doubt heading for an after-school treat at *Maxine's Ice Creamery*, the finest and only ice cream parlor in Lilith. Like most of the island's restaurants and stores, it stood upon Clifftop, the village's industrial core.

William took in their surroundings and tried to set aside his irritation with Serena. She'd been the one who'd gone on and on about needing to put aside personal desires and train for Shet. *Now she expects me to enjoy the day with her?* He suppressed a grimace.

"Why don't we get something to drink?" Serena suggested, apparently not picking up on his annoyance.

On again, off again with her. He mentally sighed. *So be it.* William managed a smile and indicated for Serena to lead on.

William wanted to take Serena's hand as they walked toward *Maxine's* but he held back. Work and worry kept them apart. He guessed that's how Serena wanted it so he never spoke of how he sometimes thought about her. He feared her response. As a result, he remained quiet as they ambled past long, narrow buildings made of brick, stone, or a combination of the two. Other people were out and about, shopping or taking a stroll. William called out loud 'hellos' to most of them, while Serena was more reserved in her greetings.

A few minutes later, they reached their destination: *Maxine's Ice Creamery.*

Selene and a few of her friends—Emma Lake and Janine Dale— were already on their way out the door. All of them clutched waffle cones heaped to overflowing with ice cream.

"We're going for a hike through Janaki Valley," Selene said. The young girl was a mirror image of her older sister, almost the same height and with a promise of beauty once she grew into her gangly frame.

Serena laughed. "Have fun."

"See you later." Selene and her friends clomped off in a wild show of girlish giggles and squealing laughter.

William and Serena entered the ice cream parlor. It was cool inside, brightly lit and smelling of chocolate, vanilla, and melted sugar. Maxine waited behind the counter. She was an elderly, bespectacled woman with sparkling, lively eyes and a generous manner. Everyone loved her.

"Can we have two lemonades?" William asked.

"Of course, dears," Maxine said. She drew the drinks from a wooden keg, filling two mugs and passing them over. "If you add a touch of Air, it changes the flavor from lemonade to cider." She didn't need to remind them, but she always did. "Add Fire for orange juice and Earth if you want soda."

William chose Earth since he loved a good soda. He sensed Serena source her *lorethasra* when a touch of mint floated on the air. The rustling of Earth indicated that she'd also gone for soda.

"Thanks, Ms. Maxine," they called as they left the ice creamery.

William took a long drink of his soda before they set out. They wandered Lilith's streets, bridges, and alleys, not really paying much attention to where they were going.

A half-hour later, Serena squeezed his arm and pulled him to a halt. "I want to stop in here." She pointed to Robert Weeks' smithy and led William inside. The ringing of a hammer from out back could be heard, but there was no one to mind the front of the store.

It didn't matter. No one would steal anything. Crime hardly ever happened on Arylyn. Anyone could take most anything they wanted and tell the storeowner about it later. The island used no currency and people were expected to pay for what they needed with reciprocal labor of some kind.

"Why are we here?" William asked.

"No reason," Serena answered. "Just browsing."

William caught the scent of roses, and he frowned, glancing about as he tried to figure out where it was coming from.

Serena's face brightened, and she drew his attention. "Look." She pointed to a small figurine, a red dragon that flapped its wings, clomped forward a short distance, and breathed fire. Next to it rested a vase full of silver-stemmed, copper roses. They were the source of the floral scent filling the room. "Robert has such a delicate touch," Serena said, sounding admiring.

"Yes, he does," William agreed in a wistful tone. He wished he had the time to learn smithing, but like everything else, he had to shove those dreams to the back burner. He had to train and become a better warrior. Maybe after Shet was dealt with, he could . . .

He sighed as he realized the direction of his thoughts. *Will I always have to defer my gratification?*

Serena studied him a moment. "Let's go." She gave his hand a squeeze, tugged him outside, and they headed back to the Village Green.

"You never did answer me," Serena said while they entered a shadowed alley. "What do you plan on doing for Western New Year's? And don't say 'training.' No one else will be."

William wasn't so focused on Shet that he couldn't set aside a single evening to give over to having fun. He also wasn't stupid enough to discount Serena's question. She'd asked him about this twice today, which meant it was important to her. "I'm not going to train," he said. "I thought I might ask a former mahavan if she wanted to go with me."

"And maybe I'll accept that offer from a certain drone," Serena said, "but only if he ever figures out that a life perpetually deferred isn't one worth living."

William scowled. Her advice seemed deeply unfair. "Weren't you the one who said we had to study? It's why we *deferred—*"

"I know," she interrupted, "and I still believe it, but sometimes you have to live for today. I realized that when we saw that movie last week during our visit to the Far Beyond, *Dead Poet's Society.*"

William recalled the movie. He'd loved it, especially its underlying message of *carpe diem*. Still, he couldn't help but wonder how he could manage that with Shet looming over them.

They continued their stroll in silence, passing from the coolness of the alley to the sunshine beaming down on the Village Green.

This was William's favorite setting in Arylyn. The Pacific Ocean surged far below while River Namaste split Lilith's five cliffs and cascaded downward as a series of waterfalls. Rainbows bathed the village's various terraces, bridges, and homes in a riot of colors. William knew without looking that the view directly northeast was dominated by Mount Madhava. To the northwest he'd find Sita's Song, a broad road made of gray flagstones that cut a slender ribbon from Lilith, through the farms of Janaki Valley, and ended at the base of the mountain.

"What do you think? Try to live for today?" Serena asked with a challenging lift to her eyebrows.

William eyed her askance. "You're not going to let this go, are you?"

"I will when you see reason, and if you do, I'll even save you a dance."

In that moment, William couldn't speak. A summons blared in his heart. Something beckoned. Fury consumed him. It took the form of a snapping, snarling beast and burned his thoughts until nothing remained but unreasoning, red rage. His fists clenched, and a vision arose in his mind, a pale, hairless creature, as tall as Kohl Obsidian and with a mouth like a gangrenous wound.

William stumbled, scared and off-balance as the vision faded. The rage receded into the depths of his mind, but he could still sense it, growling every now and then, low, throaty, and ready to leap forward.

He also remembered an anger like this from another time. It had come from Kohl Obsidian when the necrosed had killed his parents and touched him. This felt similar but far more potent, like a roaring bonfire in place of a lit lantern. And that face . . .

Serena frowned in concern. "William? What's wrong?"

"I don't know."

CHAPTER 5: PREPARATIONS AND DESIRES

D*ecember 1989*

R ukh flared his nostrils in irritation as the councilors continued their endless deliberations. He'd offered his case to them hours ago, and since then, they'd done nothing but argue endlessly about the merits of his presentation. Thus far, none of Lilith's councilors had said anything of actual meaning. Instead, all they'd put forth was a useless recitation of points made earlier.

He ground his teeth in impatience. By now, the sun lingered late in the sky. He knew it to be true despite the lack of windows in the Council Chamber. A Kumma could always tell the time, and politicians the worlds over did nothing but waste it. They loved speaking and hearing the glory of their useless voices.

Rukh mentally grimaced. He hated politics.

The others in the room—Jessira, Mr. Zeus, William, and Serena —must have sensed his agitation. They eyed him askance, stirring and shifting in their seats—the pews facing the rectangular table behind which sat the councilors. Serena even flicked a worried glance toward the single entrance leading into the drab, boring room.

"I don't think this is that hard a decision," said Bar Duba, a large man with the dark skin and hair that proclaimed his lineage as being a native born to Arylyn. "Rukh only offers to instruct those who wish to be trained as part of a militia. Nothing more." He faced Rukh. "Isn't that correct?"

Rukh nodded. "After the attack on Sinskrill, we need a military force to defend this island. The mahavans *will* respond, and Shet will follow on their heels. I think we all know that."

"I agree," Mr. Zeus said.

"You weren't so sanguine about any of this a year ago," Mayor Lilian Care said to Mr. Zeus in her aristocratic English accent.

"As you said, that was a year ago," Mr. Zeus replied as he stroked his long, white beard. "I've modified my opinion since then."

"This is old news," blurted Zane Blood, an officious man with all the pomp and arrogance of a born bureaucrat. "All of these individuals . . ." he gestured at Rukh and the others, ". . . were intimately involved in that prior undertaking. Of course they urge further action now, but I have yet to see why we should allow it. These rumors about Shet are hearsay and nonsense, as are these unwarranted fears that Sinskrill will attack us." His eyes widened in feigned amazement. "Exactly how will they achieve this miracle? They don't even know the location of our island!"

"They'll know it if Shet tells them," Serena said.

Zane snorted in derision. "Shet."

"Yes, Shet," William said, his voice edged in obvious anger.

Rukh studied the youth with a worried frown. A few days ago William had started to become angry for the smallest of reasons.

Zane chuckled in derision. "Shet is a myth."

"Think what you wish," William replied. "We only want a chance to defend ourselves. That's all we're asking."

Zane harrumphed. "Young man, matters are not so simple."

"Why not?" William challenged.

Rukh sighed as the conversation took a turn down a previously argued dead-end alley. He tuned it out.

Even if the mahavans didn't attack Arylyn, the magi had to return to Sinskrill. They had to go back and close the anchor line from Seminal. How else could they prevent Shet's arrival on Earth? As Rukh reckoned matters, it was far better to defeat Sinskrill's supposed god by avoiding him altogether than hoping to defeat him in face-to-face combat. Their chances at the latter would be vanishingly small given how difficult it had been to overcome Shet's servant, the Servitor.

When Rukh returned his attention to the discussion, he discovered that Break Foliage, a counselor and a rat-faced, rat-hearted man, was blathering on and on about prudence and cost.

Prudence and cost. What cost? Arylyn used no currency so the only cost would be the time spent by the volunteers who chose to fight. *As for prudence, was it not prudent to defend one's home?*

Rukh silently snarled. He was a man of action, not of words, and right now, he imagined himself concussing Break and bringing the meeting to a close.

Jessira noticed his anger, and she subtly shook her head. *Patience* her eyes urged.

Rukh mentally snorted. *Hot-blooded Jessira is telling me to be patient.* Nevertheless, he took a settling breath, and tried to force his simmering anger to cool.

It was of no use. Break continued to drone on, his words signifying nothing.

Rukh had enough. He surged to his feet. "Be silent and make a decision." He glared at Break Foliage. "Fight to live, or huddle like cowards and hope the hunting wolves overlook you."

Break gaped. "How dare you!" the little man shouted. "You are nothing but a late-come visitor who thinks to tell us how to live. If *you're* to be believed, you're not even from this world."

William rose to his feet as well. "Which is why you should listen to him. Rukh and Jessira come from a world called Arisa, a place none of us have ever heard of. If that's real, then why can't Seminal and Shet also be real?"

Seema Choudary, a small, quiet Indian woman with a raspy voice, rapped her fist upon the table. "Young man, we understand your passion, but curtail your surety and think. What if you're wrong?"

"I'm not," William said with a belligerent thrust of his jaw.

"What if you are?" she pressed again. "We would panic the populace for no reason." She held his attention. "You ask for far more than you realize."

"We are Lilith's councilors," Break Foliage puffed up in a self-important manner, "chosen by popular decree to uphold the laws of this land and ensure our survival. We will not lead our charges into blind panic based on wild stories without any basis in fact."

"You *are* Lilith's councilors," Rukh agreed, "and you *are* charged with ensuring our survival." He leaned forward, knuckles braced upon the bench in front of him. "Then do your job and let me train people who will help us survive what's coming. No one need panic over that."

"You want to do more than just train," Lucas Shaw said in his slow, southern drawl. "You want to attack Sinskrill."

Jessira stood. "Yes," she said, "because sometimes the best defense is a good offense. I would rather fight the mahavans on Sinskrill's soil than on Arylyn's."

"Only if they actually come," Zane countered.

"Which they will," Mr. Zeus said.

"We're going nowhere with this," Bar Duba rumbled.

"In this, I think, we are all in accord," Mayor Care said. "It is time we made a decision."

Rukh mumbled agreement and took a seat. William followed suit.

"Motion to bring this interminable discussion to an end," Bar said.

"Seconded," Seema announced.

"All in favor?" Mayor Care asked.

A unanimous voicing of 'ayes' met her query.

Rukh stood again. This might be his last chance to sway the Council's opinion, and while he'd never been good at politics and speeches —that had been his sister Bree's forte—he had to make sure the councilors heard him. "Wait a moment before casting your final decision. Please. Remember, I only want to train whoever seeks instruction. Consider it my means of contributing to the island's well-being. No one will be compelled. We only ask that you give them the opportunity to choose."

Mutters met his words, and for an instant, Rukh thought matters would descend once more into the long-winded discussion that had ended only moments earlier.

"Motion to do as Rukh asks," Bar said.

"Second," Seema agreed.

"All in favor?" Mayor Care asked.

The Mayor, Bar, Seema, and Lucas voted for the measure.

"Against," Mayor Care asked.

Break and Zane voted in negation.

"The motion carries," Mayor Care announced.

Rukh exhaled in relief.

The mayor continued speaking. "Whoever wishes to learn from you will be allowed to." She collected Rukh's attention in a stern gaze. "Let me be clear, though. This does not give you license to invade Sinskrill."

Rukh nodded acceptance, but he'd already begun planning what to do next.

～

Jake and Julius walked the flagstones of Sita's Song as it took them through the emerald heart of Arylyn's farmlands. A wispy fog enveloped the green hills, fields, farmhouses, and barns of Janaki Valley, and even this early—a little past dawn—farmers were already out working their fields.

Despite the long hike, Jake's breathing came easily. Thankfully, the hitch in his chest, the pulling sensation that lingered for months following his near-death in Australia, had finally receded.

"How are you holding up?" Julius asked in his brisk Jamaican accent. He'd cut off his cornrows and now wore his hair short and neat along with a fashionably sculpted goatee. Jake sometimes didn't recognize Julius with his clean-cut appearance.

"I'm fine." Jake took a deep breath to demonstrate his fitness.

"Glad to hear it," Julius said with an open-hearted grin. "How did your visit with your family go?"

"I wish I could have stayed longer," Jake replied, a wistful tone to his voice. "It would have been nice."

Julius's face fell into lines of concern. "Still having nightmares?"

Jake gave a bitter chuckle. "After everything I've been through, I'll probably always have nightmares."

"Can Mr. Zeus help?"

Jake shook his head. "Not really. Not for something like this. But I was better at home. Sometimes, it feels like it's the only place where I'm safe." More bitterness rose. "Back there, I could pretend that none of this real, and the future is still bright and shiny."

"The future can still be bright and shiny," Julius said in a soothing tone. He wore the expression of someone carefully choosing his words. "Your life can still be a good one."

"I already *had* a good life," Jake said with a sour chuckle. "Now I have magic, but it's brought me nothing but heartache and pain."

Julius had no response, and they continued in silence.

As they traveled, Jake stewed over the sharp left turn his life had taken, the one leading straight into a ditch. He hated most of what had happened to him. If not for *asra* he'd never have learned about Sinskrill, Arylyn, or Shet. He'd never have been stolen into slavery and nearly killed. Instead, he'd have been part of a national championship football team at Notre Dame and gearing up for another big bowl game. That had been the life he had wanted for himself. Not this one full of magic and adventure but more often of pain and suffering.

His thoughts were interrupted when a passing wagon approached, one loaded with apples and headed toward Lilith. He and Julius stepped aside, and while they waited on the wagon, a couple of farmers—Samuel Winston and Erick Fine—came over to chat. Julius shared some gossip with the two men, but Jake didn't much want to talk. He continued to brood over the events of the past few years, and the desire for a different life remained on his mind.

The conversation with the farmers quickly ended after the wagon passed, and he and Julius soon pressed on.

Minutes later, Julius pointed to a house atop a small hill. "We'll find what we came for up there."

They ascended a low rise and paused in front of a white, clapboard farmhouse with a windmill close at hand. Both structures would have been normal for an Indiana cornfield. Farther beyond the house and windmill lay a wide field of wheatgrass. It swept down to the edge of a cliff, and the Pacific Ocean rumbled hundreds of feet below, audible even from where they stood.

Julius led the way toward the windmill. "One of the leylines here is polluted."

"We're going to clean it?"

"It's what I do," Julius said. "Especially since only certain Water adepts and *raha'asras* can see *lorasra*."

"Weren't you an engineer at Purdue before you came to Arylyn?" Jake asked.

"A student, and before that the black sheep of the family." Julius chuckled. "I don't think my father and mother believed it when I finally grew up and focused on my studies."

"Do you see them much?"

"Several times a year," Julius said, "but it's not easy. There aren't any *saha'asras* in Jamaica, and it's a long trip to get there."

Several times a year. Jake grimaced. If he had his way, he would spend forever in the Far Beyond.

"Can you see the leyline?" Julius asked as they approached the creaking windmill rotating slowly in the wind.

Jake searched for the leyline and quickly found it. For those who could see them, leylines pulsed like streams of gold, like trunk-sized, ghostly arteries that branched off one of the island's Primal Nodes and spread root-like extensions throughout the island. They flowed several feet underground but were still visible to those with the skill to see it, and this one pooled around the windmill, containing a pus-yellow color.

"You know about *therasra*, polluted *lorasra*?" Julius asked.

"On Sinskrill, they collected it in *theranoms*."

"So do we," Julius replied. He gestured at the leyline. "You see how this one has a kink in it?"

Jake bent to peer closer. The leyline, normally beating with the island's lifeblood of golden *lorasra*, held a deep pinch, as if someone had squeezed it shut. He had no idea how it had happened. *Maybe a shifting rock?* "Will Sioned or Afa have to fix it?"

"Yeah, but first we'll clean what we can," Julius said.

He unlocked a cellar door next to the windmill, and they descended into a small, dirt-floored, underground chamber. A musty smell permeated the space. The leyline entered from the far wall before branching into individual arms that passed into a rack of terra cotta urns centered inside the cellar. From there, the leyline reformed as it exited the room's near side.

"Those are the *theranoms*." Julius pointed to the urns. Each one had a pair of handles and an opening sealed with a thread of Earth. "They're going to be full of *therasra* since the break is downstream of them."

"You know, the mahavans spaced their *theranoms* at regular intervals along a leyline."

"Seems like a lot more walking that way."

"But since this one broke downstream of these *theranoms*," Jake said, "the entire section upstream is polluted. That wouldn't happen if the *theranoms* were placed more regularly."

Julius grunted. "I guess even evil bastards can have good ideas." He lifted an urn off the rack and set it down before unbraiding the seal. It popped open with a hiss.

Jake peered inside. Within the *theranom* floated a brackish liquid that smelled like sewage. He covered his nose. "It smells like Sinskrill's *lorasra*," he complained.

"It does, doesn't it?" Julius noted with a wrinkle of his nose. "No wonder that place sucked so bad."

Jake glowered. He hated thinking about Sinskrill. His time there had been one of unending misery and horror, and while Mr. Zeus had removed or eased many of those horrific memories, he couldn't calm all of them. Certainly not the lashing.

Yet another reason to wish for a different past and a different future. He wondered if magi could turn back time.

≈

A few days after helping Julius with the kinked leyline, Jake awoke and yawned mightily. He padded downstairs and stepped through the French doors leading outside to the flagstone patio behind Mr. Zeus' home. He noticed the others waiting for him, William, Jason, and Mr. Zeus, along with Julius, who must have stopped by for breakfast. They sat at the table stationed beneath an ivy-wreathed pergola, sharing conversation and laughing with one another.

The sun had yet to rise high enough to crest the ruddy-veined, black-granite wall that formed the rear of the property, and much of the back yard remained in cool shade. A rivulet from one of River Namaste's cascades slid down the cliff's stony face before forming a small pond. Orange and mango trees as well as a number of flowering shrubs edged the water and the patio while a thin strip of grass and a firepit finished out the space.

Jake caught William's grin of welcome. "Woke up late?" William asked.

Jake yawned again. "Went to sleep late is more like it."

William gestured to an unoccupied chair. "Have a seat."

Jake nodded his thanks.

"We saved you some food," Jason said.

Jake's attention focused on breakfast as Jason passed him a plate piled with pancakes, eggs, and bacon. "Thanks," he said. He was about to tuck in, but he noticed Jason grinning. "What?"

"You really must be tired," Jason said. "You didn't even ask if anyone licked the pancakes."

Jake grunted and plowed into his food. Most mornings he couldn't get anything done until he'd had breakfast. "Hangry" was what William called it, probably some made-up word Serena had told him.

"It's his teenage brain," Mr. Zeus said, and Jake heard the smile in his voice. "He never knows when to sleep or wake up."

"Where's Serena?" Jake asked when he finally surfaced for air. She, Selene, and Fiona often had breakfast with them.

William answered. "She had work to do. Sile needs her help with one of his fields."

Julius pointed west to the Triplets, a trio of rounded mountains, where a bank of dark clouds headed their way. "Looks like they'll be catching some weather."

Jake eyed the clouds and chuckled as a stray thought came to him.

"What's so funny?" William asked.

Jake gestured to the pregnant clouds. "Serena doesn't have much skill with Air. She can't make the weave that shucks the water off your clothes," he explained. "When that rain hits, she'll be wet as a cat."

Jason groaned. "That's a terrible simile. Wet as a cat. What does that even mean?"

Jake shrugged. "It means you're as smart as a limp rag."

Mr. Zeus spoke before Jason could respond. "No arguing."

Jason clicked his mouth shut, and Jake grinned at him. Needling each other was how they passed the time, but sometimes it irritated Mr. Zeus.

"The rains here remind me of home," Julius said, sounding fond. "They always come on quick and leave just as fast."

Jake glanced his way. "It sounds like you miss your life back home as much as I do."

"I miss my family," Julius clarified, "but I've made a new life here. A good one."

Jake shrugged. "I'd give up magic in a heartbeat if it meant I could go home."

William snorted. "Hi kettle, I'm Jake."

Jake bristled. "What does that mean?"

"It means you're always getting on my case about not being happy with what I've got."

"It's true," Jake replied. "You're always going on and on about how you'll worry about being happy in the future."

William wore a triumphant expression. "How's that any different than looking back and wishing for what you don't have?"

Jake opened his mouth, wanting to disagree with William's statement, but as he searched his mind no answer came to him. The seconds stretched, and Jake scowled. He hated when William used his own words against him. "Shut up," Jake eventually replied. "It's not the same."

"How?" William challenged, laughing in satisfaction.

"Because it isn't," Jake retorted. He still scowled. His answer sounded stupid—he even thought so—but he couldn't take it back. "It's no secret that I want to go home," he said, "but my situation is different from yours. You can have happiness right now if you want to. It's a choice you can make any time you want. I can't to do that. What I want is impossible. It can never happen. I'll have to settle for having my brother healed. Rukh and Jessira said they'd help me with that."

William perked up as he always did whenever Rukh and Jessira were mentioned. "When do you plan on going?"

"Between the Western and Chinese New Years," Jake answered. "I was going to ask Steve Aldo and Sonya Bowyer over to my parents house, too."

Jason eyed him with a skeptical air. "Your old girlfriend? You sure that's a good idea?"

Jake shrugged. "It's a terrible idea, but I feel like I owe Sonya an explanation about why I dropped off the face of the earth."

"I'll come with you if that's all right," William said.

Mr. Zeus cleared his throat. "If you plan on telling Sonya and Steve the truth, make sure you—"

"I remember," Jake interrupted. "I'll put a braid on them. They won't be able to tell anyone about us."

Mr. Zeus gave a single, grave nod. "Then you have my blessing." He leaned forward and stared Jake in the eyes. "And while you're there, think about what you have here. It isn't all gloom and doom here, you know. Your future is also a choice, and it can be a wonderful one. All you need do is open your heart and accept it."

CHAPTER 6: UNEXPECTED EMOTIONS

January 1990

A fast-moving cloudburst caught William and his friends as they hiked to Linchpin Knoll. After it moved on, he braided a fine weave of Air and Fire to quickly dry himself off. The weave took a level of control that William had mastered only a few months ago, and once he'd wrung out most of the wetness, he levered his rucksack onto his shoulder and ascended the short incline to the top of the hill.

He shivered when a stiff breeze blew. It carried the scent of the recent thundershower and the perfumed scent of jasmines growing along the base of the knoll. The full moon hung in the sky like a luminescent pearl. It flooded the island with a bright, ivory light while Mount Madhava wore a glowing crown of clouds. Crickets chirped, and William caught sight of a small lizard dashing away from their path.

He watched the little reptile leap into a bush, and his inattention almost cost him his footing when he slipped on the damp grass. His arms wind-milled as he sought to regain his balance and avoid a humiliating fall. Once he no longer threatened to pitch over, he furtively stared about to see if anyone had noticed his near tumble.

Rukh had. He winked.

William shrugged in embarrassment and made sure to climb more slowly across the rain-slick turf and stones that formed the path to the top of Linchpin Knoll. This time, he was more careful in trailing after Rukh and Jessira while Jake, Serena, and Selene followed him. The others held silent, apparently concentrating on their own thoughts or maybe their own footing.

They soon reached the hill's crest, and Rukh and Jessira paused to check their weapons: swords, daggers, and pistols. Despite everyone expecting it to be a simple trip into the Far Beyond, the two of them insisted on traveling fully armed.

Jake watched them with a frown of puzzlement. "Guns don't work on a necrosed," he supplied.

"They work on everything else," Rukh said.

William stood next to Selene. It surprised him anew how tall she'd grown. In his mind, she should still be the little girl he'd helped rescue from Sinskrill, but instead, she'd somehow transformed into a long-legged, coltish, almost-woman with striking hazel eyes that contrasted strikingly against her dusky skin and the scattering of freckles sprinkling her nose. In a few years—if not now—the boys would come pestering her. He shook his head in disbelief at the idea. *How did she grow up so fast?*

Selene momentarily eyed him in curiosity. "Are you going to ask Serena to marry you?"

William's jaw dropped. *Where did* that *come from?* He liked Serena, but in all their time together marriage had never once come up. *Of course, neither has dating, and whose fault is that?* "What are you talking about?"

"It's simple," Selene explained. "You love her, she loves you. Why don't you get married?"

William scowled as he tried to wrap his head around the unexpectedly bizarre notion Selene had come up with. The growling beast of anger that had somehow settled in the back of his mind like an unwanted houseguest awoke then. It stirred, black-furred and red-eyed, and he snapped his response. "Who put you up to this?" he demanded. "Fiona?"

He knew his voice had come out harsher than he intended, and Selene's eyes widened in alarm. She took a step away from him. He took a deep inhalation and managed to smooth over his features. "Sorry about that."

Selene stared at him for a moment longer in concern, but an instant later she collected herself and managed an eyeroll, something she apparently mastered when she turned thirteen.

William found himself irritated anew, and once again, the strange, red-eyed creature he'd come to associate with his anger rumbled. He had a moment of panic. He didn't know where the beast had come from, but ever since that day of shopping with Serena, when he'd had a vision of that skeletal, albino monstrosity, his anger seemed ready to rage at a moment's notice. He hated it. He closed his eyes, taking more calming breaths.

The anger slowly simmered to sleep.

"No one put me up to it," Selene said in answer to his earlier question. "I came up with it on my own. Just me."

William gave her his hardest disbelieving stare, but she didn't flinch. "I think you should stay out of this," he finally said.

"Fine. But you should tell her how you feel." Selene waited a beat. "Unless you're fine with her moving on to someone else."

"Uh, huh." William didn't know why Selene was doing this, but it was time to flip the script on her. He tapped his chin in apparent thought. "Say, who was that boy I saw you with the other day?" he asked, making stuff up since he'd seen no such thing. "If I didn't know better, I'd think you liked him." He paused a beat. "A lot."

Selene frowned in clear suspicion and worry. "What boy?"

"The one you shared an ice cream cone with," William said, coming up with answers on the fly. "If I didn't know better I'd think the two of you planned on kissing."

Somehow he'd guessed right, and Selene paled. "How did you know about that?"

William grinned and touched the side of his head. "I may be old, but I'm not slow." He grinned wider as Selene sputtered and begged him not to tell Serena or Fiona. "I won't say anything, but only if you tell the truth," he said. "What was with the marriage thing?"

Selene's shoulders slumped. "It was just a thought," she said. "I know you're going back to Sinskrill. So is Serena. I only want both of you to be happy before then."

William didn't know what to say. Selene's fears were real and true. He and Serena, one or both of them, might not survive what was to come. Jake, Jason, Mr. Zeus . . . they could all die, including Selene. He drew her into a hug and kissed the top of her head. He spoke words, a vow he couldn't keep with any certainty, a gentle lie. "We'll be fine. I promise."

She nodded against his shoulder before pulling away and going to speak with her sister.

William drifted to where Rukh was talking to Jake. "We'll do what we can for your brother," the Indian-looking man was saying, "but we make no promises."

"I understand," Jake said. "Even if you can't do anything, it'll be nice seeing the family."

Rukh wandered off to check on something else, and William noticed Jake smiling. "What's got you grinning like an idiot?"

"I was imagining what Sonya will think of what we can do."

William chuckled and wondered the same thing. For the longest time Sonya Bowyer had been his life's lodestone. He'd had a huge crush on her, right up to the moment a certain former mahavan had sauntered into his life.

Serena.

She would also be going with them on this trip, stating that she wanted to make amends with Jake's family, but William didn't think it likely. He worried for her.

Serena was speaking softly to Selene, but she must have noticed his regard. She flashed him a crooked grin, the one he loved where she seemed secretly amused by the world in general.

"Are we ready?" Rukh asked, interrupting William's thoughts.

Everyone nodded or muttered. "Yes."

"Then let's go."

The scent of iron filled the air as Rukh sourced his *lorethasra*. An instant later, a vertical line split the air and rotated on its long axis. A two-dimensional doorway opened onto a kaleidoscope of colors and patterns. The smell of sulfur took the place of iron as Rukh rhythmically pulsed a thread of Fire. Seconds later a deep-noted bell tone rang out, and the colors took the form of a rainbow bridge extending into infinity.

Rukh and Jessira crossed first, and William let the others go next. His turn came, and he tethered to the anchor line. When he stepped onto the rainbow bridge a single thought filled his mind. *Marriage?* He laughed, recalling the impressive clergyman from *The Princess Bride*.

~

Serena stepped through the anchor line and entered a small, West Virginia meadow covered in a dusting of snow. Golden light spilled from the windows of a few log cabins standing perimeter around the edge of the field. They reminded her of sentinels remaining in watchful wariness, with their lanterns held aloft to dash away the dark. The nearby forest held quiet except when an errant wind blew. Then the branches rattled and clacked like a blind man's stick over pavement.

Serena's breath frosted in the pre-dawn air, and she shivered despite the jacket she wore. Her Sinskrill heritage, which had inured her to a harsh life, had been eroded by Arylyn's warmth and the generosity of its people.

"I think I should have brought a heavier coat," she said to William.

He stepped closer. "You're sure you want to go through with this?" he asked in a hushed voice only she could hear.

She understood what he meant, and while she really didn't want to meet Jake's parents, she also felt like she owed them the deepest, most sincere apology she could muster. She didn't let her uneasiness show, though. While her time in Arylyn had given her freedom to laugh without reserve, her Sinskrill training remained, and it wouldn't allow her to display weakness or vulnerability. Instead, she managed a dismissive shrug. "At some point, I have to apologize for what I did."

"If it doesn't work out—"

"I'll stay at a hotel," she finished. She imagined that would be the most likely scenario, but she had to try. She wanted to make amends to the Ridleys. It was a burning need, one she couldn't fully explain, a desire to face the sins of her past and ask for forgiveness.

William gave her shoulder a sympathetic squeeze and her forehead a brief kiss before gesturing to the parking lot. "There's the T-bird."

He strode off, and Serena watched him go. Her forehead tingled where his lips had pressed against it. She would have called him back but Ms. Sioned's admonishment from many months earlier, before they'd saved Fiona and Travail, kept her in place. *Work hard, dedicate your life to what must be done. Let nothing distract you, or you will surely fail.*

Jake took William's place at her elbow. "I can't promise things will go well with my folks, but I'll make sure they hear you out." He wavered. "Or at least I'll do my best."

Serena managed a smile. "It's better to face your demons before they face you," she said, quoting an old aphorism from Sinskrill.

"My parents aren't demons," Jake said, sounding offended.

"No, but my actions were," Serena said.

Jake's demeanor relaxed, and a moment later, he moved to help William pack their gear into the T-bird's trunk.

Serena inhaled deeply and tried to settle her nerves.

Jessira approached then, and Serena silently groaned. She didn't need *everyone* wishing her well. Sometimes too much support felt less like sympathy and more like an aggravation.

Jessira surprised her, though. "When this is over, tell me what you require and I'll do it, even if it's simply to leave you alone." She quirked a grin, a winning expression on her striking if not lovely face. "I'll even move aside those who seek to annoy you with their over-exuberance of empathy."

Serena started, surprised at Jessira's guess at how she was feeling. "How did you know?"

Jessira laughed, and her long, honey-blonde hair, currently tied in a braid, bounced. "Because that's what Sign would have wanted, and as I've mentioned once or twice, you remind me of her."

Jake smacked the roof of the T-bird to get their attention. "Ladies, hurry up! Geez."

Rukh, standing near him, gave him a shove.

"What?" Jake squawked.

Rukh said something inaudible, and Jake's eyes shot toward Jessira. He paled. "She wouldn't," Serena heard him say.

Rukh chuckled, soft and low, in answer.

Jake took in Jessira's stony expression once again. His face went slack, and he dove into the back seat.

Serena grinned as she slid into the T-bird's back seat, while Jessira entered from the other side. Jake sat squeezed between them.

"This is cozy," Jessira noted to Jake, a teasing glint in her eyes.

Jake never noticed. He studiously ignored her and Serena laughed.

Rukh slid into Serena's usual spot in the passenger seat. With his long legs he needed the space more than she did.

William got them going, and they quickly rumbled out of the meadow. The road they followed cut through a forest and followed the contours of the various hills and hollows. Snow, blackened, dirty, and often interspersed with a littering of leaves, had piled in drifts alongside the road, and occasional winter-bare fields broke the monotony of the trees.

"Has it always taken this long to get out of West Virginia?" Jake complained.

Serena privately wondered the same thing as they switch-backed across the hills and changing elevations. She judged that they likely traveled four miles for every straight mile they needed to go.

William flicked his gaze through the rear-view mirror. "Bit excited to get home?" he asked.

Jake shrugged. "I don't mind being squished between two beautiful women—"

"Well spoken," Jessira said with a smile.

"—but, yeah, I'm looking forward to getting home," Jake finished.

"It's a lot prettier in the spring," William noted.

"Everything is prettier in the spring," Rukh replied in an unexpected note of complaint.

"Not everything," Jessira said. "Teardrop Lake was always lovelier in the winter."

Rukh shifted about and faced her. He shook his head in mock disgust. "Only an OutCaste would think so."

Jessira smiled. "Or maybe your Pureblood heritage was simply unable to appreciate it."

"I remember the first time I saw Teardrop Lake," Rukh said. "I didn't think much of it."

"Is this some place on Arisa?" Jake asked.

Rukh nodded. "I was Jessira's prisoner. Do you remember that, *priya?*" he asked her.

Jessira scoffed. "You were never anyone's prisoner."

"What does *priya* mean?" Serena asked.

"Nothing important," Jessira said with a chuckle. "It's only Rukh's way of believing himself funny."

"As you say, *priya.*" Rukh said.

"My mom called my dad *priya*," William said. "She said it meant beloved."

"Interesting," Rukh replied, still facing backward.

"You can't leave us hanging," Jake said to Rukh. "What happened? Why were you Jessira's prisoner?"

They reached a state highway—four lanes with two in each direction—and the road straightened. They journeyed on, and Rukh told more about his and Jessira's history from Arisa. He spoke of his banishment from his home.

"The first time I was born . . ."

Serena caught Jakes's eyes widen in confusion.

". . . I lived in Ashoka, a glorious city-state, one of many scattered throughout the land," Rukh said. "The rest of the world, though, was ruled by Suwraith, the Sorrow Bringer, an ancient power who plunged the world into darkness when She murdered Her Parents. It happened two thousand years prior to my birth, and the only reason Humanity survived is because in His last act, Suwraith's Father created the Oases, a powerful manifestation of *Jivatma*—*asra* as you would call it. The Oases proved impervious to Suwraith's power, and the cities sheltered within them were able to ride out Her fury. Afterward, a new civilization arose, and the remaining cities developed a means to maintain contact with one another."

"The Trials," Jessira murmured.

Rukh nodded. "They were large caravans of wagons or ships that traveled from city-to-city, carrying goods and materials but especially knowledge, such as new means of farming, more effective medicine or architecture. Most prized, though, were newly minted pieces of poetry, music, and plays. But we always had to be cautious of the Sorrow Bringer and her Plagues of Chimeras. Stepping beyond the boundaries of an Oasis often times meant death."

"You're saying you lived in some post-apocalyptic hell?" William asked.

"It wasn't as bad as that," Rukh said, moving to face forward. "For instance, Ashoka, my birthplace, was as lovely as Arylyn.

"How many people lived there?" Jake asked. "Ashoka, I mean."

"Two-hundred and fifty thousand," Jessira answered. "And Rukh is right. Ashoka was a precious gem of a city, set on the sea like Arylyn but with the history and culture of London or Paris."

Serena's mind swirled as she tried to take in all the information Rukh told them. "You've been to London and Paris?" she asked.

Rukh shook his head. "We've only read about them."

"Ashoka sounds like Atlantis," William said.

"Or Numenor," Jake added.

Serena tilted her head in puzzlement. "Atlantis is a name I know, but what's Numenor?"

Jessira spoke. "He refers to a fictional island from *The Silmarillion*."

Jake's mouth dropped, and Serena was no less surprised.

"I read," Jessira said in response to the shock on their faces.

"At any rate," Rukh continued, "I was born into Caste Kumma—

"What's a Caste?" Serena asked.

"A grave mistake," Jessira said. "An evil one."

Rukh flashed her a grimace of annoyance. "Would you like to tell the story?"

Jessira grinned unrepentantly. "You go ahead. You always do such a good job."

Rukh eyed her a moment longer. "Castes were the means by which my society was structured. There were seven Castes, and each one had a specific task to perform. For instance, mine, Caste Kumma, was warriors. Murans were farmers and singers. The Duriahs were artisans. The Sentyas were accountants and musicians, and Shiyens were Healers."

Serena considered Rukh's words, unsure as to Jessira's antipathy. "That doesn't sound too bad."

"A person is born in to a Caste and can never leave it," Jessira said. "Their lot in life is set forever more, and they can never do anything other than what their Caste dictates."

William scowled. "Well that would suck."

"You haven't heard the worst," Jessira said. "Not only does the birth Caste set your station in life, every person of a Caste has a similar physical build and features to every other member of that Caste."

"Do you mean all Kummas look like Rukh?" Serena asked.

"Yes," Jessira said, "and it was because men and women of different Castes could never marry. They were even prohibited from ever touching one another."

William blinked. "No touching? At all? That's stupid."

"And yet it worked," Rukh said. "Our society wasn't flawless, but we kept Humanity alive for two millennia in the face of a goddess trying to kill us. The Caste system allowed us to build our cities."

Jessira still scowled. "But what about the *naaja*, the OutCastes? People like me."

"It wasn't as if the OutCastes were unburdened by bigotry," Rukh said to Jessira.

Serena sensed an old argument brewing. "Can we skip to the part of how you met?"

"Of course." Rukh cleared his throat. "I was on my first Trial. We were attacked by the forces of the Sorrow Bringer—the Chimeras—and my caravan was destroyed. Somehow I obtained Talents that didn't belong to Caste Kumma." William opened his mouth, a question on his face, but Rukh cut him off. "That's too long of a story," he said. "Those of us who survived the attack tracked down the Chimeras, and discovered two miracles. First, we learned that the Chimera commanders, the Baels, hated Suwraith and actively opposed Her will. They sought to protect Humanity. I was about to speak to the commander, Li-Dirge—"

"I liked Li-Dirge," Jessira said. "He had a calm presence about him, almost like Travail."

"Yes, he did," Rukh agreed.

"What was the second miracle?" Serena asked.

"I found Jessira," Rukh answered. "The love of my life."

William and Jake groaned in disgust.

Rukh grinned. "Actually, I captured her and was about to kill her."

William seemed to sit up straight at the steering wheel. "Seriously?"

"Of course," Rukh said. "Jessira's features immediately told me what she was: the child of two Castes, a *naaja*, an abomination. Based on everything I was taught, she should never have been born, and I was expected to kill her for being alive."

Serena viewed Jessira sidelong, wondering at her thoughts and if this was true.

Her features remained steady and unwavering. "It's all true," Jessira said, "and since I'm here, Rukh obviously let me live."

"Suwraith attacked us right after all these discoveries," Rukh said, "but we managed to escape Her wrath, although Jessira was injured."

"There was a lot of running, hiding, and fighting after that, but in the end—" Jessira said.

"In the end, I was banished from Ashoka because of Jessira."

"That wasn't my fault," Jessira protested.

"No, it wasn't," Rukh agreed. "It was mine. I was an idiot to think I could bring you home and not be judged."

"It wasn't bringing me home that brought about your downfall," Jessira said. "It was the dinner we had. You shouldn't have taken me to Dryad Park."

Rukh smiled ruefully. "I suppose not, but I'm glad I did."

Part of Serena couldn't wrap her mind around the depth of Rukh and Jessira's obvious love for one another and another part wanted it for herself. She studied William and wondered if there would ever come a time when a looming crisis didn't take all their attention. So far they'd become good friends, but nothing more. Maybe someday that would change.

"At any rate," Rukh continued, "since I had no home, I followed Jessira to hers." He spoke on, describing a severe injury he'd suffered struggling to reach Jessira's home, the mountain city of Stronghold, and winning some fighting tournament.

By the time he finished, they'd passed out of West Virginia, rambled into Ohio. There, they had to stop for gas in an area of farms and fallow fields. The wind bit through their coats when they stepped outside the vehicle to stretch their legs.

"I'll pump the gas," Serena offered William, "if you get me something to drink."

William grinned. "Consider it done."

Jake stepped out of the car as well. "What are you two lovebirds talking about?"

Serena glanced his way, and a sly thought crossed her mind. She returned her attention to William and offered him a lazy, inviting smile as well as a wink. "We were talking about that song we heard the last time we were in the Far Beyond." She gazed into William's eyes and laced her arms around his neck. "You know, the one by Kevin Raleigh. 'Moonlight on Water.' There was a line in there about sex on the beach."

Jake groaned. "Get a room." He clambered back into the car.

Serena and William laughed.

"That was mean," William said.

Serena crinkled her nose. "Weren't you supposed to be getting me something to drink?"

William doffed an imaginary hat and went inside the gas station.

Minutes later, they got back on the road. This time Rukh let Serena have the front seat, and they traveled through Ohio's rolling hills and farms. Not many cars were out. They had the state highway to themselves and made quick time, passing an endless series of small convenience stores, gas stations, and restaurants. Soon thereafter, they began started seeing signs for Cincinnati.

Serena's heart thudded. Only an hour to go to meet the Ridleys. *Lord help me.*

~

W illiam glanced in the rear-view mirror when Rukh spoke up in complaint. "What is this disgusting music?"

"It's not music," Serena said. "It's noise set to a beat."

Temptation stirred inside William. *If it's too loud, you're too old.* He wanted to crank up the radio, which had been blaring "For Whom the Bell Tolls" by Metallica. Instead he turned the sound down.

"Killjoys," Jake muttered. "That was a great song."

William privately agreed. He'd never heard the song before, but he loved it. It reminded him of gunshots and something dark and terrifying. Badass music at its best. In fact, he'd never heard of Metallica either, and he made a mental note to look them up if they had a chance to hit a record shop during this visit to Jake's family.

They rolled on and soon reached Cincinnati's outskirts. William took I-275 toward Jake's home, driving in the cloudy gloom of a typical Midwestern winter's day of gray sky meeting gray pavement. A drizzly rain fell, and a river of headlights reflected off the wet concrete.

"I take it back about moving home full-time," Jake said. "Maybe I can spend winters in Arylyn."

"Amen to that," William said, even while he hoped Jake would find a way to make peace with the life he had.

"This weather reminds me of Sinskrill," Serena said.

William flicked his gaze toward her. "Which is one of many reasons we'll never miss that shitty island."

Serena might have said something, but William wasn't listening any more. The coolest tagline in all of radio, *The Lunatic Fringe of American FM*, had come on, followed by a song with an infectious guitar hook.

"Turn that up," Jake said.

"You ever hear this before?" William asked him.

"No," Jake said. "Now shut up. I want to listen."

William turned up the sound to a song called "Sweet Child O' Mine" by some band named Guns N' Roses.

William heard Rukh mumble something about noise again but

paid him no attention. No chance he was going to turn *this* song down.

A few minutes later "Let the Day Begin" by the Call came on and William found himself wondering how much great music he must have missed during his time on Arylyn.

They eventually reached their exit and were soon driving along suburban streets lined with shopping centers, fast food restaurants, and gas stations. William hummed along to the songs that came over the radio, all but the last one. "She Drives Me Crazy" had him glancing at Serena and thinking about her as the song played.

It ended at around the same time they reached Jake's house. He keyed off the engine and stepped out of the car, into a quiet neighborhood of elegant mansions.

"You *did* grow up rich," Serena told Jake.

"I know," Jake said, sounding smug. He led the way to the porch where he rang the doorbell once before unlocking the door and letting them all in.

William noticed Serena hanging back. She wore an unhappy, uncertain expression, possibly even anxious, all of which were atypical for her.

"Come on," he said, tugging her inside.

They found themselves in a two-story foyer with a massive chandelier.

Mr. Ridley, a big, balding man who looked like an older, heavier version of Jake, came out from a second floor hallway, crossed a catwalk ending at the stairs, and trundled down to meet them. "Jake. William," he said, a happy grin plastered on his face as he enveloped his son in a hug and shook hands with William. "Come on in," he said to all of them. "We'll sort out your coats and everything later."

He directed them to a large, open kitchen with oak cabinets, blue-tiled counters, and a double oven. Mrs. Ridley waited behind a large island. She had hot turkey sandwiches and tomato soup ready. Jake's brother, Johnny, sat on a leather sectional couch in the family room, watching a basketball game on a large-screen TV. He reminded William of a slightly-built, more bookish version of his father and brother. Mrs. Ridley stepped around the counter with a grin every bit as broad as Mr. Ridley's and hugged Jake and William. Her once-blonde hair had gone gray and laugh lines nested at the corners of her eyes, but she retained much of the beauty she must have had when she'd been young.

"Hey, Johnny," Jake called out to his brother.

"Hi, Jake," Johnny said with a shy smile, his eyes flicking to the others standing in the kitchen. "I'd come over and give you a hug, but today's a bad day." He gestured to his legs, which were shackled in braces, and the wheelchair resting against the couch. Johnny had some kind of muscular disease that waxed and waned. Last year he'd been able to hobble around without crutches but during the past few months things had gotten worse again. He now needed a wheelchair to get around.

"Those bad days are part of why I've brought my friends with me," Jake said.

Johnny viewed the others in interest.

"Who are your friends?" asked Mr. Ridley.

"This is Rukh and Jessira," Jake said. "They're the ones I told you about. The ones who might be able to help Johnny."

"It's a pleasure meeting you," Mr. Ridley said with a broad smile. He shook hands with Rukh and Jessira, as did Mrs. Ridley.

Jake moved to stand next to Serena. He put an arm around her shoulders. "And this is Serena." He inhaled deeply, and his words tumbled out. "Before you say anything, you should know that I think of her as a friend." He gave Serena's shoulders a brief squeeze.

William appreciated Jake's gesture, but he doubted it would be enough. He winced when an instant later he was proven right. Mr. and Mrs. Ridley's eyes hardened and their faces became flat and uninviting.

William's heart sank. Serena's intentions in coming here had been good, but intentions didn't count for much, not after what she'd done. He figured there might never be a way back from that. She should have stayed on Arylyn. But he'd do what he could to help her out. "She's my friend, too," he said, moving to stand at Serena's other side.

"A good friend," Jake added.

William caught Serena's grateful smile. She faced Jake's parents once again. "Mr. and Mrs. Ridley, I know I've done something unforgivable to the two of you . . ."

"Yes, you did," Mr. Ridley growled.

Serena nodded acceptance. "I came here to tell you how sorry I am for all the pain I put you through."

"You should be," Mrs. Ridley said. Her features remained unfriendly. "Jake and William have spoken up on your behalf, but it isn't enough, not for me."

The angry, red-eyed beast that William couldn't seem to get rid of uttered a soft growl. *Not now.* He couldn't let the anger take over.

He imagined sailing *Blue Sky Dreamers*, the wind blowing in his hair, the spray on his face, and the sun beaming down on a perfect day. He gave a mental sigh of relief when the beast went silent.

In the meanwhile, Serena's face had gone drone-unreadable. "I understand."

Mr. Ridley scoffed at Serena. "I seriously doubt you understand anything about what you put us through." He held up a hand, forestalling any further words. "One day maybe we can forgive you, but we'll never forget what you did. You should leave."

William's heart ached for Serena, but he also understood the Ridleys' response. He'd expected it, in fact. Once more the red-eyed beast rumbled, and again William took a moment to imagine something calming. This time Meldencreche, the dwarven village.

"Mom. Dad," Jake complained.

"It's fine," Serena said. Her voice and face still held a flat affect, but William could sense her embarrassment, her humiliation. "I'll wait outside."

"I'll take you to a hotel," William said. "I know a nice one pretty close by."

CHAPTER 7: FULFILLING HOPES

J anuary 1990

W illiam walked with Serena to the T-bird, uncertain what to say after the humiliation inside, and he remained quiet as he unlocked the car and waited for Serena to settle into the passenger seat. He got them going.

"I'm sorry," he said as they pulled out of Jake's driveway.

"Don't be," she replied, facing him with a tight-lipped smile. "I expected it. If I were in their shoes, I'd probably react the same way. I'd never forgive someone who hurt Selene."

William had no response to that, and they drove in quiet. He waited to make a right-hand turn onto Compton Road and scowled when a little, old lady in a Cadillac trudged along. She traveled fast enough so he couldn't pull out in front of her but so slow that it felt like an eternity before she reached them. She finally passed, and he slipped in behind her car, quickly swung into the left-hand lane, and gunned ahead of her. He glanced at Serena. "If you expected their reaction, why'd you come?"

She shrugged. "I had to do it. It's not something I could avoid." Once again she offered him a tight-lipped smile. "It was part of my New Year's resolutions."

William recalled a joke, and he smiled at the memory. "You know what they say about New Year's resolutions?"

Serena shook her head. "No. What?"

"They're made in one year and out the other." He grinned.

Serena smiled faintly. "That was a horrible pun."

"But it got you to smile," William said.

"You're an idiot," Serena said with a chuckle, affection in her voice.

William shrugged. "It's how I'm made. Besides, you like me this way."

"Or maybe you just grow on a girl." A beat later. "Like a fungus."

William laughed. "You stole that line from Jake. He's always saying things like that."

"Sometimes even simpletons have wisdom."

William arched his eyebrows. "Jake's a simpleton? Better not let his parents hear you say that."

Serena's face went drone-flat and William mentally kicked himself. "Too soon?"

She nodded. "Too soon."

They fell once more into silence, and William flicked on the wipers and headlights when a drizzle kicked in. With the clouds and misty rain, visibility had dropped. They drove along the outskirts of a country club and William noted some golfers still out on the course. *Typical. Some people can't get enough of that lazy person's sport.*

Serena broke the silence. "May I ask you a question?"

William shrugged. "Sure."

"Why do you push so hard? I mean, I know what I said to you that night a few months ago is part of the reason, but that can't be the only thing."

"What do you mean?"

"I mean you're the hardest working, most intense person I know," she said, "and I was a mahavan. That means something. But when you let yourself relax, you're fun and funny, more like you used to be when we first met."

William smiled wryly. He missed that part of himself too and often wished he could go back to the way he'd once been: carefree and happy. "I push so hard because my family is dead. My brother is gone, and you know why."

"Kohl Obsidian."

William shook his head in negation. "No. It's because of *asra*, my potential to do magic. My family paid for my *lorethasra* with their lives, and I have to make sure their sacrifice was worth it."

Serena frowned, obviously confused. "I don't understand."

William took a few seconds to gather his thoughts. "I want to protect everyone I love. I don't want anyone else to die because of me, because I wasn't good enough or strong enough. When I meet God, I want to be able to tell Him that I left it all down here, that I gave everyone everything He gave me."

"The God I believe in also gives you love and joy."

William sighed. "I know." The problem was not that he didn't want joy in his life. The problem was that he had so many responsibilities and worries, and he didn't know how to let go of them. Or at least accept them and still find a way to happiness and love.

William drove automatically, not really paying much attention to the road or traffic. Instead, he thought about what Serena had said.

She shifted about and faced him, and he met her disconcertingly intense gaze, the one that always put him off-balance. "The world doesn't rest on your shoulders," she said. "Other people are willing to take the burden, too. I have some of those same responsibilities. So do Jake, Jason, Rukh, and Jessira."

"You mean everyone who volunteered to protect the island?"

Serena nodded. "Rukh said he's still figuring out where and how to train us, but yes, them. They want the same thing that you do. It's not all on you."

William had thought about that as well. He knew Rukh and Jessira could better protect Arylyn than he ever could. Nevertheless, the self-imposed burden weighing him down had yet to shift, possibly because he didn't want to shift it. The insight startled him, and his mouth pursed as he pondered the notion. Maybe he had to *want* to be happy in order to be happy. Maybe it was conscious decision.

"Think about it," Serena said, giving his bicep a gentle squeeze.

They drove another few miles and soon reached the hotel. William grabbed Serena's bag.

"I can carry it myself," she said.

William dropped her bag.

Serena's mouth gaped in shock, and he laughed. "Just kidding," he said before stooping to retrieve her luggage. "I know you can carry it yourself, but sometimes it's nice to do things for others."

The sun seemed to breach the gloomy clouds when Serena smiled. "That's a sweet thought."

～

After dropping Serena off at the hotel, William drove back to Jake's house and went inside.

Mr. Ridley greeted him in the foyer. "I'm sorry for treating your friend like that, but you have to understand—"

"Forget it," William said, not wanting to rehash any explanations. He especially didn't trust that the red-eyed beast wouldn't wake up. The last thing he wanted was to have it unleashed on Mr. Ridley. "Did Jake tell you about Rukh and Jessira?"

"They're the ones who saved him last summer?"

William nodded, although he didn't like thinking about how close Jake had come to dying. It had been a matter of seconds. "You know, I hated having to tell you what happened the whole time after it occurred."

"I hated having to hear it," Mr. Ridley said, "but Jake's fine now, and I don't care if he still talks about Rukh and Jessira like they're royalty."

"No," William corrected. "He talks about them like they're divine."

Mr. Ridley grinned. "I don't know about that, but Jessira looks the part. She's about as divine as any woman I've ever seen."

"I can hear you," Mrs. Ridley said from the rear of the house.

Mr. Ridley's grin became sheepish.

"I'm betting Jessira heard, too," William whispered. "Same with Rukh. He hears everything."

"William, we might need your help," Jessira called.

Mr. Ridley's smile utterly departed, and William chuckled. He raised the pitch of his voice, making sure those in the back of the house could hear him. "Besides, Jake feels the same way about her. You know, like father like son."

"You jackass!" Jake protested. "That goes against the bro-code, ratting me out like that."

William laughed, and he and Mr. Ridley entered the kitchen. In the family room, he saw Rukh and Jessira looming over Johnny, who sat on the couch, wide-eyed and still. Mrs. Ridley fretted nearby.

"Hey, Johnny," William said.

"He goes by John now," Jake replied, standing next to his mom. "He says he's too old for Johnny."

"How old are you, John?" Rukh asked.

Jake answered instead of John. "Last birthday he turned fifteen-years-dumb."

"Ha, ha," Johnny—no—John replied.

"We need your blood," Jessira said to William.

Mrs. Ridley twisted her hands in fear but didn't say anything. Mr. Ridley went to her, put his arm around her shoulders, and drew her close.

Jake spoke. "Why? If you're thinking of transforming John into a *raha'asra*, it won't work. A *raha'asra*'s blood doesn't transform every normal person like that. It's unpredictable."

Rukh nodded. "John doesn't have a magical malady, but William's blood might make the Healing easier. The necrosed portion in it might, anyway."

Mrs. Ridley stepped out of Mr. Ridley's arms, and fear lit her features. "It won't change Johnny into what Jake is?"

"It shouldn't," William said. *At least, I hope not.*

"I need to cut your forearm," Rukh told William, displaying a kukri. "Don't worry, I'll Heal it. You won't have a scar."

William held out his arm, and Rukh made a shallow slice. The cut stung, and an instant later, blood welled. William winced, but the beast within, his simmering anger, held the pain at bay.

"You're next," Rukh said to John.

Jake's brother had grown pale, but he bravely held out his arm as well.

Rukh quickly sliced it and immediately grabbed William's bleeding forearm. He pressed their wounds together until the blood mingled. After a few seconds, he grunted in satisfaction and separated them. "We'll see if that helps," he said before focusing on William. "Ready for a mild Healing?"

William took several deep breaths and readied himself. He hated this part. "Go ahead."

Rukh sourced his *lorethasra*, and the tang of iron filled the air. It was a scent only an *asrasin* could smell. Rukh held William's arm, and his eyes went blank as he stared at the wound. A moment later, lightning poured out of his hands.

William's muscles went taught as the Healing entered him. He became hot and cold at the same time. The pain from the lightning rippled outward from the wound and spread to his fingertips. It traveled up his shoulders, across his chest, and through the rest his body, all the way to his scalp. William imagined his hair standing on edge. The pain went on for what felt like minutes but in reality was probably less than a second. When it ended, the wound on his forearm was healed without a scar.

Jessira moved to kneel beside John. "I need you to lie down."

John shifted until he lay on the couch.

"Do you mind if I put my hands on your head?" Jessira asked.

John gave an uncertain nod but then firmness filled his eyes. "Do whatever you need to do."

Jessira took John's head in her hands, and her eyes went blank, like Rukh's had only a few moments prior. "This is going to hurt," she warned. Her hands glowed, and so did her green eyes. Her honey-blonde hair, hanging loose for once, billowed about her face. Lightning coursed out of Jessira's hands and into John's head.

Immediately, he spasmed, stiffening as if all of his muscles had clenched at once. The lightning continued to bleed out of Jessira, and John's mouth gaped and closed, gaped and closed.

Mrs. Ridley pressed a fist to her lips and made a horrified sound. Mr. Ridley drew her again into his embrace. Jake went pale. His jaw clenched, and he took a single step forward before coming to a lurching halt.

William gave him a brief nod of support before returning his attention to John. The lightning still poured from Jessira and into Jake's brother. He continued to gape and close his mouth while his posture remained rigid and unmoving.

This was a far longer Healing than William had expected. He sought reassurance from Rukh, but he had his attention focused on Jessira and John.

William swallowed heavily.

The lightning finally ended, and John groaned once before going limp. Mr. Ridley rushed to his side, crouching down and hugging his son while Rukh moved to support Jessira.

"John?" Mr. Ridley said. He cradled his son, peering into his vacant face. "Can you hear me?"

John's head flopped, and he didn't reply. Mrs. Ridley cried out.

Mr. Ridley's head snapped toward Rukh and Jessira. "What's wrong with him?" Terror filled his features.

"He's only asleep," Jessira answered. William noticed dark circles under her eyes. Her entire bearing spoke of overwhelming tiredness. She swayed on her feet, barely able to stay upright.

"Then he'll be okay?" Mr. Ridley asked.

"He'll be fine," Rukh said as he helped settle Jessira on a nearby chair.

"But is he healed?" Mrs. Ridley asked. She knelt next to Mr. Ridley and stroked John's head.

"It's too soon to tell," Jessira replied. "We'll know more when he wakes up."

Mr. Ridley rose with John in his arms. He took him to his bedroom, which was on the first floor, while Jake huddled with his mom.

William watched the scene play out and wished Landon could be similarly Healed and his memories restored.

~

Several hours after John's healing, Jake checked in on his little brother. He still rested, hopefully comfortable and at peace as he slept in his room full of nerd stuff—a life-sized Alien, like from the movie, some wizards and dragons, a poster of Robocop, another of some silly show called "V," U2 from *LiveAid*, and a final one of Cindy Crawford. His mom didn't approve of the latter, but Jake did. Cindy Crawford was gorgeous. As for the geek stuff, he couldn't care less. Everything else in John's room belonged in a nerd lair, like something William, Daniel, or Jason would have wanted. Then again, John *was* a geek. He always had been.

Jake smiled. He still had trouble referring to his brother as anything other than Johnny, but time never stopped and they all had to change and grow up.

Jake further darkened the room by closing the blinds. He softly tiptoed out the door, shutting it softly behind him and making his way to the family room.

His dad was talking to William. "College is like mal-tuition. It's a waste of good money." His eyes sparkled. "Get it?"

Jake rolled his eyes. It was an old topic that always got his dad on his soapbox, and the pun hadn't improved with time.

"All you need are some math and finance classes at the community college," Dad continued, "and you'll be fine."

"Unless you want to do liberal arts or history," William said. "Or major in theater or music."

Dad scoffed. "All that does is train you to ask if you'd like fries with that."

"What's wrong with working in fast food?" William asked. "It's hard as hell."

Jake did a double-take. "When did you ever work fast food?"

"During the summer between sophomore and junior year,"

William said. "It sucked, but it also taught me a lot, like giving me respect for those who do it. Those people are busting their humps."

Jake's dad held up his hands as if placating William. "There's absolutely nothing wrong with fast food," he said in agreement. "I spent every summer in high school and college flipping burgers for tuition."

Rukh smiled. "Ironic. You went to college, but now you decry it?"

Mom laughed. "He's got you there, Steven."

Dad shook his head. "No, he doesn't," he said. "See, the thing is, back then a person could flip burgers *and* afford college. It was affordable. Now everyone needs student loans." He harrumphed. "It's disgusting how much colleges charge nowadays, and don't get me started on making a living in fast food. It can't be done."

The doorbell rang.

"I'll get it," Dad said.

Mom met Jake's gaze. "That'll be Steve and Sonya."

Seconds later, Steve Aldo and Sonya Bowyer, Jake's girlfriend throughout high school, entered the kitchen. He hadn't seen either of them since that night when Adam Paradiso had kidnapped him to Sinskrill, had barely spoken to them, in fact, since he'd escaped to Arylyn, only a few phone calls. Steve had grown a goatee and might have put on some weight around his middle, but his dark eyes remained curious and alive, and the hint of an easy grin remained at the edges of his mouth.

Sonya had also changed. Her face, always beautiful, had gained character and she remained fit and fashionable with big hair—maybe bigger than ever—and snug jeans. Both of them wore curious expressions that became welcoming smiles when they saw Jake.

He hugged Sonya and Steve, while William, Rukh, and Jessira shook hands with them.

"That's our signal," Dad said. "We'll leave you kids to get reacquainted." He and Mom said their goodnights and headed upstairs.

Rukh and Jessira rose to their feet as well. "I think we'll also leave you to do whatever the young do," Rukh said.

Jake caught Steve watching them exit and eyeing them in speculation. "I remember a Rukh and Jessira from St. Francis," he said, "but they were freshmen."

"Those two are the same Rukh and Jessira you knew from before," Jake said to his old friend.

"How's that possible?" Sonya asked. "They were freshmen when we were seniors. Now they look way older than us."

"Life," Jake replied, knowing his enigmatic response didn't really answer her question.

Steve studied him. "You've changed, too," he said. He shifted his focus to William. "Both of you."

William smiled in reply. "Lots of things have changed. Jake is going to tell you about it."

His words sparked a reminder, and Jake sourced his *lorethasra*. He quickly wove a braid to prevent Steve and Sonya from speaking of what they were about to learn.

"So, what happened to the two of you?" Sonya asked. Her pleasure at seeing Jake seemed to have dissolved, and she stood with arms crossed. "You guys disappeared one night, and I hear you've been back for months. Only now you want to talk?"

"You might want to sit down," Jake said. "We've got a story to tell."

He and William spent the next hour explaining about *asra*, Arylyn and Sinskrill, and the ongoing ancient war between the two hidden islands. They didn't bother mentioning Seminal or Shet.

Sonya barked in disbelief in the middle of their explanation. "You really expect me to believe this?"

William answered by causing a ball of fire to flicker on the palm of his hand. Jake made one of water and sent it colliding into William's braid. A puff of steam exploded from the point of contact.

"You see?" Jake said. "What you saw was nothing. And that's how it always begins. Very small."

Sonya had always been a tough sell, though, and it took a few more demonstrations before she believed they spoke truth. She didn't like it one bit when Jake told her she wouldn't be able to tell anyone else about what she'd learned.

"That's bullshit!" she exclaimed, rising to her feet.

William didn't back down in the slightest. "Those are the rules we've got to go by. So do you."

Jake eyed his friend in surprise. Prior to Sinskrill William had always been tongue-tied around Sonya. He'd acted like a doofus, really. Now here he was standing up for himself.

Sonya sputtered to a halt, apparently put off by William's unwillingness to bend to her will. She eventually resumed her seat next to Steve on the couch.

Jake changed the subject. "What have you two been up to?"

Sonya gave William one last glare. "We're both going to *the* Ohio State University," she said, "and we're both working toward getting into dental school, but Steve won't cut it if he keeps trying to graduate Summa Cum Lauderdale."

Jake shared a puzzled frown with William.

"It means he parties all the time instead of actually studying," Sonya explained. "You know, like Spring Break at Fort Lauderdale."

"I've gotten better," Steve protested. He waved aside whatever Sonya might have been about to say. "Enough about us. You guys seriously live on some paradise?"

"We do, although Jake wishes none of this had happened," William said with a smile.

Jake didn't smile. "I have my reasons," he said to Steve and Sonya, who stared at him in curiosity. "I had to pay too much for my magic."

Sonya eyed him in sympathy. "It sounds like you've been put through the ringer." She reached for Jake's hand and squeezed it briefly. "Sorry if I came off kind of harsh."

Jake managed a weak smile. "No biggie." He gestured to William. "But can you believe my best friend in the world is this dork?"

Steve cracked up. "Three years ago, I never would have believed it."

"Me, neither," William added.

Sonya stared from Jake to William and back again. "You've talked about fighting your way off that one island, and that Serena was one of those mahavans or whatever, but which one of *you* is better?"

Jake frowned. "You mean stronger with *asra*? Or the better fighter?"

"Both," Steve said.

"William. In both categories," Jake answered without hesitation.

Steve's eyes widened in surprise. "Seriously?" Disbelief tinged his tone.

Jake nodded. "The last two years of high school, he spent every night learning to fight. He could have kicked all our asses if he wanted." He smiled wryly. "I'm only glad he never had a reason to."

"What about Serena?" Sonya asked. "Other than being a bitch—"

"Careful," Jake said. "She's our friend now."

Sonya waved his words away. "Whatever. How tough is she?"

Again, it was Jake who answered. "William could probably take her, but I'd have trouble. She's so damn focused. She and William are a good pair. They're both too intense for their own good."

Sonya eyed William in speculation. "You and Serena are . . ."

"Friends," William said. "Nothing more."

Although they could be, if William wasn't such an dumbass, Jake thought.

CHAPTER 8: TROUBLESOME TRUTHS

January 1990

Although he'd only come back from visiting Jake's family yesterday, William wanted to get right back to work.

He'd talked Ward Silver, the magus who had taught him how to weave multiple braids, into helping him out. The two of them stood in an empty field north of Linchpin Knoll, getting ready for a sparring session. All combat training began with governors, the leather helmets meant to restrict their ability to source *lorethasra*, and they placed them on their heads. While William didn't need one any more —he could control his braids well enough to not hurt someone with whom he was sparring—he and Ward both figured it was better safe than sorry. Plus, William couldn't tell when the angry beast lurking in the back of his mind would surge to life. He hadn't told anyone about it, but most of his friends had realized something was bothering him. They occasionally walked on eggshells around him, and he hated that.

Some had even mentioned that his self-inflicted stress about stopping Shet was turning him into a dick.

It wasn't true. The stress part, anyway. Something else was going on, and he wasn't sure what it meant, but he knew it probably wasn't anything good.

William tried to shove aside his worries and took a moment to study his opponent.

Ward was in his mid-twenties and had the dark-skinned, dark-haired, dark-eyed features that proclaimed him as a native of Arylyn. He also was a skilled craftsman and could wield *lorethasra* as a weapon more effectively than anyone William knew, except for Rukh and Jessira.

William set his governor in place, attaching the flaps across the front of his neck and buckling the straps under his chin. The helmet tightened on its own until it fit snugly over his head. He took in a deep breath and rolled his shoulders. The warm, humid air had him sweating, and he fanned himself with his shirt. The loamy smell of wet leaves and mold filled the clearing as birds cried out from the surrounding forest. An occasional breeze rattled the branches and stirred the leaves, rustling them until they sounded like cicadas in song. It also helped to keep the clearing from growing more stifling than it already was.

Ward finished with his governor. "Remember. No draining *lorasra*."

"I know," William said.

Draining *lorasra* was something only *raha'asras* could do, and Ward couldn't defend against it. However, it would have also wasted their time. William wanted to beat enemies who could fight back and were every bit as talented as Ward.

"Think you can hold me off this time?" Ward asked with his ever-ready smile. From most people a question like that would have sounded arrogant or teasing, but not from Ward. From him it was merely a part of who he was, happy-go-lucky.

Kind of like how Jason used to be.

William mentally scowled. *Focus.* While he could hold Ward off on most days, he hardly ever won, and he wanted to win. He had to. He'd worked too hard for anything less. Of course, Serena would have told him he needed to ease up a bit and enjoy his life. Or would she? He couldn't tell anymore. He mentally frowned. Maybe she was right, but then again, what did she know? She . . .

He cut off his circling thoughts with a scowl. *Focus,* he chided himself once more. The grass remained slick from the morning dew, and he set his feet. He didn't want to slip. His vision narrowed. *Ready.*

"Go!" Ward shouted.

William sourced his *lorethasra* and blocked the rise of freezing water meant to trap his feet—one of Ward's oldest tricks. He also split a blistering line of Fire and whistling arrow of Water sent his way.

Fire rippled down William's arms and sulfur filled his nostrils. He leapt into the air, powered upward with a braid of Air, and evaded another arrow of Water. He landed and launched a wide wave of Fire. Ward blocked with a shield of Earth. Dust and mud billowed from the contact, along with a low rumble William sensed as a vibration rather than heard.

Ward whipped out a cracking line of Water. William bent backward at the waist beneath it. Another line of Water surged toward him, and he dug his feet into the wet ground and rolled to the right. Twin weaves of Air barreled off his hands straight at Ward . . .

Who wasn't where William expected.

William searched about, frantic to find him. In the periphery of his vision he caught sight of a curling weave of Fire and threw himself aside. The flames passed over his head. A rushing sound like a breaking wave filled the air. William rolled and guessed right. Freezing water surged up from where he'd fallen.

He still couldn't see Ward.

Move.

He got to hands and knees. The ground trembled, and he shot forward. He guessed right again. Buckshots of earth exploded as if from a gun toward him. He levered himself upright and instinctively sent out a fan of hissing Air. More buckshots hammered his way, but the braid of Air and a hastily erected shield of earth protected him.

Frustration at his lack of success had the angry beast growling to

95

life. Redness tinged William's vision, and he snarled. *Where the hell is Ward?*

There!

Ward waited vigilant on the far side of the field. Braids of Water snaked around his forearms. William sent a blast furnace of Fire at him. *Let's see him put that out.*

Ward managed it, but super-heated steam burst all around him. He cried out. Some of the steam must have boiled back at him.

William didn't let up. His anger wouldn't let him. He sent a looping arrow of Air. It clubbed Ward, knocking him off his feet. The rage exulted, and so did William.

An instant later shame and horror overcame him. *What have I done?*

William ran to where Ward lay face down in the dirt, mud, and grass. The world around the field had gone silent. Even the wind had quit blowing. William rolled Ward over and stared in shock at the red burns blistering his face. *Oh, God.*

Ward groaned.

William tried to help him sit up, but Ward waved him off. "I need to heal the burns or they'll blister. Get the governor off of me."

William did so and took his off as well. "How can I help?"

Ward sat with his eyes closed and spoke. "Spirit is what *raha'asras* are best with. I need that along with Earth and Water. Copy what I do."

William peered at the weave Ward worked on himself and quickly duplicated it. He poured it into Ward's burns and watched anxiously for a response.

Seconds passed, and he continued the healing braid. More time, minutes maybe, and sweat beaded on William's face at the effort needed to maintain the weave.

Most of the redness faded from Ward's face, and William sat back in relief. The healing wasn't as complete as what Jessira could have managed, but at least Ward wouldn't be left with scars all over his face and chest.

"How are you feeling?" William asked.

"Like crap," Ward replied. He reached out a hand. "Help me up."

William levered Ward to his feet and waited with his heart in his throat.

Ward glared at him. "What was that about?"

William could barely meet his friend's eyes. "I don't know. I was losing, and I got angry, and—"

"And you braided too heavily and nearly burned me to a crisp," Ward finished. "You would have if it wasn't for the governor."

William hung his head in shame. The rage that had come upon him . . . He vowed to never let it control him like that again. At the same time, he worried he wouldn't be able to keep his promise.

～

Jake yawned as he stumbled through Mr. Zeus' living room. They'd only gotten back to Arylyn a few days ago, and between the time difference and sleeplessness from missing his family, he hadn't gotten much rest.

Leaving them had been harder than usual, especially with John— Would he ever get used to calling him by that shortened version of his name?—recovering from his Healing. His brother still had a long way to go, and while he'd never be an athlete, Jessira felt pretty sure he'd be able to live out a normal life, not doomed to die young, something the doctors had said would happen ever since John's birth. With physical therapy, he might even be able to walk without crutches.

The smell of fresh donuts—frying dough, melted sugar, and sweet chocolate—shook off the last of Jake's lethargy. The deliciousness filled the house, hypnotizing him with its aroma, and he drifted toward it like a sailor toward a Siren. He entered the kitchen and found everyone already gathered there: Mr. Zeus, Jason, William, and Serena, all of them helping make Saturday morning breakfast.

Jason was frying the donuts while William dipped the cooked ones in a melted chocolate glaze or dusted them with sugar. Serena washed and dried the dirty dishes.

Mr. Zeus wasn't doing much of anything. He leaned against the counter and chatted with the others, wearing a ridiculous purple robe. A robe like that, Jake almost expected to see stars, planets, and crescent moons decorating it. Toss in a pointy hat, and the old man would have looked like a prototypical wizard.

Jake cleared his throat. "Anything I can do to help?"

"We got it," William replied over his shoulder.

"Took you long enough to get up," Jason noted.

"I was tired," Jake replied as he took a seat at the rectangular dining table. Sunlight poured through the picture window that opened onto the courtyard, and he soaked in the warmth and light, briefly closing his eyes.

When he opened them again, he noticed Mr. Zeus bending toward William. "Stop being so stingy with the sugar," the old man said, sounding waspish.

"I'm not being stingy," William answered. "It's just that I have long pockets and short arms."

"What the hell does that mean?" Jason asked.

"Something my dad told me. It means my hands are too short to reach the cash in my pockets."

Jake scoffed. "Is this the same dad from Ireland who quotes NASCAR?"

Jason laughed. "I remember that. *If you ain't cheatin', you ain't tryin',*" he quoted in a southern drawl.

William grinned in response, which was a better reply than the rages he seemed to have all of a sudden. Jake didn't know where they came from, but they had started a few months back and had gotten worse over time. He'd asked Serena about it, but she didn't know anything, either.

Jake realized then that a few people were missing. "Where's Selene and Fiona? They're usually here for donuts."

Serena answered. "They decided to have an early breakfast and take a walk through Janaki Valley. I think they're meeting Travail. Fiona wants Selene to know him better."

Jake grunted and briefly stared out the window before resuming his attention on the others. Guilt gnawed at him for sitting there doing nothing while William, Jason, and Serena worked. "Are you sure you don't need any help?"

"Come on over," Serena said. She had her arms up to her elbows in suds. "I'll clean. You dry."

Jake went to help her. A few minutes later, they got the dishes cleaned at roughly the same time that Jason and William finished with the donuts. Everyone gathered at the kitchen table, but Jake got a cup of coffee first.

They kept the pot near the sink, and he stirred in cream and sugar. The familiar ritual of preparing his morning coffee, something Jake had done since sophomore year of high school, bridged the gap between past and present. He grew lost in his musings. After visiting his family and seeing Steve and Sonya, he realized he had some choices to make. He was a *raha'asra*, and nothing could change what had happened to him, which meant he was stuck on Arylyn. This was his life, and he had to get busy living it.

"You all right?" William asked, apparently noticing his quiet.

Jake glanced his way and didn't reply at once. He took his seat at the table next to Mr. Zeus and stared out the window at the lovely courtyard out back. Thoughts still percolated in his mind like water dripping through coffee grounds. He had to find a way to fit in on Arylyn. He thought of one way that would work better than any other.

Jake cleared his throat. "You know how I've been complaining about how my life hasn't ended up the way I wanted?"

"Whined is more like it," Jason said.

Jake dipped his head in agreement. He had been whining. "After visiting home, I'm thinking I need a girlfriend. It's probably the most surefire way of making Arylyn my home."

His words caused a resounding silence, and he found himself the focus of everyone's attention.

Jason and William stared at him with mouths open while Mr. Zeus and Serena smiled as though sharing some secret.

Serena clapped, breaking the quiet. "It's about time you came to that realization," she said. "If you want, I can ask Lien if she knows any girls who might be worth pursuing."

Jake perked up. There were some girls he was interested in, too. An instant later, his enthusiasm deflated. *Wait a second.* He frowned in suspicion. Serena was a friend, but it didn't mean he fully trusted her. She could lie too well. "You're not making this up, are you?"

"Of course not," Serena said, sounding offended. "You think I'd lie about something like that?"

Jason grinned. "Remember when we used to say Serena has lie-abetes?"

Serena grinned back at Jason. "And remember when I promised to set your pants on fire if you ever said that to me again?"

"You never said that."

"I just did." Serena's smile dropped like an anchor.

"Touchy much?" Jason muttered under his breath. "Anyway," he said to Jake, "when you find a girlfriend, promise not to end up like Daniel and Lien." He shook his head in disgust. "Those two don't have time for anyone else any more."

William gave Jason a hard nudge. "He only said he wanted to date someone, not marry them."

"I know," Jason said, "but you've got to plan for these things."

Jake rolled his eyes. "Mr. Zeus was right about you," he said to Jason. "You're a gossip."

"What? No, I'm not!" Jason protested. He turned to Mr. Zeus. "You don't think that, do you?"

William kept his head bent to his donuts, but Jake could see the smile lurking at the corner of his mouth. "Methinks he doth protest too much," he whispered loud enough for everyone to hear.

"He most certainly doth," Mr. Zeus said equally as quietly.

Everyone chuckled while Jason glared. "Fine. We'll see how you like it when no one tells you anything about the island's happenings."

"Anyway," Jake said, "I'm tired of being alone. I'm thinking of asking out Daniella Logan to the Chinese New Year. You know, Karla Logan's sister." He looked to Serena. "She wouldn't happen to be one of the girls you were thinking about?"

Serena lips briefly tightened as if his question made her uncomfortable. "I hardly know any other girls," she said. "Like I said, I was going to ask Lien for you. I'm sure she'd know about Daniella, though. The two of them are friends."

Jake smiled in gratitude.

William addressed him. "If you find yourself a girlfriend and all that, at least you won't be looking down the barrel of a normal life." He glanced around. "Isn't that what Sting said in "Invisible Sun"?"

Jake shook his head in pity. "That's not at all what he said."

"Do you ever say anything that makes sense?" Jason asked William.

"Gossip," William replied.

"Why don't you take that donut, shine it up real good, and stick it—"

Mr. Zeus slapped a hand on the table, interrupting their bickering. "You know this is a big step," he said to Jake. "I'm glad to see you make it."

It *was* a big step. It would mean accepting Arylyn as his home now, that this place was his life. Despite his earlier words, Jake still wasn't sure how he felt about that.

~

Jason huffed alongside William, struggling to keep up with his friend as they trotted up the Main Stairs of Cliff Spirit. He gulped air, and his heart raced. *Only a few more terraces to go. Then I can kill William for torturing me like this.*

Jason wanted to ask for a break, but pride kept the words sewed inside his mouth. He grimaced when he recalled that a few years ago, William would have been one straining to maintain the pace, but Kohl Obsidian had changed all that.

They finally reached Clifftop, and William thankfully eased down to a halt. Jason hunched over at the waist and panted.

"Too fast?" William asked.

Jason couldn't answer at first. He hadn't yet caught his breath. Every time he thought he'd grown used to William's stamina, his friend surprised him by going even harder. Today they'd gone to Clifftop for the farmer's market. Mr. Zeus wanted chard, apples, and a few red onions for a salad to go with dinner.

"You okay?" William asked.

Jason straightened and took a deep breath. "Next time, I'll ask Jake to come with me. Jackass."

William grinned. "It was too fast."

Jason wanted to punch the smugness off his face, but William had also long since outstripped him when it came to unarmed combat. He settled for a scowl. "Anyone ever tell you how unattractive smugery is?"

"Smugery?" William lifted his eyebrows.

"It's a word," Jason said, still bent at the waist. "It's related to buggery. Why don't you look it up? It has your picture next to it in the dictionary."

William smiled wider, a better response than the waspish bitchiness he'd been afflicted with for the past few weeks. Jason had no idea what bee had burned a hole in his friend's bonnet, but he hoped William would kick out of his funk.

Jason straightened. "Let's get the food." He set off toward the farmer's market, which took up most of the Village Green.

"Are you going to ask anyone out for Chinese New Years?" William asked.

Upon hearing the question, Jason knew his face became guarded. He'd never been able to hide his feelings, not like those who had once lived on Sinskrill, like Fiona, Serena, and Selene. Or William and Jake for that matter

Resentment about William and Jake's closeness flared, even though Jason knew such sentiments were childish. Before the mahavan island, Jason had been William's best friend, his protector and trainer, the one others looked to for leadership. But William didn't need him anymore. More often than not, Jason was the one following, and if it came down to it, he'd be the one needing protection, not William.

In addition, the title of 'best friend' now belonged to Jake Ridley, William's one time nemesis, the boy who had bullied him most of his life. Their closeness sometimes—maybe often—left Jason feeling like a third wheel in their presence.

Jason inhaled deeply and exhaled slowly, doing his best to let the resentment pass through him. There was no point in glomming over the matter.

William never noticed his internal conflict. "Who are you asking?"

"I'll tell you after I ask the girl," Jason said, his answer truthful and yet not the entire truth.

Jason had always been a private person growing up, and Arylyn had never changed that. More importantly, Jason had no idea who to ask. He felt like he had to say he would, though, especially if Jake did ask out Daniella Logan. William had Serena. Jake might end up with Daniella. And who would Jason have?

No one, he thought sourly.

Plus, his life would have been a lot easier if could trust more easily. Jason found it hard to open his heart ever since his parents abandoned him. When his *lorethasra* had flowered, when he'd discovered he could become a magus, his father and mother—despite the stories about the family history, about Mama Layla and where she came from—thought him devil-cursed.

His mother had told him so when Mr. Zeus had arrived to take Jason to Arylyn, *"Thou shalt not suffer a witch to live."* She'd quoted from Exodus 22:18. Afterward, she'd added a final warning." *Leave and never darken our door, boy."*

And Jason never did. In hindsight, he was surprised his parents hadn't tried to kill him before Mr. Zeus' arrival.

"You alright?" William asked, his face filled with concern.

"What do you mean?"

"You looked like you were somewhere else, someplace dark."

"I'm fine," Jason said. He brushed past William, not wanting to discuss it. "Let's go find what Mr. Zeus wants."

"Want some iced tea first?" William asked. He pointed at *Jimmy Webster's Restaurant.*

Jason smiled. "Only if you're buying."

"I'm buying." They walked toward *Jimmy's.* "You sure you're ok?" William asked after a moment.

Jason nodded. "I'm good."

William apparently struggled with wanting to say something and frowned.

"What is it?" Jason asked.

"I know we aren't as close as we used to be, as close I wish we could be," William said. "It's all the training and things we've got to do."

Jason managed a faint smile. "There's the William I know, always going on about training." He meant it as a joke, but William scowled, and Jason groaned. *Here comes the anger.*

William surprised him. His scowl disappeared. He seemed to shove it aside and exhaled heavily. "Sorry about getting angry like that," he muttered. "I think it's the stress of training."

"Don't worry about it," Jason said. "I know you have a lot on your plate. We all do. I know Sinskrill's coming for us, and I believe Serena about Shet." The last made him want to gag. Believing Serena should have been impossible, would have been a year ago, but lots had changed since then, including his opinion about the one-time mahavan.

"Then we're good?"

Jason stopped and eyed him in surprise. "Why wouldn't we be? We're still friends. We always will be."

~

Serena shifted her weight forward and made minute changes to her stance, maintaining her balance as she rode the wave she'd been waiting for all morning. She focused her attention both inward and outward, the moment in which she existed, embracing all of the world's sensations: the gusting wind, the shifting water, and the newly risen sun warming the world.

The wave changed, and Serena felt power building behind her, a lifting motion. She flexed her hips, thighs, and calves as well as her core. All the muscle contractions occurred in an automatic sequence, one she didn't have to consciously focus upon.

She cut across the water, carving the wave. A barrel readied to form. Serena could sense it, and she aimed for where she anticipated the entrance would open.

It did so, right where she expected.

She ducked low to enter the tube. The world became a tunnel of endlessly falling water. Rainbows glittered in her wake. Spray splashed, warm and salty, across her body and face, trickling into her mouth. Her vision obscured momentarily. Wet hair clung to her scalp. Distantly, she noticed the cry of a petrel.

The barrel unrolled endlessly before her even as it collapsed behind her. It hammered like the steady beat on a drum. The far end never seemed to get closer but it never stopped moving and she made minute corrections, a flex there, a twist here.

Serena ran a hand through the wave. It felt like warm, liquid cotton, and alive.

On she sped. With a breathtaking suddenness, the far opening arrived, and the barrel spat her out like a seed. Serena shifted her weight onto her back foot and brought the board to trim. She stood tall, arching her back. The wave petered out, and she slid into the water.

She whooped as the ocean enveloped her. *What a rush!*

Too bad William had been too impatient to wait for the better waves. He had set off a half hour ago for his morning run and after that, his work as a *raha'asra*. He never stood still long enough to enjoy the moment.

Whose fault is that? her conscience asked.

Serena had no answer. She'd pushed William away, told him he could only be a friend until Shet was dealt with. Sure, it had been Ms. Sioned's advice, but the truth was the words had been an excuse that Serena had latched onto like a drowning woman clinging to a lifeline. She lacked the courage to open her heart.

Maybe her rejection of William was the cause of his inexplicable anger.

She wondered about it even as she did her best to ignore the guilty thoughts that swam to the surface of her mind similar to how she swam to the water's surface. She clambered atop her board and sat facing the ocean's depths, managing to set aside her self-reproach, trading it for the experience of the world. Once again, she heard petrels call as they soared the trade winds. Waves surged against the shore, and she knew without looking that some of them crashed high against Lilith's red-veined, black cliffs and left jewel-like rainbows in their wake. The sun climbed higher in the sky, and it beamed through vagrant, fluffy clouds that resembled stretched cotton balls.

Serena surfed for an hour more and wished she could have stayed far longer. Lilith Bay in the winter had some of the best waves on the island. Best of all, it was a short stroll to her cottage, as well as an easy climb up the cliffs and a short bike ride to Sile Troy's fields where she still apprenticed as a farmer.

Farming. Anyone who had known Serena from Sinskrill would have scoffed at seeing her engaged in such mundane work. In Sinskrill only drones, those whose capacity for *lorethasra* had been removed— slaves, really—farmed but not here. On Arylyn, farmers were honored. Not that it mattered to Serena. She would have farmed no matter the supposed esteem of her chosen profession. Farming felt like a natural extension of her years of pent-up longings, her desire to create rather than destroy, to see things grow rather than burn.

And to hear the song of the Lord.

The last was a private notion, one she hadn't shared with anyone, not Sile, Selene, or even William.

When she dragged her board to shore, she noticed Lien waiting on the golden-sand beach. "Hi," Serena called in greeting.

She recalled her promise to Jake, to ask Lien about girls who might be interested in him. Of course, right after breakfast, Jake had asked her to hold off on asking for Lien's help. He'd said that he wanted to get the lay of the land on his own, so to speak. Serena had agreed to his request, but at the same time, she realized something Jake probably didn't realize about himself. Despite his words about wanting to make Arylyn his home, he was like her: unready to open his heart.

Serena high-stepped the last few yards to shore. "What are you doing here?"

"Waiting for you," Lien said. "It's too hard finding you any other time. You're either here, farming, or doing who knows what with William."

Serena's eyes narrowed, and she tried not to scowl. "That sounded a touch judgmental."

Lien held her hands up in placation. "No judgment. I just wanted to talk."

Serena's irritation left her, and she accepted Lien's explanation. "We couldn't talk at the enrune fields?"

"Sure, but who knows when you would show up," Lien said. "I already knew you'd be here."

"What did you want to talk about?" Serena asked as she braced her surfboard in the sand and began drying off with the towel she'd left on the beach.

"I think you should make some friends."

Serena paused and stared at the other girl. "I already have friends."

"I mean girl friends."

"You're not a girl?"

Lien held up a finger. "First, I'm *one* girl. That's a singular." She held up a second finger. "Two, I'm talking about more than one. That's plural. Hence, girl *friends*."

Serena resumed her toweling. For some reason Lien's proposal filled her with trepidation. Maybe it had to do with her Sinskrill upbringing. All mahavans saw one another as competitors but amongst women it was even worse. Vindictive didn't begin to describe the level of abuse they flung at one another. "I see," Serena said. "What if I say 'no?'"

Lien sighed. "Stop being intentionally dumb. I won't introduce you to a bunch of catty, mean girls," she said. "You know me. Do you really think I'd be friends with people like that?"

"I suppose not," Serena said, still unsure about Lien's offer. She finished drying off, wrapped the towel around her waist, and slipped on her sandals. She then pulled the surfboard free of the sand.

Lien shuffled alongside her as they headed back to Serena's cottage. "Plus, as much time as you spend with William I'm sure you're looking for someone who can provide more stimulating conversation. Him and his mission. Shet. Training. Shet. Training. Blah, blah, blah."

Serena paused to face Lien. She had long ago grown tired of the other girl's snipes toward William. "I know you don't think about him like that," she said, "and even if you do, I'd appreciate you not speaking about him in such a fashion."

Lien's face filled with amusement. "You really do like him, don't you?" Even with her mahavan training Serena couldn't entirely hide her reaction, and Lien grinned. "I knew it."

Serena sighed in disbelief. It was impossible to keep up with Lien's thoughts. "That's why you insulted William? To see if I'd come to his defense?"

Lien smiled smugly. "Of course. And it worked." Her amusement faded and confusion took its place. "If you like him so much, why haven't you kissed him yet?"

Serena blinked, and once more her mahavan training failed her. "What?" she asked, flustered. For some reason, kissing William in the West Virginia *saha'asra* right before Kohl Obsidian attacked didn't count in her mind. "How did you know we haven't kissed?"

"I didn't," Lien said. "You just told me."

Serena silently applauded the girl's cleverness while at the same time, she seethed at her intrusiveness. Serena was a private person, and she didn't like people prying into her life.

Lien blithely spoke on. "I figured after Australia, and all the time you spend together, you'd have at least kissed."

Serena's mahavan training finally kicked in, and she managed to prevent her face from reddening. She wouldn't have minded kissing William, maybe more than kiss him, but Ms. Sioned's words still echoed in her mind, as did her own fear. *Will I ever have the courage he deserves?* She mentally frowned at the thought. *Then again, he hasn't asked me to Chinese New Year's.* He had for the Western New Year's, and they had spent an awkward few hours pretending to dance. Mostly, though, they'd watched everyone else have a good time. After she'd made her statement about friendship, it was like they didn't know how to act toward one another as anything other than friends.

Lien patted her shoulder. "Don't wait too long on him," she said. "I know every once in a while I give him a hard time but—"

"Rarely," Serena murmured with a smile. "You rarely give him a hard time."

The other girl grinned. "Right. Rarely. I know I *rarely* give him a hard time, but he does have a cool, dangerous quality to him, doesn't he? Girls like that." Lien's fond words were ruined an instant later. "Too bad he's such a dork."

CHAPTER 9: THE PAST REACHES

November 1989

Jessira quietly observed her husband and reflected upon how much their lives had changed since they'd first met.

Rukh wasn't quite as handsome in his current form compared to how he'd been on Arisa. His nose was a tad larger and his mouth a mite narrower. However, his coal-dark eyes, his black hair, and his dusky skin, the color of tea touched with milk, remained unchanged. So, too, did his lean but well-built physique and his incomparable grace.

Jessira knew that she was also different. Her hair was a lighter shade of blonde, her lips fuller, and her body slightly more curvaceous. She liked the last. On Arisa, she'd always considered herself boyish in build. Rukh had claimed otherwise, but his opinion didn't overcome her feelings of self-doubt.

She continued to study her husband and wondered at his thoughts. For once, she couldn't sense them.

Rukh frowned at the round, red entrance to Meldencreche, the dwarven village. Sunlight beamed down upon the meadow at the foot of Mount Madhava. Birds called from the nearby forest, and bees hummed amongst the early spring wildflowers. The gray-black bulk of the mountain towered overhead, and a crisp wind blew.

The latter two features reminded Jessira of Stronghold, her long-dead birthplace and the home of her heart.

Rukh surprised her then by reaching for the large knocker mounted on the red door. He rapped several times before pushing his way inside. Jessira followed, and they entered the dwarven home. No Memory greeted them this time, since Rukh had asked to be left alone for this visit.

"Why are we here?" Jessira asked.

Rukh paced along the long corridor and didn't reply. Instead, concentration filled his features.

Jessira strode alongside him and accepted his silence. He'd tell her when he was ready.

Regularly spaced lanterns lit the long passage, another feature that reminded Jessira of Stronghold. However, one obvious difference between Meldencreche and her birth home were the numerous frescoes adorning the granite walls here. Stronghold had been spare and undecorated, a fortress prepared for battle. Here, though, colorful images embellished the walls, and almost all had humans in positions of importance and reverence. Despite knowing how the dwarves had come to be, the obvious adulation made Jessira scowl.

Rukh halted in front of a mosaic. It depicted a dark-skinned man with smudged or rubbed-out features as he knelt amongst a small group of dwarves who stared at him as if he was holy. It was a rendering of the creation of the dwarves.

"This one soothes my mind," Rukh said.

"The dwarves tend to soothe the mind."

Rukh grunted. "Yes, they do. I think it's part of their magic." He fell mute again as he stared at the fresco.

Jessira waited on him to explain more, but he remained quiet, and her patience finally ended. "Why are we here?" she asked again.

Rukh twitched as if in uncertainty, staring off in the distance. He answered after a few seconds. "Because my memory of our past life feels like his face." He pointed to the faceless man of the mosaic. "We can see his skin and body, but the visage is missing."

Jessira eyed her husband in concern. Their shared ability to sense the other's thoughts continued to fail her. "What do you mean?"

Rukh's mouth moved as if he struggled to piece together the words. "My memory, my sense of self isn't complete," he said. "I don't remember most of my childhood, which is terrible enough, but I worry I'll lose even more. I fear that the heart of us, who we are to one another, might similarly fade away and perish."

Jessira didn't understand the nature of Rukh's concern. "We already have the heart of us." She took one of his hands in both of her own. "We're together. We know one another, and we have our love."

Rukh shook his head. "The heart is there, but too many memories remain missing." He frowned. "I worry I'll never recover them."

Jessira brought his hand to her chest. "It will. Give it time."

"It's been three years. That should have already been enough time."

Jessira smiled as she cupped Rukh's face. "You delayed taking corporeal form when you placed Aia in William's path. I didn't. That has to be why you haven't recovered all your memories."

Rukh remained unconvinced. "It isn't only that."

Worry began gnawing at Jessira. "What else are you missing?"

"Fear."

Jessira's eyes widened in surprise. "Fear? I've never known you to be afraid of anything. Even when you should have been."

Rukh smiled at her. "I'm afraid all the time, but I'm usually too busy risking my life to pay it any attention."

Jessira chuckled. "I'm sure." Her amusement departed when Rukh's features became serious once more.

"I worry about the future, but I don't fear it," he said. "I should. Shet is coming, but before he arrives, the mahavans will come first."

"You truly think so?" Jessira asked, although she already agreed with him.

"I don't remember everything, but I remember Shet's daughter. She would never allow what we did to Sinskrill go unanswered. If the mahavans are anything like her and her father, they're coming."

"The magi don't think the mahavans can learn the key to Arylyn's anchor line."

"They don't need to if they discover Arylyn's location. They can sail here, like we did to Sinskrill," Rukh said. "Plus, Shet's daughter discovered our world and look what they did to it." He put a hand to his chest. "Which is why I should fear, but my heart is empty of it. It shouldn't be."

Jessira cocked her head. She finally had a sense of what had Rukh upset. "Our travels amongst the worlds isn't yet complete, and you worry that if fear and your childhood can be stolen from you, love can as well."

Rukh nodded and drew her into his arms. "What do you know of Jareth, Wren, Sinder, and Brinatha?"

Jessira stiffened. The names caused her joy and pain in equal measure.

"You know who they are, don't you?" Rukh asked. "I can't see their faces. I only know the names."

"They're our children," Jessira told him.

"And two are dead."

His words fell like a stone, and Jessira could only nod. Pain at what they'd lost stole her voice. After a moment, she managed to collect herself. "They were born without flesh and yet were mortal." A tear leaked down her cheek.

Rukh traced the tear. "You've known all along?"

"I knew," Jessira said. "It came to me when I first entered Meldencreche."

Rukh tilted up her chin. "You carried the burden of their loss alone. Why not tell me?"

"They are only names until you remember their lives," Jessira replied.

Rukh hugged her. "It's why I came here, to remember all I lost. To know our children when we see them again."

Jessira stepped out of his embrace and took his hand. She tugged him forward. "Let me show you what stirred my memories. It's a mural of the Lord of the Sword and the Lady of Fire. You'll know who they are when you see their faces."

❧

William, Jake, and Jason hunkered alone in a quiet, dead-end alley that opened onto the Village Green and the hundreds of people overflowing its confines in celebration of the Chinese New Year. Those who didn't want to deal with the hassle of the horde up on Clifftop held celebrations in their homes. Those parties could be every bit as raucous as the one up here.

Electricity coursed through the throng, and William imagined this might be how Times Square felt and looked on New Year's Eve . . . if Times Square had glorious waterfalls, majestic, awe-inspiring statues of magi from history, and a massive escarpment that overlooked the Pacific Ocean. Nevertheless, while the crowd's energy could be intoxicating, the tumult, along with the music blaring from the gazebo, made it hard to think. As a result he, Jake, and Jason had retreated to this out-of-the-way alley, each of them withdrawn into their own thoughts.

William studied the others and for the first time noticed the faintest hint of crow's feet at the corners of the other boys' eyes. He wondered if he had the same set of wrinkles. The three of them were only twenty-two, and a few years ago all their faces had been smooth and innocent, but time and dangerous living had aged them. Their lives had changed so dramatically since their senior year of high school and those alterations had marked them in ways other than the age lines on their faces. Jake was no longer the brash, smug, cocky football player he had once been, and Jason had traded smooth confidence and self-assuredness for doubt and uncertainty.

As for himself . . . William sighed in disappointment at the direction his life had taken. Dedication and focus. Work and train. That's all he ever thought about, and he wondered if the pressure would ever let up.

Why didn't I ask Serena to the Chinese New Year's festival? She would have said 'yes.' *At least, I think she would have.* Instead here he moped, alone and unnoticed in an alley, separate from the excitement, while the rest of the village celebrated.

"Where's Daniella?" Jason asked Jake. "Didn't you say you were interested in her?"

Jake's shoulders hunched. "I'm working on it."

"I thought Serena was going to talk to Lien about her," Jason said.

"I told her not to bother," Jake answered. "Like I said, I'm working on it."

Jason snorted. "By working on it, you really mean you're delaying?"

"Says the guy who also doesn't have a date," Jake countered.

Jason held up his hands in surrender. "I know I sound like a hypocrite, but believe it or not I've got a date lined up for next week."

William's head shot around. "Since when did you start dating?"

Jake followed up. "Yeah, with who?"

Jason smiled smugly. "You'll find out."

Jake viewed Jason in study. "I don't believe you," he eventually said.

"And I don't care," Jason replied in a haughty tone.

"Then who is it?" Jake asked.

"None of your business," Jason said.

"Then why didn't you ask her out to New Years?" Jake asked.

"Because she already had plans." Jason scowled. "Leave it alone, all right?"

William looked from Jake to Jason and considered their shared situations. "We're a trio of losers," he decided.

The other two stared at him, brows lifted in either offense or annoyance.

"We are," William said. "All of us keep putting off asking out girls we like because of all the crap we've been through."

Jake nodded agreement. "We suck. I mean, look at us. Hiding in an alley like this."

"Speak for yourself," Jason said. "I plan on living again." His eyes drifted over the crowd and he pointed. "Look. It's Lien and Daniel."

William searched for where Jason indicated. Lien and Daniel danced close, swaying slowly in time to the music. He smiled as he watched them move. "They look good together."

"Check out Jean-Paul and Thu," Jake said with a chuckle.

Jason laughed, too. "Is Jean-Paul having a seizure?"

William shook his head, amazed and appalled at the herky-jerky nature of the Frenchman's movements, especially compared to the gracefulness of his Vietnamese husband. "I think that's just how he dances."

They watched a few minutes more until the song ended.

"Lien and Daniel are coming over," Jason said, and they waited in silence for the couple's arrival.

"What are you guys doing here all alone?" Lien asked.

"Nothing," William answered. "Talking about people who shouldn't be dancing in public."

"You mean, like you and Serena?" Lien asked with an arch of her eyebrows. "You really should have asked her out."

William grimaced. Lien always gave him a hard time. "Yeah, well some of us are born dumb."

"You should find her and at least ask her for a dance," Daniel said, giving William a nudge and a wink.

William feigned cool unconcern.

"Just do it," Lien said, giving him a shove toward the crowd. "Don't be a dumb-Shet."

William dug in his heels, preventing Lien from pushing him forward. "A what?"

"A dumb-Shet," Lien said. "You know what I mean. Now, get going." She gave him another shove toward the Village Green.

William kept his feet dug in.

"Even Rukh and Jessira took the day off to celebrate," Lien said, pointing out the strange couple.

William watched them. Lien was right. They were having a good time, although both had seemed morose a few days ago when they'd come back from Meldencreche.

His gaze wandered then, but it locked in place when he saw Serena. He couldn't look away. She wore a sleeveless dress, sunshine-yellow, that hugged her form and swirled about her long legs as she eased through the crowd. She gracefully twisted to avoid those dancing, smiling or laughing every now and then, her expression open and warm. William swallowed heavily.

"Go dance with her," Lien urged. "We all know you want to."

William blinked, awareness of his surroundings returning.

Daniel laughed. "I think our friend here *wants* to dance with Serena, but he doesn't know how to ask her." He wore a knowing leer. "Or maybe he's thinking about doing the horizontal bop."

"Gross!" Lien exclaimed at Daniel, her face pinched in disapproval.

Daniel spent the next seconds apologizing profusely to Lien, but William had stopped paying them any attention. His focus remained on Serena, and he found himself moving toward her like iron to a lodestone. Shet could wait. Danger could wait. The world could wait. Right now, he wanted to dance with Serena.

"I'll see y'all later," William called over his shoulder.

He strode toward Serena, and she turned on the moment of his arrival, somehow sensing his approach. She broke into a smile, the secret smile of amusement that set his heart to beating faster. He didn't have to say anything. Serena held out her hands, and he took her in his arms. They swirled into unison, flowing like they'd danced together a thousand times.

Serena laughed, and William wondered what her lips tasted like. He'd once felt them pressed against his own, but he wanted to know it again.

The music slowed, and Serena rested her head against his shoulder. They swayed in time to the rhythm, and through the fabric of her dress and his button-up shirt, he felt her heartbeat. It raced faster than it should have. He thought she trembled, and he wondered at it.

She pushed off his chest when the song ended and smiled at him. Not the secret one he loved to see. This one was the smile of a friend, and somehow also sad.

"Thank you for the dance," Serena said before disappearing into the crowd.

CHAPTER 10: ADVANCING ELEMENTS

M *arch 1990*

"W hy are we here?" Serena asked Lien.

The two of them stood in the early morning sunlight outside of an abandoned townhouse on Cliff Fire. The two-story structure clung to the very edge of Terrace Ten on a long, narrow lot, and the structure could have easily fit in amongst the rundown tenements of Over-the-Rhine, the ghetto Serena remembered from her time in Cincinnati. Despite the shadows cast by the looming cliff toward the rear, the townhouse had the same slumped, disheveled disrepair apparent in most buildings in that Cincinnati neighborhood. In addition, similar to Over-the-Rhine, a hint of something beautiful lay hidden beneath the grime and grit. *Deeply hidden.*

Serena ran her eyes over the boarded windows, the rotted door, and the sagging porch with columns ruined to little more than sawdust by wood ants or termites.

At least someone had made an attempt to maintain the grounds.

They'd trimmed the weeds and kept them at a manageable ankle-high level rather than allowing them to grow to a person's waist.

Lien threw her arms wide as if to embrace the slouched structure. "This is my home," she declared in answer to Serena's question.

Serena lifted her eyebrows in disbelief. "This place?" It had to be a joke. *Why would Lien want to live in such a broken-down hovel?*

The other girl nodded, though. "It's actually mine and Daniel's. He proposed to me last night." She displayed a gold band with a small diamond encircling her ring finger and nearly squealed in delight, a strange sound from the normally blunt and razor-tongued girl.

Serena smiled at Lien, amused by her friend's reaction but mostly glad for her. "Congratulations," she said. "Have you set a date?"

"Next spring," Lien answered. "We're hoping to move into the house right after the wedding."

Serena opened her mouth to reply but caught sight of two girls heading their way. She recognized both of them—Karla and Daniella Logan—native-born sisters a year apart in age who could have almost passed for identical twins.

Karla, the taller and older of the sisters, had native-born dusky skin, but rather than dark hair, hers was a sandy-brown and clipped short at the nape of her neck. In addition, she had startling, bright blue eyes rather than dark-colored ones. They were somewhat hidden by the round glasses that fit her face. She wore jeans and a T-shirt with the logo of the Episcopal Church. Her grandfather had been a rector.

Serena had gotten to know Karla pretty well during the times they played enrune and had immediately been struck by her bubbly personality and generous manner.

Daniella, on the other hand, was more reserved. She left her hair longer, letting it drape around her lean, pretty features. Maybe she wanted to hide her face, but nothing could mask her blue eyes, every bit as vibrant and startling as her sister's. Daniella also wore clothing similar to Karla's, but for some reason she had a lantern in her hand. She smiled shyly.

Serena smiled in reply and realized an opportunity had presented itself. Jake couldn't seem to muster up the courage to talk to Daniella, and here she was. Maybe Serena could push the issue for him. He'd likely resent her intrusiveness, but if all went well, then all would also be forgiven. She'd have to find a subtle means of broaching the topic,

"Hi," Karla said in her open, forthright manner as she directed her attention to Lien. "You wanted some help cleaning up your new homestead?" She shoved Daniella forward. "I nominate my little sister to clear the cobwebs."

Daniella offered Karla an amused smile. "And I nominate my much *older* sister to clear out the mice droppings."

"Gross," Karla said.

Serena chuckled. "Is that why you invited me up here?" she asked Lien.

"You don't mind?" Lien asked.

"Of course not. What do you want to do first?"

Lien wore an unaccountably uncertain expression. "I'm not sure. I've never fixed up a house before. What did you start with when you repaired your cottage?"

Daniella addressed Serena. "By the way, your cottage is an absolute gem," she said. "When you had us over a few months ago, I couldn't believe it was the same place I remembered from before. I always knew it as that ugly dump by the lagoon."

"I especially liked the gardens," Karla said.

Serena's feelings toward the Logans warmed. "Thank you," she said. "It took a lot of work getting it to look like it does."

"Do you think we can do the same thing for my house?" Lien asked.

Serena shrugged. "Hard work can fix nearly anything. Let's go inside and take an inventory of what needs repairing."

They climbed the short flight of steps to the front porch and entered the house. Serena rocked back at the stench, a nostril-burning stink of mouse-droppings and bat guano, and the fetid rankness of mold mixed with the reek of stale air. In addition, with all the windows boarded up she had trouble seeing anything.

"Here," Daniella said. She held up the lantern she brought.

Serena silently applauded the other woman's foresight when bright, white light chased away the darkness. It also disturbed the bats roosting in the chimney. They chirped and fluttered, disturbed in their sleep as other vermin scuttled across the floor, seeking shelter from the sudden illumination.

Lien held a handkerchief to her mouth and nose. "What's that smell?" she asked, her voice muffled by the fabric.

"Bat guano and mouse droppings," Serena answered. "Amongst other things."

Daniella snickered at Karla. "Cleaning that stuff is your job."

"No, thanks," Karla quickly said. "I think Serena and Lien can handle that part, right?"

Serena didn't answer. She was too busy creating a mental inventory of what needed doing. A thick layer of dust covered moth-eaten or termite-damaged furniture. All of that would have to go. The plaster walls had cracks extending like lightning from the ceiling. Massive chunks were missing. *Maybe a water leak upstairs?* In addition the flooring sagged, with a pronounced drop-off from the front of the house to the back. Serena bounced experimentally a few times, confirming her suspicions. Some of the floor joists had gone bad.

Serena addressed Lien. "I think we'll have to take the house down to the studs first. After that, we can figure out what we want to do with it."

Lien sighed. "It sounds like a lot of work."

Serena nodded. "Let's start with the furniture. We need to get rid of all of it." She looked to Lien. "Do you have any more handkerchiefs? We shouldn't breathe too much of this stuff."

Lien pulled three handkerchiefs from her back pocket, and they got started.

"We'll have to toss the furniture outside," Serena said.

"I've got a better idea," Karla said. She sourced her *lorethasra*, and the smell of dandelion briefly washed away the room's stink. She wove whip-like braids made of Earth and Air and sent them into a sofa. They reached out with grasping, root-like fingers. "Watch." Wood cracked as the sofa buckled. Legs snapped, the spine broke, and sawdust rose.

Lien sneezed. "Ugh."

Serena automatically pushed the sawdust away from her face with a weave of Air.

A few minutes later, Karla had torn the furniture into small pieces of kindling. "If we hold the pieces in a mesh of Earth, we should be able burn them to ashes."

Serena smiled. "Good idea. Let's get it done."

They quickly had the rest of the furniture torn down and burned to ash. From there, they moved on to the rest of the filth. Hours later, by common assent, they broke for lunch. All of them were covered with dirt and grime.

"We got a lot done," Daniella said, sounding proud of herself.

The four of them rested outside on the front porch, enjoying the fresh air.

"We did get a lot done," Lien agreed. "Breaking down the furniture helped a lot."

"That was a handy trick," Daniella said to Karla.

"We still have to tear down the walls and pull up the flooring," Serena reminded them. "We'll eventually need help with all that or we'll be doing demolition until Christmas."

"What about Daniel?" Karla asked. "What's he doing?"

Lien scowled. "He has to repair the leylines near Mount Madhava or something like that. Lucky guy."

Serena swatted at a smear of dirt on her pants. "I can ask William to help."

Lien smiled knowingly. "I'm sure he'll do anything for you."

Karla and Daniella grinned as well.

Serena mentally sighed. After dancing with William at the Chinese New Year's celebration, their relationship had resumed its normal platonic pattern of friendship and nothing more. "William's a good friend. That's it," she said, knowing her statement sounded weak as soon as the words left her mouth.

Daniella laughed. "I wish I had a good friend like that."

"Same here," Karla said. She leaned in for a conspiratorial whisper. "He's handsome but so intense. I like that."

Lien nodded vigorously and grinned. "But don't forget that he's a dork."

"Isn't Daniel the one who memorized the theme song to *Star Blazers*?" Serena asked. She'd seen the show once in Cincinnati. Daniel had chosen it for movie night. Between the absurd plot, ridiculous bug-eyed women, and silly weapons—*A Wave-Motion Cannon. Really?*—Lien had no right to mock *anyone* as being a dork given the man she loved.

Lien only smiled wider. "Daniel's a dork, but he's the kind of dork William only wishes he could be. My man is the king of dorks."

Serena laughed in reply, genuinely amused by Lien's take on the situation.

"What about Jake?" Daniella asked. "Why's he such a snob?"

Serena privately thanked whichever god had placed Jake's name in Daniella's mind. "He's not like that at all," she said. "He's actually quite kind and generous, but he's had a hard time coming to grips with everything he's lost and been through. Give him time, and I think he'll surprise us all."

Karla wore a puzzled frown. "That sounded like an oddly ringing endorsement." Her eyes widened an instant later. "You're trying to set him up with one of us."

Serena quietly cursed the god who had apparently given Karla supernatural insight into the thoughts of others. "No, it's only—"

Thankfully, Lien rescued her, interrupting and cutting cut her off from having to comment on Karla's astute observation. "Rukh starts training his fighters tomorrow," Lien said. "He says the mahavans will eventually attack us. Are you going to be there?" she asked the Logans.

Karla's humor fled. "They're training somewhere north of the enrune fields, right? On the other side of Lakshman's Bow?"

"Middle of the morning," Serena said.

Daniella frowned and shifted about, clearly troubled. "Maybe we *should* be there, too," she said to her sister.

"I don't know," Karla hedged. "It seems a lot to accept."

"I hope Rukh isn't too hard on us," Lien said.

Somehow, Serena doubted it. They'd all have to work hard and focus if they wanted to defeat the mahavans. *Another reason to pursue nothing more than friendship with William,* said the cowardly part of herself.

~

W illiam waited alongside twenty other people on a wide, grassy field bereft of any shade or the promise of relief from the sun's mid-morning heat. No clouds rode the sky and no breeze blew. Instead, bugs flitted about, droning and buzzing while a few lizards slithered from bush to bush. A swampy oppressiveness trapped the air.

The alluring rush of River Namaste flowed from several hundred yards away, and William eyed the cool water wistfully as he sweated.

"I see what you're eyeing there," Jake said, standing to William's left. "I'd rather go swimming, too."

Serena, who stood to his right, nodded agreement. "I'll even take Sinskrill's rain to this muggy heat."

William didn't bother replying. His mind was filled with visions of sipping icy lemonade beneath the shade of a tree next to a cool mountain lake.

"I think we're about to start," said Ward from nearby as well.

William drew his attention back to the present and glanced down the line at Jason, Daniel, Lien, and the others. Everyone here was young—the older folk either didn't believe in the approaching danger or had other work to do—and today would be their first day of training. They all wore shorts, t-shirts, and comfortable boots in which to run and eyed Rukh and Jessira, who stood in front of them.

Rukh gave Jessira a brief nod before clasping his hands behind his back. He paced the line of those present and viewed them with quiet scrutiny.

William instinctually drew back his shoulders and straightened his spine until he stood at attention, stiff as a fence post. Rukh continued to study them, and the pregnant quiet became charged, as if a storm or something powerful were about to occur. It continued to build and William found himself holding his breath. He didn't want to ruin the moment. He wanted to freeze it, capture it forever in his memory. His eyes went to the white-capped waters of the river, to Lakshman's Bow, all the way to the enrune fields where games were being played.

William closed his eyes. *This* was the instant when Arylyn's defense began.

Rukh's voice broke the spell. "I have no grand words to inspire you."

William opened his eyes, and only then noticed that *everyone* stood as ramrod straight as he did. Rukh had that kind of effect on a person.

"I only have what's in my heart," Rukh said, "and what I believe you already know. The people of Arylyn lead cosseted lives of peace and tranquility, and a true warrior would want that to continue. Though others doubt our mission, better for this island's beautiful life to continue uninterrupted than for us to be proven right."

William silently agreed.

Rukh continued. "However, I fear such will not be the case. While others may laugh at what we do, scoff at our fears and mock our preparations, they will nevertheless bless all of you when the storm breaks." His gaze swept over them. "And the storm will break. It is why you are here: to shelter your brothers and sisters." He held up a fist. "Faith, dharma, and duty." He ticked off each word with a separate finger. "Though you may not realize it, these three hallowed words ordain the purpose of your lives. They define what impels you, why you are here, and what you seek to become."

William wanted to shout agreement. Rukh's speech touched a core of desire inside him. The words resounded rightly, and he buzzed with the adrenaline rush of wanting to do something mighty—anything, really—so long as it was meaningful.

Jessira moved to stand beside Rukh. "We'll begin with an explanation of what we expect from each of you," she said. "The council has granted those volunteering for the Ashokan Irregulars absence from most of the work details you would usually do." She shared a private smile with Rukh.

Jake leaned in toward William. "What are Ashokan Irregulars?"

William shook his head. "No idea," he answered. He shushed Jake when Rukh started talking again.

Rukh took up the explanation. "The Ashokan Irregulars is the name for our unit. It is who you now are."

"Therefore," Jessira said, "starting this morning and from now on, we'll meet here and train. We'll start with a run, which will grow progressively longer and more difficult. None of you can train if you aren't fit." She stared at them in challenge. "After that, we'll take a short break and then drill. We'll teach you how to fight as a unit."

"Like you and Rukh do?" William asked.

Jessira quirked a questioning eyebrow.

"When you fought the Servitor, you moved . . ." William struggled to find the right words. "You moved like you had one mind."

Rukh dipped his head in acknowledgement. "We did move as one. It's a type of weave, which on our world is called a Duo. We can add up to two more, which is then a Quad, and it's essentially a hive mind."

A hundred questions raced through William's mind, but he didn't have a chance to ask them.

Jessira had already moved on. "After drilling, we'll break for lunch, and follow that with another training session in the afternoon." She held up a hand as a few other people tried to ask questions, and she shouted over them. "Before we begin our run, I want to emphasize one point. Some of you are already somewhat skilled with the sword." Her gaze briefly rested on William and Serena. "But a great swordsman isn't as useful to the Irregulars as unit cohesion." She made a fist of her hand. "We need you to learn to fight as a fist formed from five fingers."

"What about you and Rukh?" Serena asked. "You're both great at fighting individually."

"We fight as one," Jessira said. "It only seems like we fight individually."

"Right," Rukh said. "Remember, when we spar, it is not meant to be to the death. You'll all wear governors." He pointed to a stack of leather helmets piled several feet behind him. "I'll remind you of this from time to time."

William went still. He remembered how close he'd come to hurting Ward a few weeks back and how he'd vowed again to never lose control of his anger . . . especially since he feared where it came from.

~

W illiam settled himself with a groan into a wicker chair on Afa Simon's lanai. He imagined himself melting underneath the noonday sun. Thankfully, a thatched roof provided shade from the unbearable heat. William sighed in appreciation as he closed his eyes and basked in the cool air stirred by the overhead fans, the steady breeze, and the mist from one of River Namaste's innumerable cascades.

"You look how I feel," Jake said as he flopped down in a chair next to him.

William didn't bother replying but merely opened his eyes a crack. Large, red tiles floored the lanai, which overlooked the tropical gardens that made up Afa's front yard. Several more pieces of wicker furniture, one of which Jake currently occupied, provided additional seating. Afa sat nearby as well.

William's gaze went to aqua-blue Lilith Bay, a hundred feet below and a half mile away. At such a distance the surf couldn't be heard above the sound of the whispering waterfall in Afa's backyard.

William waved away an annoying bee that drifted into the lanai from the tropical gardens and momentarily wondered how Afa maintained his flowerbeds. As old as he was—older than both Mr. Zeus and Ms. Sioned—and with his perpetually stooped posture, how did he manage to get it done?

"I'm beat," William said.

"Same here," Jake agreed with a wheeze. "It was that final drill. I think Rukh was trying to kill us."

"It's the sun," William disagreed. "The drill wouldn't have been so bad if there had been a breeze or a few clouds to cool us off. We've had this muggy weather for weeks now."

"Training with the Ashokan Irregulars again?" Afa asked. Polynesian warrior tattoos decorated his thin arms and chest, and an omnipresent wide-brimmed hat rested on his otherwise bald head. He took a sip of his lemonade, and William caught him smiling. He likely found their exertions amusing.

The notion of someone laughing at his difficulties caused the red-eyed beast within him to shift and growl as if in question, and William quickly thought of something else. For some reason his mind latched onto Serena. Thinking of her, though, agitated him in other ways, especially thinking of her hair, face, and lips. He cut off that line of thinking and shifted them to *Blue Sky Dreamers*. It had been weeks since he'd been able to sail the dhow.

Afa cleared his throat. "Was it truly that painful?"

"You have no idea," Jake said. "Thrust, parry, shield. Thrust, parry, shield. Now sprint!" He mimicked Rukh's drillmaster cadence.

"I'm sorry to hear that," Afa murmured in sympathy.

William sat up, wanting to get the meeting over with. "What did you want to talk about today?" he asked. "Is it to go over the work schedule? Do you need me and Jake to pitch in more?"

While training with the Ashokan Irregulars allowed him and Jake relief from most of their work duties, it didn't let them get out of all of it. As *raha'asras*, no one else could do what they could. They created *lorasra*, the magic of a *saha'asra*, something an *asrasin* could then use to create their braids and weaves. While there were three other *raha'asras* on Arylyn—Fiona, Ms. Sioned, and Afa Simon—the others were older and it wasn't fair to leave all the work to them.

Afa didn't have a chance to answer because Ms. Sioned hobbled into the yard. She leaned on a cane, which William hated seeing her have to use. When he and Jake had first come to Arylyn she hadn't needed it. Nevertheless, her blue eyes remained bright and curious behind her thick glasses, and her seamed face broke into a smile when she noticed William and Jake.

Trailing close behind her was Arylyn's third elderly *raha'asra*, Fiona Applefield. She had her gray hair pulled back in a braid, and her friendly face held a smile of greeting. She looked like someone's kindly grandmother, although she'd once been an unholy terror to William and Jake. It had occurred in a different life, during their imprisonment on Sinskrill with Fiona as their not-so-kind jailor.

Ms. Sioned eased into a wicker loveseat, and Fiona sat beside her. The two women had become good friends.

Ms. Sioned addressed William and Jake. "Thank you for coming so soon after your training, dears," she said in her Irish lilt.

"What's this meeting about?" Jake asked.

"William," Afa answered.

"What about me?" William asked.

Ms. Sioned eyed him with frank disappointment. "Your anger. Everyone has felt your barbed tongue."

The monster inside William's mind murmured in its slumber, and he shifted in his chair, willing it to remain asleep.

Fiona stared at him for a moment. Her eyes widened in astonishment. "It isn't of you, is it?"

William's mouth gaped. "How did you know?"

Fiona offered a secret smile, one eerily similar to Serena's. "A lucky guess."

Afa held a frown. "What is this?" he asked William. "What does she mean, 'it isn't of you?'"

William glanced around the lanai, feeling trapped. The red-eyed beast growled, and he forced it back into the recesses of his mind. The sensation of being caged passed, and he was able to tell the others about when the anger had first occurred. He spoke of the albino creature he'd seen right before the fury entered him. He described its appearance, a snarling, red-eyed monster, and how it resembled the way he'd felt after Kohl Obsidian first touched him when the necrosed killed his parents.

As he spoke, relief and guilt washed over him in equal measure. It felt good to finally let someone else know what he'd been going through, and he also realized he should have spoken up much sooner.

Ms. Sioned scowled at him in obvious anger. "And you never thought to tell anyone of this until now?" she shouted.

William wanted to shrink into his chair and vanish.

Jake shook his head. "You dumbass."

Fiona, however, stared at him pensively. "Sapient Dormant is said to be an albino. As Overward of the necrosed, he could have been the one you saw, calling you through Kohl's blood."

Afa hissed, appalled. "It must be purged from him."

Fiona nodded. "But we must first learn the truth of what has happened."

Ms. Sioned shook her head in disappointment at William. "You will set aside your work, up to and including your training with Rukh and his Irregulars if we deem it necessary."

William opened his mouth to protest.

Afa, usually even-tempered, glared and rapped his cane on the lanai's floor. "This is not a matter for negotiation. You *will* attend us."

"Yes, sir." William bent his head in defeat and acceptance as well as relief. At least he'd have some help dealing with the anger if it truly did come from the Overward of the necrosed.

"We do have one piece of good news for you," Ms. Sioned said.

The anger had left her voice, and William lifted his head, hoping she was no longer upset with him. Ms. Sioned smiled at him, and the worried fist clenching his heart eased a little.

She continued to smile. "Your search for information about the anchor lines reminded me of a book I once read in the library. It was decades ago, and I no longer recall the title. However, when I described it to Julius, he sounded certain he could find it."

William's curiosity piqued. "What's it about?"

"Anchor lines," Ms. Sioned replied. "Did I not tell you that a moment ago?"

William grinned. "Of course."

Jake also smiled, more of a leer, really, and a gleam sparkled in his eyes. William mentally prepared himself. "Maybe you can ask Serena to help you out," Jake said. "I'm sure she'd love to spend time alone with you in the dark corners of a library."

Afa's eyes lit with interest. "What's this?" He sat forward.

William rolled his eyes and pretended long-suffering forbearance. "It's nothing. Just Jake thinking he's funny."

"William won't ask Serena out on a date," Jake helpfully filled in.

Afa harrumphed and faced William, his eyes wide with disbelief. "Am I to understand that you have yet to court the young lady in question?"

"Yes, sir," William replied.

Afa sighed in disappointment. "My boy, you're being a biblical donkey."

William's brow creased in confusion. "What?"

"A jackass," Afa said.

Ms. Sioned cleared her throat, appearing unsure for some reason. "Perhaps it's for the best that you aren't courting Serena."

William shot her a surprised look but was distracted a moment later.

"He hasn't *courted* her because he only lives for tomorrow," Jake said.

William tensed. With no warning, the angry beast broke its shackles, and he spoke without thinking. "And you live for yesterday." His voice became cruel. "Or did you ever get the stones to ask out Daniella Logan?"

William stared at Jake, aghast and horrified. The anger snuffed out like a light bulb and self-loathing filled him. His heart pounded. *How could I have said that?* "I'm sorry," he said, the words inadequate to express his remorse.

Jake's face had gone pale. His fists clenched and unclenched. He jerked upright. "You're lucky we're friends," he finally said. He addressed Afa. "Find out what's wrong with him before I kill him." He stomped off the lanai.

The other *raha'asras* stared at William with mingled expressions of pity and horror.

CHAPTER 11: KNOWLEDGE AND STRIFE

M*arch 1990*

A dam held back a scowl of frustration as he waited for his brother's arrival. They were supposed to meet in Shet's Hall, which was otherwise empty since Axel was late. Again. It was a common occurrence, one likely meant to emphasize his brother's importance, and there was nothing Adam could do about it. Axel was the Servitor, and until Shet's arrival, his brother was the unchallenged ruler of the mahavans.

Adam paced about in impatience, and his breath frosted in the chill air of the unheated Hall. However, he didn't allow the cold to touch him. He crossed his arms and ignored his discomfort. *Cold means nothing.*

Rattling sounds from the ceiling drew Adam's attention. He stared upward where gusts of wind shook the stained-glass windows depicting scenes from *Shet's Counsel*. His eyes narrowed as he took in details he hadn't noticed earlier.

With Sinskrill's omnipresent clouds, sunshine rarely beamed

through the windows, but today a late winter sun made itself known. Beams of light poured through the stained glass and lit the Hall in a rainbow of colors. They also brightened the images and made them more easily visible. In some of them, Shet wore a patient visage, calm and loving, while in others, resoluteness filled his features. But in every single stained-glass picture, blood lay splattered and the right side of Shet's face was unmarked.

Which meant the images were a lie, something Adam had long suspected. He smirked at the stained-glass images but quickly wiped away all emotions from his face when the tall, gray double-doors to the Hall opened.

In strode Axel, proud as the sun but currently wearing a frown on his heavy-set features.

Despite his brother's obvious irritation, Adam smiled to himself. In some ways Axel resembled a troll. He contained his amusement as he bowed low to the Servitor. "Something troubles you?"

Axel thumped the steel-shod heel of Shet's Spear—he no longer traveled anywhere without the weapon—against the Hall's dark, marble flooring. The sound rang out, and he spoke above its lingering echoes. "I want us ready to assault Arylyn by late summer."

Adam hid a grimace, not daring to let his antipathy show. *Not this again.* "Why so soon? The recovered drones are progressing, but—"

Axel cut him off with a chopping motion of his hand. "Those who were healed of their stripping, their training . . . How goes it?"

Adam forced an uncaring smile, something at odds with his true feelings toward the drones. He'd come to pity them, but it was a weakness no one could ever learn. "They are focused," he answered. "They know what will happen if they fail a second time."

Axel nodded. "Another stripping. And should they fail beyond that, a short journey from the Judging Line." He took on an introspective countenance, possibly even regretful. "I wish we didn't have to do this to our people."

Adam's mouth nearly dropped in shock, and by the barest margin, he managed to bite back his surprise.

Axel noticed, and he smiled knowingly. "I know I shouldn't say it, but I pity the drones."

Adam struggled to contain fresh amazement, and Axel laughed. "I know you feel the same way. They are our people, and though their purpose is to support us in our undertakings, we can still sympathize with their plight."

Adam knew he had to choose his next words carefully. Agreeing too readily could be seen as an implicit criticism of the path the Servitor had chosen. Disagreeing could be seen in the same light. He chose to pretend ignorance, which in this case wasn't entirely feigned. "I may have some level of empathy toward the drones, but I would appreciate a further explanation of what you mean."

Axel dipped his head as if in regal assent. "The drones are my people."

They are Shet's people, Adam wanted to say.

"And their care has been placed in my hands," Axel continued. "I would not see their lives wasted."

Which is what the coming assault on Arylyn would be: a waste of lives and resources.

Rather than voice such treasonous thoughts, Adam mimed a grave expression of agreement. "I understand," he began, "and to that end, instead of invading Arylyn with the full might of our people, I've finalized plans to land a small breaching party along the island's northern shore and map it out first." *And perhaps learn a way to end this mad venture.*

"A good idea," Axel mused as he stroked his chin, "*if* our mahavans are not discovered."

"They won't be," Adam said. "The magi will be too busy lazing away their hours to search for our people."

Adam knew the magi were slothful through Serena, his once-bishan and the daughter of his heart, although it had been Axel who had fathered her. She had once told him of Arylyn through a lucid dream, something only close family members or those who loved one another could share. It had been months since she'd replied to him though, and he knew why: his actions in Australia when he'd killed Jake Ridley. The thrust had been clean, straight through the young *raha'asra's* chest.

"And then?" Axel pressed. "We can't assault the island with only one hundred and fifty mahavans. From what Serena apparently inferred to you about their population, they'll still vastly outnumber us. We need more mahavans."

"And we'll have them," Adam said, "but first we need intelligence."

Axel hesitated still, and Adam frowned in confusion. "What is it?"

"Jeek Voshkov and Arcus Elder, the unformed Primes, have heard Shet's call," Axel said, the words coming slowly and reluctantly. "They were told to attack those with *lorasra* who are not allied to Lord Shet."

Adam realized the true reason for Axel's unhappiness. "The necrosed," he breathed.

Axel nodded. "If the unformed have been called, we can guess that the necrosed have as well, along with their Overward, Sapient Dormant." He spat out the name.

"But didn't Sapient bend knee to the Servitor's Chair?"

"He did," Axel said, although his words didn't sound convincing. He made his way to the clear windows overlooking the balcony and stared outside. "Or did he bend knee so he could learn Sinskrill's location? I've often wondered."

Necrosed. Adam shivered, and in that moment he didn't care about hiding his weakness. In the face of those abominations, especially Sapient Dormant, there was no such thing as strength. "You've changed the key to the anchor line?"

Axel chuckled without humor. "More times than I can count," he said. "But as the magi have twice taught us, there are other paths to Sinskrill." He faced Adam. "Recall any mahavan in the Far Beyond. We need to maintain ourselves and defeat the magi before Shet's woven come against us. We need to earn our lord's approval." His words spoken, Axel swept toward the Hall's exit. "See it done," he shouted as he departed.

Adam watched his brother's retreating back and worried. He wondered if he should reach out to Serena again and dream to her what was to come. Fighting the magi when the necrosed might menace them was the height of lunacy. But would she listen? He doubted it. Not after what he'd done to Jake. Besides, she was a magus now. She'd fought against the mahavans before, and he was sure, she'd do so again. *But does that make her wrong?*

~

T he morning sun shone in William's eyes, forcing him to squint as he and Julius ascended the final steps of Cliff Air. Thankfully, they soon reached the top and found themselves upon a rounded promontory consisting of a grassy sward bordered by pale yellow flagstones. Centered upon the knuckle of stone arose Arylyn's library, William's destination. The building resembled a church: high walls made of blocky stones and a peaked roof interrupted by evenly spaced, stained-glass windows. A nearby finger of River Namaste plunged downward, raising a mist that washed across the flagstones and grass.

Julius broke into a grin. "Mind the rocks," he said. "Don't slip on them like you did the last time I brought you here."

William remembered, and he flushed in embarrassment. Lien had witnessed the fall and mercilessly needled him about it for weeks afterward. He took Julius' advice to heart and carefully made his way across the slick pavement to where the pathway ended at a pair of tall, dark-brown double-doors.

Julius pulled one open, and once inside, William paused to get his bearings.

Had the library been the church it resembled, he would have stood within the narthex. Round chandeliers the size of wagon wheels and wall-mounted lanterns containing lights resembling warm, incandescent bulbs provided illumination. Several patrons sat at large, rectangular tables placed in what would have been the nave, and rows of shelving, all of them holding a plethora of books, scrolls, and documents, marched away from the rounded center. A few patrons briefly glanced at him and Julius before returning to their reading.

William closed his eyes and inhaled the musty odor. He smiled as they pressed deeper into the heart of the library. As always, no matter how many times he'd been here, the beauty of the place took his breath away. High above soared a vaulted ceiling with wooden beams the color of chocolate. The supports resembled the ribs of a ship, and breaking the long line of the keel were stained-glass windows telling stories through imagery. They contained scenes from the world's past:

135

idyllic vistas with mythical creatures such as graceful unicorns, whimsical faeries, protective dragons, and peaceful dwarves. Included was one of the Lord of the Sword and the Lady of Fire. They held calm countenances as they knelt facing one another with their foreheads pressed together.

William loved the smell of old books, and Arylyn's library—its ancient tomes and millennia-old scrolls—had a comforting scent that bridged the ages. Every time he came here, a calm filled him, a joyful serenity made from the various scribblings, the turning of pages, and the whispered conversations of shared information. The peace, one held by libraries the world over, washed across William and soothed the aching anger inside of him.

Julius grinned. "You look like you're catching the aroma of a fine steak or the world's most delicious dessert."

William could only smile back.

"Let's go." Julius guided him through the shelving, and his eyes searched along the lines of books.

William followed in his wake as they bypassed sections on the practical uses of magic, presumed structures of anchor lines, and the forging of ancient weapons. He had already read many of the books in this section, or at least thumbed through them. So far, he hadn't found them useful, except for the ones about weaponry. Those had inspired some vague notions about cannons. The beastly anger always stirred whenever he thought about weapons and fighting.

Right now, though, he was more interested in the book Ms. Sioned had mentioned. Julius hadn't remembered the title, but he said he remembered where it might be shelved. William paced a few feet behind the other man, and they continued down a long shelf.

Julius frowned. "This is the wrong section." He cut down an aisle, and they entered a different area of the library. Julius' frown soon cleared. "This is it. You need to know more about the underlying theories of magic. Powerful *asrasins* like you usually have to know the basics more than the rest of us."

"You're sure it's here?" William asked.

Julius nodded. "Positive." A moment later, he stopped and pulled a tall book off the shelf. *Treatises on Travel—A Translation.* "See. Here it is."

Blue leather bound the yellowed pages and William gently took the book from Julius. He traced the gold lettering on the cover and binding and inhaled the musty smell of the old pages.

"Good hunting," Julius said.

William looked up from the book. "Thanks."

"No worries," Julius said before departing.

William resumed his inspection of the book, and a sense of impending glory, a ringing of horns echoed in his mind. *This is it. I'll finally learn how to stop Shet.*

His burgeoning excitement crashed to utter disappointment a second later when he cracked open the book. It was written in some kind of old version of English, like something from Shakespeare. *Damn it.*

He sighed and took the book to an unoccupied table, where he dropped into a seat and began reading.

Hear ye, O diviner of Truthe, to this mine question posed. Though misfortune be laid in full iniquity afore ye who are Awakened, our path doth yet remain to be trod. The Word ye seeketh, though it may be shackled and laid low, doth never slumber, but desireth to be known. Be like unto a leaf afore the wind, and the leaves these pages turn, that ye may learn what Truthe there be herein. Thus say I, Flye on and Read!

William mentally groaned but forced himself to do as the author instructed. He also planned to take the book to Ms. Sioned or Mr. Zeus. Maybe they could read the middle English in which it was written—or whatever it was—and translate it for him. Until then, he'd have to do his best to decipher the text on his own.

Hours of eye-burning effort later, with irritation and impatience rearing their twin heads, he finally came across a clue of what he might need. Roughly stated, the author posed a question. *What if two travelers entered an anchor line from opposite ends? Could they meet one another in the middle?* William thought it strange that something like that hadn't already occurred, and according to the author, it did happen, but rarely. And in those few recorded episodes, the travelers had *not* seen one another, except in one instance. On that occasion, an *asrasin* had stood athwart the anchor line and forced the other traveler to halt.

William stared at the passage, trying to figure out what it might mean. Minutes passed as he considered the question. The large grandfather clock near the library's entrance ticked off the seconds as William pondered, but in the end, he made no headway.

Disgusted, he flipped the book closed and stared at the title: *Treatises on Travel—A Translation.*

He frowned. *Wait.* William wanted to smack himself in the forehead. The book was a translation, which meant he needed the original.

He stared around the library and wondered where it might be, or if the original existed anymore. Plus, it surely wouldn't be written in English, so how would he possibly read it?

Frustration boiled at the impossible task he'd set for himself, and the beast within roared to life. William saw nothing but red for a moment, could conceive of only rage. A vision filled his mind, a quietly chuckling creature, an albino monstrosity, sadistic and cruel, with centuries of blood on his mangled claws. The hideous thing had a name. William knew it. Sapient Dormant.

"So you are the one who ended Kohl Obsidian," Sapient said in a cultured, elegant voice, utterly at odds with his form and visage. "You have his blood within you."

William swallowed, terrified. He clawed at his hair, trying desperately to break whatever connection he and Sapient might have.

The Overward of the necrosed frowned. "You have something else. Kohl changed you." Sapient snarled. "The fool touched your Spirit." His wasted features filled with rage, and William's head throbbed. "You will not live to master his gift."

The connection broke.

~

Sapient Dormant kept still, not caring that his back was to his fellow necrosed. They waited behind him, and all of them faced the ruins built by an unknown people in what was now called Mexico.

Night had fallen but the dim light didn't impede Sapient's sight. He gazed about, thinking of the boy he'd discovered several days ago, the one Kohl had touched and somehow given the strength of his blood *and* Spirit. Sapient growled in outrage. In so doing the fool had granted the *asrasin* the Wildness, an ancient weapon and one of the few things that could kill a necrosed.

He cursed Kohl anew, wishing him alive so he could flay him. His brother necrosed rustled as they sensed his anger. Several of them backed away.

Sapient calmed himself. The boy was of no significance. When Shet returned, no *asrasin*, not even one wielding the Wildness, would pose a threat. The matter settled in his mind, Sapient returned his attention to the reason for his presence in this abandoned place.

The jungle grew all about the area and had overgrown what had once been a temple. Silence, however, filled the air, and no animals dared raise their ruckus here. Even the trees seemed to hush their leaves and branches, keeping them quiet and bending their limbs away from the structure. Whatever warning the other foliage and animals sensed emanating from the building went unheeded by ugly vines with small white flowers. They covered the structure in a cloud of green, camouflaging the building and covering it in a perfume of corruption. The temple endured underneath it all, invisible and inviolate.

Sapient had no fear of the vines or the temple, though. He found the cemetery-like air charming. Hidden inside all the foliage was the first temple to Shet. Clarity Pain was its name, and this was Sapient's birthplace. It was the place where the Lord had resided when he'd created the necrosed. It had taken him a hundred years and the torture of a hundred holders to forge the first of the necrosed.

Sapient smiled as he recalled the past. Shokan's greatest warriors, the holders, converted into pitiless, undead assassins. *How delicious.*

He frowned when one of his brothers shuffled forward, stumbling. *How far have we fallen.* The necrosed had once possessed the grace and speed of their holder predecessors, but now they shambled about, unkempt and clumsy. They existed as nothing more than walking stains upon creation. At least the terror they were meant to inspire remained. The necrosed had been created as black reflections of the dwarves, large rather than small, instilling fear rather than peace, and bringing death instead of prosperity.

The dwarves and their peace. Sapient silently snarled.

The dwarven gift for serenity had extended even to the dragons, causing the great beasts to slumber peacefully in deep caverns. The dragons, black-hearted monsters whose only purpose had been the acquisition of gold and gems, should have been Shet's natural allies. But not in the presence of dwarves. Then they had slept, leaving the world untroubled by their fearful presence.

Sapient brought his anger to a crashing halt, stilling it as he'd been taught. Work was required. Within the temple, deep in its bowels, lay a sword guarded by Grave Invidious, the progenitor of their kind. History stated that Sapient had been the first of the necrosed, but it was untrue. It had been Grave, the first-born of those hundred tortured holders, and the greatest necrosed of all. To him had been granted this lonely *saha'asra* of death and mutilation, and to him had been granted the greatest of Shet's prizes: *Undefiled Locus,* a diamond blade of ancient forging that the Wildness lit to life. This was the weapon by which the Lord had conquered empires, built the anchor lines of this world and Seminal, and destroyed all who dared oppose him.

Except Shokan, who had somehow turned the blade against the Lord and banished him to Seminal. Well did Sapient remember Shokan. The two of them had once been close as brothers. Those fraternal feelings had died upon Sapient's rebirth, and especially when he betrayed Shokan and caused the death of the Lady of Fire.

A rank smell drifted to Sapient, ending his recollections, and a fresh growl rose in his throat. *Death. Corruption. Evil.* None of the acrid aromas should have bothered him, but something worrisome underlay the stench.

The necrosed behind him, even Manifold Fulsom, the largest and most dangerous of them, shifted in uneasiness.

Sapient didn't give his brother necrosed a chance to offer any questions. He led them into the temple, into air as still as a body in a grave. They passed through dark, cobwebbed halls and rooms he'd last seen seven thousand years ago, shortly after his birth. He'd been young and powerful then, fresh-bodied and fresh-blooded rather than decayed and weak as the millennia slowly robbed his strength.

Early in his life, he'd raged forth from Clarity Pain and battled the traitorous dragon, Antalagore the Black. He'd even faced off against Shokan's steed, the mighty Aia, a great cat. His thoughts grew grim as he recalled that battle. Aia had raked the right side of Shet's face, ruining it permanently.

As they pushed forward, the worrisome smell, the one Sapient couldn't identify, grew stronger, and fear, an unknown sensation, wormed its way into his pustulant heart.

"One of our kind died here," said Manifold, his harsh voice a curse against the tomblike silence. "I know not who."

Sapient gestured sharply in rebuke. Sound was a sacrilege in Clarity Pain. No one ever spoke loudly here. "Silence," he hissed in a voice like a drawn knife.

They strode more swiftly toward the heart of the temple. The smell grew stronger, and Sapient's fear climbed.

They eventually reached a crumbled doorway, the wood rotted to sawdust, and the fear-inducing smell became blinding. On the other side of the doorframe was a broad room, deep and tall. The ceiling stretched yards above, held aloft by a bevy of jeweled columns and arched beams. More vines, brothers to those outside, had found purchase here, and dim urine-yellow lanterns, still alight these thousands of years later through Shet's incomparable weaving, brought a wan illumination to the space.

Sapient didn't require their luminescence. His eyes easily penetrated the deepest black, and he noticed the cobwebs filling every corner, covering crumbled chairs, sofas, and the altar at the far end of the space. He also discerned spiders the size of his forearms scuttling about. They had a scorpion's stinger and seemed to stare balefully at the necrosed. One, larger and prouder than her brethren—definitely a female given her size—crawled too close.

Sapient crushed her. The creature stabbed at him, but the poison couldn't harm that which was already dead. The other spiders took this as a sign to flee, and Sapient pressed on.

He marched across the room, his bare feet raising dust from the threadbare rug that stretched from the entrance, past the altar, and all the way to the massive throne from whence Shet had once ruled. As he paced forward, Sapient saw that the dust had already been disturbed. His mouth twisted in outrage. *Human bootprints and the paw prints of some kind of cat. A small one.*

On the far side of the altar Sapient climbed the dais leading to the throne. There, the fear inducing smell was greatest. Hidden there he found the source, the crumbled corpse of Grave Invidious. A hole the size of one of Manifold's sizeable fists had been punched through the dead necrosed, penetrating through both face and chest.

Sapient blinked in astonishment, and a single word reverberated in his head. *How?*

His head shot toward the throne.

Undefiled Locus.

Sapient spared Grave no further study. The sword should have rested next to the throne, in a sheath made from the hide of Antalagore the Black. He found nothing. Human footprints had gone to where the diamond blade should have rested, and there the boot marks had paused.

"A human killed our brother," Manifold said, sounding bemused.

"No human did this," Sapient growled. "It was a holder." Fury rose in him, too hot to contain, and he forced his necrosed to experience it. He wanted them to share in his lava-hot rage.

He screamed, suspecting who the holder might be: the one touched by that fool, Kohl Obsidian. He'd murder the boy.

In that moment he also recalled his Lord's final command, and he carried it out. *Good. I'll inspire the boy, guide him to the Treatises and have him learn of firewagers. And with that false hope implanted, I'll destroy the boy.*

CHAPTER 12: SEEKING HELP

A *pril 1990*

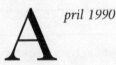illiam tried not to scowl like a sore loser when the drill ended. His squad had been defeated by Rukh's and they shouldn't have been. All they'd had to do was defend a fortified position and prevent Rukh's unit from getting past them.

They hadn't been able to. They'd lost. Badly. It had been swift and sudden, as if they hadn't spent any time training at all during the past two months. It shouldn't have occurred like that, and William couldn't figure out what had happened. Was it because Rukh was that skilled a commander or because Ward Silver was that poor of one?

The anger inside of him—the snarling animal of hate—was ready to rage, but William managed to keep it under control while stomping away from the others and toward the stacked canteens.

Ward called to him. "We're not done yet!"

"I need a break," William shouted over his shoulder. It was the truth, but not all of it. The *truth* was he needed distance from the rest

143

of the Ashokan Irregulars. There were twenty-five of them now, and right now, one wrong word from any of them was sure to set him off.

William reached the far end of the field, where it bordered Sita's Song and wiped the sweat from his brow. The muggy weather had returned, and he cursed it anew. Only a few, scattered clouds drifted across the blue sky, and they did little to shield anyone from the sweltering mid-day sun. River Namaste rumbled and gurgled and far away, those playing enrune seemed to be having a fun time of it.

William unstopped his canteen, drank the warm water, and eyed the enrune fields and those playing resentfully. *Enrune. A stupid game played by stupid people. They have such an easy life, no worries to keep them up at night. For them, Sinskrill and Shet are as far away and unreachable as the moon.* William sipped more water and continued to glare at those leading carefree lives while his thoughts returned to the recently lost drill. *We should have won. We would have if Ward had done what I told him to.*

Rukh approached, and William offered him a sullen nod. "Commander."

A scowl of disappointment or disgust swept across Rukh's features. "You may have your notions of what should be done," he said, "but your unwillingness to carry out Ward's commands is the biggest reason your squad keeps losing."

Outrage at Rukh's criticism rose in William's heart. So did the red-eyed beast. "I do what I'm told," he said. He kept his tone civil by the barest of margins.

"No, you don't," Rukh said, "and even when you do, you act like a jackhole. Do what you're told next time and do it without complaint. If you'd only followed your orders today, we wouldn't have rolled your left flank, the side you were meant to protect."

"But then the center wouldn't have held."

"Yes, it would," Rukh said. "Jake, Lien, and Daniel attacked you there, but Ward had Jessira held in reserve to defend the center. There was no need for you to rush in like some stupid, avenging angel. You allowed Jason and me to collapse the flank, and Jessira fought unassisted against us."

William smirked. "Is that the real reason you're angry? Because

Jessira was defeated?" The words made him want to smack himself, and he mentally gaped at his stupidity, but the anger wouldn't recede. He couldn't control his words.

Fear slowly overcame anger when Rukh stepped into his space, obviously furious. "This is only a drill. Jessira has little to fear, and I have little to fear on her behalf. This criticism is the truth of what happened," he growled. "Stop griping like a child and take this criticism to heart. Anything less is pathetic." He stepped closer, his face inches from William's. "Or quit. Right now. You're not doing anyone any good. You're useless to me, behaving like this."

The last of William's anger collapsed, and the beast of anger snarled fitfully as it faded. He could think again. His shoulders slumped, and he struggled to meet Rukh's eyes. "I'm sorry, sir. I can't stop being so angry all the time." He hesitated. "I need help."

Rukh exhaled heavily. "Yes, you do, and I commend you for recognizing your need."

William took heart from Rukh's mild praise. At this point, with a sense of failure and fear hanging upon him like a wet blanket, anything the slightest bit positive felt like sunshine on a cloudy day.

"Your anger stifles your every attempt at success," Rukh added.

Silence grew between them, and William shifted in nervousness as Rukh measured him. "I've heard about the cause of your anger," Rukh eventually said. "Have you heard anything from the *raha'asras*?"

William nodded mutely. "They're looking into it, but . . ." He shook his head. "They haven't figured out anything that can help me."

"Then consider this: grave odds can break the strongest of warriors. Rather than confront such obstacles head on, remember the green reed. It bends in the wind and is stronger than the mighty oak, which breaks in the storm."

William recognized the words as a saying attributed to Confucius, but the aphorism didn't offer any illumination. He frowned in confusion. "Sir?"

"Perhaps you need to approach the anger from a different direction," Rukh said. "Rather than banishing it or mastering it, perhaps you should seek to channel it. Have you tried to engage it? Let it flow through your mind and into your muscles, nerves, and bones? Once it passes, only then will you be able to fight with clarity."

William thought about Rukh's advice, but it made no sense. Once awakened, the beast raged. It would never pass out of him. It would storm inside his mind like a lightning-laced, bruise-colored cloud. Plus, he knew the anger wasn't a part of himself. It came from elsewhere, from Sapient Dormant, similar to how it had once come from Kohl Obsidian.

"Think on it at least," Rukh said.

"Yes, sir," William replied.

Rukh gave his shoulder a supportive squeeze and left him.

While watching the other man return to the other Irregulars, William took a sip of water and considered what to do. A moment later, his head snapped to the east, and he spun about. He stared into the distance, somewhere far away. The monster inside him erupted to life. He couldn't think straight, see straight. He worked his jaw, clenching and unclenching it in rage.

An image rose in his mind, the same one he had seen twice now, the albino necrosed, Sapient Dormant, diseased, decayed, and furious. The desire to bend a knee to the creature came over William as well as a notion to find something lost, a book perhaps.

The image and notion faded, and he shuddered.

A hand landed on his shoulder. He flinched and spun around, a shout at his mouth.

"What's wrong?" Serena asked. She stood in front of him, eyes wide and frowning.

William shuddered again and explained what he'd seen. He rubbed suddenly chilled arms. Goosebumps had risen on them. "I keep seeing him. Sapient. Hearing him. Kohl's blood gives me a connection to the other necrosed, and it scares me."

"It scares all of us."

"What am I going to do?" William asked, despair filling his mind.

～

Serena flung a small stone into the ocean and lost sight of it the instant it hit the waves. She stared at the water for a moment longer while the wind whipped her long, dark hair. She and William had decided to wander along a rocky stretch of beach directly north of Lilith Bay. Here, the soft, golden sands gave way to glassy stones the size of marbles. A shingle beach, Mr. Zeus would have named it. A briny breeze blew off the water, and it carried a sulfurous stink like an *asrasin* weaving Fire. This stench, though, came from algae and seaweed.

William took a step toward the ocean and threw a stone as far as he could. A gusting wind held it up, and the rock barely made it twenty yards. It plunked with a pitiful splash.

Serena chuckled.

William shot her a look of dismay. "The wind held it up."

"Of course." She dipped her head to hide her smile.

William muttered something under his breath, and they continued their walk.

They had the beach to themselves, the first time they'd been alone together in weeks, and the only sounds to be heard were those of the crashing surf and a few white birds crying out as they skimmed the water's surface. The wind whipped again, and Serena's hair got in her eyes. She made a mental note to braid her hair or put it in a tie next time she came here.

"Hold up," William said, pointing to the horizon. "Look. It's almost sunset."

They paused and faced west, watching the sun. It glowed red and sullen, hanging only inches above the western horizon. They stood in companionable silence as the sun briefly dipped behind a cloud. It re-appeared a moment later to cast a few final bars of light. The beams reflected off the glassy stones of the beach and set them gleaming like the iridescent patterns of an anchor line.

Serena broke the silence. "This afternoon could have gone better."

William didn't reply. He stared at the sunset. His jaw clenched, and he scowled. An instant later, the anger seemed to leave him in a rush. "Yeah," he replied with a sigh. "Sapient Dormant can talk to me."

Serena gave him a sympathetic gaze. "I already figured as much."

William faced her, surprise on his face.

"Most everyone else has figured it out, too," Serena said in reply to his unspoken question.

William rubbed his arms as if they were cold. "Do you know what it means? To hear the Overward's call?"

Serena frowned. "We know he's the reason you keep flying off the handle, but . . ."

"I can sometimes hear his thoughts, too," William said. "He's always angry, furious, and all he ever thinks about is killing." He grimaced. "He fantasizes about it. It can be pretty graphic."

Serena tried to imagine what that was like, but she couldn't. To have someone else's blood-soaked thoughts in her mind . . . She shuddered. It would be horrible.

William scowled and stared at the water. "Remember how mad I used to get back at St. Francis?" he asked.

"A little bit." Serena vaguely recalled his anger, but for her it hadn't been much to remember. What she recalled most of William at St. Francis was a sweet, young man and his friends, all of them innocent. She missed that about them.

"My anger nowadays is like that," William continued, "but the last time it wasn't nearly as bad, and it only happened because Kohl did something to me after he murdered my parents. At least that's what I figure must have happened because that's when I started getting faster and stronger."

"I thought you got faster and stronger when Kohl's blood got in you."

"I did," William said, "but the changes really started with the murder of my parents. I've thought about it a lot. Anyway, after we killed Kohl the anger kind of went away. It sort of vanished."

"And now it's back, and you think Sapient is the reason?" Serena guessed.

William gave a hesitant nod. "I think so, and I think I can hear Sapient because of Kohl's blood."

Serena tilted her head in thought as she assessed William's hypothesis. It made sense, and she wished it didn't. She also wished she could see him smile more. Even prior to the intrusion of Sapient Dormant, he'd been too serious. She couldn't recall the last time she'd seen him truly happy. Maybe at the Chinese New Year celebration, but that had been months ago.

She viewed him through considering eyes. Sometimes he laughed when she made fun of him. "What makes you think it's Sapient and not you being a jackhole?" she asked.

William groaned. "You've been spending too much time around Rukh."

Serena wore a wide-eyed look of innocence. "What did I say?"

"Jackhole," William answered. "That's something Rukh and Jessira say all the time."

"It's a portmanteau," Serena said in a tone meant to convey that she thought she was being helpful. "It's a word that means—"

William cut her off. "I know what a portmanteau is."

"Ah. In this case jackhole hole is a combination of—"

"I think I get it," William said with a wry chuckle.

Serena smiled, happy to see him laugh. "At least now you know why you've been a jackhole for the past few months."

William didn't respond. Instead, he stared quietly at the last of the day's light with a pensive cast. The tiniest rim of the sun hung above the horizon.

While they waited for it to dip below the ocean's line, an idea formed in Serena's mind. "If the *raha'asras* can't help you, maybe you should talk to Travail."

"Why?" William asked.

"Because he's calm and controlled *all the time*," Serena said. "Maybe he can help you figure out how to be the same way."

William's brow creased, and his mouth pursed in apparent thought. He gave a slow nod. "That's not a bad idea."

They fell silent again until Serena spoke up. "Has Jake talked to you about Daniella Logan? I was given to understand that he was interested in her."

"He is. Interested, I mean," William answered. "But no, he hasn't asked her out yet. I think he's still having trouble letting go of the past."

Guilt crawled up Serena's spine. "His life since I came into it has been nothing short of a disaster. Kidnapped, brutalized, tortured, and nearly killed in battle. It's understandable that he'd hate what he's become."

"Understandable, but there's nothing he can do to change that, either." William's voice held a hard, brittle quality and his face betrayed judgmental anger. His jaw clenched. A second later, his entire body shuddered. "Sorry about that," he murmured, bending his head and sounding contrite. "The rage-beast woke up."

"Is that what you call it?"

William shrugged. "That's what it reminds me of: a red-eyed, rage monster."

"Then we'll have to find a way to kill it."

"Or kill Sapient."

Serena nodded agreement. "An even better solution." She only hoped they could manage it before William lost himself to the anger.

~

William and Travail perched on the edge of a cliff, their feet dangling as the ocean stretched out far below them. The surf surged, smashing against the dark expanse of the cliff and the boulders strewn along its base. It sent spray climbing high but none of it came close to reaching them. A rainbow arched through the mist raised by the pounding water, and a gusting breeze carried a mixture of brine and minerals. The sun, still early in the sky, beat down on their backs and slowly warmed the black stone upon which they sat.

Travail listened quietly, not offering any comments or questions while William explained his dilemma.

"It's why I've been angry all the time," William said. "I can hear the Overward's voice or his thoughts. Or something like that. The *raha'asras* are working on a weave to block him out or maybe get rid of the necrosed part of my blood, but I asked them for help weeks ago." His shoulders slumped. "I don't think they know what to do."

"You're certain of this?" Travail asked. "About Sapient Dormant?" His mouth curled as if the very name of the necrosed was poison.

"I'm sure. The other *raha'asras* are certain, too." William stared at the ocean, trying not to let the glumness of his situation get to him.

Travail clapped him on the shoulder. "All is not lost. You came to me for help in controlling your anger," he said. "You'll have it."

William smiled in gratitude even though he hadn't expected anything else from Travail.

"Tell me what happens," Travail said. "How does the anger overcome you?"

"At first, I could control it," William explained. "All I had to do was imagine something calm, and it would go away. Now it comes on like a motorcycle. Too fast to stop it . . ." He struggled with the words. "I never know when it's going to wake up and take over."

"This is how it happens every time?"

"Not every time. Sometimes it's a slow acceleration."

"Have you tried to burn it off with your weaves?"

William frowned. "I didn't know that was possible."

Travail smiled. "You *asrasins*, so limited in what you think can be done," he teased. "Do you not have weaves to change the feelings of others, to make them calmer?"

A slow-kindling hope filled William. "You think I should weave something like that on myself?"

Travail barked laughter. "Certainly not. You can't weave on your own mind."

"Why not?"

Travail blinked, obviously not expecting the question. "Because it's not possible. No one can do that. The strength of will, the elegance of the weave required to accomplish something on that order . . ." He shook his head. "No. I'm saying you should ask someone else to perform that calming braid to burn off Sapient's hold upon you, his anger. The *raha'asras* for instance. Ask them to help."

William wanted to smack himself in the forehead. "Why didn't I think of that?"

Travail smiled in fondness. "The better question is why did you wait for such a long time before asking for help? Rukh would say you've been a jackhole."

William chuckled. "That word again. Everyone seems to be using it these days."

"It's a useful descriptor," Travail said. He pointed east, to a place behind where they sat and the hills of Janaki Valley that marched north and south in their verdant glory. "Rukh and Jessira live only a few valleys over."

William viewed the distant hills and considered Rukh and Jessira's supposed history. "Do you believe them?" he finally asked.

"Believe whom? Rukh and Jessira?"

William nodded. "Do you believe them about Arisa and all those things? That evil goddess, Suwraith, the Sorrow Bringer?" For some reason, upon saying the name, his anger stirred, but rather than the red-eyed beast, this time it reminded him of a lightning-laced, bruised cloud. Alive somehow. It rumbled, and a cackling voice drifted on an unfelt breeze. William's mouth curled into a furious snarl.

"Be easy," Travail said softly.

Some of the anger receded.

Travail spoke on, his voice soothing. "Do as Rukh suggested. Let the anger flow through you."

William closed his eyes and exhaled slowly and controlled. He pretended to breathe away the anger. He didn't want it. He never had, and he kept his eyes closed. He took more cleansing breaths, thinking of his parents and Landon, their love for him and his for them. He imagined the anger washing through him. Slowly but surely, it flowed out of him. When he opened his eyes, he found Travail staring at him. *It worked.*

The troll broke into a broad grin. "Well done."

William broke into a shaky smile. "Thank you."

Travail nodded gravely.

"You believe them?" William asked, reminding Travail of his original question.

"You don't?"

William stared aside as he thought about the question. "I do. I always have but I wanted to know what you think. I mean, according to what they say they were essentially gods."

"No," Travail said. "They were very powerful beings, but not gods, and although they don't say it, the war against Shet's daughter and children nearly defeated them, or at least brought ruin to their world. It was costly, and they lost many whom they loved. Gods would have done better for themselves."

William had sensed the same when Rukh and Jessira spoke of their home, but the knowledge only made him wonder how they kept going. How they continued to fight despite all the apparent losses and sorrows they'd suffered.

Travail hesitated, and William sensed that something troubled the troll.

"What is it?" William asked.

"I sometimes think I have an unusual connection toward Rukh and Jessira, as if I've met them previously. Sometimes visions fill my mind, or I recall a name: Li-Dirge."

William's curiosity roused. "Who was he?"

"I don't know. When I try to visualize him, I see a creature much like myself. A Baél, as Rukh and Jessira described." He sat up straighter. "Did you know that the bridge, Chimera Seed, contains images from Arisa?"

William rocked in surprise. "Seriously?"

Travail nodded. "When I gaze upon it, or sometimes when I speak to Rukh and Jessira, I see flashes, fragments of memories, but I can't retain the visions. They leave as soon as I see them. The name Li-Dirge is the only item I can recall and keep. That and a deep sense of gratitude toward Rukh and Jessira."

William fell silent and tried to make sense of what Travail had told him. "What do you think it means?" he asked after a few minutes of thought.

Travail shrugged. "I don't know."

"Did you ask Rukh or Jessira?"

"I did," Travail said. "They refused to answer, which is an answer of its own."

William waited for the troll to say more but he didn't. "Well, if Rukh and Jessira could defeat an insane goddess, maybe they can defeat a cruel god."

Travail shook his head in disagreement. "We can't leave it all on them. We must do our part to stop Shet, too. No matter what it takes."

William smiled. "How do you always see to the heart of the matter?"

"It helps that I'm a vegetarian," Travail replied. "All that meat inside your belly rots your mind."

William frowned in confusion. "I always thought 'vegetarian' was an ancient slang word for the village idiot who couldn't hunt, fish, or barbecue."

"You're very funny."

William grinned.

An instant later he screamed in terror. Travail had shoved him. He tumbled forward, threatening to go off the edge of the cliff.

Travail yanked him short, his massive hand all-but enfolding William's waist.

William scowled, but for once the red-eyed demon didn't rouse. "That wasn't nice," he complained.

Travail chuckled. "No. But it was funny."

~

William sat with Fiona and Ms. Sioned at a small, glass-topped table in the enclosed garden behind the latter woman's house. Azaleas provided shade for low-lying verbenas that were dotted with pink flowers and astilbes, bleeding hearts, and hostas. The plants bordered black boulders settled upon a bed of fine, white stones. A line of water trickled down the cliff-face forming the rear of the property, and the water fed the koi ponds centered like liquid sapphires within the gardens. Like most yards, Ms. Sioned's was beautiful, but William's favorite part of her home was the delicious scent of fresh-baked cookies that she loved to bake. The aroma wafted through the open patio door leading to the kitchen.

The mouth-watering joy of that smell held no interest for William today, though. "Do you think you can do it?" he asked. Desperation and his discussion with Travail had brought him here, and he peered anxiously at Ms. Sioned and Fiona, awaiting their verdict. He couldn't tell what they were thinking.

The two women wore nearly identical serene expressions and neither responded at once. They shared a long, assessing gaze before returning their attention to him.

"You want us to weave a braid to take away your anger?" Fiona asked.

William nodded. "It's getting worse. The anger. It's always there, and if I'm not careful every second of the day, it erupts on its own." He swallowed. "I don't know how much longer I can control it."

"Taking away your anger might also take away some of your drive, your fire," Ms. Sioned warned.

"I'll take the chance," William said. "Besides, I could use less drive and fire. Serena says I spend too much time worried about work anyway."

Fiona smiled knowingly, and William ground his teeth. *Why does everyone think my relationship with Serena is amusing? More importantly, how can I give her anything other than friendship when I have this raging beast dwelling within me?* His irritation rose, quickly becoming the all-too familiar anger, and he scowled. *Damn it! Not now.* He closed his eyes and thought about Lilith at sunset—the orange and red beams streaking the sky, lighting Clifftop, setting the buildings afire, and turning the waterfalls into liquid gold. He also thought of Serena standing by him, the wind catching her raven hair and blowing it about like a flag. All the while, he let the anger rage through him. He let it spend itself empty while he held still.

The fury ebbed, and he opened his eyes.

"The rage again?" Ms. Sioned asked.

William nodded.

The two women shared another assessing gaze along with whispered words he couldn't make out. After a few seconds of hushed conversation they faced William with somber expressions.

"We'll study what can be done," Fiona said, and William's heart soared. She held up a cautionary finger, and his hope stuttered in its flight. "It will take time," she continued. "The weave must be perfect.

Neither of us have attempted this, and we don't want to see you harmed."

William's heart sank. "The way Travail talked about it, I assumed you already knew how to do it."

Ms. Sioned shook her head. "Would that it were so simple. Until we have a means to cure your rage, you must practice extreme caution and control your anger as best you can." Her features took on a sympathetic cast. "I know it won't be easy."

A huge understatement.

Fiona's face became sad, and William wondered why. "What's wrong?"

"I've harmed you many times, and by doing what you ask, I fear I'll harm you again," Fiona said. "When we first met, do you remember how often I disciplined you? The pain I caused? I never apologized for it."

William shifted, made uncomfortable by the turn in their conversation. "You never had to. Jake and I understood why you did what you did."

"Perhaps," Fiona said with a shake of her head, "but it doesn't absolve me. I did as I did because you couldn't afford mercy. It would have weakened you, and we both know that Sinskrill isn't for the weak. You needed hate to make you sturdy, and the brotherly love you had with Jake to keep you whole. Nevertheless, I'm sorry."

William took both of her hands in his. Her apology touched him, but it wasn't necessary. "You're forgiven. You know that."

Fiona nodded and wore a wan smile. "Thank you."

Ms. Sioned leaned forward. "Fiona is correct, though. What you want us to do could be very dangerous. We should talk to Afa."

Fiona nodded agreement. "Odysseus's opinion would also be of benefit."

It took William a moment to realize that 'Odysseus' was Mr. Zeus, his real name, and now it was Ms. Sioned who smiled knowingly. William wanted to grin, too. A few months ago Fiona and Mr. Zeus had begun to spend more and more time together, and it quickly became obvious that the two of them had become close in a romantic sort of way. It made William chuckle to think about it, but it also made him happy for the two old people he thought of as grandparents.

Another question, one more pressing, took precedence in William's thoughts, and he glanced from one woman to the other. "How long do you think it'll take to get the braid ready?"

Ms. Sioned exhaled heavily. "I don't know. Give us a few weeks. We should know whether it's possible by then."

CHAPTER 13: ELDER ADVICE

A *pril 1990*

Serena wove a braid to keep as much of the rain off of herself as possible as she and Ms. Sioned walked Sita's Song. Wind lashed, and trees bent but didn't break before the gusts. Gray clouds hid the sun, and the temperature dropped.

Serena shivered. Her braid kept off most of the water but not the wind's sudden chill. She chided herself an instant later. Arylyn's tropical ease had made her weak. This supposed coolness would have been considered a warm spell on Sinskrill.

"The rain will pass soon," Ms. Sioned said in her Irish lilt as she hobbled along, hunched over a cane. She had obviously mistaken Serena's shiver for true discomfort. "It always does."

Serena nodded understanding of the unnecessary advice, and kept their pace slow, holding out a hand in case Ms. Sioned slipped on the rain-slick pavers. She glanced up when a sunbeam broke the cloud cover. More sunlight shone down, and within seconds the road steamed as the rain dried.

Ms. Sioned chuckled. "See. It can't rain all the time." She shuffled along, her wispy, white hair collected in a bun beneath a broad-brimmed hat, and Serena eyed her in concern. A few months ago Ms. Sioned hadn't required a cane, but then she'd fallen, and her great age had caught up with her all of a sudden.

Serena frowned in unhappiness at the idea.

At least Ms. Sioned had found a late-in-life friend in Fiona. Over the past year both women had discovered the commonalities they shared, how much they needed one another, and Serena enjoyed watching them travel about the island, thick as thieves and sometimes giggling like school girls. Their friendship was especially fulfilling for Fiona. Other than Travail, Serena's grandmother had never had a true friend on Sinskrill. Decades of loneliness, without even the comfort of her children to keep her company, had been her lot in life.

"I don't think Sile needs you to clear his garden. I can take care of it," Serena said.

Ms. Sioned chuckled. "If I didn't help *him*, I'd hardly get to see *you*. Between your training with the Irregulars and working with my grandson, you're a busy woman."

Serena smiled. "I think I serve too many masters."

Ms. Sioned eyes widened in surprise. "Master? I thought only Sile had that title."

"He does," Serena quickly clarified. "But Rukh and Jessira ask a lot of all of us."

Ms. Sioned frowned. "Those two appear no older than you, but I swear someone ancient peers out from their eyes."

Now it was Serena who chuckled. "You're only now noticing?"

Ms. Sioned smiled ruefully. "I noticed a long time ago, but I try not to think about it." She feigned a shiver. "It's disconcerting."

"Yes, it is," Serena agreed with feeling.

Ms. Sioned smiled for a few seconds more, but then her features grew pinched.

Serena's lips pursed in worry. "What's wrong?"

Ms. Sioned didn't reply at once. Her face remained tight and unreadable. "I fear I owe you an apology," she eventually said. "I've not advised you as you deserve."

Serena's brow remained furrowed. She didn't know what Ms. Sioned was talking about, and she remained quiet, waiting for the other woman to continue.

"When you first came to Arylyn, you and your sister, I didn't trust you. I asked you to stay away from William and not give him hope for anything more than friendship. I didn't want his heart broken."

Serena already knew this, and in some ways, she even agreed with the old *raha'asra's* counsel. The advice had been couched as a soft warning from several years ago. She said as much. "Why do you think you need to apologize to me?"

"Because I've kept you and William from happiness," Ms. Sioned. "After you came back from Sinskrill, returning with Fiona and Travail, I should have advised you to pursue William if that's what you wanted. Instead, I told you to stay focused and dedicated, allow yourself to ease your way into your emotions, to protect your heart. I was wrong. You could have managed all of that on your own."

Serena remembered their conversation from many months ago when they were tilling Sile's garden. Part of her wanted to be angry with Ms. Sioned for nosing into her business, but she couldn't manage it. It wasn't the old *raha'asra's* fault. At least, not entirely. Ms. Sioned's advice had merely mirrored Serena's fear about risking her heart to love. As a result, rather than speak with anger, Serena chuckled in bitterness. "You weren't the reason William and I have remained nothing more than friends."

"You're certain about this?"

"I'm sure," Serena said. "It wasn't your doing. I could have ignored your advice, but I didn't. I was afraid of my feelings."

Ms. Sioned peered at her with a still-troubled mien. "Regardless, I hope you'll find it in your heart to forgive an old woman's supposed guidance, no matter how terrible."

"It's already done," Serena said. She surprised herself when she realized the words were true. "Besides, if you haven't noticed, William's not exactly been himself lately. Even if I wanted something more with him, now isn't the time to pursue it. His anger overwhelms all his senses."

"That it does," Ms. Sioned muttered, staring into the distance. "I hope we can do something about it. He came to us with an interesting approach."

"To weave away his anger?" Serena asked. William had already told her about it. Another notion came to her then and she gave voice to it, wondering what Ms. Sioned would say. "You once told me you thought Shet was real. Do you still feel that way?"

Ms. Sioned grimaced. "I had always thought he and the ancient *asrasin* war nothing more than a fable. I still wish they were."

"So you believe in him?"

Ms. Sioned smiled. "The way you put it makes it sound like you're asking if I worship him. I most certainly do not." The smile left her face. "But I do believe he's real. I've said so before, and I also believe we have to prepare for his coming." She took Serena's hand and gave it a gentle squeeze. "More than that, I believe this, a phrase from my misspent youth. *Collige, virgo, rosas.*"

Serena translated the Latin in her mind. *Gather, girl, the roses.* She frowned as she tried to parse the meaning.

Ms. Sioned smiled. "Enjoy life. Do it now. Do it before it's too late. Consider it much better advice from a sometimes foolish old woman."

~

R ukh frowned as he watched his warriors train. Nearly forty magi had decided to join the Ashokan Irregulars. They currently fought one another in groups of ten, drilling upon the training grounds north of the enrune fields. The late afternoon sun blazed within a blue sky, but rain would soon come. Dark clouds rolled toward them from the Triplets with the precipitation heralded by a gusting breeze. Until the promised downpour occurred, though, dust still swirled and billowed as magi fought with governed *lorethasra* and swords. Their stomping feet beat the grass flatter and more life-less than it already was, and Rukh reckoned that even the fabled farmers of Caste Muran would have struggled to maintain the training field's green grass.

Rukh frowned when one of the warriors engaged in the drill tripped on his own feet.

Jessira, who stood at his side, nudged him. "Your scowl is scaring them."

Rukh momentarily eyed her askance. "Better that they're scared now than when the mahavans arrive."

"This isn't Hellfire Week," Jessira reminded him, "and those aren't Kumma Trims who've trained their entire lives for battle."

"No, they aren't," Rukh agreed, "and I know this isn't Hellfire Week. This is more serious. Hellfire Week ended with the Advent Trial. What these warriors will face is far deadlier."

Memory made him pause as he recalled his youth, the years spent training at the House of Fire and Mirrors in Ashoka. He'd been a prodigy then, a swordsman of unparalleled skill, and later on the one to defeat the Sorrow Bringer. Now he had to teach these children to fight, to battle the forces of another false god. *When will I earn some rest?*

Jessira moved to stand directly in his line of vision. She cut off his view of the Irregulars and shifted when he tried peer around her. He was forced to meet her green-eyed gaze.

"I understand what you're saying," she said, "but these people are young at this. They weren't born with swords in their hands and songs of martial glory in their hearts. They need time to learn."

Rukh studied his wife's sober expression and considered her words. She was right—at least partially—but she was also wrong. In an ideal world with bountiful time, Rukh would have allowed the Ashoka Irregulars to learn more slowly, afforded them greater understanding and patience. But this wasn't an ideal world, and time wasn't on their side. The Irregulars had a lot to learn, and they had to learn it quickly. The mahavans were coming, and after them, Shet.

The link he and Jessira shared allowed her to sense the direction of his thoughts. He didn't need to speak them aloud.

She understood. Nevertheless, she shook her head in disappointment, and Rukh wondered about her. While the fierce, unflinching heart of her, the indomitable will and courage he'd immediately noticed when they first met, hadn't changed, in some important ones, it had. Jessira had softened here, become more patient.

He smiled at the thought. On Arisa, Jessira had been stern as a mountain, hot-tempered as a volcano, but as generous as a favorite grandmother.

"What is it?" Jessira asked. She obviously sensed his amusement, but apparently, their link didn't tell her why.

He explained, and she scoffed. "We both know that 'soft' and 'patient' characterize me as accurately as 'raven-headed' and 'fine-boned.'"

Rukh chuckled. "I'll try not to glare so much," he said.

"I'm sure you will," Jessira said before drifting away.

Rukh watched her a moment before returning his attention to the drilling Irregulars. His brow furrowed as he focused on a particular pair of squads, the Silvers and the Reds. Six warriors remained, three from each group.

As he watched the sparring Rukh realized what would happen. *The Silvers will lose.*

Though the two squads possessed equal numbers, they weren't evenly matched. William should have been the deciding factor to give the Silvers victory but he never fought with discipline. He'd already drifted out of position, seeking to take on the other side more independently.

Rukh tsked. *How many times do I have to tell him to battle alongside his brother warriors and fight as a unit?*

Jason—one of the Silvers—took a braid of Air to the belly. He gasped and fell to a knee. Lien 'ended' him with a finishing blow of Earth. Meanwhile, Daniel fought to reconnect with William, but Ward Silver—ironically named since he was one of the Reds—cut him off. A lance of Fire that Daniel couldn't quench figuratively torched him. An instant later, William landed a telling blow against Ward—a bar of ice to the chest—and put him out of the fight.

The remaining two Reds, Jake and Lien, flanked William. Jake feinted. William spun to keep his 'enemy' in view. Lien darted forward, fearlessly, recklessly. William tried to trip her with a braid of Earth. He succeeded, but his distraction allowed Jake to land a killing blow: a blazing bar of Fire.

The fight was over. No one had been seriously injured, but the Silvers muttered in aggravation while the Reds preened proudly.

Rukh's jaw clenched. He waited a moment for some of his frustration with William to pass. Only then did he confront the boy. "Why did you step out of line?" he asked. "Your unit lost the moment you did so."

William's jaw thrust out, his shoulders squared, and his brows furrowed. He appeared ready for belligerence.

Rukh mentally sighed. *Not this again.* He pushed closer. "You have something to say?"

For once, William's anger fell away as quickly as it arrived, and he stared at the ground. "I know it was wrong, sir," he said. "I knew as soon as I did it."

An abashed air filled his features, and Rukh's ire abated somewhat.

William continued. "I can't think straight when we drill. I don't know why. My mind goes blank, and all I see is redness from the anger."

The last of Rukh's irritation left him, and he eyed William in sympathy. There was no reason to castigate him. He plainly felt bad enough already. The anger dwelling inside him was more punishment than anyone deserved. "It isn't easy, is it?"

William shook his head. "It's like fighting a storm cloud. When I try to let the anger wash through me, it's like I'm drowning in a flood."

Rukh gestured for William to follow and led him apart from the others. A dozen feet away, with a little more privacy, he stopped and faced the young man. "Is there no way to help you?"

"I don't know." William hesitated. "The *raha'asras* are looking to do something about the anger, maybe break my connection to Sapient Dormant."

"Did they give you any hint when this might occur?"

William nodded but didn't hold a hopeful mien. "Tonight, I think. At least, I hope so. There's a weave they want to test out."

Rukh wordlessly scrutinized William. The boy appeared simultaneously scared, angry, and humiliated. "Why do you want to fight?" Rukh eventually asked. "Would it not be easier to manage your anger if you chose a different avocation?"

William blinked, clearly taken aback. "Excuse me, sir?"

"You heard the question. Why do you want to fight?"

"Because I'm good at it, and it needs doing," William said. "The mahavans are coming. Shet, too. What else am I supposed to do?"

Live free and laugh, Rukh wanted to tell him. Instead, he sighed at the ignorance of youth. "When you see me tomorrow, tell me if the weaving helped," he said. "For now, go get something to drink, and take the rest of the afternoon off."

"Sir—"

"It's not a punishment," Rukh said, placing a hand on William's shoulder and giving him a supportive squeeze. "I think you'll need the rest for whatever happens tonight."

"Yes, sir," William said.

Rukh gave William's shoulder a companionable slap. "Good luck and remember to come see me tomorrow."

William still wore a disappointed cast, but he snapped out a sharp salute and departed.

Rukh watched him leave and glanced aside when Jessira arrived again to stand next to him. He saw her smiling at William's departing back.

"He could be a fine leader if his anger didn't destroy his ability to think clearly," she said.

Rukh nodded, and for some reason, in that moment, he remembered his brother, Jaresh, born of Caste Sentya. He had been a great leader, but the pride of intellect had nearly ruined him. He hoped William's anger didn't similarly ruin *him*.

CHAPTER 14: FIRE TO HEAL

April 1990

urry up," Jake shouted from the bottom of the stairs.

"Stop pestering him," Jason said, sounding like he was standing right next to Jake.

William tuned out their bickering and slipped on clean clothes. After Rukh had dismissed him, he'd gone home and taken a nap, only awakening when Jake and Jason had rambled inside.

The other two men had been hot, dirty, and sweaty, and since the *raha'asras* who were coming tonight would be less than thrilled about sharing a living room with three very smelly twenty-something-year-olds, Jake and Jason had showered as soon as they got home. William waited for them to finish before cleaning off, too. He presently toweled his shoulder-length hair one final time and combed it into a semblance of order. He could have used a braid of Air and Earth to do it but that would have been wasteful.

Once done, he trotted downstairs and discovered that Mr. Zeus and the *raha'asras* hadn't arrived yet. Only Jason and Jake were present. They waited in the living room, sitting on the couch and speaking in hushed tones. They glanced up when William entered the room and fell silent, shifting apart.

"What are you talking about?" William asked, although he already had an idea. It didn't take a genius to figure out he was the subject of their conversation.

William took a seat on one of the two Queen Anne chairs facing the large picture-window that opened onto a view of the Pacific Ocean. The western sun hung a few hours above sunset, and the waves glistened like a cracked sapphire as they washed against the shores of Lilith Bay.

Serena was probably down there with Jean-Paul. The Frenchman had taken her under his wing and taught her to surf. She had asked to be here tonight but Mr. Zeus wouldn't allow it. He thought she'd be too much of a distraction.

Jake leaned forward and the soft, cream-colored leather of the couch squeaked. "You sure this is what you want?" he asked. "What if it goes wrong? They say they might burn out more than your anger. They might burn out your ambition."

"Then they burn it out," William replied. "Nothing can be as bad as what I'm going through right now. I can't think straight. I want to hurt people. It's like I'm being poisoned with rage." He viewed the scenery outside the window, viewing Lilith's beauty, and in that instant, he felt strangely apart from it all, separated by his rage from everything he loved here. He wondered if after tonight, when he next viewed the village would he see it through eyes still glistening with fury or view it with the lifelessness of a drone? He hoped it would be neither, that he'd see the village with the same awe as when Jason had first shown it to him.

Jason wore doubt on his face. "I know it must be hard to—"

"You have no idea what you're talking about," William snapped as he faced him. He lunged to his feet, his fury making it impossible for him to sit still, and paced. The only sounds in the room were his footfalls and the grandfather clock in the corner marking time. The angry beast raged, wanting to take over, to exit its dark cave and overwhelm, dominate, hurt, kill . . .

No. William stopped his pacing and closed his eyes. He counted to ten, thinking again about the first time he'd seen Arylyn, the glory of the place, and the fury slowly ebbed. He thought about Serena, and the anger drained further. Only then did he open his eyes. "I need this." He filled his voice with all his longing.

Jason stood, and his face contained wariness as he approached William. "I didn't mean to question you. I only want you to know we care about you."

The quiet moment between the two longtime friends was ruined by Jake. "Get a room."

William shook his head. *Jerk,* he thought fondly, and the last of his anger broke. He flung a throw pillow at Jake.

Jason wore a tight smile. "I think I should get going," he said. "This is something only for *raha'asras* and someone with mastery of Spirit like Mr. Zeus. I don't want to be a distraction to them or to you."

William nodded agreement and watched as Jason departed the house. He resumed his seat, propped his feet on the coffee table, and stared at the Pacific Ocean and its many blue hues. All the while he tried to ignore his nervousness. Jake must have sensed his need for quiet because he didn't say anything more. The two of them waited in silence for the *raha'asras* to arrive.

～

Jason jogged up the Main Stairs, not really paying attention to where he was going. However, his feet carried him automatically toward his destination—the Karllsons' home—while his mind remained on William, hoping today's healing would fix him, get rid of his anger. He sent a prayer to the Lord on his friend's behalf.

Minutes later, he reached the Karllson's home, a peaked-two story house of German design. He gave the front door a single rap and let himself in. He didn't need the formality of an invitation, not anymore. Not for years now. The Karllsons had long ago basically adopted him, and he could come on and go as he wished.

"Hello?" he called out.

"In the kitchen," came the clear voice of Mrs. Karllson.

Jason passed through a wood-paneled study, the quickest way to the kitchen, and waiting for him there were Daniel, Lien, and Mr. and Mrs. Karllson. Jason's attention, though, went straight to the strawberry cheesecake standing front and center on the butcher-block island.

His stomach grumbled, and Mrs. Karllson noticed. She quirked a grin, and her white teeth flashed against her Ethiopian dark skin. She moved in her easy, graceful way to a cabinet and withdrew a small plate. On it, she placed a large slice of cheesecake. "I should have known you'd want one," she teased in her east African accent.

"Thanks," Jason said, with a fond smile. Pretty much from the moment he'd arrived on Arylyn, the Karllson's had treated him like their own son. It didn't make up for what his own parents had done to him, but it helped.

"What is happening to William?" asked Mr. Karllson in his deep baritone.

"The other *raha'asras* hadn't arrived when I left," Jason said. "I didn't think they'd want me in the way for something this serious." Bubbling worry for William rumbled to life again. To be fair, it had never much faded.

Mrs. Karllson shook her head. "This should have never happened," she said. "The boy deserves some peace."

"If Afa's plan works, he'll have some," Mr. Karllson said.

"I know," Mrs. Karllson said, "but William's suffered more than all of us here, and he's so young." She sounded upset, which wasn't surprising. In the Far Beyond, the Karllsons had also taken in William, loving him as a close part of their family.

"And that doesn't even include what happens when the mahavans show up," Daniel said. "They're coming."

Jason shot his friend a disbelieving look. Reminders of the mahavans weren't what any of them needed right now.

Mrs. Karllson's features hardened, growing angry, and she reminded Jason of a roused mama bear. "If the mahavans come, we'll drown them in the sea."

Mr. Karllson moved from where he'd been sitting at the kitchen table to stand behind his wife. Despite her willowy height, he towered over her, massive as an oak, as he silently rubbed her shoulders and supported her.

Their quiet love for one another stood in stark contrast to what Jason recalled of his own parents volatile relationship. They'd argued all the time. Sometimes violently. Pots, pans, cutlery, even hammers would fly when they went at it. Their fights had always terrified Jason, and whenever an argument threatened, he'd run outside to hide under the porch until the dust settled.

At the time, he thought that's how life was lived. He never saw any different, including from his cousins, aunties, and uncles. As far as he knew, fighting was what all parents did.

Finding out otherwise might have been the biggest shock of Jason's life. He'd learned it when he'd come to Arylyn and gotten to know the Karllsons. He'd learned that their relationship was built on respect and friendship, which were better foundations as Jason reckoned matters than love. After all, his parents always said they loved each other, but that never stopped them from fighting all the time.

Until that understanding, for months after meeting them, he'd always thought Mrs. Karllson was so soft spoken because she was afraid of her husband. After all, Mr. Karllson was a giant, and a younger Jason had been sure the massive man would break his wife in half if she ever spoke cross to him. It took awhile to realize that Mrs. Karllson's soft-spoken manner of talking was just her way, and Mr. Karllson was as gentle as they came.

"But when the mahavans *do* come," Daniel continued. "We'll beat the brakes off them."

Lien shook her head. "You've been spending too much time around Jake. He's always saying stupid things like that."

"Rukh said it the other day," Daniel said, sounding defensive.

Lien rolled her eyes. "Then if Rukh said it, it must be the gospel truth."

"First of all, that doesn't make any sense," Daniel said. "And second, don't make fun of me because I admire Rukh."

"More like worship him," Lien muttered.

"Like you're any better when it comes to Jessira," Daniel countered.

Jason slapped the countertop. Most times, he found Daniel and

Lien's squabbling amusing, but not today. He was too wound up and worried. Everyone's attention fell on him, and Lien, in the process of speaking, snapped her mouth shut. "Can we talk about something else?" Jason asked. "I don't feel like joking around or arguing tonight."

"Agreed," Mr. Karllson said. "Perhaps we should have a quiet meal and pray that the Creator provides Afa the skill needed to heal William."

"I don't have anything prepared," Mrs. Karllson said. "All we have are bread and some leftover chicken.

"That is plenty," Mr. Karllson said. "We can have sandwiches. I'll make them."

Mrs. Karllson smiled. "Make enough to feed seven since Daniel and Jason eat as much as two people each."

"I wonder how Serena's handling things," Daniel mused.

Jason had spoken to her earlier in the day, right after Rukh had sent William home early from training. He'd discussed William's upcoming healing with her and found himself surprised by her reaction. Serena could lie like no one Jason had ever met and hide her emotions better than a statue. But this afternoon, fear had lurked behind her eyes, easily missed but present. Which meant she was terrified.

Jason had never seen her afraid of anything, not even when they battled Kohl Obsidian.

"She is with Fiona and Selene?" Mrs. Karllson asked.

"As far as I know," Jason answered. "At least that's what Fiona said. I ran into her after training."

Mr. Karllson nodded. "She shouldn't be alone during this. She likely cares about William more than any of us."

"Too bad she's too afraid to do anything about it," Lien said.

"Isn't William just as much to blame for that as she is?" Daniel asked.

"William's an idiot," Lien said, a sentiment Jason privately shared. "Serena's wise. She knows what she wants. She should go get it."

"But isn't it the guy who's supposed to chase the girl?" Daniel asked. "Not the other way around. That way, the guy gets to be in charge."

Jason gaped at Daniel's stupidity. Even Mrs. Karllson chuckled.

Lien, though, kissed Daniel on the cheek. "That's a silly thing to say."

~

Several minutes after Jason left, the front door opened. In walked Mr. Zeus, Fiona, Ms. Sioned, and Afa. They took whatever seating was available.

William's heart thudded harder. Further anxiety birthed a sheen of perspiration on his forehead.

"Are you ready?" Mr. Zeus asked. He sat in the other Queen Anne chair.

"Yes, sir," William replied.

"Good." Mr. Zeus gave a nod. "Let's get started. Afa will be the one to do the actual weaving."

Afa cleared his throat. "I insisted," he said from his place next to Jake on the couch. "I may be old but I can still weave more tightly than the others. It should help."

William tilted his head in thought. "If we need tight weaves, shouldn't Rukh or Jessira do it? They can weave more tightly than any of us."

Ms. Sioned shook her head. "Not for this." She sat on the other side of the couch from Afa with Jake in between them. "We consulted them. While Jessira's Healing is impressive, it won't help you. They can't do what you need."

"If Afa's doing the weaving, why are the rest of us here?" Jake asked. "I thought you needed us to help you somehow."

"We're here to watch and learn," Fiona answered from her chair in front of the picture window. "We'll observe Afa, his weave, and its effect on William. We should all pay close attention in case something like this is ever required again."

William clapped his hands once, getting everyone's attention. "I want to get this over with."

Afa gestured. "Come closer, then. It's best if we're close enough to touch."

William stood and dragged the coffee table the short distance to the couch. He sat on it so he could face Afa.

The old *raha'asra* briefly took William's hands in his palsied ones. "We begin." He let go of William's hands and sourced his *lorethasra*. The scent of wet leaves momentarily filled the room.

William focused on Afa's weave. It mostly consisted of a thick thread of Spirit that glowed silver and contained flecks of amber. It swirled about the old *raha'asra*'s forehead and then flowed into his hands. Afa used it as a scaffold, and onto it he attached short strands of Earth, Water, and Air. He kept at it, and the pattern gained more and more complexity. William lost track of the weave, at the number of threads Afa wove into it.

Through it all, the other three *raha'asras* and Mr. Zeus offered occasional suggestions.

"That thread of Air is a mite thin," Ms. Sioned commented.

Afa nodded and thickened the thread she'd pointed out.

"That one is too short. It doesn't reach far enough," Fiona said.

Again, Afa merely nodded and made the correction. Moments later, he inserted a long coil of Fire into his work. "Done," he declared. A flashing, pulsing weave rotated in mid-air before him.

The others sat in silence for a moment and studied Afa's creation. William shared an awestruck expression with Jake. The dexterity and complexity took his breath away.

Mr. Zeus leaned forward with a puzzled frown. "I'm still not convinced about the need for that last thread of Fire. As thick as it is, what if it burns out William's passion?"

Afa shook his head in negation. "It won't. I thought about this last night." He pointed. "See? I placed a strand of Air directly below it."

William saw the thread in question and realized what Afa intended. "The Air will cause the Fire to burn hotter but it'll also burn out faster."

Afa nodded. "It'll also allow the weave to do its job more quickly. Less chance of damage to you this way."

Mr. Zeus sat back with a grunt and rubbed his chin in thought. "That makes sense." He surveyed the room. "Anyone else have any suggestions?"

Ms. Sioned and Fiona shook their heads.

William exhaled heavily. His heart hammered ever harder in his chest.

"Then we'll start," Afa said, addressing William. "Are you ready?"

William could only manage a nod. His mouth had gone dry. *Here it goes.*

Afa reached for his creation and held it carefully. "It'll burn at first," he warned before passing over the weave.

William took it and allowed it to melt into his hands. From there the weave traveled up his arms, past his shoulders, and into his neck. It moved into his head and burned like Afa had warned.

William stiffened. *The pain.* He gritted his teeth and clenched his fists. *I've been through worse.* He breathed slowly and deeply and willed himself to ignore the discomfort, waiting on it to fade. Once it did, he exhaled in relief.

A whooshing noise, like his heartbeat in his ears, became audible. It grew louder and then ebbed. He tilted his head in confusion. Again came the sound, louder and then softer, but this sound didn't follow the rhythmic cycle of his heart. It had an odd, four-beat pattern.

A trickle of worry began when wetness leaked from the corners of his eyes. It wasn't tears, though. William touched it. It had a gritty texture. Next came air hissing from his ears. His eardrums popped. Worry turned to fear. *Is this supposed to happen?*

"What's happening?" Jake asked.

William's anxiety spiked, and his gaze darted about. He opened his mouth, but his throat clenched and no sound came out. He couldn't breathe. Panic threatened.

Fiona moved to sit beside him on the coffee table. She took his hand. "All is well," she said, her voice soothing. "The weave is doing what it was intended to."

William took in her words, and his fear eased. His throat loosened, and he took a stuttering breath.

Afa peered closer. "The weave is working exactly as I hoped. How do you feel?"

"Terrified," William said. "And slow. Like my thoughts are in quicksand."

He caught the worried glances shared by Mr. Zeus and the three older *raha'asras*.

"What is it?" Forming the words took effort. William's tongue wanted to trip on itself. It felt like when the dentist had done a root canal, and his mouth had been too numb to work right.

Fiona met his eyes. "It's nothing. It's likely a temporary side effect."

"We expected it," Afa added. "It won't be permanent."

Their words didn't slow William's gnawing fear. His mind remained dull, and he found it ever harder to give thought to his worries. *Will I be like this forever? Not angry anymore, but permanently slow and stupid?* It took an eternity to find the words.

The four-beat pattern he'd heard earlier continued, but after a few more minutes, it quieted. The gritty water no longer leaked so readily from his eyes, and the air no longer puffed so easily from his ears. More minutes passed and the sounds, wetness, and air faded away.

In their place lay silence. The brooding anger, the beast William hadn't been able to control, was no longer quite as menacing. He smiled. Despite his fears about whatever else the weave might have done to his mind, he realized he was himself again.

A faint growl echoed in his thoughts.

Mostly.

CHAPTER 15: PROGRESS AND PERIL

M *ay 1990*

S erena led Selene and Fiona through the still-crowded streets and bridges of Clifftop. With sunset approaching, the clouds had taken on an abundance of vivid colors: pomegranate-red, luscious violet, and burnished indigo—the latter hue reminded Serena of the Norwegian Sea around Sinskrill. Night always fell quickly on Arylyn, and shadows crept across Lilith's alleys and streets. Nevertheless, groups of people still strolled about, caught up in conversation and laughter, and some took the time to stop and call greetings to the three of them.

Serena replied with smiles and salutations of her own, but most of her attention lay elsewhere. She and William had agreed to meet at *Maxine's Ice Creamery* tonight and she didn't want to be late. It wasn't only about seeing William again—it had been a week since his healing, and she hadn't talked to him once in that entire time—but almost as important, tardiness irritated her.

She caught sight of Lien and Daniel and gave them a warm grin and a wave, a sentiment she wasn't certain she entirely felt. While she was happy enough for the young couple, did their obvious love for one another ultimately mean anything to her? Serena didn't know if it should. How could it? She wasn't the one in love with Daniel, and she wasn't the one intent on marrying him. However, a proper manifestation of joy for the couple was generally required, and she supplied it. It came easily and naturally.

Fiona tsked. "You worry too much about what behavior others expect of you," she said. "Simply let them flow."

Serena frowned at her grandmother. "How could you tell what I was doing?"

"Only another mahavan would."

Serena paused as a woman with a miniature lioness on a leash walked past, miniature being a relative term since the animal stood larger than a bullmastiff. The cat craned its neck to sniff at them, but a tug on her leash had the lioness resuming her place at the woman's side.

"Neither of us are mahavans any longer," Serena said.

"But we still have our training."

"Of course," Serena replied, "and there are times when that training helps me fit in."

Selene put a finger to her lips and shushed them. "Just don't tell anyone what Serena's doing," she said, her tone mocking. "It's her big secret. No one else is supposed to know."

Fiona laughed while Serena rolled her eyes. She wondered when Selene had become such a smart-aleck. She was about to point it out when the lampposts along Clifftop's streets flicked on and surprised her. Darkness crept in from the east, but the bright, yellow lights from the lamps shoved back the shadows.

"Do you wish to fit in because this is your home?" Fiona asked.

Serena paused to consider her answer. "Among other things," she replied. "These people are also my friends. I enjoy their good opinion."

"Though they don't enjoy yours?"

Serena flashed her a frown of true annoyance. While the crowds had thinned, a few stragglers still wandered about, and some of them might have caught Fiona's last comment. Upon hearing it, they wouldn't have thought kindly about Serena. Besides, old habits died hard. *Walkers hear all.* "Of course not. I simply can't be happy all the time like everyone else can."

Fiona nodded her head in understanding. "Too much darkness from Sinskrill persists within you."

Serena continued to scowl, not bothering to hide her emotions and not wanting to discuss whatever Fiona apparently had in mind. Since her arrival on Arylyn, her grandmother seemed to have made it her purpose in life to challenge Serena upon every aspect of her bearing that might reflect a lingering influence from Sinskrill. It could be wearying. "What of you?" Serena demanded. "Are you truly friends with Ms. Sioned?"

They turned down an alley containing strings of lights that criss-crossed the passage like sutures. These connections, though, were warm and inviting rather than cold and clinical. They exited the alley, took a right turn, and came upon their destination: a tall, brick building with a simple, illuminated sign that read 'Maxine's Ice Creamery'. A bank of windows opened onto the street and through them they could see one of Maxine's helpers working a large lump of vanilla ice cream on a slab of cold marble. He moved it about like flour, mixing in cocoa, slivers of almonds, and marshmallows. The delicious scents of chocolate, baked sugar, and vanilla wafted from the confectionary, drifting at least a block in all directions.

A crowd of people milled near the creamery and Serena made a moue of annoyance.

"And for your information, I *am* friends with Sioned," Fiona said, replying to Serena's question.

"And for both your information, I'm hungry," Selene announced.

"You're always hungry," Serena said. Irritation at Fiona lingered, and her words came out sharper than she intended.

Fiona laughed at Selene. "Overindulge in food, child, and you won't enjoy the unnecessary weight."

Selene ran her hands across her bony frame. "I think I can risk it." She pointed. "There's William."

"Hey, everyone," William said, having seen them as well.

Serena smiled in welcome and immediately gave him a surveying gaze. She studied his features, his posture, searching for changes. *Was the anger truly gone?* She searched for it, continuing her assessment.

After a few seconds, she breathed out relief. The anger was gone. Her friend had returned. She smiled more broadly. "It's good seeing you," she said, only then noticing the two waffle cones in his hands.

He smiled in return at her. "It's good seeing you, too," he replied before addressing Selene. "How was school, Tiny?"

Selene gave an imperious sniff. "I sagged off today."

Serena's eyes widened in outrage. She didn't know what the phrase meant, but it sounded vulgar. "Language, young lady!"

Selene viewed her with a shout of triumph and broke into laughter.

Serena's eyes narrowed. She sensed she'd just made herself the butt of a joke.

"'*Sagging off*' means skipping school," Fiona said in a dry tone. "The child has been planning this jape for some time."

Serena made sure not to smile at the joke—she couldn't encourage Selene—but she did think it clever.

"Grandmother Fiona and I will leave the two of you alone now," Selene said in a queenly tone. "We know how much you value your time together." She offered a grin that was barely short of a leer. "Besides, Grandmother Fiona also says that a well-dressed man is a woman's best accessory, but given William's lack in that department, maybe that means Serena will have to undress—"

Selene squawked when Fiona gripped her arm and gave her a sharp tug. "Have a good time," she said as she dragged Selene away.

Serena momentarily viewed the two of them with a fond smile as they departed. She pointed to the two waffle cones in William's hands. Both held mounds of chocolate ice cream. "One of those for me?" she asked.

William passed her an ice cream cone. "Want to eat these by the Village Green?"

"Sure," Serena agreed. For some reason, she slipped her hand into the crook of William's elbow. She'd never done it before, and she decided after a few paces that she liked it. It felt natural.

They strolled through a relatively empty part of Clifftop. Stars lit the firmament, and a fitful breeze blew through the quiet lanes. A few other couples were out for a nighttime stroll, and it struck Serena anew that she and William could be considered one of them. It wasn't true, but maybe—

She cut off the line of her thoughts. *When did I become such a romantic sap?*

She eyed William askance as they continued toward the Village Green. "I haven't seen you since when . . ."

He faced her and smiled. "It's all right. I know you're curious. When they removed my anger."

Serena scowled. "Mr. Zeus wouldn't let me see you. Every time I stopped by, he said you were resting."

"I was," William said with a nod. "I was asleep pretty much non-stop until yesterday."

"Did it work? Afa's weave?" Jake, Jason, and Mr. Zeus had all said it had, and while she couldn't see a hint of the rage in his bearing, she wanted to hear the words from William's mouth. She needed his confirmation.

"I think so." William paused and appeared to think over his words. "Or at least I hope so. The anger, the beast, it's still there, but it's not like it used to be. It's smaller and not as violent. I can control it."

Serena smiled in relief, and they continued on their leisurely wandering.

She didn't realize she was humming until William pointed it out. "What is that?"

"It's called "There is a Balm in Gilead"," she said and recited one of her favorite verses from it. *"There is a balm in Gilead to make the wounded whole."*

"I like that. Is it your new favorite spiritual?" William teased.

He'd guessed the truth, but Serena didn't like admitting it. She remained a private person, even to William. She merely smiled in reply.

Minutes later, their walk brought them to the Village Green, and they took a seat on a bench overlooking the cliffs and cascading waterfalls.

As Serena worked on her ice cream, she noticed William shifting about and frowning, his countenance troubled. "What is it?" she asked.

He continued to frown as he stared at the darkened waters of the Pacific. "While I was laid up, I was thinking about things. You and Jake —everyone really—keeps telling me to live for today instead of always for tomorrow," he said. "But I don't know how. With everything we've been through and everything we still have to do, and especially fighting the anger, I think I forgot how to relax."

Serena didn't have an easy, rational answer for him. She chose instead to speak what was in her heart. "Maybe you need to recognize the special moments in your life and treasure them instead of always hoping they'll be there waiting for you tomorrow."

"I wish I could, but you know Sinskrill is going to—"

Serena put a finger on William's mouth and silenced him. "You're an idiot, William Wilde. I'm talking about right now. Us." Her heart thumped when she realized what she'd said. *Us.* A word freighted with heavy meaning.

Thankfully, William missed her slip-up. "I just think—"

"You shouldn't believe everything you think." Serena managed a chuckle at the small joke meant to hide her newly risen uncertainty. *Us. What did I mean by that?*

"Are you trying to be annoying?" William asked, smiling to take the sting out of his words.

Serena grinned, a true expression, but one driven by relief rather than amusement. "Only if you keep making every one of our conversations about life and death."

William's eyes flashed in warning, and Serena worried for him. *Maybe his anger isn't entirely banished.*

An instant later, he quirked a wry smile. "Fine. What do you want to talk about?"

"Anything but Sinskrill."

"Then what?"

"How about when are we going to the Far Beyond again?" she asked. "I want to try that rib place you, Jason, and Jake keep going on about."

"Montgomery Inn?"

"Yes."

He wore a hopeful cast. "Can we rent *Batman* afterward? I never got to see it." He chuckled. "I can't get over how they cast Mr. Mom as Batman."

Serena tilted her head. "Is he related to Wolverine?"

William groaned, which was exactly what she hoped he would do.

~

A ia sat up and yawned wide, wondering who had disturbed her nap. She yawned again and searched around, quickly locating the disturber of her sleep. Shon, her tawny-furred brother. He'd kicked her in his sleep. One of his rear legs twitched while Aia observed him.

Her ears flicked in annoyance. The big pest likely was dreaming of chasing a gazelle on the Hunters Flats on Arisa. As she continued to watch Shon slumber, Aia unconsciously crouched low. The temptation to pounce on her brother and scare him senseless flitted through her mind.

She hesitated for a few seconds before straightening and choosing instead to shake out a paw and lick it clean. Jumping on Shon was something only kittens did. It wasn't an acceptable behavior for someone of Aia's august nature, especially now that she remembered herself, her long life and the many miracles and wonders she'd witnessed and experienced. As the bearer of such a lofty heritage, she had to maintain the grace expected of a regal Kesarin.

Kesarin.

The word echoed in Aia's mind, and she wondered if she'd ever regain her prior stature. Would she ever again stalk the Flats and pull down a full-grown water buffalo? Or cause an elephant to move aside for her? Full-sized, she'd been more than seven feet tall and twenty-five feet from nose to tail tip, and Shon had been even bigger.

She examined her body and snorted in disgust. *Now look at me. Landon says I'm the size of a mountain lion, but I'm still less than a quarter of what I once was. Pathetic.* Her ears flattened in depression.

An instant later she shook her head in irritation at her self-pity.

Enough. She stood, arched her back, and stretched, digging her front claws into the cool dirt. She leaned forward and did the same with her hind legs. Next, she set to grooming herself. Her calico fur held a coating of dust from where she'd been napping in the patch of sunshine beaming down between the trees surrounding Landon's cabin.

While she worked on her coat, the hunter side of her made a mental note of the people moving around the small, tidy village in which she had settled the past few years. Sand was its name.

Aia and Landon had washed up in this place, and shortly thereafter, Shon had joined them. He should have arrived alongside her, but her brother had somehow managed to get himself lost during the long journey from Arisa to Earth.

Foolish kitten. The thought held a deep well of affection.

Her grooming complete, Aia sat with her tail curled about her front paws and studied her current home.

Roughly fifty cabins made up the village, and wide lawns of soft grass separated each of the rough-hewn homes. Most were made of logs stacked atop one another and rose only one or two-stories, but all of them had broad, deep front porches leaning over the streets. Smoke curled off most of the chimneys, and there was no mystery as to why. This place, Idaho, remained cold all year long, even in the summer. At least it did for Aia.

Her kind, the Kesarins, had been bred to hunt on wide, warm savannas, not cold, evergreen forests.

Aia watched as the Wrin, the people of Sand—witches and warlocks as they were known elsewhere—moved along their streets. They talked and laughed with their neighbors, friends, and family while the occasional ringing of a blacksmith's hammer drowned the sounds of the surrounding forest of pine, cedar, and aspen.

Aia hissed when someone laughed, a high-pitched, yelping sound. *Humans are as loud as thunder.*

Shon sat up and noticed her annoyance. He blinked. *What's wrong?*

Nothing, Aia replied. *We've napped long enough. It's time to hunt.*

Shon swished his tail. *Hunt what? We aren't allowed to kill any of the* tasty animals here.* He blinked again. *Do you think Landon would miss it if we ate his goat?*

I'm certain of it, Aia said. *Rukh and Jessira would.* She rubbed Shon's forehead with her own. *Let's stretch our legs and see what trouble we can rouse.*

Shon rose and stretched in the same languid fashion Aia had. Once he was ready they padded away from Landon's home to skulk around the perimeter of the village. Aia took the lead, and they prowled along the edges of back yards that ran to the evergreen forest soaring all around Sand.

That's a lonely looking cow, Shon said. He gestured with his nose toward a solitary bovine placidly munching grass.

Aia warned him. *That one belongs to Elaine. She'll skin you if you kill her cow.*

Shon grumbled a complaint, and they continued on their way.

A stream that bisected Sand interrupted their wandering. They eased down the bank, leapt the water, and clambered up the other side. There they encountered a farmer tilling his field. The heavy-set, balding man growled noisily at them and made broad gestures with his hands.

Farmer Ted, Aia said. *I wonder what he tastes like?*

Probably disgusting, Shon answered. *Isn't that what Thrum said about Humans?*

Aia recalled their long-deceased brother. Smart, brave, but a bit of a braggart. How would he know what Humans tasted like? Jaresh wouldn't have allowed it.

Her thoughts must have leaked to Shon since he answered, *You know Thrum. He did whatever he wanted. No one could tell him otherwise.*

Aia grunted and they continued their exploration and passed more fields, some of which were ripe and ready for a harvest. Others were only now being made ready for a planting.

This isn't at all like Ashoka, Shon said, sounding approving. *It's much more peaceful.*

Ashoka was peaceful, at least Dryad Park was, Aia said as she flicked an ear to ward off an annoying fly. *But there was no peace after They came.*

Shon hissed. *They were worse than the Demon Wind.*

Aia was forced to agree.

Their short journey eventually led them back to the center of Sand. There, Aia came to a crashing halt. *Granny Castor,* she warned, pointing out the old human with her nose.

Elaine's grandmother was a wiry woman who wore glasses and the pinched, pursed lips of perpetual irritation. Aia and Shon always stepped warily around her.

How does she wield such a swift broom when she can barely see or walk? Shon asked.

Aia didn't know, but they held still until the old woman wandered away.

I miss Jessira, Shon said, exhaling heavily once Granny Castor passed from view.

And I miss Rukh, Aia replied.

When can we go to them?

When our Trial here is complete.

Shon flicked his tail. *Trial? That's something Rukh or Jessira would say. They're Human. We're not.*

Aia smiled, a perking of her ears and widening of her eyes. *Some of what they so often say must have rubbed off on me.* She licked Shon's ear. *Just as it has rubbed off on you.*

Much to Aia's chagrin, Shon behaved as a kitten then. She yowled when he tackled her.

~

Walker Brandon Thrum of Sinskrill stepped out of the rowboat and marched ashore. Once he reached the beach, he knelt and cupped a handful of fine sand and let it slowly drift through his fingers. *Arylyn. We actually made it.*

Brandon's feet were proudly planted upon the home island of the hated magi, perhaps the first mahavan in all of history to be able to make the claim. He smiled, watching as the final grains of sand drained away from his hand. He rose to his feet then and took in the warm breeze blowing off the ocean, the soft waves washing against the shore. A fruity fragrance drifted on the wind, emanating from the surrounding jungle and treed hills that lined the beach and stretched out in all directions. Palm trees swayed, and their rustling fronds masked the sounds of his mahavans as they gathered their belongings from their rowboat and approached him.

The excitement of arrival gave way to the necessity of work, but it was a labor for his lessers. Brandon merely observed the mahavans over whom he'd been given command as they collected the supplies. He made no effort to assist in their work, choosing instead to merely wait on them. He could easily able to make out their features as they trekked toward his position. The realization made him curse. The night was too bright. Unlike Sinskrill, Arylyn apparently had no ready cloud cover to provide shelter from prying eyes. Here, despite no illumination but the Milky Way, the night still gleamed brightly enough to make out *Deathbringer*, their ship, floating in the harbor.

The ship would soon depart, though. Already the rowboat returned—even now oars rose and fell as it moved steadily back to the ship. As soon as it arrived, *Deathbringer* would cast off. Then Brandon and his mahavans would have to fend for themselves. They'd have to survive by their wits and skills alone, avoiding detection while simultaneously learning all they could about Arylyn and the magi. They need to learn the island's state of readiness and strengths, their culture, and also their weaknesses—especially their weaknesses. Of those, Brandon reasoned there would likely be many.

After all, consider the island itself. If the magi were anything like Arylyn, Brandon reckoned that he and his mahavans had little to fear. Arylyn was warm, tropical, and comfortable. Soft. Her people likely would be, too.

A nagging voice pestered him from the recesses of his mind. It was the part of him that refused to simply accept orders. *How, then, had the magi defeated the mahavans? Twice thus far, including on Sinskrill, no less?*

Brandon hid a grimace. *Perhaps the magi aren't as weak as their soft island.*

A moment later, he threw off his concerns. *No matter.* He had a duty to perform, a tremendous challenge to overcome, but with success in this, the greatest of pilgrimages, mighty rewards awaited.

Again came his nagging voice. *What if those two, the man and the woman who cut through the mahavans like a spinning saw through straw, find us? The World Killers as the Servitor had labeled them. What then?*

Evelyn Mason, a Rider, took that moment to address him, thankfully breaking his worried thoughts. "Your orders?" she said in a tone short of a demand. Time and defeat had possibly robbed Evelyn of her prior breezy self-confidence and lackwit manner. In fact, she was now a woman of few words and most of them terse.

It was all a façade.

Evelyn remained as arrogant as a storm. Her quietness didn't indicate serenity. Rather, it was a mask, hiding a truth that Brandon knew about her. Evelyn raged for revenge. She wanted to be the one to capture Serena, and barring that, kill the traitor.

Brandon eyed Evelyn for a moment before responding. "From what we could tell when we scouted from afar while aboard *Death-bringer*, there's only one village on the island, to the southwest of our current location. We'll make our way there and learn what we must."

Evelyn's blue eyes—rare for a mahavan—widened in excitement and her auburn hair billowed about her. "And burn this place to the ground," she breathed.

"Perhaps," Brandon said. "It is for the Servitor to decide."

"We should find cover," Samuel Ingot said. "We're exposed on this beach." Samuel's pinched features flittered about in worry and his clothes flapped like sails around his scrawny frame. Despite his lack of physical stature, Samuel was a powerful mahavan, a Rider, a Water Master, but his unfortunate sense of fair play and lack of ambition would forever deny him a chance at greatness. Samuel was doomed to follow rather than lead.

His suggestion made sense, though, and Brandon quietly called out orders.

They moved away from the beach, pushing past the hillocks of grass growing along the edge of the sand and a half-built tower commanding the bay. No one was about, and they pressed farther inland. They soon reached the trees, and Brandon breathed a little easier when they crept beneath the shadowy canopy of a jungle.

Preeti Amal, also a Rider like Samuel and Evelyn, and the final member of their group, stiffened as if she'd been stabbed.

A spike of worry shot through Brandon. He could neither see nor sense any injury to the sharp-faced, sharp-tongued Rider. "What is it?"

However, it wasn't pain that caused Preeti's reaction. It was awe. Even in the jungle gloom Brandon could make out the wonder on the woman's face. "Has anyone linked to the *lorasra* yet?" she asked.

Brandon cursed himself. Just as he'd been the first ashore, first linkage to Arylyn's *lorasra* should have also been his. *I'll have to make sure the history texts say I did,* he silently promised as he sourced his *lorethasra* and reached for a golden thread of *lorasra*.

He gasped. None of the *saha'asras* he'd ever visited in his life compared to what he experienced now. Arylyn's *lorasra* tasted pure, like a perfect, fruity beverage, not overly sweet and with a sharp, tangy taste. No pollution marred its flavor. No sewage taste as on Sinskrill. Brandon could have luxuriated in Arylyn's *lorasra* for hours, and based on the expressions of his fellow mahavans, they felt the same way.

Brandon snarled. *No. I won't be seduced by this island's charms.*

He gathered himself, strengthened his spine, and forced sternness to his visage. "The *lorasra* is lovely, but we came here to work. We came to conquer this island and make it Sinskrill's." He glared at the others. "We will not act like simpletons who've never seen the sun. Let's go."

He marched into the jungle's darkness and tried to ignore the golden glory of Arylyn's *lorasra*.

CHAPTER 16: LONGING DREAMS

M *ay 1990*

D espite the vow he made prior the Chinese New Year to make Arylyn his home, Jake had yet to make good on his promise. He hadn't asked out Daniella Logan, and he hadn't made any new friends amongst the other magi. He mulled again about what he wanted in life while he had lunch with Mr. Zeus, William, and Jason. They'd made fresh-cut potato chips, peanut butter and jelly sandwiches, and boiled peas and sat at the dining room table that adjoined the kitchen to have their meal. The others joked, laughed, and talked about what they had planned, but Jake kept quiet.

The heavy aroma of hot oil lingered in the air, but Jake didn't mind the smell. He liked it. It reminded him of summers at his Aunt Vivian's restaurant when he'd helped out in the kitchen. Memories flitted through his mind, and he mechanically chewed and swallowed his food while staring out the picture window. He remembered something Rukh had once told him. *The only things in life worth keeping are love and innocence.*

Jake thought about the words. His innocence had been stolen when the mahavans had kidnapped him to Sinskrill. He scowled at the notion. So many bad experiences in that place. So many terrible things. He wished . . .

He realized the direction of his thoughts and did his best to redirect them. He could never regain his innocence, but what about love?

Before all this *raha'asra* stuff and magic, he and Sonya Bowyer had had something. Maybe it would have been special, but that too, had been in a more innocent past. It was long gone and irretrievable.

What about now? Why can't I love again?

Jake considered the question and took another bite of his sandwich, shoveled down a spoonful of peas, mechanically chewed and swallowed, and took a sip of lemonade. He planned on saving the potato chips for last. He always ate the best food last, a weird habit from childhood.

While he chewed and swallowed, he realized that he loved Arylyn. After all, he'd volunteered for the Irregulars. He'd probably even put his life on the line for the folks here. He even loved lots of people: William, Selene, Mr. Zeus, Fiona, Jason. Even Serena.

So what's my deal?

"Earth to Jake," William said. He sat at the other side of the table and snapped his fingers in front of Jake's face. "You spaced out there. Mr. Zeus—" he gestured to the old man, "—has been asking you the same question over and over again."

Jake shook off his reverie and smiled sheepishly. "Sorry. I was thinking about something."

Jason grinned. "Is that why smoke was coming out of your ears?"

Jake smirked. "Yeah, because I was imagining what it's like to be like you."

"A mind on fire cause I'm so smart?"

"More like a dumpster on fire," Jake said. He waved his hand in front of his nose as if he smelled something stinky.

William chuckled, which was a way better reaction than the anger he used to have. Afa's weave seemed to have restored William to his normal self, and Jake was grateful for it. He had missed his friend.

"Seriously," William said, "what was going on in that pea-brain of yours?"

Mr. Zeus spoke up, cutting off Jake's response. "Who wants the last sandwich?" He addressed Jake. "That was what I was asking you."

Jason reached for the sandwich. "I'll take it."

"You've already had three, you dumpster fire," William protested. "I've only had one."

Jason grinned. "You snooze, you lose." He waved the sandwich like it was a banner.

William snatched it out of his hands, took a massive bite, and put it back on Jason's plate. "You can have it now if you want," he said around the bolus of food.

Jason stared at the sandwich a moment before wordlessly passing it to William.

Jake laughed at them while scooping up the last of his peas. Unfortunately, half of them fell off the spoon and onto the table.

Jason groaned in disgust. "Stop *peaing* on the table."

Jake didn't bother responding. He hated puns, and his lack of reaction would tick Jason off.

"Get it?" Jason asked. "*Pead* on the table."

Jake kept a blank expression on his face.

"You never answered my question," William said. "What were you thinking about?"

"You know cause we're eating *peas*," Jason said. When Jake didn't respond, he grumbled something under his breath.

Jake hid a smile. "I'm thinking about getting on with my life," he said to William.

Mr. Zeus stared at him. "If I recall, you said this once before."

Jake shifted in his seat, unable to meet Mr. Zeus' eyes. "I know, but this time it's different. I wasn't ready then. I am now."

"What's changed?" Mr. Zeus asked.

Jake's mouth opened and closed a few times as he struggled to explain his thoughts.

"You don't have to convince us," William said. "You were kidnapped, lashed, and nearly killed. You've had a lot to deal with."

"Well, it's time I dealt with it," Jake replied. "I had a good life in the

Far Beyond, but I've got a pretty good one on Arylyn, too. A lot of people would kill to live here, to do what I get to, and for the past year, I've acted like I hated it."

"No, you haven't *acted* like you hated it," Mr. Zeus corrected. "You *did* hate it. But as William indicated, it's a natural reaction after everything you've experienced. You've been through far more trauma than anyone should have to experience at any age."

Jake smiled in appreciation, touched by the old man's words. "Thanks," he said, "but I meant what I said about getting on with my life. If I keep longing for my old life, I'll never appreciate what an even more awesome life I have now."

Mr. Zeus smiled at him. "I'm glad to hear you say so."

Jake nodded. "Anyway, I'm thinking I should do more with myself than train with the Irregulars or the *raha'asras*." He quirked a grin. "And don't take it wrong, but I also think I need more friends than the ones I have."

Jason smirked. "What's her name?"

Jake's mouth dropped open in surprise.

Jason noticed his response and tapped the side of his head. "I know things. Mind on fire, remember?" He grinned. "What's her name?"

William shook his head and rolled his eyes. "He's talking about Daniella Logan, oh wondrous Mind-On-Fire."

"Oh, yeah. I forgot about him liking her," Jason said.

"Speaking of asking a girl out, didn't you say you'd be asking someone out after New Year's?" Jake asked.

Jason's face grew guarded. "It didn't work out."

The table fell silent, and Jake regarded Jason in silent consideration for a moment before deciding to let the matter drop.

William spoke up. "You're really going to give up this brotherhood," he gestured to everyone around the table, "for some girl?"

Jake leaned back in his chair and aimed a Cheshire-cat grin at William. "Aren't you and Serena going on a morning stroll tomorrow? That's the fifth time in the past week you're spending time with her." He shook his head. "I think you've already broken our band of brothers."

~

William probed the inside of his mind, searching for the anger, but he couldn't find the beast.

He continued to search for it as he and Serena walked along Sita's Song. They journeyed through Janaki Valley, and the morning dew glistened on the fields. Bees and early-rising butterflies flitted about while birds wheeled in a blue sky filled with thick clouds built like wispy castles. Farmers in straw hats and overalls paced their fields. Some took the time to call out greetings while others surveyed their crops, a few bent low as they studied the plants. Underneath it all, River Namaste rumbled toward the falls, sounding like the distant murmur of a thousand indistinct conversations.

William caught Serena staring at him, frowning in bemusement.

"What are you doing?" she asked.

"What do you mean?"

"You have this scrunched-up expression on your face." She mimicked what she meant.

William flushed. "Oh, that." He shrugged, not sure how to explain things. "I know the anger is gone, but I keep expecting to find it. Like it'll still be there if I search for it hard enough."

Serena's features brightened in understanding. "Like a missing tooth your tongue keeps trying to find?"

William's face cleared, and he nodded. "Yeah. Like that."

They strolled on, shaded by the trees of an orange grove on one side and an apple orchard on the other. A fitful breeze played with William's long hair, and he made a mental note to have it cut. It was becoming too much of a pain to maintain.

Serena chuckled. "I still can't believe Rukh gave us a rest day."

"I know, right?" William agreed. He especially had needed the time off. Afa's weave still had him groggy, clumsy, and foggy-headed. "I didn't think Rukh noticed things like tiredness and stuff."

"We deserved it, though," Serena said. "With all the hard work we've put in, I think he was probably impressed at how far we've progressed."

William chuckled. "When has Rukh ever been impressed by anything we've done?"

Serena started. "You're right," she said, a note of surprise in her voice. "Most of the time he acts disappointed in us, like we're not measuring up to the people he knew from his home. He finds us wanting."

"Arisa and Caste Kumma," William said.

"You think they were really as good as Rukh says?"

"I do," William said, surprised by her question. "Don't you?"

Serena wore a doubtful expression. "I don't know."

"Well, if Rukh is anything to go by, then the answer is 'yes.' Kummas were badasses. I don't think any of us will ever be as good as Jessira, much less Rukh."

"Jessira's not far behind what Rukh can do," Serena said.

"Maybe," William said, although he privately disagreed, "but she's definitely a lot nicer than him."

Serena's eyes widened in shocked disbelief, like he'd grown an extra head or something. "Are you serious? You don't remember what it was like when she was in charge of our training?"

William eyed her in befuddlement. "Yeah, I remember. She wasn't that bad."

Serena continued to stare at him in incredulity. "Yes, but during those times when she led the training, Jason was the one who kept messing up. He got the brunt of her temper. Not you or me. That's why you didn't notice her yelling."

"She doesn't yell," William corrected. *Well, maybe a little.* "She's stern."

"Yeah, well she definitely gets in your face and lets you know when you've screwed up."

"She did that to you, did she?"

Serena nodded. "To Lien and Daniel more than me, but yes, I've caught the bad side of her a few times." She shook her head. "Let's talk about something else. We've got the day off, and I don't want to talk about training."

William nodded agreement.

They continued on their hike, and with his mind no longer taken up by searching for his anger or talking about training, William finally noticed how Serena's lime-green sundress swirled around her tanned, toned legs. With every step she took, it rode to her mid-thigh, and William caught himself staring sidelong a little too intently, a little too appreciatively. He made himself focus on something else, the surrounding crops.

Thankfully, Serena didn't notice his overly intense regard, but even if she had . . . He wondered. *Would she care? Or better yet would she enjoy the attention?* He stared at the ground, lost in thought. A moment later, he glanced at her askance. That's when he noticed her secret smile of amusement.

Serena *had* noticed. She winked at him, and he flushed. His reaction elicited a warm, throaty chuckle.

"At least I was paying attention," William said.

"Paying attention to what?"

"To a beautiful woman." He didn't know if he was pressing his luck, but the words felt right.

Serena smiled at him, this time in a pleased fashion. "Good response."

She tucked her hand into the crook of his arm, a habit she'd picked up shortly after his healing, and William allowed it. He didn't mind, liked it actually. Since his healing, a new closeness had arisen between them.

They continued along Sita's Song and paused at the peak of a low rise. Janaki Valley spread out all about them, the vineyards, the orchards, the lines of banana trees and orange groves, the fields of tasseled corn, and of course, the golden wheat and barley.

"I want to show you something," Serena said. She tugged on his arm, and he followed her onto a narrow, cobblestoned path. They had to walk single file. On either side of them grew beets. A tall, bespectacled farmer with an Amish-style beard, Rainn Mose, ambled amidst his crops and waved at them.

They waved back before proceeding on.

"This way," Serena said.

The cobblestone path ended at a two-story, brick farmhouse with a wraparound porch. There, a hound dog lifted his head and peered at them with sad eyes. His tail thumped hopefully a few times, but when they showed no signs of stopping, he slumped on his paws and closed his eyes.

"It's right here," Serena said.

They reached a gravel pathway that meandered through tall grass, and William's ears perked when he heard the croaking of frogs and buzzing of dragonflies. Grasshoppers leapt before them. "Where are we going?"

Serena pressed on without answering. She strode a single pace ahead of him, and when she reached back, it felt like the most natural thing to take her hand and follow.

Once again, William caught himself watching the sway of her hips, the way her dress swirled around her legs or rose to her thighs as she high-stepped through tall grass.

"Stop staring," Serena said without turning around.

He tried to brazen past the potentially embarrassing situation. "I'm not staring. I'm admiring." He privately congratulated himself on what he thought was a pretty good answer.

Serena offered him a wry smile. "I'm sure that's all you're thinking about."

William didn't have a chance to reply.

"We're here," Serena said.

She came to halt, and William moved to stand beside her, still holding her hand. They'd come upon a small pond centered within a large copse of trees. Cattails ringed the water and swayed under a gentle breeze. The croaking of frogs came clearer, and puffy clouds reflected off the mirror-sheen pond. A broad live-oak with limbs dripping Spanish Moss extended over the water and provided shade.

"I found it last fall," Serena explained. "Lots of people probably know about it, but it's always quiet in the morning."

"What do people do here?" William asked. He knew the question was inane the moment it left his mouth.

Serena laughed. "I imagine they play." She pointed at a rope swing that hung from one of the live-oak's branches leaning over the water. "They probably also renew friendships and try to enjoy their lives."

William noticed a tear leaking down Serena's face. "What's wrong?"

Her face took on a serious note. *"There is a balm in Gilead to make the wounded whole."*

William remembered the song, and he provided the next line. *"There is a balm in Gilead to heal the sin-sick soul."*

Serena smiled. "You remembered."

"I always remember the important things." He wiped away the wetness from Serena's cheek, and she lifted her face. William's mouth grew dry and his heart thumped, but not with fear. Instead, a richer emotion inspired its beating. Time halted. The world became more vivid, colors brightened, and sounds rang like clear bells. The moment reminded William of the first time he'd stepped into a *saha'asra*.

He folded Serena into his arms and dipped his head. When his lips met hers, a slow-burning lamp went off in his heart, a warm light telling him he should never let this woman go.

~

B randon shifted slightly as Evelyn crowded him. The two of them crouched within a small clump of trees containing a marshy smell. Preeti and Samuel hunkered several yards away.

Brandon stared at the scene playing out a several dozen yards away. Tall reeds and cattails ringed a mirror-like pond while frogs hiccupped and insects chirped. Puffy clouds, like something from a painting, drifted sedately across a summer sky that would have been perfect if not for the harsh sun mercilessly beating down. Thankfully, the shade from the trees brought comfort from the heat, which was sweltering for someone used to Sinskrill's chill.

A line of sweat trickled down the back of Brandon's neck, and perspiration beaded uncomfortably on his forehead. It dribbled down his face and obscured his vision. More sweat formed on his chest and his armpits, soaking his shirt. It clung uncomfortably, and Brandon grimaced. He didn't like Arylyn's heat, its constantly sunny days, or its effortless beauty. It offended his mahavan sensibilities. He preferred

Sinskrill's icy weather, its dreary rain, and the rugged, harshness of its environment.

Nevertheless, the weather and lovely scenery wasn't what held Brandon's attention. It was the man and woman on the other side of the pond.

"Do we take them?" Evelyn asked. Though her voice remained soft and controlled, she couldn't entirely mask her excitement. Her blue eyes gleamed, and her auburn hair seemed to move about in defiance of the generally absent wind.

Brandon studied the object of Evelyn's eagerness. Across the water William embraced Serena, and they kissed. They might have been drowning in one another, clearly in love.

Brandon mused. *Love.* A sentiment he had long considered a ploy, a ruse foolish poets wrote about in order to seduce even more foolish women. Brandon had always believed love to be a feigned feeling, something spoken of but not truly experienced.

Apparently he'd been wrong, or the possibility arose that he *might* have been wrong. William and Serena loved one another. It was as apparent and obvious as the blue sky above, and part of him envied them their passion.

"Do we take them?" Evelyn repeated.

Brandon shook his head. "No," he whispered. "William is a powerful *raha'asra,* and whatever Serena's faults, she is still an *asrasin* of repute."

"There are four of us," Evelyn hissed. Her jaw clenched momentarily. "They would be easy meat."

Brandon turned to her, and his eyes lit with irritation. While Evelyn might have learned to control her fire and fury, she had never mastered the art of reasoning before speaking. "Is the Servitor easy meat?" he challenged. He hoped his question would force the idiot to think, but no such luck.

Evelyn's anger was replaced by her dullard's confusion. "Of course not."

Brandon rolled his eyes at her stupidity. He pointed to William and Serena. "They fought the Servitor and lived to tell the tale. Or have you forgotten what happened on Sinskrill when they stole Travail and Fiona?"

"No. The Servitor allowed them to—"

"What? Allowed them to flee?" Brandon asked. "You really credit that the Servitor would have allowed Fiona and Travail to escape as well?"

"No, but perhaps our liege was tricked in some way."

Brandon scoffed. "Save such simple explanations for a child. Those two fought the Servitor and survived. They are not easy meat." He pointed again to William and Serena, who were wandering away now. "Discount everything else if you wish, but yesterday you also witnessed their training. You saw what they can do. Those two are skilled and dangerous."

Evelyn's jaw clenched in a mulish scowl. "Well, now it's too late to find out if they're as powerful as you fear," she muttered. "They're leaving."

"Which is fine as far as I'm concerned," Brandon said. "We're only here to observe and learn, remember?"

"We've been here for two weeks," Evelyn said. "We've learned all we can of this valley. What more is there to know?"

"Their capital, the village of Lilith. We haven't yet scouted it," Brandon said. "We need another two or three weeks to fully learn what he came for."

"Then what?"

Now it was Brandon who frowned in confusion. "Then our pilgrimage will be complete," he answered. "What else?"

Samuel slithered near and whispered to Brandon. "For a moment I was afraid you'd order us to attack them."

Brandon shook his head. "I won't risk our pilgrimage on behalf of a vendetta," he replied. "When we're done here, we'll dream a call to *Deathbringer*, sail home, and report to the Servitor."

Preeti shifted closer. "All of this would have been a lot easier if we'd thought to bring satellite phones. We could have been in constant communication with Sinskrill if we had."

Brandon nodded. A mistake they would rectify the next time they came to Arylyn.

Evelyn still wore an unhappy scowl but apparently for a different reason. "We should let the magi know we were here."

Brandon's mouth curled in anger. "We will do no such thing," he hissed. "We came to scout and learn. That is all." He wondered anew why the Secondus had ordered Evelyn's inclusion on this pilgrimage. "The less the magi know about our presence, the better."

Evelyn nodded, but Brandon didn't miss the way her hair floated about her face. He silently cursed. He'd have to watch her and make sure the idiot didn't do something foolish.

~

William's brow creased as he tried to focus on the text he held in his hand, *The Intervention*. The book, dry as three-day-old baked chicken and written in a convoluted fashion, supposedly described the founding of Arylyn. So far, William had made it to page three—on five separate occasions. After that, his eyes began to swim, his thoughts wandered, usually to kissing Serena again, and whatever he'd read only minutes earlier melted from his mind.

One blessing was that his frustration with the impossible-to-decipher book hadn't triggered his anger. The beast remained quiescent. No glowing, red eyes or growls ready to erupt at a moment's notice from the depths of his thoughts.

Mr. Zeus cleared his throat, his head bent as he puffed steadily on his pipe while reading a book of poetry. The westering sun beamed through the tall, mullioned windows bracketing the desk where he sat. The cozy smell of old paper and pipe smoke permeated the study. They had the house to themselves since Jason was at the library studying up on anchor lines, and Jake was with Afa, trying to master the anger-easing weave the old *raha'asra* had placed on William.

Just then one of Mr. Zeus' infernal roosters chose to crow. William leaned forward in his chair, trying to spot the stupid bird. He considered weaving a braid of Fire and roasting the rooster. He hated them, always waking him up at dawn. *I wonder what one of them would taste like fried.*

After a few seconds, William gave up his search for the rooster and

returned with a sigh to the open book on his lap. *Time to give* The
Intervention *another go.*

"Why don't you try something else?" Mr. Zeus asked without bothering to lift his gaze.

"I don't like to lose."

Mr. Zeus glanced up at that. "You think it's a contest between you
and the book?" He snorted in eloquent dismissal before returning to
his poetry.

William stared out the window and wished he could chuck *The
Intervention* into the ocean and go have some fun. After a few seconds,
he shook his head. *Duty required obedience.* It was something Rukh
talked about. He bent his head and went back to reading the dry
history text.

This time he managed to make it to page four, but his concentration broke when Jason stomped inside and called a loud "Hello." He
pushed into the study and flopped into a chair, visibly exhausted and
annoyed.

"What's your problem?" William asked.

Jason rubbed his temples. "I was doing what you asked," he said.
"Reading up on anchor lines. You have any idea how boring that is?"

William glanced at *The Intervention.* "I think I have an idea."

"Ugh." Jason continued to rub his temples. "I've been studying my
ass off, and now I've got a headache."

William burst out laughing. Even Mr. Zeus's mouth curled into a
smile and he made suspicious coughing sounds into his fist.

Jason flicked his eyes from one of them to the other. "What did I
say?"

William never had a chance to answer because Serena barged into
the house. Fear pinched her features. "We need to get to Clifftop," she
said, sounding breathless. "All of us. Rukh says he needs our help."

William's hackles rose, and he rose to his feet. *What could be so bad
that Rukh needs our help or would make Serena afraid?* A terrifying notion
occurred to him and his eyes widened in alarm. "Have the mahavans
come?"

Serena shook her head. "No. Someone's been murdered."

CHAPTER 17: INCURSION CONFIRMED

June 1990

William gaped.

"Murdered?" Mr. Zeus breathed out the word as if it made no sense.

Serena cleared her throat. "We have to go."

William was the first one out the door, and the others scrambled after him. They trotted up the stairs, and Mr. Zeus huffed as he struggled to keep up. William brought them to a halt and stared down at the older man. He stood several stairs below with hands on his knees and his face red.

William took a step toward him. "We can—"

Mr. Zeus waved him away. "I only need to take it slower," he said. "I'm fine. Go on. I'll get there."

William flicked worried eyes at Jason.

"I'll stay with him," Jason assured them. "You go."

Mr. Zeus protested, but Jason shushed him.

William took a moment more to make sure Mr. Zeus was fine before once again ascending the stairs. His heart pounded with adrenaline and fear as he approached Clifftop.

This evening remained no different than any other. The sky held a splash of reds and oranges, and a cool breeze blew off the aqua-blue ocean. The perfumed aromas of a hundred different flowers mingled with the mineral-fresh scent of River Namaste's cataracts pounding down the falls, but the world *had* changed. Someone had been murdered. Who, though? He should have learned beforehand.

"Who was it?" he asked Serena.

"Jeff Coats."

"The farmer?" William blurted. "How?"

"Someone cut his throat."

They reached Clifftop, where a crowd had gathered on the Village Green, nearly as many as had been present for the Chinese New Year's celebration. Only this time, they weren't celebrating. People shuffled about, speaking in hushed tones of fear and shock.

William followed Serena to the bicycle rack, and they hopped aboard their bikes once they were free of the crowd.

"Where are we going?" William asked.

"The enrune fields," Serena answered. "Jeff's body washed ashore there."

William's gaze went to hers. "What do you mean?"

"That's where he was pulled out of River Namaste."

William grunted. "Meaning he was murdered somewhere else," he said. "Did Rukh say why he wanted us?"

Serena shook her head, and they pedaled in silence.

William had a million more questions, but they'd have to wait until they reached Rukh.

They swiftly reached the enrune fields but no one was around. No one was playing.

William stared about. "Where are Rukh and Jessira?"

"I don't know," Serena said. "Jeff's body was right here."

"Maybe they moved it?" William guessed.

Serena pointed to people crossing Lakshman's Bow. "Or maybe the real murder took place wherever those people are going."

It made sense. William led them across the bridge, and they pedaled hard. Their bicycles wide wheels smoothed out some of the rough pavement of Sita's Song, but an occasional rut still made the swift ride teeth-jarring.

They quickly passed the pedestrians, rose and descended a shallow hill, and swept by the field where they trained with the Irregulars. They reached Janaki Valley. For once, its beauty didn't capture William's attention. *Someone had been murdered.* He still couldn't come to grips with it.

At a long turn where Sita's Song bent toward the river, they reached their destination. Tall reeds grew along the bank here, and the land sloped down to the water. William readily identified Rukh and Jessira and the entire village council standing near the river. A number of farmers had set up a perimeter, a rough barricade of wood and wagons to keep the curious from approaching too closely.

William dismounted his bicycle.

"Let them in," Rukh shouted to the farmers blocking the passage.

Sile Troy ushered them through.

Rukh and Jessira stood near a puddled patch of red with more scattering swatches surrounding it. Only a few feet away, River Namaste flowed sedately, uncaring of the violence done so close to its waters.

William's gorge rose as he approached and realized what the redness meant. He swallowed heavily and tried to breathe past the overwhelming stench of blood that filled the air.

"Is this where Jeff was murdered?" Serena asked. Her voice was steady and clear, and no sense of horror marred her features. William shot her a questioning glance. Serena had a drone-flat affect. Maybe the murder *did* bother her.

"This is where Jeff Coats met his demise," Rukh confirmed, pointing to a clump of torn-up reeds. "He wasn't taken unawares, though. He fought. He might have even injured his enemy."

Bar Duba startled. "Enemy? How do we know this wasn't a crime of passion?"

Jessira answered. "Are throats often slit in crimes of passion?" she asked. "Or the victim's eyes removed?"

Bar Duba appeared shaken. "No. I suppose not."

Jessira nodded. "Then, no, it wasn't a crime of passion. Jeff's murder was a message. Someone wanted us to know that it was done deliberately."

"Do you know how many people attacked Jeff?" Mayor Care asked.

"One," Rukh answered. "He fought a single enemy, likely a woman. I found boot marks. Based on the size and shape, I suspect they belong to a woman."

"You're sure?" Mayor Care pressed.

"I'm sure."

William still had trouble ordering his thoughts. The smell of blood overwhelmed his senses, and a strange hunger growled in the recesses of his mind. In some ways, it resembled his recently rid anger. Fear flashed through him at the notion, and he took slow, steady breaths, trying to settle his emotions.

His attention returned to the here and now when Rukh addressed him. "I need you to examine the area and tell me what you find."

"Me?" William asked in surprise. "Why?"

Jessira answered. "Because you've got the blood of a necrosed in you. They're supposed to have an incredible sense of smell. We need that." Any softness William might have imagined she possessed was gone. Instead, Jessira wore a coldly furious visage.

William nodded, although doubt filled his mind. He'd never noticed that his sense of smell was more acute than anyone else's. Nevertheless, he did as Rukh and Jessira asked and breathed deeply.

The first sensation that came to him was that of blood. The smell of it suffused all his senses. He could almost imagine seeing it, hearing it, tasting it. The animal-like hunger he'd noticed earlier rumbled to life. It growled, and the sound and sensation of it was like the red-eyed anger but also different. The hunger wanted blood, and William figured it must be another part of the heritage of a necrosed. His fear of it faded somewhat when he recognized he could use it.

The hunger lifted William's head, made him inhale more deeply. He tasted the air, searched for something beyond the blood. He paused at where the blood pooled thickest, but the hunger carried his footsteps past it. He tracked back and forth, not sure where he was going but listening closely to the growling desire.

"What are you doing?" Serena asked.

"I don't know," William said, "but there's this sensation in me. It wants something."

"Something from the necrosed?" Jessira asked.

"I think so," William said. "Now be quiet, I'm trying to listen or smell or whatever."

He circled around a boggy stretch of reeds and detritus. The hunger wanted something here. William squatted, and his sandals squished in the mud and muck. *Within the tall grass,* the hunger seemed to whisper in a harsh tone. A flash of light in the dimming day caught his attention.

William reached for whatever had shone and discovered a long knife, a dagger with a horsehead pommel, partially sunk in the mud. He pulled it free. Despite the muck covering it, he could smell the blood upon it—Jeff's blood. His mouth went dry. He knew where this knife had come from.

Rukh and Jessira stepped closer. Serena did, too. They all studied the blade.

"Do you recognize it?" Rukh asked.

"It's from Sinskrill," William said. His heart raced. *The mahavans are here.*

"You're sure?" Jessira asked.

"It's from Sinskrill," Serena confirmed.

Mayor Care, who had also followed, gasped in fear. "Heaven save us."

Serena leaned in toward the knife and peered closely. "I think there's a . . ." She trailed off and plucked something off the handle, a strand of auburn hair.

"What's that?" Mayor Care asked.

Serena straightened, wearing a furious scowl. "It belongs to the mahavan who killed Jeff Coats. I know her."

~

E *velyn Mason.*

The name echoed in Serena's mind, and a rushing sound filled her ears. Vertigo stole her balance. *Sinskrill has found me.* She swayed like one of the reeds along the riverbank, caught in the tug of an unseen force that threatened to spill her onto the ground.

Evelyn Mason.

The mahavans knew Arylyn's location, and who knew how long they'd been spying on the people here. What information had they learned? What plans had they developed? Were they still on the island? And if they *had* left, when would they return?

Serena started when William gripped her shoulders. He stooped and brought himself to eye level with her. "Are you all right?" he asked.

Dusk had fallen. Serena couldn't easily see his features, but she could hear the concern in his voice. She stared into his eyes, but her thoughts remained elsewhere as she tried to answer his question. She realized she didn't know how to respond. Sinskrill had found them. The mahavans had watched them. They threatened the wonderful life Serena had built for herself and Selene.

The moment she recalled her sister, Serena snarled. *No one will harm Selene.*

"Serena?" William said.

Serena's resolve firmed and so did her spine. She leaned on her mahavan training and hardened her heart, allowing nothing to touch her, no fear, no anger, no uncertainty. She would do whatever was needed to keep her family safe. She pushed back the fear.

"I'm fine," she said to William.

Rukh stepped closer to them. Even in the rapidly encroaching darkness Serena could sense the sorrow on his face. "There's nothing more for you two here," he said. "The council can handle the rest."

"Yes, sir," William said. He reached for the crook of Serena's arm and gently urged her away from the riverbank.

She let him lead her away and glanced to where Mayor Care and the council clustered near Jessira like worried hens. They spoke in hushed tones. With the fall of night only minutes away, Serena couldn't make out their features, but she imagined they all wore expressions of fear and worry. She also saw that Jessira still held the dagger William had found.

For a few moments Serena had forgotten the smell of fresh-spilled blood, but with the reminder of the blade, she noticed it once more. It filled the air, and she stared at the pool of red, gone black now under the falling light, where poor Jeff Coats had died.

Serena's jaw clenched again, and anger took the place of worry. *Evelyn will pay for what she's done.* "Let's go." She jerked her arm free of William's hand and pushed out of the reeds.

William trailed her. She heard him say something to Rukh before jogging to catch up with her.

By the time he reached her, Serena had reached their bicycles. They mounted up, and with darkness full upon them, they each braided a weave of Fire and Air, creating cool, silvery flames that bobbed in the air ahead of them to light the road back to Lilith.

Serena fumed the entire way in grim determination. *No one and nothing will hurt me or my family.*

They passed a few last stragglers heading toward the murder scene, and Serena scoffed at them. With night falling they'd see nothing.

"What do you think will happen now?" William asked.

Serena didn't want to discuss it. "Let's talk about it later." She immediately winced at the harshness of her tone.

William thankfully disregarded her rudeness and merely muttered acknowledgment.

They traveled in silence. The only sounds came from the chirping of crickets and other insects and the droning of their bicycle tires. They were soon rattling over the knobby surface of Lakshman's Bow and across the enrune fields. They reached Clifftop, and Serena let the silvery light dissipate. She no longer needed it with the streetlights turned on.

Small groups of people still clustered along Lilith's streets. Everyone wore somber, distraught, and even fearful casts to their features. As they approached the Village Green the streets grew more crowded, and they had to dismount their bikes and walk them to the bicycle rack.

After putting the bikes away, William pointed. "There's everyone else."

Mr. Zeus, Jason, and Jake were heading toward the Main Stairs of Cliff Spirit. They must have never left the village because Serena couldn't recall seeing them on Sita's Song.

William called out, and Jake heard him. He signaled the others to a halt, and they waited.

Jake spoke when Serena and William reached him. "You saw what happened?"

William nodded. "Jeff Coats was murdered by Evelyn Mason."

Jake's mouth momentarily dropped open in shock. "What?"

"Who's Evelyn Mason?" Mr. Zeus asked.

"A mahavan," William replied.

"You're sure it was her?" Jake pressed. "How? Why?"

"The why doesn't matter," Serena said, and explained what they'd seen at the riverbank.

Mr. Zeus sighed. "At least we have the beginnings of an army if Sinskrill ever attacks us."

"They will attack," Serena said in distraction. She already had her mind focused on what she needed to do to keep Selene safe.

William eyed her in concern before addressing Mr. Zeus. "Why don't y'all head on out?" he suggested, his North Carolina drawl leaking a bit more than usual into his voice. "I'll tell you everything I know when I get home."

Mr. Zeus' worried gaze shifted from William to Serena and back again. He must have settled whatever matter troubled his mind because he gave a sharp nod and led the others down the Main Stairs.

Serena watched them leave. "We'll have to train harder than ever."

William smiled. "Isn't that my line?"

"You were right," Serena replied. "All along, you were right." Speaking the words hurt less than acknowledging her own stupidity. She'd been a fool, playing and laughing, thinking her life so wonderful while danger closed in on them.

William's smile faded. "What do you mean? About doing nothing but work?" He shook his head. "No, I wasn't. Part of why I said and did that was because of the anger. It was the only way to take my mind off of it."

"The reason you were right doesn't matter."

"Yes, it does." William exhaled heavily. "I'm guessing a lot more people will want to join the training now, and they'll do it because you were right about our lives here."

Serena frowned. "A bit apropos of nothing," she said. "I understand the more people joining part, but how was I right?"

"Because people will fight to protect their lives here. They won't let it die without a fight." He took her hand and held her gaze. "Because a life without joy isn't a life worth fighting for."

Serena's cold, hard knot of anger loosened a little, and she couldn't help but smile at his words. He'd thrown her own sentiment back at her. Nevertheless, despite the slight unclenching of her fury, her resoluteness—her determination to defend what was hers—didn't fade in the slightest.

William gave her hand a squeeze. "We should tell Selene and Fiona what's happened."

Serena squeezed his hand in response and gave it a gentle tug. She wanted something she couldn't name and somehow he understood. William pulled her into his arms and she rested her head on his shoulder.

"Do you think Fiona, Selene, and I can spend the night at Mr. Zeus' home?" she asked.

William kissed her forehead her in response.

~

Adam Paradiso gave a brief bob of his head to Gerald Fine, the mahavan guarding the entrance to Shet's Throne Hall, before pushing open the double-doors leading inside. He paused within the room's entrance, as his eyes needed a few seconds to adjust to the darkness.

He glanced back when the doors swung shut of their own accord and faced forward again. In front of him stretched an aisle of onyx amongst a sea of white marble that made up the rest of the floor. The black stones formed a passage between a forest of gold enameled columns, and the pillars ascended from the floor. They held up a ribbed ceiling containing stained-glass images and mosaics from Sinskrill's holy book, *Shet's Council.*

Adam didn't bother scrutinizing them. He'd studied the scenes plenty of times and by now had them essentially memorized. He didn't need to view them again. Instead, his focus remained on his brother, who sat upon the Servitor's Chair and waited for him at the far end of the Hall. Above and behind Axel, Shet's empty throne squatted like a toad atop a raised dais, and farther back loomed the grotesque, six-armed statue of their Lord.

His brother shifted in his Chair, an uncomfortable-appearing leather seat framed in noble, purple wood. Shet's Spear lay across Axel's lap, and while his thick-set features might have been inscrutable to some, Adam knew his brother too well. Axel brooded with impatience.

Adam approached, bowed low to his brother and straightened. "I have news from the pilgrimage to Arylyn," he began.

Axel leaned forward. "Tell me what you've learned." His face remained unreadable, but his grip tightened upon Shet's Spear. Adam could sense that tension and excitement suffused the Servitor's being.

Adam held out a satellite phone, the clever means by which Brandon had suggested they communicate. The young mahavan had had Evelyn Mason dream the notion to her parents. A short trip to the Faroe Islands, and Adam had returned with a satellite phone. Brandon had obtained one for his own use in some port where *Deathbringer* had stopped during its long voyage back to Sinskrill.

"I can call them if you wish," Adam said.

Axel waved the phone aside. "Summarize what Brandon told you. If I deem it necessary, I'll call him myself."

Adam dipped his head in understanding. "Brandon, Evelyn, Samuel, and Preeti spent most of the past month on Arylyn. The island sits in the tropics, a paradise, warm, lush, and soft. Larger than Sinskrill, with remnant Memories from various *sithes* of elves and *creches* of dwarves."

Axel stroked his chin. "The magi waste their *lorasra* maintaining these Memories."

"They have five *raha'asras*," Adam reminded him. "Apparently, I did not kill Jake Ridley as I thought. He survived, and Arylyn obviously has the *lorasra* to waste on the Memories."

The Servitor merely grunted, but Adam could tell Arylyn's wealth of *raha'asras* bothered him. "Go on," Axel ordered.

"A single village by the name of Lilith houses some seven thousand magi."

Axel sat up straight, shock evident on his face. "Seven thousand? You're certain? They have that many when we have little more than one thousand mahavans and drones in total?"

Adam nodded. "I pressed Brandon on this point, but he was adamant. However, he also said that only thirty or forty of them have any training as warriors. The rest lead peaceful, indolent lives."

The Servitor leaned back in his chair and steepled his fingers. "Continue."

"A long valley is the source of most of their food. Janaki Valley is its name. Brandon advises that if we burn their crops, we can inflict heavy losses upon them by robbing them of their food."

Axel wore a mocking smile. "How? By starving them? They live on an island surrounded by fish in the sea, and they likely have fruit trees growing wild throughout their island paradise. Burning their crops will accomplish nothing."

Adam had come to the same conclusion, but wisdom dictated he keep quiet. It was better for his brother to ferret out the flaws and merits of a plan on his own. Doing otherwise risked Axel's wrath since the Servitor did not like anyone outshining his intelligence. The last secondus who had done so had been hurled from the Judging Line.

Axel steepled his fingers once again. "Tell me more. What of the enemy? You know the ones of whom I speak."

"Rukh and Jessira," Adam said. "Those are their names." He hesitated. He knew of a way to learn more about those two, but he also didn't want to broach the topic even though he knew he had to. "Perhaps Lord Shet will know more of their nature if he were to learn their names."

Axel eyed him with a suspicion. "Are you so eager to speak with the Lord again?"

Adam forced his face to stillness and suppressed a surge of sudden nervousness. "I did not mean to overstep my authority," he said, choosing his words as carefully as if he edged through a minefield in the Far Beyond. "I had thought *you* could relay the information."

"Of course," Axel said, still eyeing him with vague distrust. "But I will not be the one to meet with him next time. It will be you."

More anxiety spiked like a stiletto through Adam's heart. *Meet with Shet?* He mentally groaned. He'd rather put his hand on an anvil and have a blacksmith hammer it flat. Nevertheless, he kept his face composed. "Yes, my liege."

Axel's suspicious mien faded, and his visage grew distant. "Do you think this Rukh and Jessira truly battled Shet's children on some distant world? When last I spoke to Shet, he said they probably did so."

Adam started. He hadn't considered such a possibility. "Truly?"

The Servitor eyes narrowed in thought. "It would make sense. Only someone with the skills to battle a demigod could have defeated me."

A flash of emotion passed across Axel's face, and Adam didn't miss it. It was fear, and upon witnessing it, he couldn't entirely hide the shock on his face.

His brother chuckled. "In some cases fear is not something to be denied. I fear those two, and I am wise to, especially because I believe Shet is correct. Those two defeated his children. They defeated me. They've earned my respect *and* my fear."

"I still don't understand why they've come here. Shet said they battled his children on some other world, so why come to Earth?"

Axel made a dismissive gesture. "Who can know?"

Adam offered the only explanation he could imagine. "Perhaps they were exiled from their world?"

"Supposition."

"It's also likely," Adam argued. "Why else leave their home? To protect ours from Shet?" He snorted. "I believe in many things but not in selfless heroes."

Axel chuckled. "Is there anything else?"

Adam took a deep breath. There was one other thing, and his brother wouldn't like it. "Evelyn murdered one of Arylyn's farmers and plucked out his eyes." He spoke softly, knowing he had to tread softly here since the hot-headed Rider's inclusion in the pilgrimage to Arylyn had been his decision.

No one could ever know why he'd chosen her, especially since she had done exactly as Adam had hoped. She'd recklessly killed a magus, and the people of Arylyn now knew of Sinskrill's presence on their island. They were forewarned, and perhaps Axel would now put aside this mad plan to attack the magi.

Axel hissed, and his eyes glowed with anger. "Idiot! She will be punished for her incompetence. Let Brandon know. Let *her* know. I want her stewing in her fears the entire journey back to Sinskrill."

"Yes, my liege." Adam answered while a distant part of him pitied Evelyn. She would suffer for her stupidity, but then, such was the fate of the stupid.

Axel resumed his reclining repose upon the Seat and steepled his fingers once more. "Matters advance as I have foreseen," he said. "I want us ready to sail as soon as possible. Forty magi, even with this Rukh and Jessira, won't mean anything against our hundreds. We'll burn Lilith to the ground."

Adam wanted to grind his teeth in frustration.

CHAPTER 18: FULFILLING FATES

June 1990

A squirrel paused in her scratchings, and while her simple mind understood the fear of foxes and the terror of stooping hawks, this danger was something different. Her nose quivered, and her tawny fur twitched. The squirrel took an uncertain step toward an acorn lying like a lure on the ground only a few feet away. The nut rested in the sunshine, on the edge of a glade in a world made strangely quiet. The squirrel listened. Leaves rustled, and the earth shook. Peril approached, and the squirrel darted away, rushing to the safety of a nearby oak.

From the forest burst five people. They never noticed the squirrel or the other animals of the forest who rushed away from the glade. Work occupied their minds.

"Form a trip-line here," William ordered. "Karla, get on it. Five inches high and five feet of ice-slick grass behind it. Keep it hidden.

We might get lucky and take out a few mahavans if they charge through." He addressed Daniel. "I need you on shield works."

Rukh, one of those who'd entered the glade, silently observed Red Team. The small unit commanded by William included Daniel, Jason, and Karla Logan, and while they dashed about, Rukh remained quiet. His purpose here was to do nothing more than observe. Later on, after the battle's conclusion, he'd meet with the members of Red Team and offer critiques. Until then he'd simply watch.

The Reds—the magi in this exercise—drilled against the Greens— the mahavans—a much larger group of fifteen with Jessira as their observer. Both teams wore governors. Rukh and Jessira, in addition to their roles as observers, would call out injuries and deaths during the running battle.

Thus far, the Reds and Greens had been at it for fifteen minutes. William's unit had steadily retreated through the high-mountain forest close to Rukh's cabin, but they couldn't fall back any farther than this glade, which was meant to represent Lilith.

This would be the site of the final clash, and while Rukh didn't expect the Reds to win, so far, William had performed far better than expected. His original five-man group, now four, had whittled the Greens down to ten. The odds still weren't with the Reds, but they'd done well. William had done well. Ever since the *raha'asras* had rid the young man of his crippling anger he'd progressed far and progressed fast.

Karla, who had been kneeling as she carried out William's command, quickly rose to her feet, dusted off her pants, and strode to William's side. "Trip-wire's ready, sir."

"Good. Go help Daniel with the shield works."

Karla snapped off a salute, and Rukh smiled. She was one of the more recent additions to the Ashokan Irregulars, but she too, had progressed far and fast. Everyone had. The dedication of the magi, the four hundred additional folk who had enrolled in the defense force after the murder of Jeff Coats, had taken Rukh by surprise. He hadn't expected so many to volunteer, and he certainly hadn't expected their dedication and intensity. At times, he found himself amazed by it. In this, they resembled his Kumma brethren, for whom battle had been a way of life.

Of course, their skill lagged far behind their desire, but over time that, too, would improve.

Rukh waited at the edge of the glade, arms folded as he watched the preparations unfold.

William called out more orders. "Jason! Get me a line of shield works there and there." He pointed. "Don't worry about making them thick. I only want them tall enough so they look the part. If it works, it might trick the Greens and funnel them into a straight-ahead charge."

Threads and weaves blurred across and through the ground. The sulfur stench from crackling braids of Fire filled the glade, along with the rustling of Earth, the hissing pulse of Air, and the rushing of Water. Dust drifted on the breeze, and the small forest meadow, once pristine and green lay ruined, pockmarked, and torn apart.

Rukh frowned at the waste, but what other choice did they have? The Irregulars had to train. They had to learn to fight. Later, they'd do their best to restore what they'd destroyed.

A sound came to him, and he peered into the forest. Greens approached, and Rukh silently applauded Ward Silver, their commander. He'd sent scouts, and they moved carefully, slowly, and quietly. Rukh smiled. They'd learned caution. *Good*.

William must have noticed their nearby presence as well. "Hurry up," he warned the others.

"Almost there, sir," Daniel replied. "Done!" He scooted back to where the rest of Red Team hid behind an overlapping series of bulwarks.

The world seemed to further quiet when three members of Green Team stepped farther into the glade. They momentarily studied the bulwarks placed throughout the ruined area before slinking back into the forest.

Seconds later, the rest of the Greens pushed out of the trees, and Rukh nodded to Jessira, who trailed them.

Three Greens apiece went after the false bulwarks flanking the Reds' main shield wall. The other four raised moving shield walls of their own, and rocks cracked as more dirt and stone flowed out of the ground.

While the Green warriors advanced toward the two false shield walls, Rukh noticed William whispering something to Daniel, who nodded in reply. His interest piqued, and he stared intently at the Reds, wondering what they had planned.

A hissing band of white wrapped around William's shoulder and down into his forearms. He thrust out a hand, and a rushing bolt of Air blasted into the right-hand bulwark, exploding it into the oncoming Greens. Though they huddled behind their own shields, several of them took blows.

"Marcus, broken arm," Jessira called. "Daniella, a concussion. You're both out."

The other false bulwark also exploded, and the Greens approaching it fared no better. Lien, reckless as usual, always thinking to attack, had moved outside the range of her earthen shield. Her aggressiveness cost her. She took a blow to the chest and was deemed killed in action.

It left the Greens with seven warriors and the Reds with four. Rukh pursed his mouth and wondered if William could actually pull this off.

Ward shouted orders and the Greens advanced. Two of them stumbled over the trip line and went down. Jason blistered one with a sizzling line of fire while Karla held down the other fallen Green with a braid of Earth and finished her off with looping line of Water.

Jessira called out the injuries. "Urban, Suzanne, you're out."

Five against four. Rukh eased forward, interested to see how the rest of the battle would play out.

Daniel stepped out from the shield wall. He prepared to unleash an attack but Ward took him down with a shotgun blast of pebbles.

"Daniel, you're dead," Rukh said. *Five against three.*

"Dammit!" Daniel flung himself on the ground, falling to where he'd been 'killed.'

Another shotgun blast took out Karla, and Rukh called it.

Two Greens fell to Jason and another to William.

Two against two.

Jason took on Stuart Hart, a Green, and they simultaneously killed one another with bolts of Fire. It left only the commanders still alive, William and Ward. The two teams gathered as one group to watch the battle play out.

"Get him," Jason shouted to William.

"Destroy him," Lien exhorted Ward. "Victory before dishonor!"

Of one accord, William and Ward stepped beyond their bulwarks. They paused a moment in seemingly silent assessment until William broke the tableau. Then, he raced forward and dodged a pulsing arrow of Air, rolled beneath a sizzling line of Fire, and leapt over grasping braids of ivy that erupted from the ground. A braid of Air pushed him higher, and at the peak of his leap, he hurled a weave of Water. It poured out of his hands with a sound like a breaking wave.

Ward crossed his arms and pulled up a wall of dirt. A screaming-banshee wind ripped at his shield, and he steadily gave ground. He suddenly halted his retreat and unleashed another bolt of Air.

William dodged right, rolled and straightened and hurled a whip-thin line of water.

This time Ward split the braid apart with a weave of Fire but had to leap away when the ground shifted beneath his feet. He leapt again, and his eyes widened when he slipped and fell. His retreat had carried him onto the patch of ice William had ordered placed behind his trip-line. Ward landed on his butt and William finished him off with a bolt of Air.

"Dead," Jessira called.

"Red wins," Rukh said with a smile to William. He approached the jubilant, young magus who stood surrounded by his cheering team. "Well done."

"Thank you, sir."

"A word."

William separated himself from the rest of Red Team, and Rukh led him a few feet away. "I meant what I said to you once about how I can see you commanding the Irregulars if Jessira and I fall. I hope you see now that isn't such an impossibility."

~

W illiam listened quietly as Rukh and Jessira discussed their plans to the village council for beefing up the island's defenses. Historically, the councilors didn't do much more than attend a few relatively unimportant meetings, but now a decision of immense significance weighed upon them. They actually had responsibility for something more consequential than officiating at a wedding.

The nondescript municipal building and the bare, spartan council chambers where they generally met was the scene of this decision. Three wooden benches, each one hard as granite, faced a large, rectangular table behind which the councilors sat and listened as Rukh described what he thought they needed to do.

For some reason, William had been asked to attend as well, which he thought odd. Odder still was the fact that the meeting was closed to the public, another first for Arylyn.

Rukh stood at a lectern and rifled through a stack of papers. "I have a list of all the landing sites on the island," he said. "We need manned watchtowers guarding them."

"How many are there?" asked Mayor Care

"Nine," Rukh answered.

Zane Blood, the Councilor for Cliff Spirit, lurched to his feet and pointed an accusing finger. "We'll need hundreds of people to man that many watchtowers. We can't afford that. We need our people working for Lilith's betterment." The balding man, every bit as nondescript as the municipal building itself, looked about for support.

"They *will* be working for Lilith's betterment," Rukh argued. "They'll be defending the island." He sighed. "I would much rather that no magi ever learns the true meaning of battle. I love Arylyn as it is, the peace, the lack of turmoil, the tranquility, but our enemies have decided we must change."

"Sit down," Mayor Care said to Zane.

"But, Lilian," he protested.

"Please sit," the mayor said.

Zane tugged his shirt straight and resumed his seat. "Of course. Forgive me."

Bar Duba, the Councilor for Cliff Air, shifted, and his chair creaked alarmingly. The normally affable, thickly-built man appeared as intense as William had ever seen him. "I accept we have to defend ourselves, and I accept your words on what is needed," he said. "What I truly wish to know is this: how long will it take for our people to learn to fight?"

Jessira, who had been seated next to Rukh, took the lectern. "Many of them already know some of the rudiments, but to become a proper fighting force they'll need at least three months of training, and even then it'll be only the bare essentials."

Rukh muttered something under his breath.

Mayor Care's gaze sharpened. "What was that?"

"Nothing," Rukh replied.

Jessira shifted an annoyed gaze to Rukh. "He continues to struggle with accepting what the people here can do compared to those of his Caste."

Seema Choudary of Cliff Earth seemed simultaneously curious and puzzled. "How long would it take to train our people to that level of proficiency?"

Rukh resumed the lectern. "A lifetime. Kummas train from the moment we can walk." He smiled faintly. "It's not required in this situation. Jessira is right. It will take three months to get the warriors of the Irregulars pulling in the same direction. After that, time permitting, we'll teach them to fight more truly."

Councilor Break Foliage of Cliff Fire sat forward. "I still have trouble accepting that we're expected to make such a momentous decision," he said in his nasal voice. William imagined the man's nose twitching like the weasel he resembled. "I wish we could turn back time and return to overseeing the refurbishment of a Clifftop road or something menial like that."

Lucas Shaw harrumphed. "We all do," he agreed in his refined South Carolina accent. "Yet we cannot shirk our duties or our responsibilities. They are ours to bear."

Bar briskly nodded. "Well spoken, Lucas."

Rukh cleared his throat. "We aren't quite finished with our recommendations," he said. "In addition to the watchtowers, we need an offensive capability to deny the mahavans a beachhead if they do try to land."

Mayor Care peered up and down the line of councilors before returning her attention to Rukh. "You have a suggestion?"

Jessira stepped to the lectern, "We'd like to use cannons."

"Impossible," scoffed Zane. "Guns and bullets don't work on Arylyn. No chemical reaction encased in metal does."

"Exactly," Lucas Shaw said, "and even if didn't, powder driven shells might be beyond our industry. It takes a great deal of metallurgical knowledge, which we unfortunately don't have."

Rukh shifted and William caught his sidelong urging, as if he wanted William to speak.

William's eyes widened. He understood now why Rukh and Jessira had asked him here. "We already have what we need," he said.

All eyes went to him, and he squared his shoulders.

Mayor Care gestured to the lectern. "Care to elucidate, Mr. Wilde?"

William marched to the lectern. A few years ago, speaking at a council session would have made his tongue go limp, his mouth dry, and his mind empty, but he'd grown since then. "I've done a lot of reading," he said. An instant later, his mouth twitched into a grin. "I was inspired. What I learned was that during the island's founding, a number of weapons were placed upon Lilith's cliffs and every possible entry point, in case the mahavans learned the island's location and attacked. A few of them might still be around. There should even be one in the Village Green."

Lucas Shaw stroked his chin. "I don't recall seeing any weapon upon the Village Green."

"That's because it's under the gazebo," William answered. "It was buried."

His answer birthed silence, one that was broken by Councilor Duba. "You wouldn't happen to know of any others, would you?"

William grinned. "As a matter of fact, there are a few more buried in front yards throughout Lilith. They were stored in stone chambers. Some of them might have even survived intact."

Mayor Care addressed him. "And what do these weapons do?"

"They work as Rukh and Jessira want. They're basically magical cannons."

The room broke out in eager conversation.

Rukh clapped his hands sharply once, twice, and the room quieted. "Temper your excitement," he warned. "We first have to ensure these devices are present, determine how they work, and barring that learn how to make them. We may have to learn to fashion them from scratch. Beyond that issue, however, lies another, final matter. If we place the cannons on the watchtowers, and one of the watchtowers is over-run, our own weapons could be used against us."

William had an answer for such a dilemma "The ancient *asrasins* had a protection against that. They put fatal flaws in all their cannons so they could blow them up if they ever fell into enemy hands. You only have to be able to see the cannons to trigger the fail-safe."

The meeting quickly broke up after that, and William caught up with Rukh and Jessira as they were leaving the building. "You already knew about the cannons," he said. "Why did you really need me here to tell the council about them?"

"If Jessira and I fall, someone has to lead the Irregulars," Rukh said.

~

Serena smiled as she reflected upon the recently finished afternoon's training session with the Irregulars. She'd led the Greens in battle today and managed to defeat William and his Reds, something no one else had managed in the past three weeks. However, the idea of how to achieve victory had come from Jessira, the notion of holding back a portion of her forces as a reserve. It sounded so obvious in retrospect, but until today, no one had ever done it correctly.

During the engagement, as he always managed, William had inflicted heavy damages on her forces. The tide might have turned his way, until Serena called in the two magi she'd held in reserve. They'd entered the battle and made all the difference. As a result, the day belonged to the Greens, and Serena still held a rosy glow of success at the accomplishment.

Also, as the losing side the Reds were the ones tasked with cleaning up the field of engagement. They had to dismantle the various, scattered bulwarks, smooth out the many gaping holes littering the ground, and heal any trees or bushes damaged in the battle.

Meanwhile, the Greens were already dismissed, and they biked back to Lilith along a gravel track. Their tires crunched on the loose stones.

Serena pedaled alone behind the others, wanting privacy to savor the day's victory. Crops of corn towered on either side of her, and their leaves rustled like braids of Earth while their tassels shook in the stiff breeze funneling through the fields. The wind was refreshingly cool, especially with the downpour of no more than fifteen minutes ago, which lingered in the smell of wet leaves, dirt, and muddy water.

Despite the day's normal Arylyn heat, in some ways the weather reminded Serena of Sinskrill, especially when the sun drifted behind a cloud. She smiled again.

"You seem pleased," Jessira said in her confident contralto. She'd drifted back from the others, and her green eyes sparkled. "You should be. You did well today."

"Thank you," Serena said. "And thank you for your advice."

Jessira raised a single, elegant eyebrow in query.

"Your mention of holding back a reserve force."

Jessira smiled modestly. "It is an old concept, and certainly not of my own unique design."

They passed through the last of the corn, and the track they followed dead-ended into Sita's Song. Jessira took the left-hand turn toward Lilith smoothly and evenly, demonstrating the grace and restrained power that were innate to who she was. Serena eyed her enviously. Despite being in Jessira's presence almost every day for months on end, she still found the woman intimidating. Serena had never grown used to her, to her confidence, or her sense of unrelenting resilience.

"It was unique to me," Serena replied with a grin, "and William had no idea about it, either."

Jessira chuckled. "Oftentimes that's more important." They traveled in silence for a few more seconds until Jessira broke the quiet. "Why do you ride alone?"

Serena shrugged, not wanting to talk about it. "I prefer not to intrude on the happiness of others."

Jessira gestured ahead. "Is that the only reason? Are they not your friends?"

Serena didn't know how to reply, unable to truthfully answer Jessira's questions. A ripple of indefinable unease coursed through her.

"I notice you've formed deep friendships with some of the people of Lilith. In their presence, you don't hesitate to speak," Jessira said. "There are other times, though, when amongst those you don't count as friends, you fade into the background and listen only. Why is that?"

Serena didn't like the turn in conversation. She preferred not to speak of her motivations and passions. "I don't need to be the center of attention. Lien does that well enough for both of us." She smiled at her joke.

Jessira smiled in reply, and they fell again into silence. They pedaled on, passing vineyards and orchards as twilight's glory splashed across the sky.

Despite the late hour, farmers still worked their fields, finishing the last of their chores and tipping their hats as the Greens rode past. Serena nodded to those she didn't know well and waved to those she counted as more than an acquaintance. On they journeyed, with shadows lengthening and darkness creeping across the farms and rolling hills of Janaki Valley. One field contained massive pumpkins that were weirdly spectral in the coming night, while another held banana trees that shook their fronds like rattles whenever a stray gust blew.

During all of this, Serena considered Jessira's question. She *did* retreat when others were around. She allowed others to direct the conversation and acted as a spectator rather than a participant. *Why is that?*

She pondered the question, and the answer she determined left her frowning. It was as William had told her long ago. Serena had paid any price that could be asked for the sins she'd committed, and yet had she truly forgiven herself?

Maybe she had, but that wasn't the same as believing she merited acceptance and fellowship. Maybe that's why she held back when others were around. She didn't believe her voice needed to be heard because she didn't feel worthy.

"My questions trouble you," Jessira said. "You need not answer them, but if you ever wish a receptive ear, you only need ask."

Serena's natural reticence reared its head, and she hesitated. This time, though, she pushed past her inhibitions and spoke up. She explained the epiphany that had come to her.

Jessira listened in silence. "Self-worth is something only you can determine," she eventually said, "but as your friend and instructor, I will say that you are worthy of all the respect and friendship you've achieved." She gestured to the other riders. "Everyone believes you can lead. You should believe it, too. Forgive yourself."

Upon hearing Jessira's words a tightness in Serena's chest, a tenseness she hadn't realized had been there, loosened. Maybe it was a good step toward her ongoing self-acceptance.

CHAPTER 19: UNEXPECTED SECRETS

*J*uly 1990

Willliam paced around the cannon and gave it a final once over, checking it out from every angle. He had to make sure he hadn't missed anything. He'd spent too much time rebuilding the cannon, and he couldn't afford to let any errors slip through the cracks. Not today. Today was too important. For the first time ever, they'd fire the cannon at full power, its first true test, and everything had to be perfect.

After a few more minutes of study, he stepped away and rubbed his chin, recalling the time spent getting to this point.

When they had first dug the cannon out from beneath the gazebo in the Village Green, William had despaired of ever repairing it. It had been little more than a pile of rubble, and the notion that the broken pieces of steel and stone they'd discovered might become a functional weapon seemed laughable.

However, luck had been with him. During his research on anchor lines, sometime before his anger had been healed, William had run across a pamphlet called *Treatises on Ranged Weapons*. Blind luck had drawn him to it. A tickle in the back of his mind had sent him questing through the library, spurring him on. At the time, he hadn't even known what it was he sought until he'd found the pamphlet. He'd discovered it lost in a dusty corner of the library, but from the moment he first held it, he could tell it was important and that his search was over.

Later on, he found out that the pamphlet had once been a famous book, a translation of a more ancient text, but no one had bothered reading it in decades. Why would they? In all the long millennia of Arylyn's existence, the island had never been attacked, and the slim book had literally been written in Greek. Thankfully, Mr. Zeus had been able to help with the translation. They learned the basic tenets of how the ancient cannons had operated, including a helpful series of prints detailing how to build or repair one. Through the work and dedication of a number of skilled craftsmen, they'd managed to bring the cannon back to life.

Now here it stood, next to the shores of Lilith Bay and placed atop a wooden platform large enough to hold the eight people who would hopefully witness the weapon's first true firing. William, Ward Silver, Mr. Zeus, Rukh, and Jessira—all of whom had been instrumental in either shaping the barrel or helping interpret the text—and a few members of the Village Council, Mayor Care, Bar Duba, and Lucas Shaw.

William couldn't help noticing that the councilors—today was the first time they'd seen it—viewed the weapon with antipathy. It was an understandable reaction, since the cannon didn't inspire much confidence on first inspection. It consisted of a short, black, marble barrel squatting between two heavy, steel-shod wagon wheels with a wheel-crank attached to a gear to allow for adjustment of the weapon's elevation. In fact, more than anything the cannon reminded William of a toad with its mouth stuck open.

There was also a cluster of stacked, marble platters near the cannon. Each one was nearly the same diameter as the barrel's basket-ball-sized opening, and each one was a special type of *nomasra*.

Now for the big test. William offered a silent prayer for their success and watched as Mayor Care stepped carefully around the weapon, apparently studying it.

She came to a stop and addressed William. "I wasn't present during the meetings when the weapon was reconstructed. Explain to me how it works."

William moved to the front of the cannon. "You load a shell into the muzzle. Right now all we have are these platter-types," he pointed to the frisbee-shaped shells stacked in front of the cannon, "but we might be able to invent other kinds in the future."

Lucas Shaw tapped the barrel. "Why did you make it out of marble? Would steel not work better?"

William answered. "According to the book we used, *Treatises of Ranged Weapons*, steel might be a better long-term solution, but for what we need marble will do just fine."

"And why not use black-powder cannon like I mentioned earlier?" Lucas asked. "I know the metallurgy might be beyond us, but not for those from the Far Beyond. We could have simply purchased what we need from them. Would that not have made more sense, since that design is essentially perfected?"

Jessira looked up from where she'd been examining of the cannon. "Correct me if I'm wrong, but other than at extremely short range, I would think most *asrasins* could easily deflect nearly anything other than modern munitions."

Rukh spoke then, finishing Jessira's thought in that creepy way they had. "Even at close range, they could probably do enough to deflect the full impact of the incoming shell."

Mr. Zeus nodded. "A skilled *asrasin* could do that." He patted one of the platters. "They'd have less success with one of these."

"Why is that?" Mayor Care asked.

Ward was the one to reply. "Because the platters are *nomasras*. They can be controlled from the instant they're blasted from the cannon's mouth all the way to the target."

One of Mayor Care's eyebrows lifted. "Fascinating. How many does it take to operate one of these cannons?"

"Five," William said, "or several very powerful *asrasins*. The crew has to be skilled in all five Elements."

"The Spirit Adept is the one who controls the shell," Mr. Zeus added.

"A strange sort of cannon, is it not?" Bar Duba mused. He glanced up from his inspection of the weapon. "

William smiled. "That's because this one is unique."

"In that case, do we still call it a cannon?" Bar asked.

"It looks like one," Rukh said. "It shoots like one and damages like one, too. What else is it?"

Ward mumbled something under his breath about, "Looks like a duck, walks like a duck, quacks like a duck . . ."

"What did the ancients call them?" Lucas asked.

"*Firewagers*," Mr. Zeus answered. "A clunky name, if you ask me."

Mayor Care cleared her throat. "Why don't we have that demonstration now?"

"An excellent idea," Rukh said. "However, a word of caution. We've never fired the cannon at full power. This will be the first time we see what it can really do. Perhaps it would be best if you waited below, on the sands." He gestured. "William is the strongest one of us in Spirit. He'll control the shell. Jessira is skilled with Water. I'm best with Air. Mr. Zeus will provide Earth, and Ward will do the honors by igniting the shell with Fire."

William waited for the councilors to descend from the platform before lifting one of the marble platters. "I'm loading the cannon," he told the others as he placed a *nomasra* within the weapon's barrel. He used a large rod topped with a wide piece of wood to shove the shell all the way to the bottom of the cannon.

"Ready?" Rukh asked.

Butterflies flitted about William's belly. He took a deep breath and exhaled it, slow and controlled.

Jessira sourced her *lorethasra*, and the scent of a mineral-fresh mountain stream filled the air. She formed a braid of Water, and it gurgled across her shoulders and forearms. Next came Rukh. The smell of iron replaced the mountain stream while a hissing braid of Air twined around his chest and pulsed down his arms. Now came

Mr. Zeus, and a vanilla flavor wafted for a moment at the same time that a thick, ivy-like strand of Earth rustled around his stomach and waist. He gathered it in his hands and held it at the ready. From Ward arose the minty aroma of his *lorethasra,* followed by a sulfurous, white-hot braid of Fire that rippled around his chest.

Each braid formed by the other magi was thicker than anything William could have managed on his own. He took a final steadying breath. *Here it goes.*

He sourced his *lorethasra* and created a thick braid of Spirit. It swirled around his forehead, noosed around his throat, and swept down his arms. From there, it pooled in his hands, laying like a limp rope. He nodded his readiness. "Go!"

The other four magi united their braids upon the *nomasra* within the marble barrel. The shell lit up, easily visible through the weapon to someone who could see *lorasra.* William attached his braid of Spirit to the munition and closely watched it. The *nomasra* expanded and took on the shape of a ball. With time and practice, William knew he'd be able to transform the shell into whatever form he wanted, but for now, he'd stick with a hollow globe that would break apart on impact.

The shell glowed, filling with the power from everyone's braids, but William's Spirit locked it in place. The *nomasra* vibrated within the cannon, and the glow deepened. William knew he couldn't hold it much longer. He had to release it, or it would explode in the barrel.

He thinned his braid, and the shell erupted out of the cannon with a thunderous boom. The explosion rumbled through William's stomach and rocked him. Nevertheless, he maintained his balance and his connection to the *nomasra.* He directed its movement and shape with his thread of Spirit.

In the midst of its flight, he transformed the marble ball into an arrow and sent it shooting skyward. At the peak of its arc, he transitioned the *nomasra* into a ball and juked it right and left. The shell lost power and speed the farther it traveled. It also became more difficult to control. William sent the munition toward the water, and when it was only yards above the waves, he clipped his thread of Spirit. The *nomasra* struck the ocean with a dull plop. A second later, a plume of water blasted twenty feet into the air.

"My God," Mayor Care whispered, sounding appalled and impressed at the same time.

William silently echoed her sentiments. Nausea filled his gorge when he considered having to use such a weapon against flesh-and-bone foes. Nevertheless, he was also proud of the work he and everyone else had done.

"A terrible weapon, but necessary," Rukh said. He faced William. "Can we miniaturize them to use as rifles?"

"We could," William said, "but only a *thera'asra* would be able to use something like that."

Rukh's mouth thinned, and he nodded in understanding. "Of course. Because only someone able to strongly and simultaneously wield every Element could power it." His brow furrowed, and he studied the cannon. "We need thirty of them ready in two months, along with crews trained to use them."

William silently swore at the amount of work he'd have to put in to meet Rukh's request.

~

Adam's Spirit traveled once more to Seminal, and upon his arrival, he slowly drifted toward Shet's palace. It was a fortress now, built onto the ledges of the same titanic mountain that he remembered from his previous visits, the one that dominated all the other peaks surrounding it. Halfway up the slope rose the bones of the citadel proper. The fortress' tall towers and walls melded perfectly with the menace of the mountain on which it perched, ascending in jagged climbs and flanking a ribbon of road that snaked upward from a grim, shadowed valley. Down there, where the very sunlight seemed afraid to penetrate, the fortifications continued with many parts likely burrowed deep into the bones of the mountain.

Adam scowled. He didn't want to be here, even in Spirit only, facing the bleak citadel that gave the appearance of swallowing the light, that carved darkness into the heart of the world like a black, gangrenous cancer. This terrible place was the home of Sinskrill's so-called god, the one who intended to return to Earth. The being who promised to bring his rule to Adam's home. He shivered at the notion.

An instant later, he forced discipline to his thoughts. Such traitorous musings couldn't be allowed. At least not here. They'd be reflected on his face and in his voice.

Adam clenched his figurative jaws and girded his loins. *Report to Shet, allow no fear to show, and then leave. That's all I need to do. Anything else can wait for tomorrow.*

He descended to an open courtyard where, on the far side, Shet reclined upon a throne made from the jaws of a dragon. A black spear lay across his lap, and his presence, his power, dwarfed everything around him. All the proud necrosed, elegant vampires, and black-eyed demons collected in the courtyard huddled timidly in comparison. Even the red dragon slumbering beside Shet's throne, with his massive, horned head resting on his clawed forearms, didn't come close to approaching the lord's power or his puzzling sense of charisma and menace.

The monsters spread out from Shet in arcs of importance, and they turned as one when Adam alighted. He scanned them. Closest to the throne were the demons, followed by the necrosed, and then the vampires. Hovering on the fringes of the court were gray ghouls wearing tattered clothing, and at the very periphery of Shet's orbit were the scourskins, vermin who did nothing more than feed on *therasra.*

Adam steeled his spine and marched through the courtyard of horrors. Terror lined his stomach as hissed promises of violence whispered to him from the various monstrosities. He did his best to hide his fear and display nothing but resolve. He strode forward and finally reached the dais. There, he fell to a knee.

"Rise," Shet commanded, "and tell me news of my home."

Adam relayed what Brandon had learned. "In addition," he said, "we learned the names of the World Killers. Rukh and Jessira Shektan."

"Rukh and Jessira Shektan." Shet seemed to taste the names. "I know not these two, only what I have gleaned regarding their nature."

"Yes, my Lord," Adam said. "We will incinerate them and all of Arylyn in your honor."

Shet smiled. "I'm sure you will try, but what will I do when I come home if my great enemies are already defeated?"

Adam blinked, uncertain how to respond. "Will you not rule the mahavans, your people?"

Shet nodded, and the smile flittered away. "Of course, but though I will soon come to reclaim my birth world—two years hence—matters on Seminal require my attention. Those who dared claim Seminal for their own during my long sojourn, resist my guidance."

Adam couldn't help it. His curiosity was piqued. "Shokan and the Lady of Fire are dead, and the World Breakers are on Earth. Who else dares contend with you?"

"Those who will beg me for death," Shet promised. "The Holy Seven, my greatest titans, shall be unleashed, their power fully unchained. They will bring ruin upon my foes. None shall be spared."

Adam dared again to question the lord. "Who can chain the Holy Seven?" An instant later he cursed his boldness and waited with bated breath, certain Shet would punish him for his temerity. Axel would have.

The lord surprised him, however. Instead of smiting him, Shet deigned to answer the question. "Long ago, my Holy Seven were placed in an endless sleep by the Orbs of Peace, creations of my greatest enemy." His grim visage caused Adam to involuntarily shiver. "In time, there arose others upon Seminal who falsely named themselves gods. They still think to rule this world, daring to defy my might and my law." His voice throbbed, tolling like a bell and gaining power. "But I am the restless tide, vast and endless, and I will wear away the will of my foes."

Adam took in the figure of Shet, the power of the being, as evident as a thundering cataract. He understood then why the god was worshipped. A part of him wanted to do so as well.

Right then, a large figure—taller than Travail, nearly the size of Shet—heavily muscled and wearing only a kilt and a set of broadswords on his back, thrust past the gathered monsters and crashed to a halt next to Adam. He did not kneel and spoke without being given permission. His voice sounded deep and rumbling, like distant thunder. "The human wishes to speak with you," the figure announced. "Again."

Adam stared at the thick-thewed monstrosity. He knew him only by description but there could be no mistaking that face, the scar that ran from the corner of his mouth to his collarbone, the ghost-white, short-cropped hair that stood in stark contrast to his ebony-dark skin: Sture Mael, a figure out of legend, much like Shet himself, one of the Holy Seven.

"Our time is ended," Shet said to Adam. "Leave us."

Adam bowed low.

"Before you depart," Shet said, "how goes the construction of the firewagers? I told your Servitor how to build them when last he visited us."

"We work to create that which you taught us. It will not be long now."

Shet wore a sly smile. "That is good. Be off now."

Adam bowed low once again and ascended straight off the court-yard. He didn't think he could stomach another passage through the corridor of horrors. As he rose he saw a figure in white approach Shet, a knight. He'd seen the man during a previous visit, the last one, in fact. The warrior marched forward confidently and untroubled, smooth and with no wasted motion. Elegant as a jaguar. Though Shet and Sture towered above him, they did not dominate him.

Adam wondered who the knight could be. *What kind of man can face both Shet and Sture and remain unbowed?*

~

The man known as Cinder Shade remained on one knee before Lord Shet, who sat on his white throne on a black dais. Sture Mael loomed nearby, his posture threatening, but Cinder paid him no mind. Shet's lieutenant wouldn't dare touch him.

"Rise," Shet intoned.

Cinder rose to his feet and met the Lord's gaze. Unlike the Spirit of Adam Paradiso, a man Cinder had once known, he didn't tremble in terror when facing Shet. In fact, no emotions marred Cinder's equilibrium. For now, Shet could destroy him, but it wouldn't always be the case. The time when Cinder could stand against the Lord would come soon.

"The human grows bold," Sture growled.

Cinder twisted his head to stare at Shet's greatest lieutenant and flicked him an appraising glance up and down. He took in Sture's dark skin, his short, white hair, and the brutal scar running from the corner of his mouth to his collarbone. He remembered delivering that scar. It had been years ago, centuries or even millennia. It was a flicker of memory, fleeting and fast, come and gone so quickly that Cinder couldn't determine if it was true recollection or a figment of his imagination. He sniffed once in dismissal of Sture before returning his attention to Shet.

Sture stiffened in outrage. "Bold indeed." His hand went to his massive sword. "Allow me to instruct him on the proper etiquette of humility," he begged Shet.

The monsters at Cinder's back stirred. They hissed and sought to outdo one another with promises of the cruelest deaths.

Cinder had no concern for their reactions. Fear had no place in his heart. It never had, not even in his childhood. It had always been thus. From his earliest memories, few emotions had ever plagued Cinder. He had been a formless husk, a boy discovered in the elven forests with no memory of himself.

Shet chuckled. "Set aside your anger," he told Sture. He leaned forward in his throne. "What news do you bring, slave?"

Cinder didn't allow the insult to touch him. In many ways, the description was apt. He *was* a slave. All humans born in the elven forests were branded as such.

"Anya and I have discovered another Orb," Cinder said.

Shet steepled his fingers. "Where is it? I don't sense it upon your being."

Cinder kept his words smooth and even. "The spiderkin possess it. They hold it deep in the heart of their mountains."

Shet grimaced. "I share the mountains with those vermin." He gestured around him to the peaks rising on all sides of his citadel.

"The Dagger Mountains are mine, but the spiderkin refuse to accept my authority. They will pay."

"Only after we destroy all the Orbs," Cinder said to the so-called god. "Until then, you can't move against them. You lack the power."

Sture snarled inarticulately in outrage, and the vampires and necrosed surged.

Shet held up a hand, holding his monsters and lieutenant in abeyance while his face emptied of emotion. Cinder sensed him gather his *lorethasra* as the scent of gardenias filled the air. "Be very careful of your next words." The Lord held a blistering braid of Fire, one that could melt a mountain.

Cinder tilted his head in acknowledgment. "I meant no insult. I merely speak truthful advice, doing as you instructed in your holy book." He quoted from *Shet's Council*. "*Fear not to speak the truth. Your true friends will always hear your words.*"

Shet offered a crooked grin, one full of malice. "You think me a friend?"

This time, Cinder did choose his words carefully. "I think only a fool would ever lie to you."

"All too true." Shet grunted. He let go of his braid, and Cinder breathed out a sigh of relief. "How do you and your elf princess plan on obtaining the Orb?"

Cinder smiled. "I was trained to fight the spiderkin." he reminded the god.

Shet smiled in return. "Ah, yes. Your training in the Third Directorate."

Like all denizens of the elven forests, Cinder had been tested in the spring of his thirteenth year. It had been a sunny day, cool and windy, when his life had forever changed. With his testing, when he'd died and been reborn, the elves had learned that Cinder could bond to metal, a rare talent for any, especially a human.

He'd immediately been inducted into the Third Directorate, the brutal school that forged boys into warriors and children into unflinching killers. The elves required graduates from their accursed place of blood and sorrow to battle in their endless wars against the spiderkin, the eight-legged monstrosities who, every year, spread farther and farther from the Dagger Mountains. They'd all but wiped out the vampires in their high halls of stone and blood and now threatened the elven forests.

Of course, Cinder's skill wasn't through his own work alone. A large part of it was through the work of Anya, a scandalous elven princess who had taken what some might call an indecorous interest in him. Anya had opened Cinder's mind to the truth, helping him recover the memories of who he'd once been, including their shared, ancient past. She'd lit a fierce desire for freedom in Cinder's heart.

He'd achieved it. *Freedom.* All because of Anya, a woman he knew and loved from long before this world or his current life. That same ancient past of who he truly was drove Cinder. He was free of the elves, but not of his duty. *Dharma* drove him, as unrelenting as any taskmaster, and Cinder would have it no other way. He had never been able to shut his eyes to the world's evils, especially the promised despotism of this ancient foe.

Sture snorted in derision. "I know not why you require this human scum. I could accomplish the same as he in half the time. Let me serve in his place," he pleaded to Shet.

Cinder didn't bother replying. He could take Sture, and Shet likely knew it as well. In the cold halls of the Third Directorate, the elves sought to forge the world's finest warriors and have them serve in mindless compliance. In Cinder they'd found one they thought a genius. Under elven tutelage, he'd become the finest swordsman to ever graduate the Third Directorate. He more than matched any elf in speed—never before seen in a human—and easily bested their strength. Even noble elves knew better than to challenge Cinder.

Sture would last longer, but in the end, he'd still die. And he'd certainly not survive the spiderkin, not without a Blend.

Shet shook his head at the titan's declaration. "I will not waste you when a worthless human can do the task."

A wise, face-saving decision.

Shet rapped his steel-shod spear against the floor of the dais, and Cinder recalled his attention to the so-called god.

"You will attend our needs and recover the Orb held by the spiderkin," Shet declared.

"As you command," Cinder said. He bowed again, but kept his gaze centered upon Shet's visage. While he feared no man or creature, only a fool broke the gaze of a viper. And the man known as Cinder Shade, the man who more properly knew himself as Rukh Shektan, was no fool.

CHAPTER 20: DEATH APPROACHES LOVE

July 1990

Jake wiped his hands on his pants and went so far as to use a tendril of Air to dry them. The last thing he wanted on his first date in years was to gross the girl out with sweaty palms. *Check the breath.* He exhaled into his hands. *Good to go.*

Jake rolled his shoulders and readied himself. He approached the front door of the Logan family bungalow. Their house, a gray, single-story structure on Cliff Earth, faced west, and it reminded Jake of an American Craftsman-style home. Butterflies and bees flitted about the flowering bushes lining the steps rising to the wraparound porch and front door. Potted jasmines perfumed the air while a trade wind brought relief from the late-day heat beating down. Sunbeams slanted onto the stairs and front porch, and left the area baking like an oven.

Jake swiped his palms one last time, took a deep breath, and blew it out hard and fast. *Here it goes.*

He lifted a fist and rapped on the front door.

Several seconds later, Daniella Logan answered the door. "Hi," she said with a warm smile. Some of Jake's nerves settled. "Thanks again for asking me out."

"You're welcome." Jake smiled back at her, the way he did in the Far Beyond when he could melt the heart of any girl. "You look great."

Daniella's smile broadened, and she stepped outside. She wore a light-blue, spaghetti-strapped dress that had a similar hue to her startling, light-colored eyes and contrasted well with her brown skin. Jake also liked the way her long, dark hair framed her face. He hadn't noticed the scattering of freckles on her nose until now. They were cute.

"Thank you. That's sweet of you to say," Daniella said with an easy grin. "Where are we going for dinner?"

"Jimmy Webster's," Jake answered. William had suggested it, and since Jake couldn't do much more than make peanut butter and jelly sandwiches, it sounded like a great idea. Plus, he'd eaten at Jimmy's a few times, and he reckoned it was a great place to take a girl on a date. Even William said so.

An instant later, Jake scoffed. *When did I start taking dating advice from William?*

"Are you ready?"

Daniella nodded. She held a sheer, gray shawl and wrapped it around her shoulders before they set off.

It wasn't a long walk, only a single set of stairs to reach Clifftop. Once there, Jake took a moment to get his bearings. Clusters of people wandered about with bags of fruits and vegetables in hand. They'd likely been to the recently closed farmer's market. Some were accompanied by small bears, lions, tigers, or dogs on leashes as they headed home.

"This way." Daniella pointed to a shadowed alley. "We won't have to deal with all the traffic from the farmer's market."

Jake smiled at the notion of traffic in Lilith. In the Far Beyond, this would have been considering nothing more than a scattering of people.

He followed Daniella through the alley, and minutes later they reached Jimmy Webster's restaurant. "I'm hungry," Jake declared. He immediately wanted to slap himself. *When did I forget how to talk to women?* He'd obviously been spending too much time hanging around William and Jason.

Daniella laughed. "Then it's a good thing we won't have eat whatever you would've tried to make."

Jake blinked. An instant later understanding came. "Who told you about my cooking?"

"William," Daniella said. "He said you have trouble making toast."

Jake chuckled as he privately vowed to pay William back for his stupidity. A guy was supposed to talk up his friends to girls, not run them down. Still, he shoved aside his annoyance and held the door open for Daniella.

A single, wide room held five blocky, rough-hewn tables and matching chairs. All of them contained a black sheen in the dim light. A set of wall lamps and a single candle rested in tall vases on each table, providing the illumination.

Jimmy, a hefty, balding man wearing a stained, white apron, came out of the kitchen. He could have passed as Mel from the old TV show *Alice.* "Have a seat," he said. "I'll be with you in a bit."

Jake led the way to an empty table and noticed a few other couples already there. He nodded greetings to them and held out a chair for Daniella.

"How very chivalrous," she said.

Jake smiled. "Three summers taking cotillion classes."

"Cotillion classes?" Daniella's eyes seemed to smile whenever her lips curled upward, and her entire face lit up. "Whose idea was that?"

"My dad. He insisted on them. I hated it."

"He did you a favor."

A sudden pang to see his family again fleetingly surged, but Jake suppressed the sensation. He didn't want to think about the past tonight. Tonight was about the future.

"Yes, he did," he said in agreement. "But you know, four or five years ago, I thought my parents were the biggest imbeciles this side of that blonde girl from *Three's Company.*"

Daniella's brow creased in confusion. "What's *Three's Company?*"

"That's right. You grew up without TV. It was a show from back home, and one of the characters was a ditzy blonde." *Suzanne Somers.* Like a lot of guys his age, Jake had once had a crush on her. "Anyway, I thought my parents were idiots, but the thing is—," he quirked a grin, "—they've wised up as the years have gone by."

Daniella took a moment to parse his words, and her reaction was everything Jake could have hoped for. She threw her head back and laughed, a sound like chimes ringing. "I like that." Her eyes sparkled. "Wait until I tell Karla." After a moment, speculation took the place of her humor. "Can I ask you something?"

Jake shrugged. "Sure."

"Why did you ask me out?"

Jake's brows furrowed. "What do you mean?"

"I mean exactly that. Why did you ask me out? You've been on Arylyn for almost three years, and in all this time you've never asked a single girl out on a date."

Jake better understood what she wanted to know, but he wasn't sure he wanted to explain it to her. It was too complicated. How would she react if she found out that he'd spent the past few years wishing he could leave Arylyn and never return? He doubted she would understand. Then again, he didn't want to lie to her.

Before he could answer, Daniella surprised him by placing one of her hands over one of his. "I didn't mean to make you uncomfortable."

"You didn't."

"That faraway, troubled look you had on your face says otherwise."

"You didn't make me uncomfortable," Jake said. *Not much, anyway.* "But the answer isn't something I like to talk about. It hits too close to home."

Daniella nodded understanding and gave his hand a squeeze. "Well, if you ever need to tell me why, at least you know where I live."

Jake appreciated the sentiment although he knew he'd never take her up on her offer. As he figured things, a guy who blubbered all his problems to a girl he was interested in wasn't much of a guy. "Maybe I'll take you up on that," he said and waited a beat. "If we're only going to be friends."

Daniella chuckled at his response, and Jake discovered something else. He liked making her laugh.

~

S erena twisted about in front of the full-length mirror in her bedroom as she checked her appearance one last time. Her blue, sleeveless dress remained unwrinkled and fit her perfectly. Reed Stephens, the owner and tailor at *Seville Sew*, had done his usual impeccable work, and she reminded herself to thank him again.

"You look beautiful," Selene said. Her little sister lay belly down on Serena's bed and her coltish legs paddled back and forth. The childish demeanor was ruined by the all-too-knowing grin on her young face. "I'm sure William will love it."

Serena threw a t-shirt at Selene and missed.

Her sister pealed laughter, and the sounds drew Fiona into the bedroom as well. Their grandmother—it still struck Serena as odd to call the old *raha'asra* by such an honorific—leaned against the door and offered a pleased smile. "You look lovely."

"Thank you," Serena said, unsure why Fiona appeared so self-satisfied. She noticed the clock and cursed under her breath.

"Are you going to kiss William with that mouth?" Selene asked.

"Brat," Serena replied. She slipped on a pair of toeless sandals. "I'm going to be late. Bye."

"We won't wait up for you," Selene shouted as Serena dashed out the front door.

She grimaced at her sister's parting words but quickly set aside her irritation. For the first time in months, she and William would have dinner alone together. Just the two of them. No one else. Between her hours working at Sile Troy's farm and William's laboring on the cannon, they hardly ever saw one another except when training with the Irregulars. *But not tonight.*

Tonight, William had asked her to have dinner with him. It would be at Mr. Zeus' house, but all the other men would be out. Of course, William had said that he'd do the cooking, and Serena wasn't sure about that. William wasn't exactly a fine chef. Still, as they said in the Far Beyond, it was the thought that counted.

Serena stepped quickly along the path leading through the patch of jungle that hid her beach cottage. She glanced at the darkening sky, briefly seen through the thick canopy, and cursed again. She was definitely going to be late. She cursed further when sweat beaded on her forehead. As usual, the jungle air was proving humid, heavy, and uncomfortable.

Serena sourced her *lorethasra* and linked a thread of Air to the surrounding *lorasra*. The braid she created swiftly whisked away the perspiration. *Better.* She didn't care that the weave might be considered wasteful. There was no chance she would show up to dinner covered in sweat.

Seconds later, she broke through the jungle and reached Lilith Bay. Immediately, the air cooled as a breeze blew briskly. Serena put a hand on her hair to keep it from coming undone from its braid and turning into a mess. She'd spent too much time getting it just right, and she kept her hand on her hair all the way along Lilith Bay's perimeter. She only let it go when she reached the silvery-stoned Guanyin Bridge. There, the wind faded, and a mineral scent replaced the briny smell of the ocean.

As she crossed the bridge, Serena peered down the canyon where River Namaste recollected near the base of Lilith's cliffs and traveled north. The waters surged through a broad, high-walled, moss-covered canyon carved with titanic figures from Arylyn's mythic history. A disquiet crowded Serena's mind whenever she viewed the statues. The carvings wore bleak, judging faces, even the ones who smiled, and she never felt worthy of their regard.

The wind moaned through the canyon like a dying man, a grim sort of omen as Serena reckoned matters. She shuddered and hustled on her way, thankfully managing to throw off her unsettled thoughts when she reached the crushed-gravel path leading to the Main Stairs. Cool, unthreatening stars twinkled in the sky above, and she knew a crescent moon would eventually rise, but not for a few more hours.

On reaching the Main Stairs of Cliff Spirit, Serena slowed her pace. Besides not wanting to sweat, she didn't want to be gasping like a fish out of water when she met William.

After ascending approximately two hundred steps, she reached William's terrace on Cliff Spirit and took the stone pathway that edged it. A similar walkway could be found on all of Lilith's various terraces, and in this case houses rose to her right while a steep, fenced drop-off fell to her left. Serena quickly made her way along the path until she reached William's front door. She hesitated then as unexpected anxiety filled her stomach.

She chided herself. *It's only William.*

Serena took a few steadying breaths and leaned on her Sinskrill training. Her nervousness faded and her heart-rate slowed. She eventually managed a sly smile, the one William liked when he thought she secretly found the world amusing.

Now, she was ready.

Serena knocked on the door. Seconds later William stood in the doorway.

She involuntary inhaled in appreciation as she took in his clothes and presence. He wore gray slacks, a white, buttoned-up, short-sleeve shirt, and black shoes, but it wasn't the clothes that took her aback. It was everything else. She'd grown used to seeing William as a disheveled mess, but here he stood, neat and tidy. He'd trimmed his unkempt mop of hair into something short and stylish and shaved his perpetually scruffy face.

Serena had forgotten how handsome he could be.

"You look good," he said. He blushed the moment the words left his mouth.

Serena smiled wider. In the past, she'd used William's obvious admiration of her appearance as a means to influence and control him. She'd never do so again. After the worst of betrayals she'd spent the last two-and-a-half years re-earning William's trust through honesty. It felt good to have a friendship based on truth rather than lies.

"You clean up pretty well, too," Serena said, which was an understatement as far as she was concerned.

"Thanks." William wore a pleased smile. "Come on in." He ushered her into the house. "We're eating in the courtyard, if that's all right."

"Absolutely." A wonderful aroma wafted from the kitchen. "What did you make? It smells delicious."

William grinned. "Butter chicken. It's Indian. Sort of like me."

Serena eyed him doubtfully. "You're not Indian."

"Yeah, but my mom's family was originally from there. I like to think that makes me an honorary one."

Serena chuckled as they passed through the kitchen and dining area into the courtyard in the back. William had hung a number of candles from the jasmine-wreathed pergola and placed a few of them floating upon the small pond formed by the waterfall trickling down the cliff face at the property's rear. Orange and mango trees, ginger plants, red-hearted anthurium, weeping medinilla, and broad canna bordered the water. A strip of grass and a flagstone patio with an unlit firepit and several chairs filled out the space.

William led her to the pergola, where he'd set out the butter chicken along with naan, rice biryani, spiced, roasted okra, and creamy spinach.

Serena whistled in appreciation. "When did you learn to cook like this?" *If the food tastes half as good as it smells . . .*

"Today," William said. "Mr. Zeus talked me through all the recipes." He surprised her then by drawing out a chair for her.

"You didn't have to do that," Serena said.

William grinned. "Consider it part of my Southern charm."

"I thought you were Indian," Serena teased.

"I am, but I was also partly raised in North Carolina," William reminded her. A hint of his southern drawl, something not always noticed, became evident with his last words.

Serena smelled the scent of pine when William sourced his *lorethasra* and lit a tall candle sitting upon the table. While he created his small braid, a thought came to her. She sourced her *lorethasra* and reached for William's Spirit with a thread of her own.

"What are you doing?" he asked. His voice carried nothing more than curiosity, no suspicion.

When their Spirits touched, William didn't draw away. As on the previous occasions when they'd done this, their rare connection—the bridge between their thoughts—took shape.

"What are you doing?" William asked again.

Serena didn't answer. She focused on William's heart, on his thoughts, and knew he did the same. She sensed his friendship for her, the joy he felt when she was around, the kindness he saw in her, his admiration for who she'd become, She smiled at the notion that he thought he needed to be worthy of her friendship. *He doesn't. It's the other way around.* And nowhere did she find that poisonous anger spurred by Sapient Dormant's call. She also felt William's regret for how long it had taken him to forgive her.

"That wasn't your fault," she said, knowing he'd understand what she meant.

"It was," he said.

She pressed a finger to his mouth. "There was blame enough for both of us."

~

B randon's eyes widened in amazement when the Servitor sourced his *lorethasra*. Such depth of power. Vast and endless.

A traitorous notion came to him. *How, then, had the Servitor been defeated?* Brandon shook off the worrying question.

"Observe," the Servitor ordered. "The idea to build these weapons originated as all great things do, with Lord Shet, but we've modified his original concept to suit our purposes and abilities."

Brandon waited alongside a number of mahavans, including Preeti, Samuel, and Evelyn, upon a ledge of stone that protruded off a broad cliff looming above the Norwegian Sea.

Evelyn shifted about in clear discomfort. She sported a fresh crop of bruises on her face. Since their return to Sinskrill a week ago, she'd been daily punished and healed for what she'd done on Arylyn. At one time the punishment might have been harsher, up to and including stripping, but Sinskrill needed all its warriors, including the incompetent ones.

Brandon watched about as the Servitor prepared his weapon.

The whitewashed Palace gleamed behind him while on every other side rose an evergreen forest. Everywhere except below the ledge where Brandon and the others waited. There, the docks squatted, and gulls cried harshly at fisherman who had laid out their day's catch. Thankfully, a stern wind blew from the surrounding hills and dispersed the stench of the haul. Rare sunshine breached the clouds, enlivening the afternoon as the light glistened off the indigo waters of the Norwegian Sea. However, the vibrant color only extended as far as the border of the *saha'asra,* transitioning at that point into a dull gray. The day's brightness offered little in the way of warmth. This was Sinskrill, after all.

A hard gust blew then, as if to reinforce Brandon's observations, and he shivered. He'd been too long on Arylyn, too long within her warmth and beauty.

He mentally scowled at the notion. Arylyn's beauty represented everything a mahavan hated, an easy, soft life. Weak.

Brandon shook off his wandering thoughts and returned his attention to the reason why they were here, a so-called *firewager.* It resembled a cannon, long-barreled, squat, and ugly. During Brandon's scouting mission to Arylyn, the Servitor had apparently developed and perfected this weapon. Somehow it would help the mahavans destroy the magi.

Brandon didn't see how that was possible. Lilith had seven times Sinskrill's population and every one of the magi could wield their *lorethasra.* Only three hundred of Sinskrill's one thousand could make the same claim.

Who am I to question the Servitor?

"Observe the ship in the harbor," the Servitor commanded, "as I ready the firewager."

Brandon did as instructed and studied the boat floating listlessly in the harbor. *Had it been abandoned?* A second later, his eyes widened in amazement when the Servitor created a weave to power the *firewager.* The control required astounded him, and awe once more rose in his heart. *No one can defeat the Servitor.*

Again came the traitorous voice whispering in his mind. *And yet the Servitor has been defeated. He was defeated by those two magi who also twice destroyed Adam Paradiso's mahavans. The World Killers. Who are they, really?*

Brandon didn't know, but he'd glimpsed them on Arylyn. He'd wanted to watch them for far longer, but somehow the woman, Jessira, had sensed his regard. When Brandon and his mahavans had initially hunkered down to study her, nothing had seemed amiss. A moment later, Jessira had stiffened and sent her gaze questing. She'd worn a frown, and even from the distance where he lay hidden Brandon could tell she was searching for them.

He and the others had quickly slunk away, moving before she or her husband, Rukh, the deadly warrior who moved with a sublime grace, found them.

Brandon's attention returned to the cannon when Adam Paradiso, the Secondus, pressed a round stone into its barrel.

"This is the shell," Adam announced, "a type of *nomasra*."

He shoved the ball farther into the barrel with a wooden rod, grunting in satisfaction. The Servitor leaned forward and thick braids of Fire, Earth, Water, and Air poured off his hands and into the stone. Next he created a braid of Spirit, white as bone and shining with dark flecks, and attached it to the ball. "Prepare to witness history," he intoned.

The ball of stone Adam had placed within the cannon began to glow and growl. It gave off a low-pitched snarl, like a pack of ferocious wolves. The sound increased in intensity, howling now. An unexpected boom shattered the air, and Brandon started, nearly pitching into Evelyn.

The shell exploded out of the mouth of the cannon, white-hot and raging. It arched skyward, trailing light and twisting right and left.

Brandon blinked, uncertain he'd seen the unnatural movement. Again the shell juked, proving it hadn't been his imagination. It corkscrewed as it descended, spiraling until it slammed into the boat floating in the harbor. Wood exploded in all directions. The boat blasted apart like a toy smashed by a blacksmith's hammer.

Brandon gaped in shock.

Evelyn was ecstatic, reverential. "We're going to crush the magi," she said with a triumphant laugh as she softly clapped her hands.

The Servitor exulted. "Now you see how we will destroy our ancient foes once and for all. When Shet returns he will find his people have not forgotten what it means to bring war and conquer!"

The mahavans continued to clap in delirious joy, and Brandon joined them. However, the traitorous voice in his mind wondered if destroying the magi was a good thing. In his heart of hearts, he'd liked the peace of Arylyn.

The Servitor held up his hands, calling for quiet. "This is only the first of my *firewagers*," he said. "This one will be placed aboard my own ship, *Demolition*, but we will have many more. With them we'll destroy the magi and their cursed island!"

CHAPTER 21: DECISIONS LAUNCHED

A*ugust 1990*

Adam kept pace beside his brother as they strode along Village White Sun's pier and surveyed the preparations underway for the coming attack. They still had much to accomplish but at least they'd finally collected enough ships. The vessels, all of them large, bobbed in Village White Sun's harbor. Most possessed towering masts, sails stowed on yardarms, and had the lean carriage of modern vessels, which made sense since they'd been stolen from docks as far away as England.

The Servitor had wisely decided against using only sailing ships when motorized yachts would do far better. Of course *Demolition*, the Servitor's ship, had no engine, but she could easily keep up with the modern vessels. With her wealth of sails and Axel to power her, she'd be a match for any ship on the sea.

Drones and even mahavans bent under the weight of crates and barrels, lowering them into waiting boats or carrying them up gangways to be stowed in the rapidly-filling holds of the impromptu war

WILLIAM WILDE AND THE SONS OF DECEIT

fleet. Shouted orders and questions added to the milling confusion as preparations to weigh anchor neared completion.

Adam tugged his cloak closer when a bitter gust flapped. The wind carried the scent of brine and fish and set the vessels rocking in their berths. The clatter of ropes smacking masts echoed as dreary clouds scudded across the sky. Typical Sinskrill weather.

He ignored the cold. Mahavans didn't display weakness.

"We leave in a week," Axel said.

Adam hid a quiver of worry. *Is attacking Arylyn our only course of action?* He didn't think so, but he also ensured that his lack of enthusiasm for Axel's plan never showed on his face or demeanor. Rather, he nodded in self-assurance, trying to figure out a way to bring up his doubts in a manner that wouldn't trigger his brother's fury.

"I would still prefer we take more mahavans," he stated.

The Servitor gestured and formed a bubble of Air about them. "You know why we can't. We only have three hundred trained mahavans, and we have to leave some behind to oversee the drones." He quirked a grin. "While the master is away, the mice will laze the day away."

Adam didn't find the old aphorism humorous. "If we wait but one more year, even six months, we'll have up to another five hundred ready. Our chances for success would be significantly improved."

Axel sighed. "Time is not on our side. You know this as well as I. We made a promise to Shet. We vowed to defeat Arylyn by the end of this year. Do you really wish to tell him otherwise at this late hour?"

Adam shook his head and silently wished they could tell Shet something else, something crude.

"Our plans are laid and determined," Axel continued. "You'll take two hundred mahavans and land upon the island and raze everything you come across. Meanwhile, the fifty under my command will level the magi village with our *firewagers*—"

"Cannons," Adam said, daring to interrupt his brother. "*Firewagers* might be what Shet calls them, but we all know what they look like."

Axel chuckled. "*Firewagers* is a rather stupid name, isn't it?"

Adam laughed with his brother. It felt good to do so, such a rare occurrence. "Consider who named them."

Axel laughed louder. "Yes," he agreed. "If not for his power, we would never bend knee to Shet or anyone."

His words stirred a longing within Adam, one he couldn't suppress. "Why must we then?" he asked. "Is there no way to ally with the World Killers and—"

Axel made a chopping motion. "We've discussed this already as well," he said. "I took the measure of these supposed World Killers. They are powerful, but you and I both know they would stand no chance against Shet. They cannot be our allies."

"In a frontal assault, yes," Adam agreed, "but is there no way to prevent the opening of the Seminal anchor line? Perhaps they could help us with that?"

"That knowledge is long since lost."

Adam grimaced, and his brother squeezed his shoulder. "Let it go," Axel said. "We each have our roles to play, our missions to fulfill. Only then can we hope to survive Shet's arrival."

Adam nodded agreement, although in his heart he remained rebellious.

"What about the *nomasras* that contain *lorasra*?" the Servitor asked. "How many do we have?"

"Not enough," Adam answered. "At least not enough for the number of mahavans we'll need."

"Then I'll have to make more of them," Axel said.

Early on, when Adam had been raised to his status as Secondus, he'd learned that *all* Servitors upon their ascension were granted great power. All of them were both *thera'asras* and *raha'asras.*

"I'd double the number," Adam said.

Axel grunted. "Is there anything else?"

Another troubling thought came to Adam. "What about the unformed? You're certain they'll follow my commands?"

"Absolutely," Axel said, "but I can only grant you fifty. Any more than that and I can't guarantee their loyalty."

Adam grunted in acceptance, although truthfully he'd rather *no* unformed sailed with them. Despite being one himself, he didn't trust the creatures.

Axel clapped him on the shoulder. "You worry too much. We'll destroy the magi and these Ashokan Irregulars. We'll kill them all."

Ashokan Irregulars. Adam frowned at the name. *Where have I heard that name before?*

Axel noticed. "What is it?"

The memory came to Adam, and he inhaled sharply. "*Ashokan* Irregulars. Does the name not sound overly similar to that of the Befouler, Shokan?"

Axel stroked his chin as his features went flat and unreadable, a sure sign of his concern. "Perhaps it does."

His words and reaction did nothing to allay Adam's spike of worry.

~

Jessira observed the work crews as they went about strapping the cannons into their carriages. They'd decided to place a few of them upon the lowest terraces of all the Cliffs while the rest were positioned on Clifftop. Jessira paced along the flagstones of the Village Green as the work went on, knowing her presence here was superfluous. The men and women of the work detail knew their job, and they required little oversight. However, Mr. Zeus held the opinion that the magi worked better whenever she or Rukh observed their efforts, so she remained nearby, watching the labor taking place around her. If nothing else, duty impelled her.

She smiled at the thought. It was something Rukh might have said. *He's rubbed off on me.*

Laird Reed moved to stand in front of her and interrupted her thoughts. "We're about done with the last one, ma'am." He twisted his hands and all-but bowed to her.

Jessira stilled a disappointed sigh, wishing once again that the magi would simply treat her as a woman and not an object of terror or veneration. When she and Rukh had first arrived on Arylyn, the people had given them little more than curious gazes. Unfortunately, time and events had changed the villagers' perceptions. First had come her and Rukh's rapid physical maturation. They'd largely resumed their semblances from when they'd walked the green hills of Arisa. Then had come their actions on Sinskrill and Australia, and lastly the training of the Ashokan Irregulars. Too many hard, fast changes had given the people here a distorted image of her and Rukh, a curious mix of fear and hope.

Jessira smiled at Laird, hoping the simple expression would thaw the man's frozen nervousness.

No such luck. If anything, Laird grew more disconcerted. He shifted about, tugging his hands so hard Jessira thought he'd twist them off.

She held onto the smile. "Thank you. Let me know when the work is complete and I'll examine it."

"Yes, ma'am," Laird said. This time he did bow as he stepped away.

Jessira sighed and stared westward, toward Lilith's Cliffs and the Pacific Ocean. The late morning sun gleamed on the homes and stones as clouds floated serenely in a blue sky. River Namaste tumbled in an unbridled series of misty waterfalls, making the fantastical bridges between the lush green terraces shine with rainbow iridescence.

As always whenever she considered the bridges, Jessira's eyes went to Chimera Seed. How had images of Suwraith's creatures made their way here to this other world? There could be no mistaking the Baels, Tigons, Braids, Ur-Fels, and Balants. Statues of all the Sorrow Bringer's fell creatures had been carved into the blocky, ruddy stones of the bridge.

Jessira shook her head. *A mystery for another time.*

She turned her attention to the study of Lilith itself. So lovely and elegant, it reminded her of a smaller-scale version of Rukh's home, magnificent Ashoka. That faraway city had also arisen above the shores of an ocean—the Sickle Sea—with its buildings carved onto the slopes of nine verdant hills. When Jessira had first beheld the city she had likened it to a diamond set amongst sapphires and emeralds. Rukh had gifted her with such a necklace after he'd heard her description.

More memories tumbled through her mind. She smiled as she recalled Sign, her fearless cousin, tall, strong, and proud; and Rukh's sister, Bree, with her razor-sharp intellect, humor, and enduring strength. One had been her sister-cousin and the other her sister-in-law, her *chellelu*. Both of them had been the truest sisters of her heart.

Memories of Rector Bryce came to her. He had been so upright, stiff, and judgmental. In the end, though, he had seen past his moral certitude, and it had been his final courageous grace that had allowed victory.

She also remembered Jaresh, Rukh's adopted brother. The scandal of his existence—a child raised in a Caste not of his own—had always caused him trouble, but he'd never let it slow him down. Jaresh, every bit as willful and generous as Rukh, had been Sign's equal and her husband, and they'd been blessed with lovely children.

For some reason, thinking of Jaresh reminded Jessira of William. She was glad the young man was no longer crippled by his anger.

Her smile faded as she then remembered her own children, and a tear leaked down her cheek. *What peace have they found? And what peace will Rukh and I ever have?*

~

Brandon took in the miserable morning weather and wanted to scowl. The day had dawned wet and gloomy, which meant it was a perfectly normal day for Sinskrill. Winter had yet to bite down on the island, but its harbingers—a stiff wind and a freezing rain—warned of its approach. Brandon clutched his coat more closely about himself as he stood on *Demolition's* stern and stared at Sinskrill. In the distance, mist and fog wreathed green hills that marched northward until they merged with the rugged outcroppings and mountains that towered over the island's interior. Closer at hand, puffs of smoke drifted skyward from the various barracks and houses of Village White Sun. A stray dog wandered the street and several children played in puddles. Otherwise, the village lay empty since the rest of the drones currently worked the fields, harvesting a last yield of crops to carry them through the winter.

This island was a hard land for a hard people, and Brandon had pride in having been raised here, of surviving and earning what he had. He was a mahavan of Sinskrill, an accomplishment not easily achieved, and he straightened at the thought. He would fight to stay true to who he was and what he had been born to be.

And yet . . .

The memories of golden Arylyn and her sun-kissed beaches, hills, and valleys, the glories of her fields and farms, the warm wind blowing and bringing ease to his soul . . . They weren't so easily set aside. Scouting the magi's home had given him a greater appreciation for why Serena had done as she had. While she was and always would be a traitor, part of him applauded her for escaping Sinskrill's hard life for Arylyn's soft one.

As if to punctuate the thought, another gust blew, and icy spray splashed across Brandon's face, raising a scowl.

His vague, seductive thoughts about Arylyn ended when Justin Cardinal approached. The man had once been a drone foreman, but he'd raised his hands against William and Jake, men who possessed a higher station as *raha'asras*. The man's offense had cost him, and Justin had been cast down. The punishment could have been much more severe, including death, but Shet's mercy—Brandon snorted at the ridiculous thought—as elucidated by the Servitor had instead seen the former foreman removed from his position of power.

However, after Arylyn's raid against Sinskrill last year, many of those who previously failed their Temperings were cleansed of their strippings and provided with something unprecedented in all of Sinskrill's long history, a second chance. Justin had passed his second Tempering and survived and thrived in his training as a shill and later as a bishan. Soon after, the Servitor had granted him the rank of mahavan.

Brandon bristled over this. To become a mahavan was no easy task. It was a hard-won title, a proud honorific, but with the once-drones now accorded the same name, it somehow felt sullied and less worthy.

"We're almost ready to set off," said Justin.

Brandon glanced at the deck, where a few last pieces of equipment and supplies were being loaded into the hold. He grunted acknowledgment to Justin. "Understood. As soon as the Servitor boards we'll get underway. Make sure the men on the oars are ready. We'll want to row hard and catch the natural wind as soon as possible." As a true sailing vessel, *Demolition* needed some muscle to get underway, but afterward only the wind or the Servitor's power.

"Yes, sir." Justin snapped off a sharp salute, pivoted and began shouting orders.

Brandon leaned on the railing and gazed at the other ships of the fleet. The rest were sleek, modern vessels with powerful engines to carry them forth—no oars needed for them—and all had hulls recently painted the same dark blue, even *Demolition*. While the Servitor's ship was typically black-hulled, this one time they'd changed it. They needed it to better blend with the water surrounding Arylyn.

Brandon's head rose when he sighted the Servitor marching through the streets of Village White Sun. He wore a gray shirt, white leather pants, and a black-sheathed longsword strapped to his hip.

Adam Paradiso, the Secondus, paced alongside the Servitor and wore his typical brown, leather garb of practical design. The two men had their heads bent close to one another.

Brandon didn't bother trying to listen in. As a Walker, he could have eavesdropped on anyone, but the Servitor and Adam always shielded their conversations with bubbles of Air.

Adam gave a sharp nod before breaking away from the Servitor and headed toward *Deathbringer*, his own ship.

Brandon straightened to his full height when the Servitor approached *Demolition*. Sinskrill's ruler marched across the gangplank, and Brandon moved to greet him.

"Welcome aboard, my liege," he said once the Servitor came aboard *Demolition*. "A good day to sail, is it not?"

He kept from stiffening by the barest of margins. *What foolishness! Speaking to Servitor in such an overly familiar tone.*

The Servitor eyed him in confusion. "How so?" he asked, gesturing to the miserable weather.

Brandon's heart pounded, but he managed a smile despite having to continue with what he hoped wasn't a terrible mistake. "The rain is a constant, but I like to think of it as Sinskrill's way of blessing us on our endeavor." He held his breath, hoping, praying—he wasn't sure to whom—that the Servitor would take the words as the light-hearted joke they were intended to be.

The moment stretched until suddenly the Servitor barked laughter. "So it is. At your command we will leave and meet our destiny!"

Brandon breathed relief and snapped off a salute. "Yes, my liege!" He faced the crew and bellowed orders. "Unship oars! Stroke count of twenty. I want us out of the harbor in five minutes. Pass the orders to the other ships. Have them start their engines and follow."

Oars were unshipped, a stroke count was picked up and kept by a drone with a drum, and they got underway.

Brandon stared one last time at Village White Sun, at the fog, the drizzle, and the green, mist-shrouded hills. He wondered if he'd ever see his home again.

CHAPTER 22: A PEACEFUL INTERLUDE

October 1990

Serena winced when Rukh barked instructions mere inches from her ear.

"Rack your swords," he shouted, pointing to a large, wooden tub at his feet, "and be back at three. We'll take it up again then."

Rukh and Jessira had changed things up with today's morning training session. Instead of having Red Team defend 'Lilith' against the Greens, they'd had the Irregulars sparring with wooden swords. Serena had done well—she expected no less since she'd trained with a blade since childhood—but others had not.

Ward Silver, for one. He'd taken a blow to the ribs, one that still left him in obvious discomfort despite Jessira's Healing, and he trundled alongside the rest of the Irregulars as they biked back to Lilith. He groaned. "I hate swords."

Many of the Irregulars shared his antipathy and rode quietly while others, such as Jake, Daniella, Jason, Lien, and Daniel, shared a boisterous conversation. They spoke loudly in order to be heard over the sound of the bicycle tires churning across the gray-white flagstones of Sita's Song, and Serena listened with half an ear. Most of her thoughts, though, revolved upon one notion: cool shade.

The hot, late-morning sun beamed upon all of them, and the air resembled a wet blanket. Another hot-spell lay upon Arylyn, and Serena longed for some blessed coolness. Thankfully, a downpour seemed to be in the offing. Gray clouds, heavy and pregnant, hung above the Triplets, and the wind already stirred. Occasional gusts swirled and some of them threatened to push Serena off her bicycle.

She cursed when one particularly hard blow nearly sent her careening into William. "Sorry," she muttered once she got her bicycle under control.

"It's all right," William said, sounding distracted. He had a furrowed brow and his head tilted to the side as if listening to something.

Serena grew curious. "What is it?"

"Jake's humming some song," William answered. "I know what it is but I can't place it. It's right there, and . . ." An instant later his faced cleared, and he laughed. "You nerd," he shouted at Jake.

"What?" Jake asked. He tried to maintain an innocent, inquisitive cast to his face, but Serena wasn't fooled. He knew what William was talking about.

William apparently saw through Jake's ruse as well. "I know what you're humming over there, you dork. *The Dukes of Hazzard*."

Jake's face fell while Jason guffawed. "You hick."

Lien took William's words as a reason to start a game. "If we're doing *Guess the Theme Song*, try this one." She started singing in her warbling, off-key manner.

Serena grinned. She'd never get tired of hearing Lien's terrible singing.

Jake's face clouded with disbelief. "No way," he said. "How'd you know *The Misadventures of Sheriff Lobo*?"

Lien grinned. "It was on re-runs in Cincinnati." She dropped her voice an octave. "The jungle cat is on the prowl."

"Who's the jungle cat?" Daniel asked.

"The sheriff's fat deputy," Lien answered.

"How about this one?" William began quoting something about someone named Michael Knight.

"*Knight Rider*," Jason shouted an instant before Jake.

Serena fell back, watching and listening to the others. She didn't know many of these shows or references since her time in the Far Beyond had been relatively brief.

Lien started another song.

"*BJ and the Bear*," Jason said. He shook his head at Lien. "How do you know the theme songs to all these old, goofy shows."

"Supreme talent," Lien answered.

"You mean supreme nerdiness," Jason countered. "I think Daniel's rubbed off on you."

"My turn," Jake said. He sang in his passable tenor.

William's face clouded. "Why in the hell would you know the theme to *Facts of Life*? It's about an all-girls boarding school."

Jake flushed, and his blush darkened when Daniella laughed and pinched him in the side. He eventually broke into an embarrassed chuckle.

Serena smiled. She was glad to see Jake happy, that they all could still laugh the way they used to. The theme-song guessing game continued, and she glanced to the side when William drifted to ride alongside her.

"He looks good laughing," William said, indicating Jake.

Serena agreed. "I'm glad he and Daniella are finally seeing each other. She's good for him." She pursed her lips. "Now we only need to find someone for Jason."

William's face grew guarded. "I don't think that will be nearly as easy."

Serena faced him. "Oh? Is this a secret, or am I allowed to know?"

William wore an uncertain expression, and for a moment Serena didn't think he'd answer her. "He never said to keep it private," he began, "but I think he'd rather not have us gossiping about him." He briefly eyed Jason. "Let's just say he has trust issues because of his family."

"Really?"

"Really. It was before your time, but early on he wasn't entirely comfortable with me living with him and Mr. Zeus."

"Why is that?" Serena asked. Isha had often taught that the easiest way to learn information was by asking an open-ended question. Part of Serena felt guilty for using Isha's training on William, but she was curious.

"I'm not sure," William said, "but he once said it felt like I was intruding on his space and stealing his grandfather's time." His mouth shut with a snap. "I've said enough."

"You hardly said anything," Serena said.

William changed the subject. "You know, I don't get to see Selene as much I used to. How's she doing? Other than being too busy to spend any time with me. I think the last time we talked was last week."

Serena smiled. "She's fine. She's grown much in the past year. She's almost as tall as me now, and every inch of her is know-it-all attitude and drama on a pair of giraffe legs." Serena shook her head ruefully. *Dealing with a teenage girl and her moods. How did Isha tolerate me?*

"That bad?"

Serena mock shuddered. "Be glad you aren't the one raising her."

William chuckled, but a second later his head snapped toward Jason. The others were still playing the *Guess the Theme Song* game. "I know that one," William shouted. "*The Greatest American Hero*! The best superhero show of all time."

"Only if you like dorky comedies," Jake replied.

"Says the guy who watched a show about an all-girls boarding school," William retorted.

"Try this one," Daniel said.

Serena pitied herself since she instantly knew the song and the show to which it belonged. "*Star Blazers*," she said on hearing the first three words.

Silence fell across the entire group, and Serena found herself the focus of everyone's attention.

Jason stared at her as if she'd grown an extra head. "How'd you know that?"

"I wish I didn't," Serena replied, "but Daniel forced us to watch that inane show for movie night once."

"And you call me a nerd," William said to Lien.

Serena didn't catch Lien's reply since Daniella had drifted over to join her.

"Tired of listening to them sing stuff no one else knows about?" Serena asked the other girl.

Daniella grinned. "It is fun watching them have fun, though."

Serena smiled in agreement, and she couldn't help but wonder how many more afternoons they'd have like this, silly times before Sinskrill came for them. Her eyes went to William and once more, she vowed that no harm would befall those she loved.

~

"We should arrive soon, sir," Brandon reported. "One day, maybe two at the most."

The Servitor nodded. A deep well of satisfaction rose within him as he viewed his fleet, the ships of his armada as they kept pace alongside *Demolition*. They would soon reach Arylyn and pay the magi back for their brazen attacks upon his home and his people. Did the people of Arylyn truly expect their assaults to go unpunished? That he would allow them to steal away his daughters as well as his new *raha'asras,* and follow that desecration by absconding with Fiona and Travail?

Axel smirked. If the magi believed themselves immune to his retribution, then they were wrong, and he would instruct them in this lesson. He'd teach them in the most painful manner possible. He would demonstrate to them that their supposed immunity from his vengeance was merely a temporary aberration. They would have their insults repaid fully and in kind. Axel's knuckles cracked as he unconsciously clenched his fists.

His rising anger threatened to overcome his mahavan training, his control of his passions, and he took a settling breath, exhaling slowly. He wiped aside all signs of emotion from his features and his posture. Now was not the time for unleashed passion. Now was the time for clear thinking and planning.

"Contact Adam's ship," he told Brandon in a tone he knew was drone-flat. "Let them know our status. We'll co-ordinate the assault on Arylyn once I know all my warriors are in position."

The young mahavan saluted sharply. "Yes, my liege," he said and moved off to do as he'd been ordered.

Axel watched as Brandon departed. The mahavan had all the attributes of a good leader: cunning, forward thinking, willing to learn, and hard-working. It was a large part of the reason why Axel had insisted he serve aboard *Demolition*. The Servitor wished to view Brandon's work from a more personal perspective. Yes, Adam could have used the man, but Axel needed to measure his true merit. Brandon could make a good Servitor if luck and fate allowed it.

Axel eventually returned his gaze to the wide-open ocean all around him. Here in the south Pacific the waters contained a strange shade of blue, one that was quite different from the indigo around Sinskrill, or the more typical murky gray of the Norwegian Sea farther past the *saha'asra's* borders. Even the spray had a different hue and texture. It splashed more lightly and didn't cut like a set of icy blades as it did around Sinskrill. In fact, everything was different in these climes, and Axel reckoned it might as well exist on another world. The wind blew steady and warm rather than fitfully and frozen. The clouds gathered in thick, puffy patches of white rather than constant, gray sheets. The very air had an unusual odor. It remained briny, but rather than the harsh, mineral aroma of the Norwegian Sea, Axel noticed something else. He caught a fragrance on the warm wind, an undercurrent of living, green vegetation, perhaps from the abundant kelp.

Of course the sun beat harder here. The Servitor hated that last part. He detested the heat, especially because he'd been forced to strip off his elegant cloak and heavy leathers in favor of lighter clothing.

As they sailed on, Axel spied a small island rising from the surrounding sea. It contained a single broken peak that thrust like a crumbled pyramid from the wreath of a low-lying jungle. Jagged, stony shards spilled all around the mountain's base, and a cloud possibly hung perpetually over the summit. In the waters near the island, the ocean transitioned from sky-blue to aqua-green.

Axel watched the peak from *Demolition's* deck and reflexively flexed his leg and hip muscles, maintaining his balance without consciously thinking about it. He continued to stare at the island as it passed to their stern and wondered at it. A broken mountain with jagged ruins at its base and a cloud hanging about the peak . . .

He wondered if it might be an omen. The broken mountain representing himself, the jagged ruins, his mahavans, and the cloud as Shet. A troubling harbinger. He rubbed his chin in consideration.

Brandon presented himself again, interrupting his thoughts. "My liege, we've contacted the Secondus," Brandon said. "He and his ships will break off in a few hours and make for the incursion zone. He'll contact us prior to disembarking for Arylyn and again once he's made his landing site secure."

"Wish him well," Axel said. "Let him know Shet's glory will carry him to victory."

"As it will all of us," Brandon said, offering the proper response to Axel's words.

"Dismissed."

Brandon saluted once more and departed. After he did, Axel again viewed the island with its shattered peak. *Could it truly be an omen?*

He decided to move away from his place at the railing. He no longer wished to see the troublesome isle. As he paced toward the bow of his ship, he recalled his brother's persistent question, the one Adam had asked prior to their departure from Sinskrill. *Would we not be better off allying with the magi and finding a way to deny Shet entrance to our world?*

As on preceding occasions, the question left Axel unsettled. Ally with their enemy? Madness.

Yet a large part of him wished it could be otherwise. He didn't enjoy death and punishment, but Arylyn's attacks against Sinskrill left him with no choice in the situation. Their assaults had to be answered.

The island with its broken mountain grew small, and Axel decided to set aside his worries.

In the end, it didn't matter. He was the Servitor, and no ill omen or worrisome questions would deny him his destiny.

~

S erena had the afternoon off from training with the Irregulars and
also from helping out at Sile's farm. It didn't happen very often,
and she used her unexpected free time to go surfing. Jean-Paul met her
at Lilith Bay. While the waves were softer here and less adventurous,
especially in the summer, the beach was closer to her seaside cottage,
which was always a plus. If they'd gone surfing elsewhere, she wouldn't
have been able to invite William to her home for dinner tonight.

She and Jean-Paul straddled their boards while they waited for a
likely wave. Serena stared at the horizon and studied the ocean
behind her. *Nothing*. She sighed in disappointment. The day's surfing
had turned out to be a lackluster affair, and she languidly paddled to
keep her place in the break zone.

Jean-Paul waved his hands about in disgust. "This kiddie pool is
utterly boring," he complained in his flamboyant fashion. "Why did
we choose Lilith Bay again?"

Serena told him.

Jean-Paul leered. "It is for William's sake, eh? Perhaps I can
whisper some advice in his ear about how best to repay you for such a
generous gift. Perhaps my words will thaw his cold-blooded American heart and set it afire with lustful anticipation."

Serena laughed. "Do you ever take anything seriously?"

Jean-Paul grinned. "I am serious enough for the things that require
gravity. I am serious when I train with the Irregulars, or when that
terribly handsome monster, Rukh Shektan, orders us about," he said.
"But for surfing, *non*. It is in my spirit to laugh and laugh I shall.
Otherwise, what is the point of living?"

Serena rolled her eyes. "I hadn't expected such a dramatic answer,"
she said, letting the sarcasm in her words bleed through, though she
loved Jean-Paul's melodrama.

"It is my way," Jean-Paul said. "You know this."

"I know," she said, smiling in fondness.

Jean-Paul didn't see it. He had his attention fixed behind them. "A
likely wave comes," he said. "Why don't you take it?"

Serena had seen it as well. She gave a quick head bob to thank Jean-Paul's generosity. Her gaze refocused on the oncoming wave. It barreled closer, and when Serena judged the moment right, she paddled hard. The swell reached her, and she launched herself upright, standing the board. She gathered her balance as she dropped down the face of wave. Once settled she cut right.

The wave's power carried her forward. Rainbows shimmered in the curl, the warm water washed her clean like a baptism as it poured off her skin, the offshore wind, stiff and steady, the call of a gull . . . She lost herself in the moment, a type of magic all its own.

The wave eventually petered out, and time resumed when Serena slipped off her board and into the bay.

Jean-Paul whooped from across the water. "Maybe the kiddie pool has some fun after all, eh?"

They surfed for a few more hours until Serena called it a day. She had to get clean and start dinner. She waved goodbye to Jean-Paul, who decided to stay out a little longer.

As she hauled herself and her board out of the water, she noticed a familiar figure in the distance crossing the Guanyin. She shaded her eyes to confirm who it was. *William.*

Serena toweled off on the warm, golden sand while waiting for him. As he approached his eyes flicked her up and down, widening slightly. Serena realized why. She wore a two-piece, black bikini. In front of Jean-Paul it hadn't mattered. He might not have even noticed but William most definitely had.

Although she was privately pleased by his attention, it wouldn't do for him to know it. Serena rolled her eyes, making sure he saw her reaction before wrapping herself in her towel and slipping on her sandals.

"I can take that," William said, pointing to her surfboard.

"Thank you," Serena said with a smile. She passed the board to him and he carried it under his arm. "You know I didn't expect you for a few more hours."

"I thought I'd help make dinner," he said as they made their way to her cottage. "If you don't mind the company."

"Are you sure it isn't because you couldn't stay away from me?" she teased.

William rolled his eyes. "Think much of yourself?"

Serena laughed. "Someone has to."

William smirked. "That's probably true."

Serena smacked him lightly on the arm.

"Ow," William said, feigning pain. "What are we making for dinner, by the way?"

They stepped onto the jungle path leading to her cottage, and the thick canopy cut off the sunshine and ocean's noise like a curtain. It left the trail shadowed and silent, except for the sounds of lizards scuttling across detritus, birds screeching in trees, and leaves rustling in the breeze.

"Ramen noodles," Serena answered William's question.

The surfboard smacked her on her bottom.

"Hey!" she protested.

William's wide-eyed expression of innocence was patently false. "Sorry."

"I'm sure you are," she said. "It's actually baked potatoes and hot dogs."

Another smack on the bottom.

Serena glowered at William. "You'll want to be more careful with that board."

"It was the wind."

No breeze stirred the jungle, and Serena shook her head.

"So what are we really having?" William asked.

"Sea bass with mango chutney, and potatoes and carrots in a cream sauce with capers."

He blinked in surprise. "That sounds pretty fancy. You sure you can make it?"

"You're free to make some peanut butter and jelly sandwiches instead."

He grinned, easy and free. "I'll trust your cooking."

"A wise decision," she said, her tone droll.

They reached her cottage and William set her board against the porch railing.

"Let me take a quick shower," Serena said.

"Do you need me to wash your back?" William asked, this time he didn't sound or look nearly so innocent.

"William!" Serena exclaimed in shock.

They'd kissed—a lot—but nothing more. Serena knew she wasn't ready for anything beyond that. Not yet. Not with everything they still had to do. Distractions like what William proposed wouldn't help either of them. Still, she found herself pondering his suggestion.

She flushed when she realized she'd been standing there staring at him. "Why don't you make yourself useful and get started on the prep work?"

"As you wish," William said.

The phrase sounded familiar, and Serena eyed William in speculation. The moment stretched, but the memory wouldn't come, and she shrugged it off. Whatever it was, she'd figure it out later. She took her shower, and by the time she finished, William already had the vegetables chopped and the potatoes frying on a skillet.

"You work fast," Serena noted.

"Part of my charm."

While Serena watched him move about the kitchen, his earlier suggestion returned to the forefront of her thoughts. A vision of her and William in her bed came to her, and she flushed, inhaling sharply. Her heart raced, and she had to lean on her Sinskrill training to control her reaction.

It took her longer than usual. Arylyn had spoiled her, left her vulnerable. She couldn't rein in her emotions so swiftly.

William noticed her silence and faced her. Her breath caught when he lifted her face and kissed her softly. "You were right about me. I couldn't stay away from you."

~

"I thought I'd find you here," Mink Ware said.

Jason started. He had thought himself alone and unnoticed. He sat near one of River Namaste's smaller cascades. Behind it actually on a stone bench set within a small hollow behind a curtain of water. It was a place he'd discovered early on after his arrival to Arylyn.

The waterfall broke off one of the main cataracts, washing down the face of a lumpy shelf of rock that jutted twenty feet into empty sky. The protrusion of stone extended from the distant edge of Cliff Air—the westernmost Cliff—like some misshapen mushroom. But from this vantage point, the watery screen distorted Lilith, making it more lovely, more ethereal. The view here reminded Jason of an impressionist painting, with iridescent colors, strange lighting, and broad swatches of imagery.

He loved it.

He loved the privacy even more. The bench behind the waterfall could only be reached by a slick staircase that someone had long ago cut into the shelf on the side opposite all the terraces and houses of Cliff Air. From here, Jason could see the village but remain hidden. While the hollow and the bench weren't exactly unknown, not a lot of people knew about it. Mink was one who did.

Jason moved over so she could sit down. The bench wasn't very wide, and she ended up seated close to him, within the bubble of his personal space. He didn't mind. He liked Mink. He always had.

When he'd first arrived on Arylyn, she'd wormed her way into his life. Forced her way into it was more like it. Mink was a force of nature, small yet mighty like her namesake animal, and whatever she wanted, she got. And when Jason had first come to Arylyn, she had wanted to get to know him. He was from the Far Beyond. She was native born. At the time, she had told him that she wanted to know if people from the Far Beyond were as exciting as she imagined. She'd been seven, and sadly, he'd gravely disappointed her.

Jason eyed Mink with a grin. "I didn't realize you wanted to find me. A guy could wonder about something like that."

She smiled. "You'd like that, wouldn't you? Me chasing after you?"

Jason laughed. He liked Mink, but she also intimidated him. "I don't think I could survive that kind of a hunt."

Mink's eyes sparkled with a teasing glint. "Don't tell me you're afraid of me."

Jason's grin fell away. Sometimes he *was* afraid of Mink but not right now. Right now, he had a different set of worries. It was why he was here. He had wanted some time alone, needed some seclusion to collect his thoughts. The mahavans were coming and doubt filled his mind as to whether Lilith would survive their arrival.

"What's wrong?" Mink asked.

"Nothing," Jason said.

She tilted her head in apparent thought. "It doesn't look like nothing. Tell me."

Jason sighed, knowing she'd pester him until he gave in. He was a private person who liked to gossip but didn't like being the subject of gossip. Mink, though, didn't bother with any of that. She pushed and shoved until she had her answers. Jason had never been able to hold her off once she'd gotten it into her head to learn something. Maybe her parents should have named her Badger.

He told her of his concerns.

Mink nodded her head in agreement, her face serious. "I sometimes worry about that, too."

"The Irregulars aren't as well-trained as Rukh would like, as *I* would like. I've seen what Serena can do. If the rest of the mahavans are like her, we might be in trouble."

Mink shook her head. "I think we'll be fine."

Jason frowned in confusion. "Weren't you just saying you were worried a second ago?"

"I did. I was."

"And now?"

Mink offered one of her irrepressible grins, a smile that Jason couldn't help but return. "That was a second ago," she said. "I changed my mind since then."

Jason chuckled. Mink really could change her mind that quickly. He'd seen it before.

She gave him a gentle shove with her shoulder. "This is nice. Being here and watching the village."

"Yes, it is." The peace of the small hollow crept into Jason. It pushed away some of his worries as he stared at his lovely home. "We'll keep it safe."

~

"It's a beautiful night, isn't it?" Jake said to Daniella.

They'd decided to take an after-dinner stroll along Clifftop, and thankfully, the heat from earlier in the day had broken when a pleasant trade wind kicked up. It kept the evening cool.

"Yes, it is," Daniella agreed.

The black-posted street lamps came on as they ambled along. The lights generally signaled an end to the day's labor, but someone hadn't mentioned that fact to poor Robert Weeks. Darkness had fallen, but the blacksmith continued to slave away. For weeks he'd been working day and night to forge all the cannons Rukh said they needed. His hammer rang out, sounding with a rhythmic quality as he struck the metal in what sounded like musical timing.

The ringing faded when Jake and Daniella took a turn onto a small side street. Here, Lilith held a peaceful quiet as a few other couples strolled about, all of them probably wanting to enjoy the evening's coolness as well.

Jake smiled at Daniella. "Would a beautiful woman on this beautiful night like to share some of Maxine's ice cream with me?"

Daniella smiled back. "You think I'm beautiful? How gallant."

"My cotillion classes," Jake said with an easy grin and incline of his head. "Always let the woman know when you appreciate her."

"I see," Daniella said. Her eyes twinkled. "Then, as a man who's taken cotillion classes, you won't be upset when I tell you that I know you weren't the one responsible for cooking dinner. But I thank you for it anyway." She put a hand to her lips as if dismayed by her words, but Jake saw her grin from behind her fingers.

Jake maintained his easy grin and rolled with the light-hearted conversation. "How'd you know?"

"A woman has her ways." A beat later she added, "Everyone who knows you says you can ruin boiled water, remember?"

"Well, let's just say that cooking is what keeps me humble."

Daniella laughed. "Of course. We wouldn't want you growing arrogant, especially since the food was actually quite good." Jake caught her eyeing him speculatively. "Who helped you with it?"

"Mr. Zeus. He told me what to do, and my job was to follow his instructions."

"Well, it was delicious." Daniella offered a half-curtsy. "Thank you again for inviting me."

"My pleasure." Jake doffed an imaginary hat. "But you don't have to thank me every time we have dinner together."

"Maybe you'll fall into a funk again if I don't."

Jake pretended to not know what she was talking about. "What funk?"

Daniella's face fell into lines of overwrought sadness.

Jake winced again. "That bad?"

"That bad," Daniella confirmed. They had entered a darkened, empty alley and her voice echoed in the hush between the two buildings.

Jake didn't like remembering that part of his life, and Daniella must have sensed it. "I'm sorry," she said. "I shouldn't have brought it up."

Jake managed a smile. "It's fine. I'm not made of glass."

Daniella placed her hand in the crook of his arm. "Let's talk about something else. Something fun."

"Something fun?" Jake tapped his chin, a habit he'd picked up from William. "Maybe Lien's singing from the other day?"

Daniella laughed. "No. That would be mean."

"How about the weather?" Jake teased. "That's always interesting, right?"

Daniella rolled her eyes, and he could tell she wanted him to see it. "Why don't you tell me how your day went? Like the afternoon drills."

"That's right, you had the afternoon off," Jake said. "You missed William facing off against Jason. Longswords. It was epic."

Daniella's interest perked. "Really? Who won?"

Jake paused when he caught sight of glass baubles in a storefront, *Samson's Trinkets*. He'd always liked the toys and creations in there. His mother did, too. He'd taken her a few presents from *Samson's* during his last visit home.

"Who won?" Daniella pressed.

Jake's attention snapped back to the here and now. "William. He's too fast and strong for anyone but Rukh or Jessira to handle."

"Serena could take him," Daniella said, sounding confident.

"What makes you say that?" Jake asked. He didn't think Serena could do so.

"William's faster and stronger," Daniella said, "but Serena's harder. She never quits until she wins. Her will would see her through."

Jake chuckled, remembering something Coach Rasskins used to say right before a football game: *"Whoever wills it, wins it!"*

"What's so funny?" Daniella sounded affronted.

Jake told her what he'd been thinking. "And for the record," he added, "William would roast Serena. You don't know how intense he can be."

They crossed an empty street where the only sounds to be heard were a softly moaning wind and their footsteps.

"I think I have an idea," Daniella said. "You might have moped, but William growled like he was angry all the time. Or at least really motivated. It wasn't always pleasant to be around him."

Her words made Jake feel defensive for his friend. "That was because of Sapient Dormant."

He caught Daniella eyeing him speculatively. "I heard about that. How he was linked to the necrosed king?"

"Overward," Jake corrected. "That's what the other necrosed call Sapient."

Daniella shivered. "Well, if William got his rage from the *Overward* —" she stressed Sapient's title "—then I'd hate to ever meet the creature because William's anger could be downright scary."

Jake grinned as he recalled something else. "Serena said a lot of girls thought we were gay."

"Not gay," Daniella corrected. "Not William, anyway."

"Hey!"

Daniella smiled. "Anyway, with William's intensity and then his anger, all of us were happy that he only seemed interested in Serena."

"She was the sacrificial lamb, eh?"

Daniella nodded. "A sacrificial lamb who could kick his ass."

Jake laughed. He liked Daniella's way of thinking. It was interesting, and he wondered anew how he could have seen her as shy and reserved. She had a lot to say.

"Well, if it makes you feel any better," Jake said, "I think we can both agree on two people who neither of *us* could take."

"William and Serena," Daniella said. "A matched pair, like Rukh and Jessira." She mock-shuddered. "Thank God they're on our side."

Jake grinned, and his smile widened when he and Daniella took one final turn. *Maxine's* was directly ahead, but the ice creamery wasn't the reason for his sudden happiness.

He'd caught sight of Selene ahead of them, easily picked out by her height and gangly legs. She moved like some strange stork amongst the flock of her girlfriends, all of them chattering and occasionally squealing. He wondered if he should try to embarrass Selene. She'd get so mad, which was the entire point.

His grin faded when he saw the girls meet up with a group of boys and one of them threw an arm around Selene's shoulder.

"Who the hell is that?" he asked.

The boy drew Selene close, and Jake's outrage rose.

Daniella chuckled and chided him. "Leave her be."

"She's too young to be meeting boys at night," Jake protested.

"How old were you when you started meeting girls?"

"That's not the point," he said. "Selene's a girl. She has no idea the dirty thoughts that go through the mind of a teenage boy."

Daniella quirked an eyebrow. "I bet she actually does. She might even have some dirty thoughts of her own. I did. I still do."

"Daniella!" Jake stared at her in shock.

Her eyes sparkled, and she laughed. Once again it reminded him of wind chimes, clear and lovely, and his irritation fell away in the face of it.

His easy grin returned, and he wondered what kind of dirty thoughts Daniella had.

CHAPTER 23: EXPECTED ARRIVALS

October 1990

Adam peered at the island looming nearby and a welling sense of excitement, one his mahavan training couldn't entirely contain, surged within his chest. *Mythical Arylyn*. It was every bit as beautiful as Brandon had described.

A half-moon shone, hanging like a strange lantern in the sky over a line of treed hills, and its light wavered on the waters, setting the clouds afire with a cool, ethereal glow. It reflected off the sandy beach and hills, and Adam also noted how brightly it beamed through puffy clouds. The moonlight illuminated the low-lying cliffs running east-to-west directly past the shoreline. It also brought the darkened, solitary tower commanding the small bay into clear relief. All of it easily visible in the moon beams.

Which meant so were their ships.

Adam cursed under his breath. They'd have to disembark as swiftly as possible and have the ships immediately move beyond the horizon. He called out orders in a low voice, one that wouldn't carry across the water.

While their intended landing site was on the far side of the island from Lilith, they couldn't risk the possibility that someone might be out for a late-night excursion. Plus, the tower on the cliff worried him. No lights played within it, but he couldn't tell if it was truly as unoccupied as first impressions indicated. It had still been under construction during Brandon's scouting mission, but now it rose finished. Disquiet rumbled through Adam's mind. As the mahavans scurried about and carried out his orders, he continued to study the island, searching for a sign that the presence of his fleet might have been detected.

The captain of the vessel, Hannah Yearn, moved to stand at Adam's shoulder. "We've got the boats lowered into the water, sir."

"Good," Adam said. "We'll disembark, row to the island, and send the boats back. As soon as you have them tied down, sail straight north. Get over the horizon." He held up a satellite phone and displayed it to the captain. "I'll call you with the details of how the landing went as soon as we secure the beach and that tower."

"Yes, sir." Hannah saluted and quickly filled in her sailors, all of them drones except for a handful of mahavans, on what they needed to do.

Adam stepped to where the boats had been lowered. *It is time.*

He descended a rope ladder, careful to keep his movements quiet. Waves slapped against the ship's hull, and the rowboat taking them ashore dipped and bobbed. Brief, hushed conversations reached Adam. He dropped into the boat and took his place at the bow. Behind him sat Evelyn Mason.

"Ready?" he asked the Rider in a low voice.

"Ready, sir," Evelyn said.

Other than Brandon Thrum, who sailed aboard *Demolition*, everyone else who had scouted Arylyn earlier in the summer—Evelyn, Samuel, and Preeti—had been chosen for the invasion of the island. While their assistance had helped guide Adam's steps to reach this point, he would have preferred Brandon's presence. The young mahavan had a steady common sense to him. Unfortunately, Axel had insisted on the young mahavan's presence aboard *Demolition* and had left Adam saddled with Evelyn, Samuel, and Preeti. The last two were timidity made flesh, and none of them offered anything but the most banal of advice: *"The sun will rise soon." "We're upwind of them."*

Useless.

"Cast off," Adam said to Evelyn.

The fiery Rider whispered a command and the drones manning the oars moved them steadily toward a golden-white shore.

Within moments, they reached the beach and swiftly disembarked. Adam splashed ashore and sent parties east and west to secure the site. No one could be allowed to learn of their arrival or raise an alarm to their presence.

Adam waited a nervous number of seconds until word finally reached him. The beach was theirs. He gestured, and his mahavans gathered their gear. The rowboats swiftly departed, returning to the waiting ships and bring back their next load of supplies.

He swung his attention back to the squat, rugged tower on the cliff. Arrow slits and a few wider holes pointed toward the ocean while a brick wall—ten feet tall—surrounded the structure on all sides, except where it ran into the cliff's steep drop-off. Adam's eyes narrowed, and he pointed to the tower. "We need to take that out," he told Evelyn.

The Rider nodded, and she and fifteen others went for the tower.

A whispered command had Jeek Voshkov, Prime of the unformed tribe under Adam's command, winging toward the structure as well. The creature took the form of a falcon, and four more of his kind flapped after him. Jeek's Secondus, Reem Voshkov, remained behind with the bulk of the unformed, and Adam led them and the rest of his mahavans to encircle the tower. They had to cut off any escape.

It took them several minutes to scale the cliffs and reach their positions. Adam and his mahavans hid in scattered bunches in the surrounding jungle. They crouched low, yards from a cobblestone road that was wide enough for a wagon and led to the tower. The smell of mold and wet leaves filled the air. A soft wind rustled the trees, but no other sound marred the night. Even the jungle creatures knew to keep silent. They likely sensed the impending violence.

Adam watched as Jeek made a circuit of the tower. The prime dipped his wings twice, apparently gesturing to one of his unformed, who flew to Adam's position. The creature landed and assumed the shape of a human. He could have passed for a slightly built, naked young man, and Adam briefly wondered if the unformed actually had a true form.

"We can find no one within the tower," the unformed hissed in a harsh, sibilantly-accented voice.

"Good. Go to Evelyn," Adam ordered. "Tell her to breach the entrance as silently as possible."

"It will be done." The unformed leapt into the air and transformed once more into a falcon. He swiftly flew to where Evelyn and her mahavans huddled behind a pile of stones that faced the sole entrance to the tower. The unformed landed and whispered a few words to Evelyn, who nodded and turned to speak to her mahavans. They shuffled closer to her, and Adam wondered what she was telling them.

He hoped she reminded them to be quiet.

At a sign from Evelyn, the mahavans rushed forward. An iron gate barred their path, and they blasted it off its hinges. Adam grimaced when it fell to the ground. The sound echoed loudly. From there, the mahavans swiftly reached the tower. They punched through the stout outer door leading within. This time, they managed it much more quietly and streamed inside.

Adam waited with crossed arms and a frown. Minutes ticked by. He let out an impatient breath.

The same unformed as from earlier finally returned, landing in front of him. "The tower is ours," the creature said. "No one resides within, although they may have planned on manning it in the next few weeks. Many supplies have been laid out. They also left weapons behind."

Adam's interest piqued. "What kind of weapons?"

"Three cannons, or at least that's what they might be. They're not as small and portable as ours."

Adam bit back an oath. *The magi have cannons. How?* An unsettled sensation washed over him as he considered what that might mean. A moment later, he set aside his worry and realized the magi cannons represented an unexpected windfall. He smiled as he thought of how best to use them. "Excellent news. Good work."

"Thank you." The unformed smiled, and canines lengthened in his mouth. He wore a mocking grin.

Adam recognized the challenge for what it was and smiled in response. He lengthened his teeth as well, multiplied them until they resembled those of a shark.

The unformed shrank away.

⁓

William awoke in a cold sweat. His heart pounded, and his breathing came in gasps. Something was wrong. Something terrible lurked nearby.

He sourced his *lorethasra* and shaped a braid of Fire and Air. The lamp on the nightstand next to his bed glowed golden and brightened the room. He quested about, wondering what had awoken him. Everything was fine. A pair of twin beds flanked the dormer window, with a chest of drawers on the wall opposite. A ceiling fan stirred the air, and crickets chirped outside. A half-moon shone ivory light. William smelled jasmine when a stray breeze rustled the curtains of the open window.

Early on after they'd escaped to Arylyn, he and Jake had shared this room, but with time and healing, Jake had moved into his own bedroom. William now had this one to himself.

He went to the window, trying to figure out what had roused him. He gazed about the front yard, searching for what might be out of place. The flowers and stone pathway along the edge of the terrace, the wispy cascades of River Namaste, and the inky darkness of the Pacific. Nothing seemed off, but something was. William sensed danger. He stretched his senses, straining to figure it out.

Minutes passed, but nothing came to him, and he exhaled heavily in frustration. His instincts kept screaming at him. *Something is wrong.*

William paced the room, trying to understand what it might be. He wondered if it might be something wrong inside of him, and he focused internally.

Still nothing.

Frustration led to anger, and the monster inside his mind, the one he'd thought removed or buried deep, roared to life. It snarled, furious and clawing.

William clutched his head. The anger threatened to consume his thoughts, and he forced himself to breathe deep and slow, willing the fury to soothe, to relax and sleep. After a few minutes, it drifted away, but he could sense it stirring now and then, restless and untamed though it wasn't as potent as he remembered.

Still, the matter of its return worried William. He needed to talk to someone. He quickly got dressed, paced down the hall, and knocked on Mr. Zeus' bedroom door.

"What is it?" the old man grumbled.

William told him.

"Hold on," Mr. Zeus said. Seconds later he opened the door, still in the process of tying off his robe. His beard and hair stuck out like a bird's nest, and he frowned. "Let's go to my study," he said, and led the way downstairs. There, Mr. Zeus sourced his *lorethasra*. The warm scent of vanilla wafted, and an instant later a floor lamp lit.

Mr. Zeus gestured, and William took one of the leather chairs fronting the fireplace. "What did you sense?" Mr. Zeus asked.

"I'm not sure," William said, "but the anger is back, so I figure it has to do with Shet or Sapient."

Mr. Zeus' gaze sharpened. "You're sure?"

"I'm sure."

"Then it's a good thing you woke me up." Mr. Zeus said. "I want you to close your eyes and reach for the anger."

"You *want* me angry?" William asked in disbelief.

Mr. Zeus shook his head. "No. I want you to study the anger. Find the reason for why it awoke."

William frowned in disquiet, and he hesitated.

"Whenever you're ready," Mr. Zeus said.

William nodded and took a deep breath. He closed his eyes and reached for the anger. It slumbered, and he imagined it as a sleeping lion. He eased toward it, inching closer, careful not to awaken it. As he edged nearer, impressions came to him, of hunting and prey, of Shet's exuberant call to war. Forever changing. Always restless. He struggled to understand what he was feeling.

More impressions. A soft place, warm and inviting, ripe for the kill. Forever changing. Always restless. Shapes altering.

His eyes snapped open. "Unformed," he whispered.

Mr. Zeus' scrutiny intensified. "What did you say?"

"Unformed," William repeated. "I think they're on Arylyn."

"You're certain?"

"No," William said. "I'm not certain, but that's the sense I got."

Mr. Zeus eyed him for a moment and apparently came to a decision. "Get Rukh and Jessira. Tell them what's happened. I'll send Jake and Jason to rouse the council."

Alarm stirred inside William. "What if it's nothing?"

"What if it is something?" Mr. Zeus countered. "Go!"

William nodded and left the house at a jog. The moon's beaming light guided his steps up the Main Stairs. Luminous clouds drifted sedately across the sky, and waterfalls misted and glowed with an unearthly light. Their crashing sounds were distant tonight as William swiftly passed silent terraces, sleeping homes, and ran across waterfall-slick stones. He pressed on, breathing smooth and easy like Travail taught. Better to maintain a steady pace than a sprint that ends in a walk.

While he jogged, he studied the anger within him again. Once more, sensations came to him. A notion of constant motion and change. A hunger for conquest, a match to the monster inside him, but different. Always shifting forms.

It had to be the unformed. He felt sure of it. They'd reached Arylyn.

He continued upward and onward, glad that Rukh and Jessira had moved from their isolated cabin north of Janaki Valley to an apartment on Clifftop directly off the Village Green. He shortly reached their home, knocked on the door, and waited.

Jessira opened the door. Her honey-blonde hair was tousled, and she wore a short, red-silk robe with a white slip showing underneath. It was oddly feminine attire for someone who William always considered a warrior first and a beautiful woman second.

"William?" She frowned at him. "What's wrong?"

William explained.

"Come in." Jessira opened the door wider, and he entered.

He almost ran into Rukh, who had exited the bedroom, already dressed and alert.

"Let me change first," Jessira said. She went to the bedroom and closed the door.

Rukh spoke. "I heard some of what you said, but tell me everything you know, start to finish."

For the third time that night, William repeated his story.

Rukh's brows furrowed. "If what you sense is true, then we have unformed on Arylyn."

Jessira exited the bedroom, dressed in jeans and a t-shirt. She must have caught the tail end of the conversation. "Or he's simply wrong about what he senses."

"I think I'm right," William said. "Certain of it."

Jessira nodded. "Then they could have only arrived by anchor line or by ship."

"They could have swum or flown," William said.

"True," Jessira acknowledged, "but swimming or flying would mean they came alone, with no mahavans to help them attack Arylyn. That wouldn't make any sense."

William was forced to agree with her. The unformed were here, and they likely had come under the command of the Servitor.

Jessira spoke again. "They likely arrived by ship then. Had it been by anchor line, the guards we've placed around Linchpin Knoll would have alerted us."

Rukh grunted acknowledgment. "My thoughts as well. We have to awaken the council and rouse the Irregulars."

A strange mix of excitement and apprehension built within William. *This is it.* "Jake and Jason have already started gathering the council."

"Good," Jessira said. "Then we need to gather the lieutenants."

Rukh finished her thought in that creepy way they had. "But not all the warriors. Not yet, anyway. We'll assemble at the council chambers and lay out our options there."

A thought came to William, one that left his mouth dry with sudden worry. "We've never planned what to do with Travail. Is there a way to warn him?"

"I wish there were," Rukh said. "He travels so much, there's no way to keep track of his movements." His jaw tightened momentarily. "If he'd taken the satellite phone we offered, this wouldn't be a concern."

Jessira said, "Maybe we can get in touch with him once we know if and where the mahavans have landed."

Rukh nodded. "We need to contact the watchtowers. Have them send out scouts and inform us the moment they learn anything."

"Only a third of them are manned," William reminded them.

Jessira shrugged. "Then those that are manned will have to do."

Rukh moved to a table where a map of Arylyn lay spread out. He pointed. "They'll likely have landed to the north. It's the easiest access point. From there, they'll likely press toward the heart of the island before setting south for Lilith. We'll have to cut them off before they reach the village."

"What happens now?" William asked.

Rukh's demeanor went grim. "Now we wage war."

CHAPTER 24: BATTLE'S ARENA

October 1990

Stacey Cloud crouched low, hunching as close to the jungle floor as she could manage. She'd crept within spitting distance of the mahavans' camp to peek around a fallen log. She flicked her vision across the encampment, trying to get an accurate count.

It had been two days since Rukh and Jessira had informed everyone that mahavans had landed in force upon Arylyn. Stacey and the rest of the scouts had mobilized to find the invaders. They'd begun their search at the unoccupied watchtowers and quickly discovered one of them—Ox Bow—breached and ransacked.

The mahavans *had* arrived, and now Stacey had located the Sinskrill warriors. She wished her partner, Rail Forsyth, was with her. He'd injured his ankle, and she'd been forced to leave him resting in the hollow trunk of a fallen tree a half-mile back. She hoped she wouldn't regret that decision, especially given how often Rukh and Jessira had emphasized the importance of having a partner close at hand. *No helping it now.*

A stirring rose in the camp and Stacey wondered at it. Mahavans gathered near a powerfully built man. He gestured all around the camp, including in Stacey's direction, and her heart nearly seized. She crouched lower and prayed that the darkness of the coming night and her camouflage would keep her hidden. She'd painted her face in the same green and brown shading as her light denim clothing and added twigs and leaves to her helmet for further concealment.

The meeting broke up, the mahavans drifted apart, and Stacey peeked once more around the edge of a log and continued her count. After a few minutes, she had her tally. She reckoned there might be around one hundred and fifty Sinskrill warriors, with others likely away from camp as advance scouts. Her eyes widened when she caught sight of cannons, a dozen of them, including the ones from Ox Bow Tower and others of a different design. *Maybe the mahavans have their own?*

Stacey didn't know, but she inched backward from the Sinskrill warriors. She crawled away on her stomach. The entire time she kept her eyes focused on the enemy as Jessira had taught. She ignored stray insects that crawled across her skin, kept her breathing quiet, and did her best not to brush against any of the bushes along her path.

A hundred yards from the mahavan encampment, with no sign or sound to give her away, she pulled out her satellite phone and dialed headquarters.

Councilor Duba answered.

"This is Stacey Cloud," she whispered. "I've found the enemy. They're camped a dozen miles north of Mount Madhava, a mile east of Riven Road."

Excitement suffused Councilor Duba's voice. "Excellent work."

"Thank you, sir," Stacey said. "I'll continue tracking them and provide updates as I'm able."

"What about your partner?" the councilor asked, sounding concerned.

"He's injured. He won't be able to keep up with me. I'm about to go check on him."

"Stay hidden and stay safe," Councilor Duba said, still sounding worried.

"I will, sir. Cloud out." Stacey hung up the phone and packed it away.

She never noticed the parakeet land behind her. And she never heard it transform into a rhino. Pain exploded in her back as a black horn thrust clear through her spine and out of her chest. Blood showered in a crimson-black fountain, and Stacey felt herself flung through the air. The jungle swirled and she landed heavily, staring upward. Her last sight was of a naked young man poking through her pack.

~

Aia sat up with a start. Something had awakened her. She noticed Shon rising as well. Trouble and concern marred his features.

She blinked at him, unsurprised. *You sensed it?*

Shon answered with a flaring of his nostrils. *Yes.*

Aia searched for what had interrupted their slumber. A crisp coolness filled the air. Darkness still reigned across the forest, but a rosy pink on the horizon heralded dawn's imminent rise. Aia's breath plumed, quickly lost amongst the towering evergreens rising like Ashoka's buildings around her and Shon. The soaring trees made her feel small. They would have done so even if she had her true, larger form.

An icy breeze blew, and Aia shivered. She hated the cold.

I don't like the cold, either, Shon said. Her tawny brother yawned mightily.

There is nothing to like about it, Aia agreed. She stepped away from her soft, warm bed of pine needles and stared longingly at it. A moment later, she sighed. *It was time to get moving.* She nosed Shon, urging him to his feet.

A distant echo, a sound of need and longing reached her, the same call that had awoken her. It echoed as a wordless cry heard in the depths of her mind. Aia knew who it was and it filled her with joy and excitement. Her eyes widened. *We have to go. Rukh needs me.*

So does Jessira, Shon said, his voice electric with joy. *I mean, she needs me. We need to go.*

And we will, but we need Landon's help in order to reach them.

Shon rumbled in impatience, and Aia soothed him with a rub of her face against his.

He settled down but still frowned. *She wants me to join her on Arylyn, but she wants us to save some troll-creature first. Will we have time to do that?*

We have the time, Aia said, better recalling Rukh's instructions. He'd sent them on the wings of her dreams, the same call that had roused her sleep moments earlier, and he, too, had mentioned the troll-creature. *The danger for our humans hasn't yet arrived.*

Shon remained agitated though, and his tail swished. *Will we be able to help Jessira and Rukh, or will we be a hindrance?* His ears flattened. *Look at us. We're still too small.*

Aia privately shared his worry. They had continued to grow during their time in Sand. They could now face a Bengal tiger eye-to-eye, and most people would consider them dangerous, but compared to what they had once been, they remained puny. Worse, the rest of the Kesarins, their kind, would have rightfully pitied them. Even at the size of a tiger, Aia felt inept and vulnerable, incapable of doing what might be required. She growled in frustration. She wanted—*needed* —to be what she had once been: fearsome, fast, and deadlier than any creature alive.

Shon rubbed his forehead against hers. *You feel the same way,* he said, apparently picking up on her silent anxiety.

Aia sighed. *I do, but there is nothing we can do about it. Our humans need us. We must save them. You know how they are.*

Shon scoffed, a flattening of his ears and upturn of his mouth. *I know how Rukh is. Always foolishly charging into danger,* he said. *If not for Jessira, he'd have died a thousand times.*

Aia bristled. *Rukh is the greatest of all humans. Remember, it was his blade that slew the Demon Wind.*

Shon yipped. *Jessira fought against Her, too.*

Aia swished her tail in irritation. *Let's find Landon.* She moved away from her annoying, little brother and led them out of the dew-wet pines. Aia scowled when her fur grew wet, but thankfully, they soon they stepped out of the forest's shadow.

Shon rubbed against her side. *Sorry.*

Rukh is not foolish, Aia said, still annoyed with him. *He is Jessira's mate. She chose him. He's worthy of her.*

Yes, he is, Shon agreed. *He always puts her in danger, though.*

Aia growled, irritated that he was right. Rukh *did* run to danger, and everyone else had to chase after him to keep his foolhardy hide alive. Of course, she'd never admit that to Shon. He'd only brag ever more loudly about Jessira.

Aia led Shon toward the environs of Sand, stepping quickly along quiet dirt lanes that separated fields full of green things the humans ate. Aia spotted a small herd of goats on a nearby low-lying hill. They munched grass in their caprine-contented fashion. *Stupid animals. Death passed close by, and they never looked up from their feeding.*

Shon grumbled low in his throat and eyed the goats. *They would taste much better than the stupid green things.*

Yes, they would, Aia agreed, *but humans think otherwise.* She nipped Shon when he lingered too long on the goats. *Landon wouldn't like it,* she reminded him.

Shon rumbled in reply, and they bypassed the goats and fields and entered the village proper. The sky lightened as Aia and her brother skirted across back yards that ran to the forest and fields. The Wrin, the people of Sand, had yet to awaken, but life stirred. A crow cawed at them from atop a roof, and a rooster made an obnoxious noise.

Aia flicked her ears in irritation.

They reached cold, brick roads—narrow, unlike Ashoka's wide boulevards—and walked among log homes with broad porches. For the most part, the houses remained darkened, although here and there, a light was on, shining out a window. Eventually, they reached Landon's home, the one he shared with his mate, Elaina Sinith. It was a log structure, one-story tall and similar to the surrounding houses. Aia knew a stream cut through the back yard.

Landon was waiting for them on the porch, dressed in a deerskin jacket, soft, leather pants, and sturdy boots. *You have to leave,* he said, somehow guessing what they intended in that irritating fashion of his.

We do, Aia confirmed. *Our humans require our help.*

What about . . . Landon broke off, like he always did when talking about his brother. He'd recovered some memories, but for the most part, he still didn't recall much about William Wilde. It upset him, and a sad, longing filled his eyes.

Aia remembered William. The boy was brave, strong, and willful. In some ways he reminded her of Rukh, and any Kesarin would have found him a worthy human. Him and the woman, Serena, who hid her life.

Landon cleared his throat. *Do you know how he's doing?*

I do not, Aia said to Landon in sympathy, *but if he remains near Rukh and Jessira, he'll be fine.*

Landon nodded. *How will you get to Arylyn?*

We were hoping you could help, Aia said. Despite the loss of his memories, Landon often had odd bits of knowledge. Aia trusted in that.

Landon smiled. *You're lucky I love the two of you,* he said. *There happens to be an anchor line linking Sand to Arylyn.*

Shon's ears rotated forward, and his pupils dilated. *I didn't know that.*

Silly kitten, Landon said in obvious fondness. *Did you really think you knew all the secrets of the village? Come.*

Landon led them away from the village and into the forest. The rising sun had yet to penetrate the canopy, and they walked in cool shade as the forest stirred around them. Squirrels, rabbits, and chipmunks rustled about. Aia followed on Landon's heels with Shon in her paw prints as they took an animal trail and occasionally brushed against pine needles still damp with dew. Once more she grimaced at the wetness.

A tod, a male fox, skirted close to their trail before wisely reconsidering. He cut an angle away from them, and Aia smiled, imagining the fox's thoughts upon coming across a much more powerful predator.

Landon, however, likely never noticed the tod. He pressed on without glancing around, and they soon reached a small clearing. *We're here,* he said. His eyes had gone fully white and depthless, like they did whenever he used his holder gifts. He seemed to focus on a distant sight only he could see until a line separated the air. It spun, and a doorway opened onto a rainbow bridge.

Shon moved about uneasily. He hissed and Aia sympathized. Neither of them liked traveling by anchor line.

Landon faced them. His eyes had resumed their normal color. He surprised Aia by hugging her. *I'll miss you, little kitten.*

Aia pressed her face against his and kept still. She enjoyed being held like this, but she generally only allowed it from Rukh and Jessira. With anyone else it left her feeling vulnerable. After a moment, she nudged Landon with her forehead, and he let her go.

Landon moved to Shon and hugged him as well. *I'll miss you, too, my brave boy.*

Shon made a whuffling noise. *We will see you again.*

I hope so, Landon said.

Aia noticed that the holder's eyes were shiny with unshed tears. She pressed her forehead against Landon's one last time. *You would have made a Kesarin happy.*

Landon smiled sadly once more. *Give William my best.* He hesitated. *Tell him I love him.*

We love you, too, Aia said. *Goodbye.*

She and Shon faced the shimmering anchor line, and Aia silently snarled. *I hate this part.* She took a deep breath and stepped onto the anchor line. She yowled immediately. Her body felt like it was being torn apart.

~

William helped Rukh unfurl a map of Arylyn and pin down the corners with small weights. Around them were gathered the village council and some of the senior members of the Ashokan Irregulars, such as Jessira, Serena, Ward, Jason, and Jake. They stood in the council chambers, having commandeered it as their unofficial headquarters. To give themselves more workspace they'd pushed the pew-like benches to the edges of the windowless room and added more tables. All of them were covered in clusters of maps, rulers, and various other items. Counters on the maps showed the location and number of the mahavans as well as the scouts tracking them. All the lanterns within the chamber had been lit to full brightness, chasing away all shadows from the room.

Rukh rapped the table, calling for silence, and the few whispered conversations ceased. "Let's get started," he said.

Once again, William felt unnecessary amongst Arylyn's leaders, and he wondered if the others, like Jason, Jake, and Serena felt the same way.

The mayor spoke. "Have we heard anything more from Stacey?"

Rukh shook his head. "At this point we have to accept that she and the other scouts we can no longer contact have either been captured or killed."

His blunt, hard words landed like a blow to people unused to violence. Everyone, councilors and Irregulars alike, shared worried glances. They'd heard Stacey's initial report from several days past when she had first located the mahavans but nothing after that. Her partner, Rail Forsyth, didn't know what had happened to her either. She'd never returned as she'd said she would.

Other scouts had been sent to observe and report on the mahavans. Because of Stacey, they'd quickly managed to track down the Sinskrill warriors, but some of them had also gone radio silent as well. One, however, had managed to get off a garbled message about being attacked by the unformed.

After that Rukh had pulled the rest of the scouts farther back from the mahavans, ordering them to maintain a several-mile distance. He'd also had them band together in groups of four rather than two and the changes must have worked. No more scouts had been lost.

"Where are the mahavans right now?" the mayor asked.

"Moving in toward Mount Madhava from the northwest," Jessira answered.

William leaned in closer when she pointed to a line on the map. *Riven Road* it said.

Councilor Duba wore an angry frown. "They must be using our own roads against us."

Ward appeared to study the positions of the mahavans and their own forces. "If we hurry we can muster our forces and cut them off at Jaipurana Pass."

Rukh nodded. "I agree. At Jaipurana we can lay an ambush and defeat them en masse." He rapped his knuckles again. "Then it's decided. We rally our forces and meet them at the pass."

Shuffling movements and muttered conversation met his words. Ward trotted to the chamber doors and opened and closed them a few times. The sound echoed, and after a moment everyone quieted. No one had left the room.

William met Rukh's expectant gaze and sourced his *lorethasra*. A pine scent filled the chamber and he quickly wove a block to keep the mahavan Walkers from listening in on their conversation.

Councilor Blood scowled. "Is this subterfuge really necessary?"

Rukh stared at the councilor for a long moment, his eyes icy with either suppressed anger or disbelief. "They found Drake Mill when they never should have been able to. The only way they could have learned his position was if they heard our conversation with him. So, yes, this subterfuge is necessary."

Councilor Blood grumbled something about seeing shadows at night and conspiracy theories.

William wanted to tell the officious, little man to shut it, and Councilor Duba must have felt the same. He glared at Councilor Blood. "How dare you question anyone after the number of times you've been proven wrong?" His voice rose. "These are grave matters, and if you had the slightest bit of humility, you'd never again challenge those of us who have been proven right."

Councilor Blood opened his mouth to respond, but Councilor Shaw spoke first. "Duba is right. The next election is in a few months, and you won't win it unless you prove yourself in the next few days." He peered down at Councilor Blood in his patrician fashion. "Think upon it before you say anything else."

"Enough!" Mayor Care snapped. "I'll have no more pointless bickering. It's time to organize the island's defenses. What we do today may decide if our children will enjoy the life we've been blessed to lead." She gazed about the room a moment, forcing everyone to meet her eyes.

Rukh nodded agreement. "With the unformed flying reconnaissance, the mahavans should be able to locate Jaipurana Pass without any difficulty. Riven Road leads right across it, and it's the easiest way to get across Mount Madhava's western slopes."

Ward frowned. "Why did you want them to know this?"

Jessira answered. "Because we want them to avoid the pass."

Rukh took up the explanation. "They'll skirt farther west. The terrain there is more rugged. It'll slow them down. It'll give us more time to get our forces in place. The mahavans will press through the jungle and reach the southwestern slopes of Mount Madhava while thinking we're exiting the Jaipurana far to the north. They'll likely think they have unimpeded access to Janaki Valley and Lilith."

William stroked his chin in thought as he started to get a sense of Rukh and Jessira's plan.

Rukh noticed, and William found himself the focus of the other man's attention. "Care to finish explaining it?" Rukh asked with a challenging lift to his eyebrows.

William stepped forward. "We'll get them to bypass the Jaipurana and take the Scylla instead." He pointed to a ragged line on the map. "They'll regain the Riven Road on the far side of Mount Madhava but still have to get through Charybdis Way."

Jake interrupted. "But we'll only go to the mouth of the Jaipurana. We'll wait and then fall back on them from the north."

Serena bobbed her head in mounting excitement. "If we leave a force blockading Riven Road south of Charybdis, we'll crush them in between us."

Jason frowned and pointed at a spot on the map, a foothill that commanded a valley. "What if they make their stand here? They'll have the heights and be able to rain fire on us with their cannon, even the ones they stole from Ox Bow Tower."

William laughed. "Ox Bow's cannon won't help them."

Serena shared a grin with him. "But they'll be useful to us."

Jason frowned in puzzlement. "I don't get it."

"The cannons can be made to explode on command," Jessira said. "When we realized we couldn't fully man the towers, we made sure to leave a weakness in the cannons in case something like this happened."

"You booby-trapped them," Jason said, his mouth slowly widening into a predatory smile.

Jake grinned as well.

William didn't share his friends' rising anticipation. He frowned when he noticed a problem. "If they're willing to push past our forces to reach Lilith, how did they think they'd escape off the island?"

Rukh folded his arms. "I'd guess their escape will await them at Lilith Bay. We should expect Sinskrill ships there."

"We'll have to leave a force back in Lilith then," Jessira said.

"How many do you think we'll need?" Rukh asked.

"Fifty," Jessira answered. "That should be enough to man the five cannons we have on Clifftop."

William did the math. "That doesn't leave you a lot of room if anyone gets tired or hurt."

"I can manage a cannon on my own," Jessira said.

William did a double-take. *In addition to everything else, are Rukh and Jessira thera'asras?*

Rukh's head shot up then, and he wore a grin of utter joy, one reflected on Jessira's face. "They're here. They must have finally heard our call."

William viewed them with confusion. "Who's here?"

"Our Kesarins," Jessira answered. "Aia and Shon."

CHAPTER 25: ALLIES AND PREMONITIONS

O*ctober 1990*

Aia tumbled out of the anchor line, and Shon followed her. Her head spun, and she had trouble seeing straight. A loud ringing filled her ears. Worst of all, she couldn't hear Shon's thoughts as anything other than a distant warble. Her stomach rebelled, and she yowled in pain. *I hate anchor lines!*

Aia hunched over, and her abdominal muscles involuntarily contracted. Her pupils dilated and the contractions continued until something gross emptied up her throat and out her mouth. *Disgusting.*

As soon as she finished vomiting, Aia instantly felt better. Not good, but better. She darted away from whatever she'd coughed up, and Shon did the same, also having retched. He quickly joined her.

That was grotesque! Shon said.

Aia silently agreed. At least her head no longer spun, her vision no longer blurred, and the last of the ringing in her ears had faded. She took a moment to scan their surroundings.

The sun had yet to rise, but a bright half-moon provided plenty of light. She and Shon stood in a valley, upon a small glade of damp grass with rugged boulders scattered about. Steep-shouldered hills, vined and jungled, surrounded them. A trail broke a path through the trees and ascended out of the valley. *Good. It should make travel easier.*

Aia's ears rotated, and she listened. *Rustling trees, whispering and rattling. Loud birds, not nearly as irritating as the roosters of Sand.* She also lifted her nose and inhaled deeply. Immediately, she scented a nearby stream. More sensations came to her. *Small animals, huddling in the muggy jungle, amongst fallen, moldy leaves and branches.* None of the creatures were worthy of her attention. She scented larger prey, deer or gazelles, and she salivated at the thought of fresh meat.

Her eagerness stunted when the sharp, acidic odor of large cat wafted on the wind. The animal—a male—had marked a nearby tree, and Aia growled. *He'd better not challenge us. He'll regret it.*

Aia picked out more details. Warm air played across her fur, a delight, after the bone-snapping chill of Sand—Kesarins weren't made for the cold. She smiled as she stretched her muscles and rolled her shoulders.

Shon luxuriated in the warmth as well. Aia sensed it in the way his ears lay back, and his eyes lidded. Shon rolled over and rubbed his back into the grassy glade. *Being warm is much better than being cold,* he said, staring at her from upside down.

We should have come here much sooner, Aia agreed.

Shon yawned. *To think our humans enjoyed this wonderfulness while we froze to death in Sand.*

Aia chuckled. *We're still alive,* she said. *We didn't actually freeze to death.*

Shon blinked. *We might have. Another winter, and I think we would have.*

Regardless, we survived, Aia said, *and though you found the cold painful and biting, I only thought it was uncomfortable.* For some reason she wanted to ensure that her little brother remembered that she was hardier than him . . . just like Rukh was hardier than Jessira.

Shon rolled over. *I'm thirsty.*

Now that he mentioned it, Aia was also thirsty. A drink would also wash away the terrible taste in her mouth. *There's water nearby.*

She and Shon padded to the stream. The water collected from the surrounding hills, forming a burbling stream that meandered through the valley and across pebbles and moss. Insects flitted above the waterline and amongst the reeds growing along both banks. Farther downstream Aia sensed that the rivulet deepened and widened.

She lapped water and drank until she was full, sighing in appreciation afterward. She felt more like herself, and the last lingering effects of the anchor line faded.

She caught Shon peering at her in puzzlement, his head tilted to the side. *You seem different,* he said.

What do you mean?

Bigger.

Aia studied her brother and noticed that he seemed larger as well. Thinking about it, she realized that she felt better than she ever had in Sand, more as she had once been when she'd roamed the Hunters' Flats. Stronger and more dangerous, too. *How do you feel?*

Shon narrowed his eyes in thought. *More like myself, like I used to be.*

Aia gave a blink of her eyes and a flick of her ears. *Me, too. I think it has something to do with this place, Arylyn.*

Shon grimaced, a flattening of his ears. *I told you we should have come here sooner.*

Aia sighed. *We had to help Landon first.*

We finished helping him weeks ago. We should have come here then, Shon persisted.

We couldn't know our work was complete until a few days ago.

But—

Aia batted him on the nose, no longer in the mood to talk about it. *Enough. We've wasted enough time. We need to find our humans.*

Aren't we supposed to find the troll-creature? That's what Jessira said.

Of course, Aia agreed.

Shon yawned. *Can I nap first?*

Aia considered the question. Any time they journeyed through one of the cursed anchor lines, it left her tired. Rukh needed her help, but she was so sleepy. Her eyes drooped, and she yawned, too. *Only for a short while,* she said. She curled up in a warm patch of sunshine.

~

Brandon stood on the deck of *Deathbringer*, automatically maintaining his balance amidst the ship's swaying motion. He stared astern to where the rest of the fleet followed. No lanterns lit the other ships, and they sailed as blackened silhouettes, assassins on the water. The wash of waves against the hull echoed dully, and despite night's fall Brandon could still see them relatively clearly. The light of a half-moon played on the waves, and with no obscuring clouds or mist, it provided enough illumination to easily identify the other vessels.

Brandon sighed. At least that same light also revealed that no islands or rocks sprouted from the water anywhere close by.

A gusting wind blew and filled *Deathbringer's* sails. The breeze brought blessed relief from the heat and humidity. Brandon lifted his sweaty shirt off his chest and fanned himself with it.

He'd been transferred to *Deathbringer*, his old ship, the one that had first brought him to Arylyn. The Servitor wanted him in command, stating that he trusted him to use the vessel more effectively than the previous captain, Hannah Yearn. She was a competent mahavan, much older than Brandon, but deathly averse to taking any risks, and risks might be required before the day was done.

Brandon faced the bow. Though he couldn't see it he knew that Arylyn hung directly past the horizon. The fleet had reached the magi's island home days earlier, dropping off the Secondus and most of the mahavans. Afterward, they'd pulled back and remained out of sight. Not forever, though. The Secondus was closing in on Lilith, and the fleet would soon begin their assault on the village as well, an attack that would surely result in the deaths of hundreds of the magi.

A queasy sensation twisted Brandon's insides at the thought. He wasn't entirely comfortable with the notion of bringing war to Lilith, and he wondered again how the Servitor could speak of Arylyn's destruction with such equanimity.

When Brandon had first returned to Sinskrill from the magi's home, his liege had asked him a great number of questions. Many of them had been about Serena and Selene. It was unsurprising. One of the most well-known, but least spoken of secrets on Sinskrill was that Serena and Selene were the Servitor's natural children. While Brandon had told his liege what he knew about Serena's and Selene's lives on Arylyn, an unvoiced emotion had filled the Servitor's features. Brandon suspected it was longing or even regret, and he understood.

Despite Sinskrill's harsh culture, certain things—like the love of a parent for a child—could never be entirely dimmed. Brandon recalled the pride shining in his mother's and father's faces when he'd been made a mahavan. There had also been something else in their unblinking, unexpressive drone faces, something that Brandon had long pondered. During his time spying on the magi he'd finally understood what it was. Love. His parents had loved him.

Which made what the mahavans would inevitably do to Lilith all the harder. Brandon regretted what was to come even as he accepted it as his duty. He'd take no pleasure in it. Not as he once might have. *My time on Arylyn has made me weak.*

As he pondered the truth about himself, he realized that his weakness had begun far earlier than his scouting pilgrimage to Arylyn. It started when Serena had escaped Sinskrill on her small dhow, *Blue Sky Dreams.* Preeti had gone after Selene, and Serena had nearly killed her for it. Brandon had seen the desperate love in Serena's face when Selene had been threatened. Worse, Brandon had understood Serena's actions and silently applauded them. Perhaps that was why she'd defeated them. Brandon hadn't wanted to win. He wondered if he wanted to win now as well.

Hannah approached, and Brandon set aside his traitorous thoughts.

"We've received word from the Servitor," she said. No sense of anger at her fallen status etched her voice. Hannah was one who followed orders and didn't worry about much else.

"What did he say?" Brandon asked.

"Adam's forces are two days from Lilith. We're to begin our bombardment tomorrow afternoon."

"Do we know of any forces left at the village?"

Hannah shook her head. "Expectations are that their forces will be north of the village, seeking to stop Adam. There shouldn't be anyone left in Lilith to defend against us."

"The plan relies on it," Brandon said.

Hannah blinked once, her features uncaring, as if the coming battle was of no concern. "The Servitor also states that we have nothing to fear. He says the cannons he's created and the *nomasras* he's provided will defend us from any counter-attack." Certainty filled her voice, as if the Servitor's words were unalterable truth.

Brandon wished he could be so sanguine. He recalled other aspects of his last conversation with the Servitor. Beyond regret at losing Serena and Selene, his liege had also been nervous. In fact, there might have been fear lighting his eyes. This attack wasn't quite as simple or risk-free as Hannah apparently believed.

~

T ravail sat with his eyes closed and his back to the rocky face of a spiny foothill west of Mount Madhava. Across his lap lay a staff, twelve feet in length and thick as log. Despite its massive size, the walking aid and weapon fit him. He rested his hands upon it, holding quiet, meditating and listening to the world.

An early afternoon sun beamed down. It cast the eastern half of the mountain in a shadow that cleanly bisected the peak all the way from its snowy top to its rugged shoulders. The sunshine also kept Travail warm in spite of the chill wind blowing endlessly at the heights upon which he sat. Fine dust swirled and the perpetual gusts tossed his long hair about, rippling through his thick, black fur. Travail ignored the wind and focused instead on the silence of his thoughts.

Peace, however, proved elusive as a disturbance interrupted his meditation.

Travail opened his eyes and searched for what had broken his concentration. He quickly discovered two large cats making their way up the slope toward him. One had a calico pattern, and the other was tawny with a white tuft on its chin and paws. Both were larger than any cat Travail had ever heard of. He stood to face them and readied his staff.

Twenty yards away, both cats sat down and curled their tails in front of their paws.

My name is Aia, a female voice spoke in Travail's mind.

My name is Shon, another voice said, this one a male.

Travail blinked in surprise and he tilted his head in thought. He recalled William's words about a calico kitten named Aia, from long ago during their time together on Sinskrill, one who could speak in a person's mind. But this was no kitten. She was huge.

I'm glad you think so, but we're still small compared to who we are meant to be, the female voice said.

Travail relaxed. The words told him that it must be the same animal.

I am no animal, Aia said, obviously offended. *I am a Kesarin.*

Travail smiled and planted the butt of his staff against the ground. His curiosity piqued. Something new had entered his life, something no book could properly explain. *I meant no offense,* he said. *My name is Travail. I am a troll.*

You look like a Bael, the male voiced, Shon apparently.

In some ways, yes, Aia said, *but his features aren't as thick and coarse, less bovine as well. More human.*

True, Shon agreed with a slight smile.

Travail's brows lifted as he recalled something once told to him. *A Bael is a creature from Arisa, Rukh and Jessira's world, is it not?*

Aia's eyes widened, and what Travail would have described as happiness filled her feline features. *You know Rukh and Jessira?*

Travail nodded. *I know of them, but I can't say that I know them very well. I've only spoken briefly to them. Most of my knowledge about them comes from my friends, William and Jake.* He pursed his mouth in thought before continuing. *If you don't mind me saying, Rukh and Jessira are odd humans.*

Shon surged to his feet and growled. *They are the greatest of humans.*

Travail pulled his staff closer and eyed the cats in worry. *Again, I meant no offense.*

Aia nipped Shon on his shoulder. *No offense was received,* she said, seeming to eye the other cat in annoyance.

Shon settled down, subsiding.

Travail relaxed somewhat. *Aia and Shon, what brings you to Arylyn?*

Aia shrugged—a brief narrowing of her eyes—or at least it seemed that way to Travail. *Our humans require our help. We sensed their need. We traveled to meet them.*

Travail viewed them in uncertainly. *Your humans? By this, I assume you mean Rukh and Jessira.*

Shon sighed, a long blink of his eyes. *Jessira is mine. Rukh belongs to Aia.*

They belong to you?

Both Kesarins nodded, a slight lifting of their chins and widening of their eyes. Again it seemed so to Travail, but who could truly tell with cats?

Kesarins, Aia corrected.

Travail wanted to roll his eyes at her pedantic correction.

Shon's eyes narrowed. *Are you a troll or a human?*

A troll, obviously.

Not to most cats, Aia said. *They lack the wit to see the difference. To them, you walk on two legs, which means you're human. We recognize the difference, though. We simply ask that you do the same on our behalf.*

Travail grinned at her statement. What wonderfully wise creatures. He decided he liked these two.

We think we'll like you, too, Aia said.

He'd have trouble getting used to them knowing his thoughts, though.

Shon slowly blinked his eyes. *All creatures have that problem with us.*

Travail felt oddly relieved by Shon's words, and he returned to what the Kesarins had earlier said. *And you're here because you sensed Rukh and Jessira's need?*

Aia nodded. *Our humans are always getting into trouble. I've lost count of the number of times they've required our help.*

Without us, they would have died many times over, Shon said.

Aia spoke, *Humans can behave foolishly, and ours can be the most foolish.*

Travail faced the Kesarins with puzzlement once more. When he'd called Rukh and Jessira 'odd' Shon had taken great offense. Now they insulted them? He wasn't sure how to interpret their strange behavior.

Aia smiled. *No one said Kesarins are consistent.*

Travail blinked as he considered Aia's words. He eventually shrugged. *What kind of trouble approaches Rukh and Jessira?*

Not just Rukh and Jessira, Aia corrected. *William and Serena also.*

Shon took up the explanation. *A large band of humans, deadly of intent, has come to this island.*

Along with a number of strange creatures with no shape, Aia added.

Travail frowned. *No shape?*

Aia nodded. *They constantly change their shapes. One second, they're birds, the next, something else.*

Unformed, Travail said. *You're speaking of unformed.*

Shon tilted his head. *Is that what you call them? A good name.*

A coldness settled in the pit of Travail's stomach. *And you know this how?*

Rukh and Jessira told us, Aia said. *They called us and told us. They also asked to find and warn you if at all possible.*

Travail's mouth curled, and he growled. In the ancient world, trolls had been Justices, givers of judgment. They still were, and sometimes justice required the harshest of verdicts. *Mahavans and unformed had arrived on Arylyn.* Travail readied himself for travel. *Let's find Rukh and Jessira.*

CHAPTER 26: FINAL PREPARATIONS

O ctober 1990

W illiam started in confusion when Jason nudged him.

"Pay attention," Jason hissed.

William glanced around the command tent, hoping no one else had noticed his momentary lack of awareness. He'd grown lost in his thoughts, rubbing the locket holding the picture of his family. It dangled from a silver chain around his neck. He'd been wondering how Landon was doing.

Thankfully, the others in the tent—Rukh and Daniel—had their heads bent over a map and hadn't noticed his inattentiveness. William gave Jason a brief nod of 'thanks'. Rukh had chosen the three of them to be his lieutenants, and William would have been humiliated if he'd been found staring off in the distance and not paying attention to the briefing. He returned his focus to Rukh's explanation.

Earlier in the day, the forces under Rukh's command had pushed hard, making a beeline through Jaipurana Pass. However, shortly after nightfall, with the unformed hopefully unable to see them, they'd turned around and edged back some distance the way they'd come. They'd made camp a few miles south of Jaipurana Pass and five miles north of the mahavans' last known location, which was near the entrance to Charybdis Way.

Outside the tent, a steep drop-off plunged on either side and ended in jagged scree. An intermittent wind moaned like an old man in pain. At these heights, the blustery breeze gusted cold, and William suppressed a shiver at the eerie sound and the icy chill. He'd grown too used to the rest of the island's warmth. Thankfully, Rukh had insisted they carry thick coats and warm boots and gloves. The heavy clothing was especially needed because they couldn't afford any fires. The flames would give them away.

Jason cleared his throat. "Will we send scouts to confirm the mahavans' location?"

Rukh answered. "No. The unformed might see them and give the mahavan commander knowledge of what we intend."

Jason frowned. "Assuming the trip-lines we left along the Riven Road are telling us the truth." He referred to the weaves they'd set along the road, which only went off during the passage of large groups of individuals.

Daniel shrugged. "I don't see what else the trip-lines could be picking up. It has to be the mahavans."

William tapped the map, at a point north of the Elven Tor and several miles from where the Riven Road originated off Sita's Song. "Are the rest of our forces in position, the group south of the mahavans?"

Rukh nodded. "I heard from Ward earlier in the evening. His group is in place. They've blockaded the entrance to Janaki Valley. They'll push north in the morning. We'll squeeze the mahavans in the Charybdis."

Jason was still frowning.

Rukh noticed. "What is it?"

Jason pointed at the same place William had. "Ward's group only has one hundred warriors. Are you sure it's enough to hold the line? From the last report, the mahavans number two hundred warriors and more than fifty unformed."

"Ward's also got cannons," Rukh reminded him, "and they're building fortifications and limiting the routes through which the mahavans can reach them."

Jason persisted. "What if we're late?"

Rukh offered no easy answer. "Ward's unit will have to hold."

William shifted, made uncomfortable at the reply.

"We better not be late," Jason muttered.

"We won't be," Rukh said.

"Any word from Lilith?" William asked. Since the mahavans had landed, he'd hardly spoken more than ten words to Serena, and he worried about her and everyone else. Selene, Mr. Zeus, Fiona . . . All those they'd left behind at the village. Even Jake, who was with Ward's group.

Rukh's jaw tensed. William guessed he was thinking about Jessira. "There hasn't been any sighting of the enemy," he replied, his voice flat as a drone's, "but they'll show. I'm sure of it."

He *was* worried about Jessira, and for some reason, William felt himself lifted by the thought. It was good to know their deadly, often grim and terrifying commander could still feel fear because it meant he was also human.

Jason grimaced. "Damn mahavans. Their ships are probably hanging over the horizon where we can't see them."

"That would be my guess as well," Rukh said. "Any other questions?"

Daniel spoke up. "Can the warriors talk softly amongst themselves? This is our first battle, and they'll want to discuss things."

"They can talk," Rukh said, "but only if an Air adept is available to form a block around them."

Daniel started in surprise. "You're still worried about Walkers listening in?"

William quirked a surprised eyebrow. "You're not? On Sinskrill, Walkers listened to everyone. I can't imagine them not doing the same thing here."

"I agree with William," Rukh said. "We don't know much about how the mahavans wage war, but what we know of their culture tells me that they are a deeply suspicious lot and prone to paranoia. I don't want to give our plans away when we can easily keep them secret."

Daniel nodded. "Yes, sir."

"Any other questions?" Rukh repeated. His gaze flicked expectantly from one of them to another.

A trio of "No, sirs" met his question.

Rukh clapped his hands. "Then get some rest. Be with your men. Tomorrow will be a tough day. The mahavans are on foot. We're on bicycles. Speed will be on our side. Even with a five-mile head start we should be on them within several hours." His face went hard. "After that the hard, bloody work starts. We'll drive them forward and break them against Ward."

"Yes, sir," William and the others replied.

"On final thing," Rukh said, reclaiming their attention. "Make sure everyone knows the night guard rotation. I don't want anyone taking it for any longer than two hours. That goes for the three of you, as well."

"Yes, sir," they replied again.

William quirked a grin as he thought of something. "You know, after all this is over we're going to have to come up with specific names for the small units making up the Irregulars."

Rukh smiled back. "Yes, but it's a task for another time. For now, get some rest."

~

Adam frowned as he considered what to do next.

Darkness had fallen, and his warriors had settled in for the evening, camping where the Riven Road broadened onto a wide shelf of stone before narrowing again as it entered the Charybdis. The spine of a mountain rose on one side of their position while on the side opposite, a scree slope plunged about fifty feet. Guards patrolled the camp's perimeter, a mix of mahavans and unformed. The latter paced about in the form of tigers, choosing an animal form that was both ferocious and had excellent night vision.

The only sounds to be heard were those of the surrounding jungle and the moaning wind. Adam had insisted on utter quiet, no conversations unless they were blocked. No fires, either. He didn't want anything to give them away.

While he stared about the camp, Adam considered how far his warriors had come. They'd penetrated deep into Arylyn, encountering little opposition on the way south. Only a few scouts here and there. Nothing more. Everything was going according to plan, which was what bothered Adam.

Things had gone *too* smoothly, and he should have realized it sooner. As Far Beyonders reckoned matters, Adam should have been keeping vigil for some demon named Murphy and his unalterable Law. The monster would always rear his ugly, horned head at the worst possible moment, and he had.

Earlier in the evening, Adam learned that the magi scouts they'd come across had possessed satellite phones. It meant the scouts had likely transmitted the mahavans' exact position. In fact, the magi might have known all along of Sinskrill's presence on their island. There might already be an ambush waiting for them up the road.

Adam cursed silently. *How do I plan when so much remains unknowable?*

Early in the march he'd used the Walkers' abilities to listen at a distance and eavesdrop as the magus commander, the supposed World Killer, Rukh Shektan, detailed a plan to meet the mahavans at the Jaipurana Pass. It was why Adam had forced his forces off the Riven Road and pushed them through the Scylla. It had been a hard march, longer. South of Mount Madhava he'd regained the Riven Road. They now had a clear shot to Sita's Song and Lilith with only the Charybdis to traverse.

Until tonight, Adam had thought his forces well-positioned, but thinking about it he realized the terrain ahead wasn't favorable. There were too many places to blockade the road, and Adam worried that a blockade was exactly what his forces would face.

Samuel Ingot, his second-in-command, approached. He wore his armor and arms, and Adam silently applauded his carefulness. The man stopped, his brows lifted in silent expectation.

Adam gestured and formed a block.

"You seem troubled, sir," Samuel said.

"I am troubled," Adam admitted. He reviewed his concerns with the other man.

Samuel grunted. "The unformed should have told us about the satellite phones days ago, the first time they encountered a scout."

Adam nodded agreement and glared at a passing unformed in fresh annoyance. "The magus commander, Rukh Shektan, doesn't strike me as a fool who'll run straight for where he thinks the enemy might be." He snorted in disgust. "In his shoes, I would have allowed us to reach this exact location, harry us through the Charybdis, and crush us between his forces."

Samuel stared south, as if he could see the potential ambush despite the darkness. "Have the unformed seen anything untoward up ahead?"

Adam shook his head. "Nothing but a rockslide. They can't make out much else given the fog and mist shrouding the area."

Samuel frowned, although the expression was difficult to make out in the dark. "I don't recall a rockslide on Riven Road within the Charybdis when I was here in the spring."

The young mahavan's words spurred a warning bell that jangled in the back of Adam's mind. His brows furrowed as he pondered what the rockslide might entail. "It wasn't in Brandon's report, either." He hesitated. "It could be a natural occurrence, but . . ."

"You don't believe it?"

Adam nodded as his misgivings crystallized. "It's more likely an ambush, a blockade, and Shektan's force of three hundred that we thought were rolling through the Jaipurana this afternoon might have circled back. They might be no more than a few miles north of our position."

Samuel swore. "What do we do, sir?"

Adam took a moment to think. "With first light we'll cut cross-country."

"It'll add days to our travel," Samuel said. "It'll also give the magi that much more time to prepare for us."

Adam had already realized that. "I'm open to suggestions."

As expected, Samuel had none to offer.

Adam sighed. "If I'm right about the rockslide and the location of Shektan's forces, we're liable to be ambushed if we march forward. It could be a disaster."

"Can the unformed act as a distraction?"

"They can, but despite their overall stupidity, I doubt they'll agree to suicide. Not even the Servitor could command them so."

Samuel straightened. "Our mission was to inflict death upon the enemy," he said, his tone righteous. "If you give me command of our mahavans, you and the unformed can sneak away. You can bypass the blocking forces and attack Lilith. Between you and the Servitor's ships, you can bring it to ruin."

Samuel's suggestion sounded noble, except for one fact. "How do you think I can keep up with the unformed?" Adam asked. "They can transform into birds or animals that are fleet of foot."

Nervousness etched Samuel's features, and he cautiously glanced about. Though there was no one near and a block disguised their conversation, he leaned in close. "I know about you and the Servitor. Your unformed powers."

Adam's face went flat and inscrutable. He didn't want to kill Samuel but he would if he had to. No one else could learn what Samuel had apparently discovered. Adam gazed at Samuel through narrowed eyes as he considered what to do.

Samuel swallowed heavily, but he never dropped his gaze.

"How did you learn?" Adam asked after a moment of silence.

"When we first landed, you disciplined a young unformed," Samuel said. "I saw your teeth. They weren't your own."

"You were mistaken."

"I am certain I was not."

Adam fell silent again, grimacing sourly as he cursed Samuel's clever eyes. "What do you want in return for your silence?"

Samuel straightened to a military posture, his face full of purpose. "Nothing. I only wish to serve."

Adam gazed at Samuel skeptically. "How?"

"Split the forces as I said. Take the unformed, wreck Lilith, and escape aboard the fleet waiting at Lilith Harbor. I'll . . ." Samuel's mouth tightened. "I'll ensure you have time to complete the pilgrimage."

Adam wasn't sure whether to trust the man, but he saw no other options. If he *could* trust Samuel, different opportunities might also be available. His mind flitted to other means of accomplishing what the Servitor had ordered. His mouth pursed as an idea came to him. He focused on Samuel, who still waited expectantly. "You understand what you're offering?"

"I do."

Samuel sounded earnest, and Adam trusted it. Samuel had never been able to fully control his emotions, not like Serena, who could lie to the most cynical sinner and have them proclaim her an angel. "Good," Adam said, "then this is what we'll do." He explained what he had in mind. "Do you have any final requests?"

Samuel managed a weak grin. "Can you take Evelyn with you?"

Adam barked laughter.

~

Serena stood atop Clifftop, at the place where the Village Green jutted forward like a ship's prow. Night had fallen, and she gazed at the ocean, still visible beneath the cold light of a half-moon. Waves washed against Lilith Bay's golden shore, and trees all along the village's escarpment swayed beneath a constant breeze. That same wind whipped Serena's hair, making her wished she'd braided it. The smell of roasting meat and spices wafted from Jimmy Webster's restaurant as a band set up their instruments on the rebuilt gazebo. Nearby conversations drifted to Serena. So did bright laughter. It seemed like most people were determined to treat tonight like any other.

But tonight *was* different, not simply because none of the lamp-posts had been lit—Jessira wouldn't allow it—but because tonight might be the last evening of what Lilith had always been. The peace and beauty here might be—likely would be—shattered.

Others must have realized it as well because Serena sensed a tension in the air, an underlying fear in the words and laughter she heard from those still out and about.

Serena glanced at Jessira, who stood beside her. Of course *she* had been wise enough braid her hair. It hung down her back, and her green eyes seemed strangely alight as she searched the water. Serenity, however, prevailed on her face and posture, and Serena took heart. If Jessira wasn't afraid then she shouldn't be either.

Fiona paced up alongside them. "Selene is with Emma and her family."

"How is she doing?" Serena asked.

"Her friends are treating tonight like it's some kind of wonderful adventure," Fiona replied, "but Selene knows better. She's of Sinskrill. She remembers how deadly life can be. She doesn't laugh like her friends."

Serena wished her sister didn't have those grim, childhood memories, but if nothing else, Sinskrill had made Selene wise to the world's dangers as well as strong enough to face them. Serena only hoped that strength wouldn't be needed tomorrow. She prayed that no violence would touch her little sister.

"I hope she stays safe," Serena said.

"I hope everyone stays safe," Fiona said.

Mr. Zeus popped his head over the top of Cliff Spirit's Main Stairs. Since the mahavans' landing on Arylyn, deeper wrinkles now etched the old man's craggy face, and he looked to have aged ten years in the past few days. "The terraces are empty," he told Jessira. "I've spoken to some of the older citizens, the ones who didn't want to leave their homes, and talked sense into them. The Irregulars are helping gather them up."

Jessira nodded. "Good. Get some rest. You're worn out."

Fiona stepped forward. "I've found a place for us," she said to Mr. Zeus. "Come." She held out a hand, and Mr. Zeus took it.

Serena smiled fondly as she watched the old couple drift hand-in-hand deeper into the heart of Clifftop.

Jessira smiled as well. "I'm glad for them. They deserve happiness, no matter how late in life they found it."

"We all do," Serena said. "This is a beautiful place full of good people."

Jessira's smile became distant and wistful. "It would be a tragedy to see Lilith die."

Serena had heard Jessira and Rukh's story about their homes, Ashoka and Stronghold, and she prayed Lilith didn't meet the same fate as those two fabled cities. She flicked her gaze at Jessira. "Do you really think the mahavans will come by ship?"

Jessira nodded. "Of course. You do, too."

"Where are they, then?"

Jessira pointed to the ocean. "Beyond the horizon. They're waiting there, but sometime tomorrow, they'll sail to the bay." Her face hardened. "Then it starts."

Serena, not usually one to offer hope, found herself in a strange position. "I'm sure our cannons will drive them off "

Jessira offered a crooked smile. "Something tells me it won't be as easy as that. This Servitor wouldn't have come here without a means to hurt us. Or defend himself."

Serena hoped Jessira was wrong. "Then maybe the Irregulars who went north will quickly finish off the mahavans and help us deal with the Servitor."

Jessira scowled. "Rukh leads the Irregulars." She sounded upset for some reason.

Serena frowned. "Isn't that a good thing?"

Jessira nodded, but she still scowled. "It is, but I don't like being here without him. I'm afraid."

Serena found the words stunning. Jessira had always struck her as fearless.

Jessira's face cleared. "You misunderstand," she said, obviously noticing Serena's shock. "I don't fear for myself. I fear for Rukh. He battles with reckless abandon. He'll get himself killed without me." She muttered. "I only hope Aia and Shon find him soon. They'll protect him from himself."

As an inspiring speech prior to a battle's eve, Serena found Jessira's words lacking.

~

Jake checked his sword one final time, making sure it slid smoothly from its scabbard. While he'd trained with the weapon daily during the past four or five months, it didn't mean he felt comfortable having it on his hip. The sword had a single purpose—to kill—and while Jake had killed before—Dalton the Hunter—it didn't mean he wanted to do it again. Truthfully, he wished he didn't have to, especially with a sword. To feel the blade penetrate someone else's flesh, to have it cut and slice. To stand close enough to smell their fear, their breath, and see the light leave their eyes.

Jake scowled at the thought. No, he wasn't looking forward to this, but it was happening anyway, and he'd do whatever it took to keep his friends safe.

He finished packing away his sleeping bag and the rest of his gear and racked the equipment on his bicycle. Once done, he took time to study the rest of the camp.

The sky held a rosy hue, barely visible through the thick fog that the Irregulars had raised last night. The misty air hugged the ground, eddying all around them and much of the surrounding jungle. Hopefully it hid them from the unformed, although it did nothing to silence the birds waking up with sunrise and calling out from the nearby trees. Nor did it mask the stink of nervousness coming off the Irregulars or the moldy scent like stale grass clippings wafting off the jungle.

At least the fog hushed many of the noises the warriors made as they moved around in quiet efficiency and professionalism. No pots clanged, no loud conversations emanated, and no sudden shouts of laughter rang out, only the shuffling of boots across the flagstone pavers of the Riven Road.

Jake watched the Irregulars. Some were busy stowing their gear while others had already finished their packing and gathered in small groups to share a cold, quiet breakfast of jerky and boiled potatoes. As Jake observed them, he tried not to think about how many of them might die today.

His thoughts were interrupted when Ward called for a meeting with him and Julius, the two lieutenants. Ward waited in front of his tent with crossed arms and a furious frown.

Jake arrived first and waited on Julius. The one-time Rastafarian had long since shaved his dreadlocks, and seriousness had replaced his usual happy-go-lucky demeanor.

"Word came in from Rukh," Ward said after Julius arrived. "The mahavans are on the move."

Jake's heart-rate picked up. A pulse of adrenaline pounded through him, and he bounced on his feet.

Ward scowled, though, like he'd eaten something sour. "The bad news is that they've abandoned the Riven Road."

Jake's nervous energy faded, and he and Julius shared a frown of confusion. Questions tumbled through his mind. "Where'd they go?"

"And how'd they sneak away?" Julius asked. "We had everything clamped down."

"How should I know?" Ward said. "We thought they were settled in for the night. The scouts on the rises never saw anything. But sometime in the middle of the night, the mahavans broke camp and vanished down the side of a rocky hill and into the wilderness. Rukh has scouts on their trail, but the mahavans are moving fast."

Julius swore. "I still don't understand how they knew to leave right then and there."

"Their damned unformed must have figured it out," Ward said, still scowling. "Anyway, Rukh isn't sure where they went, but he doesn't like whatever they're doing. He thinks they've split their forces."

Jake cursed. *Stupid mahavans. Why couldn't they just do what they were expected to?* He had been worried about today's battle for weeks now. He'd spent the entire night thinking about it. This morning the worry had changed to acceptance. At this point, he only wanted to get it over with. To learn it would be delayed pissed him off.

"Damn mahavans," Julius said, sounding every bit as bitter as Jake felt.

Ward nodded agreement.

Jake spoke. "If they're off the road, can Rukh follow the mahavans by bicycle?"

"No," Ward said with a sigh. "The mahavans took a rugged path.

Depending on which way they go, it can add days to their travel to Lilith, but regardless, Rukh and the others will have to follow them on foot."

Julius no longer scowled. Instead, he wore a pensive expression, and he began pacing. "What if they never intended to go to Lilith?"

"What do you mean?" Ward asked.

Julius hesitated, apparently unsure. A moment later, his energy deflated. "I don't know. Nothing, I guess. But why would they abandon the road?"

"Maybe the unformed saw the rockslide and fog, and they put two and two together," Jake suggested.

"It's possible," Ward agreed, "but at this point it also doesn't matter."

"What do we do then?" Jake asked. "Hold our position?"

"No," Ward said. "Rukh wants us to fall back. He wants us closer to Lilith in case the mahavans have separated their forces. We have to be in place to defend the village."

Jake thought about it. "Makes sense," he said after a moment. "He wants us to create a line of defense instead of chasing the mahavans all over the island."

"Is that what Rukh's going to do?" Julius asked. "Chase the maha-vans down?"

Jake answered. "He'll have to. We can't have a large group of armed hostiles roaming the countryside. We need to end this. Now."

"Amen," Ward breathed, "but that's Rukh's job. He'll call and let us know if the plans change, but for now, we break camp and head south."

"How far south?" Jake asked.

"North of Janaki," Ward said. "Here. Look." He dragged a portable desk out from his tent and unrolled a map of Arylyn. He set small stones on the corners to hold it in place and pointed to where the Riven Road branched off Sita's Song. "Rukh wants us here, directly north of the entrance to Janaki Valley."

Julius nodded. "We'd still be in position to either block them from entering the valley or bring support to wherever Rukh needs us."

Jake studied the terrain leading off from where the mahavans had made camp. "It'll take the mahavans a long time to reach us from there."

Julius frowned as well. "For some reason, I'm doubting they'll spend days or weeks wandering around Arylyn's interior. They've never struck me as stupid."

Ward nodded grim agreement. "This would be a lot easier if they were."

Jake frowned more deeply as he stared at the map. A worrying idea slowly developed in his mind. "Do we have numbers on how many mahavans left the camp?"

Ward must have picked upon his agitation. "What are you thinking about?"

Jake chewed his lower lip in thought. "If the mahavans knew enough to get off the Riven Road at the exact moment they did, then like I said, they probably knew they were about to run into an ambush."

Julius grunted. "Right, but it still doesn't explain how they figured it out."

"We can worry about that some other time," Jake said. He continued to study the map, quickly measuring distances and making rough calculations. "Rukh is worried that the Sinskrill forces might have separated, and I'm thinking about what that might mean." He finished his calculations and met the eyes of the other two men. "What if the unformed formed one group and the mahavans formed the other?"

"Why's that important?" Julius asked. "From what we know the unformed are commanded by a Prime, and while they're deadly, they don't know how to fight as a unit."

"But the Servitor and Adam Paradiso do know how to command a military unit," Jake said, "and Serena said both of them are unformed. She told us back on Sinskrill, right before me and William escaped with her and Selene."

Ward's blood drained from his face. "The unformed can fly."

Julius retrieved his satellite phone. "We need to let Lilith know what might be coming their way."

~

Adam smiled as he listened to the magi commanders discuss their plans. *So. They intend to block the passage to Sita's Song. Then we'll have to enter Janaki south of them.* He never paused from the fast march that he'd set for his forces—they needed distance from the World Killer. He unfurled his map as he strode along and quickly found what he was looking for.

Firedeep Gorge. A narrow trail. It entered Janaki in the middle portion of the valley, well south of Ward and his magi. *Perfect.*

CHAPTER 27: BATTLE JOINED

O*ctober 1990*

"Ships!" Fiona shouted.

Serena startled awake. The sun had barely risen, and the sky held the faintest pink that transitioned to a deep blue hue that slowly pushed back the black. The floral scent of gardenias puffed with every breeze, and an obnoxious rooster cawed, but Serena paid the bird no mind. Around her slumbered the fifty Irregulars meant to man the cannons mounted along Clifftop. They stirred, some wakening more quickly than others.

Serena surged out of her sleeping bag, kicking her way to her feet. She joined Fiona and Mr. Zeus at the edge of the Village Green and stared down at Lilith Bay. For once the village's beauty held none of her attention.

Jessira quickly arrived as well. She scanned the bay with a pair of binoculars.

Serena spied the ships in Lilith Bay, small from the distance. She wanted to see them more clearly and sourced her *lorethasra*.

She layered a mix of Air and Water upon a foundation of Spirit before reaching for a dendritic root of *lorasra* and creating a weave. The air in front of her eyes hardened and took the shape of a pair of lenses. The ships in the bay came into immediate focus.

Fiona and Mr. Zeus had also created braids similar to Serena's and examined the vessels, too.

Jessira noticed the weaves. "I really need to learn to do that," she murmured. She gazed through her binoculars once more, returning her regard to the ships entering the harbor.

Serena scanned the Sinskrill fleet. "*Demolition*," she noted. "The Servitor's flagship."

"It flies his standard," Fiona confirmed. "It's the one with the black chair and white spear on a field of dark gray."

"Those other four vessels are more modern, though," Jessira said, frowning in concentration as she peered at the fleet. She cursed. "They have cannons, four per vessel, two each on starboard and port, except for *Demolition*. That one has five. One on the prow."

Serena narrowed the focus of her 'binoculars' and saw what Jessira meant. The Sinskrill cannons mounted on each ship were longer than the ones William had developed, but there was no mistaking that shape.

Mr. Zeus seemed to be counting. "I make fifteen crew per ship," he said. "Including the flagship."

Jessira nodded. "Agreed, and if their cannons are like ours, they'll require five mahavans to fire each one." She tilted her head in thought. "Except for the Servitor. As powerful as he is, he can probably fire a cannon by himself."

Daniella Logan, who stood nearby, had also been staring at the ships, and she swore. "How did they learn to make a cannon?" She glared at Serena and Fiona.

Serena shook her head. "I have no idea. They didn't have any when I was there."

Fiona replied as well. "Likely the Servitor knew the secret of their manufacture all along. His bloodline holds secrets we can only guess upon."

Serena figured the same, although there was another possibility. "Or maybe Lord Shet told him."

"What makes you think that?" Mr. Zeus asked.

Serena shook her head helplessly. "I don't know. It's just a thought."

Jessira's features took on a serene but firm countenance. "It doesn't matter how or when they learned. They have cannons, and we have work to do." She barked orders. "Back away from the cliff's edge. Get to the cannons. Ranging shots first, but if possible, I want those ships sunk before breakfast."

Mr. Zeus chuckled. "Now that's a plan I can get behind."

They rolled the cannons forward and set them up ten feet from the cliff's edge. Each one had a barrel made of black marble lined with gray steel and squatted between heavy wagon wheels. The weapon's bore was wide but short, and it reminded Serena of an armless fire hydrant tipped onto its side. A wheel crank allowed for adjustment of the barrel's elevation.

"Ranging fire only," Jessira reminded them. "Save your strength and your energy. Once we have their distance, we'll make them wish they never came here."

Serena took heart from her words. She moved to her position next to Fiona, Mr. Zeus, and the Logan sisters. Karla loaded a shell into the cannon they'd been assigned. After she stepped aside, everyone sourced their *lorethasra*. The various scents of their *asra* wafted on the breeze as Daniella wove a hissing braid of Air that twined from her neck to her hips. From Mr. Zeus came a rumbling strand of Earth that curled around his abdomen and legs. He gathered it in his hands. Karla created a thick braid of Water, gurgling and washing over her shoulders and down her arms.

Serena took a deep breath. *My turn.* She formed a thick thread of Fire, not paying attention to its sulfur stink. She attached it to the corresponding Element from *lorasra*.

Finally came Fiona with her silver Spirit. She nodded her readiness and shouted, "Go!"

Serena and the other three magi united their weaves upon the *nomasra* in the cannon's bore. The black shell slowly brightened, radiating like an old-style light-bulb slowly coming to life. Fiona attached her braid of Spirit to it, and the *nomasra* plate grew thicker, transforming into a globe. The shell's glow grew incandescent.

After a few more seconds Fiona let the *nomasra* explode out of the cannon.

Serena tracked the munition's movement as it left a streak of light across the sky. Fiona remained attached to it through her line of Spirit, and she sent it hurtling at *Demolition*. The *nomasra* juked right and left, and Serena figured the mahavans sought to tear control of it from her grandmother's grasp. They failed. The shell continued to shift its flight. It eventually steadied, ripping downward. It was aimed dead-on for *Demolition*. Serena leaned forward in anticipation.

Yards above *Demolition's* mainmast, a gray webbing, something that resembled Rukh's and Jessira's Shields, crackled around the ship. The shell detonated impotently against the protective barrier, the sound reaching them seconds later.

Serena gaped in dismay. She shared an expression of shock with Fiona and Mr. Zeus. *What the hell was that?*

The other cannon crews ran into the same problem.

Jessira remained unperturbed. "Keep up the fire. Let's see if their protection weakens."

Ten more shells from each crew and ten similar fruitless results followed her command.

"Switch crews," Jessira ordered.

Serena stepped aside, tired from her sourcing and frustrated by their lack of success.

Mr. Zeus pulled her aside. "Go check on your sister. Make sure she's all right. We may have a long day ahead of us and you never know how it might end."

Serena nodded. Until the advent of that gray webbing, she hadn't believed the battle for Arylyn could end in anything other than victory. Now, she wasn't so certain.

~

W illiam crowded next to Jason, Daniel, and Rukh as the four of them pored over a set of maps spread out on a fold-up table. The late morning sun shimmered in the sky, and the air contained a thick, damp quality. It promised to be a hot day, and it didn't help that his camouflaged hemp clothing trapped his sweat. He fanned himself with his shirt, lifting it off his chest. Gnats buzzed about in the motionless air and pestered him as they flew around his head. He blew them away with a small blast of Air.

Rukh leaned close to the map. With a grimace of concern he traced the line of a narrow valley a few miles away. After discovering that the mahavans had departed from their campsite in the middle of the night, they'd been forced to ditch their bikes and chase them on foot, sending groups of scouts up ahead. After a full day of pursuing the Sinskrill warriors, they had finally brought them to bay.

Rukh had been wary of ambushes. A few minutes ago, they'd received word from a unit that believed the mahavans were readying to make a stand in a canyon with a tapering entrance and an even narrower exit. Rocky, low-lying hills surrounded it. It was the same valley that Rukh traced on the map with his finger.

William flicked his eyes across the terrain surrounding them, and he shifted nervously. He didn't like stopping here in this canyon hemmed by tall hills. There were too many places for an ambush. He gazed about, imagining who might be crouched behind the large mounds of grass covering portions of the hard ground, which was a mix of shale and clay. He worried about who might be hidden on the other side of the cluster of stunted trees growing next to a pencil-thin stream.

Rukh didn't so much as flick his gaze away from the map. "No enemy is near us."

Jason glanced up from where he'd been working a stone out of one of his boots. He'd picked it up during their pursuit of the mahavans across the rocky rises near Mount Madhava. "How can you be so sure?"

Rukh straightened to address him. "Because the scouts have already been through here, and the herd of wild goats standing on the hillsides wouldn't be lingering if there were armed men in their midst."

William studied the goats. He hadn't noticed them until now, and he grunted acceptance.

"What if they're unformed?" Daniel.

"Then they're poor scouts since all of them are busy chewing their cuds," Rukh replied. "None of them have once looked our way."

"What are we going to do when we catch the mahavans?" Jason asked. "Ward is headed back to the northern entrance of Janaki Valley—"

"He may be out of position, one way or another," Rukh said, "especially if he's right that the unformed have split off from the rest of the Sinskrill forces and taken to the air."

"Then the Irregulars we left at Lilith will have to hold," William said. He privately said a prayer for Serena and everyone else back in Lilith.

"They *will* hold," Rukh said.

Jason cleared his throat. "Point is that without Ward, we'll only outnumber the mahavans three hundred to two hundred—"

"We'll outnumber them by even less if the unformed aren't gone," Daniel said.

"Right," Jason said with a nod. "What do we do?"

Rukh pointed to the canyon he'd been studying. "What do you make of this?" he asked. "This is where the scouts say the mahavans have stopped their flight. The reports state that about one hundred warriors remain there behind a line of fortifications. Where are the others, then? We were told there were two hundred mahavans."

Jason spoke. "Unless that number included the unformed."

"It didn't," William said. "Remember, whenever the scouts saw the unformed in human form they were naked."

Jason grunted.

"Could it be a trap?" Daniel asked, pointing at the map.

Rukh nodded. "It's most definitely a trap, and we're going to spring it. But before we do I want to know where the rest of the mahavans are. They have their own cannons as well as ours."

Daniel frowned. "We can't explode ours until we can actually see them."

William peered at the map. "What about this hill? It's steeper than the others but has a relatively flat top. Wouldn't that be a good place to set up their cannons? It has clear lines of sight all the way to the canyon's entrance."

Rukh smiled briefly in apparent approval. "My thoughts as well." He pointed to another spot on the map. "And a rockslide here could wipe us out as we penetrate the canyon. They likely have units there as well."

"Unless we send a unit to wipe theirs out first," Jason suggested.

"How many do you think would be needed to eliminate the forces on that hill?" Rukh asked.

"Fifteen," Jason answered. "I'd guess the mahavans have four or five warriors over there. That's all it would take to bring down that hill. Plus, I'm guessing they won't use more men than they absolutely have to."

"I agree," Rukh said. "You'll command that unit."

William pointed to a streambed. "If we come through here it'll be a tough approach, but we'll be hidden from that flat-topped ridge."

"What about their scouts?" Rukh asked.

"We'll have to locate and neutralize them," William answered, "but I don't see them venturing too far from the main body of their forces. They'll be needed in the battle."

"Then what about the flat hill where they might have cannons?" Rukh asked.

Daniel leaned closer to the map and pointed. "This hill isn't ideal, but it seems to be taller than that ridge," he noted. "And there might boulders or outcroppings near the peak. We can set up our own cannons behind them and smash the mahavans the moment we see them."

Rukh smiled. "I like that. How many warriors will you need?"

Daniel started. "You want me to command them?"

Rukh eyed him challengingly. "Do you think you can handle it?"

Daniel slowly smiled. "Leave it to me, sir. Give me twenty-five Irregulars, and I'll wipe them out."

"See that you do," Rukh said. "The rest of us will be mincemeat otherwise."

William noticed something else. "Once we take the scree slope and neutralize the mahavans' cannons we can penetrate through the streambed and also this river valley—" he indicated the positions on the map "—and sweep down from the north and south and trap the remaining mahavans. We'll destroy them en masse."

Rukh slapped him on the shoulder. "Well done. You'll command the northern elements. I'll command the southern. Questions?"

"No, sir," all three replied.

"Then gather the men you'll need," Rukh said to Jason and Daniel. "I want you ready for a swift march in a half-hour." He turned to William. "Figure out which units you want with you." He met each of their gazes. "Let's roll."

William saluted sharply, as did Jason and Daniel, and they left to carry out Rukh's commands.

"This is it," Jason said, his eyes bright and excited.

"It's a good plan," William said. "The cannons are the key, though."

"I'll take care of them," Daniel said with a smile, "and after I take them out, I promise not to drop any rocks on you."

William barked laughter. "Even if you did, they'd only break on Jason's hard head."

The other two chuckled, but the importance of what they intended quickly stole William's humor. They were about to see battle and blood. Death as well. None of them might see another day. The other two had also stopped laughing. They probably realized the same thing.

"Stay safe," William said and gave Jason and Daniel a quick hug. "Don't do anything I wouldn't."

Jason grinned. "So, don't do anything stupid?"

William chuckled and watched them go. As he did, he once more considered the plan they'd come up with. It *was* a good plan, but the whole time they'd been discussing it, William had the sense that Rukh had already known it. Like he'd already come up with all those ideas and had been waiting for his lieutenants to figure them out, too. It was like Rukh had prescience—a word William first read in *Dune*—when it came to war. He only hoped they were as successful as Muad'Dib's Fremen when it came to battle.

~

Brandon braced himself and held onto a line as *Deathbringer* swept across the bay. The sun had long since risen, but Lilith's cliffs still shaded much of the bay. It left the area blessedly cool, which was unusual for the tropics. A stiff, onshore breeze blew, and it whipped Brandon's hair and snapped taut *Deathbringer's* sails.

Brandon squinted against the salt spray and silently urged the vessel to greater speed. He loved the rushing responsiveness of wood and wind and made a private promise to build his own ship when he returned to Sinskrill.

Shouts from Clifftop drew his attention. At this distance, the words were an indistinct blur of noise, except for a Walker. Brandon sourced his *lorethasra*, focused Air, and gathered those cries as a farmer did his crops. He listened as the magi shouted in consternation. Their cannons remained ineffectual against the Servitor's fleet. *Good. Let them fear.*

Brandon eyed *Deathbringer's* prow once again. The figurehead remained that of a demon with a horned head and glowing, red eyes, but below it had been mounted a plain, gray globe. It crackled whenever the magi shells reached the ship, and the shield it produced extended out and deflected any incoming blow. *Another of the Servitor's new weapons.*

It made the attack on Lilith child's play, but Brandon was conflicted about their success. Like all mahavans he hated the magi, but he also appreciated the culture they'd developed, the beauty of their village.

"Bring the ship about," he shouted. "Rake them again with a full spread to starboard. Reduce that village to debris." He winced internally at his words.

The drones aboard the ship carried out the orders, while the ten mahavans—two for each Element—moved to the starboard cannons and readied their next attack.

Brandon gazed upon Lilith, upon her proud terraces and lovely homes, upon her lacework bridges, and the glory of her cataracts. Thus far, the fleet hadn't accomplished much damage. A building here and there had tumbled, but most of the attacks had been aimed at Clifftop. From far below in the bay, Brandon couldn't tell how much destruction they'd managed. Part of him hoped it wasn't too severe.

His satellite phone rang. *The Servitor.* Brandon shifted his attention to the fleet and quickly found *Demolition* several hundred yards away and deeper in the harbor. He answered the phone. "Yes, my liege."

"There has been a change in plans," the Servitor said. "Adam will arrive with the unformed later in the day."

"What about his mahavans?"

The Servitor didn't answer at once. "We underestimated the magi's resolve. Their warriors vastly outnumber our own. Adam's mahavans may not survive today's engagement. They will battle for Sinskrill's glory and retreat if they can."

Brandon silently cursed. Once again, the magi might defeat the mahavans. *How can such a weak people offer such resistance against their betters?*

"Their sacrifices will not be forgotten," the Servitor was saying.

Brandon spoke without thinking. "Is there no way to save them?" He immediately bit back an oath. His question too closely resembled a challenge of the Servitor's judgment.

"No," the Servitor replied.

Brandon exhaled softly in relief. The Servitor had chosen to discount his breach in decorum. "What are my orders, my liege?"

"Raze the village," the Servitor replied. "Kill as many as possible and wreck what we can't destroy."

"Yes, my liege." Brandon hung up the phone and gazed at Lilith again. In his mind's eye he imagined the village ruined. He imagined smoke billowing from the village. Homes destroyed. Terraces wrecked, those lacy bridges shattered.

He couldn't make himself believe such an occurrence was a good thing.

CHAPTER 28: DECEPTIONS KILLED

O *ctober 1990*

J ason crouched next to Tam Emond, an older member of the
Irregulars. Tam possessed a hard-bitten, hard-eyed, calm presence, which was unsurprising since the gray-haired, gray-
bearded magus had seen action in Korea and Vietnam as a leather-
neck, a Marine. Sometime in the early seventies Mr. Zeus had found
him and brought him to Arylyn, where he'd taken up the life of a
farmer and a vintner. A few weeks ago he'd set aside his vineyards and
joined the Irregulars. He could have—should have—been one of
Rukh's lieutenants, but Tam had declined. He'd told Rukh in a firm
but polite tone that he had been a sergeant for twenty years in the
Marines and had no desire to be anything else.

Jason huddled with Tam and the others who would take the rocky
slope that loomed ahead. They waited in a copse of scruffy pine trees.
While the foliage provided only minimal coverage, minimal was
better than nothing. Fifty yards of empty plain stretched before them.
It quickly rose into a set of sharply elevated stony hills. No grass or

greenery marred the area past the trees, and the sun beat down, hot and humid. Jason ignored the sweat beading on his face and checked his watch.

Noon.

Someone nudged Jason's shoulder. He glanced aside and saw Tam gesturing. He stared to where the older magus pointed, to the southern peak of the scree slope, their objective.

Jason sourced his *lorethasra*, ignored the aroma of dandelions—the scent of his Spirit—and quickly braided a weave. The air in front of his eyes hardened and invisible binoculars brought the slope into focus. He immediately saw what Tam had noticed and nodded understanding.

Silhouetted against the sky were a group of hunched figures. From the north side of the hill they could have passed for boulders, but Jason saw legs, arms, and heads. *The mahavan ambush.*

Tam shifted closer and whispered in his ear. "If we send the bulk of the men east, they can stay hidden in the trees. They get to the slope, regroup behind that large outcropping over yonder—" he pointed, "—and attack before the mahavans realize anything's wrong."

It was a good idea, but Jason saw a flaw. "During the last five yards of their ascent, they'll be exposed," he said. "The mahavans will hear them coming. They'll be fragged."

Tam whispered, "They have that projection they can hide behind." He pointed again. "They wait there until—"

Jason saw the shape of Tam's plan and he nodded excitedly. "—the warriors we send west get in position and distract the mahavans."

Tam grunted. "It's not the best notion I ever had. Be a lot better if we had air support to pin them down."

"Be better if the fragging mahavans never showed up."

"Fragged," Tam mused. "Strange the way words carry across worlds and retain a bit of their meaning."

Jason shrugged, not sure what Tam meant. Instead, he chewed the inside of his lip as he considered the numbers and the situation. From what he could tell, four mahavans crouched atop the hill. He had fifteen magi. "How many do you think we should send east and west?" he asked.

"Ten east, five west. You take the east, I'll take the west."

"Those going west are going to have it hard," Jason warned.

Tam smiled. "Just be ready. We'll probably beat you to the top anyway."

Jason grinned, and the two of them shuffled back to where the rest of the Irregulars waited deeper in the copse.

After a quick explanation of what they intended, Jason led a group of ten magi skulking along the eastern face of the rocky slope. They passed out of the line of trees and sprinted for a large, blocky formation at the base of the hill. A scattering of stones and pebbles crunched as they ran. Jason prayed the mahavans wouldn't turn around. *Don't look down. Don't look down.* His heart thumped the entire way, and he breathed relief when they reached the rise. He and the others—a mix of men and women—hunched low.

"Everyone drink some water," he ordered. "We climb from here. Stay flat and low. Careful where you step. We don't want loose rocks or whatever giving us way. I'll lead, but you all know where we're headed." He pointed. "That knobby jut of stone. Once we get there, we wait for Tam's signal."

His Irregulars nodded, their faces trusting and alert but fearful.

Jason swallowed down a bolus of concern. *What if I'm wrong about this?* Fresh sweat beaded on his forehead, his chest, and lower back. His mouth went dry. He gulped down a final swig of water before shoving down his worries. *Hope I'm not wrong.*

A final series of deep breaths, and he shuffled out from behind the outcropping. The others followed on his heels, remaining hunched as they scuttled up the hill. Jason watched his steps, avoiding loose rocks and pebbles, and made sure the sword strapped to his back didn't catch on anything. They soon reached their target, the knobby formation.

Jason silently exulted. The rest of the Irregulars huddled close, and he could sense their excitement as well. *Now where's Tam?*

Seconds later, shouts arose from atop the hill. Elements raged. Braids of Fire crackled down the slope. They lit the air, causing a heat shimmer as they boomed. Threads of Earth growled. Bolts of Air hissed. Even Water susurrated. Answering Elements raged up the hill.

Jason gestured, and he and the other Irregulars left the protection of the rise. They sprinted for the top. Twenty yards. Fifteen. It might as well have been a thousand. Time slowed. Jason's heart pounded. Each beat stretched out, endless. His heaving breath sounded like bellows. He took a peek upward. Halfway there. No one had seen them yet. The mahavans had their attention focused westward. They hurled coruscating braids, and Jason prayed for Tam's group.

Movement in the sky caught his attention. A murder of crows—six of them—rode the currents. A warning bell pealed in his head. *Arylyn doesn't have crows. Unformed!*

Jason sourced his *lorethasra*. He wove a sizzling line of Fire that daggered upward. It branched into five reaching fingers. All of them touched a crow, and three fell to the ground dead. The other two seemed to inhale, expand, and absorb the Fire.

The mahavans noticed Jason's attack. One of them barked a command and three of them spun about to confront Jason's group.

The Irregulars pumped hard, but they still had yards to cover. Nothing for it but to fight.

"Attack!" Jason shouted. He wove Fire and Air, more to distract than anything else. The other Irregulars launched their own braids.

The crows plunged, transforming into large cats as they hit the ground. One went after an Irregular and swept her off the hill. Jason heard her cry out once, followed by a sickening crunch. He closed his ears to the sound and pounded up the hill, right to the top.

A crow darted at him, becoming a savage eagle. Jason ducked. The Irregular behind him wasn't so lucky and screamed as he was ripped off the hill.

Jason drew his sword. The eagle came at him again. A swift slash, and the creature crashed to the ground, headless. More Irregulars reached the summit. The mahavans hurled spears of Air and arrows of Water. Stones blasted outward.

Jason pulled up a wall of rock. The braids shattered against it.

Another unformed in the shape of lion came at him. A frozen line of Water cut this one in half. One of the Irregulars had gotten the creature. The last unformed transformed into a falcon and winged west.

The mahavans gritted their teeth and sent everything they had.

Jason deflecting burning braids of Fire. He blunted shafts of Air and hurled bolts of Fire. One of his braids clipped a mahavan and sent him tumbling down the hill, off a sheer cliff. Another mahavan fell, punched through the chest by a rod of Earth.

Jason rolled beneath a scythe made of Water. He rose to his knees and faced a mahavan, a grizzled older man and thrust with his sword. The mahavan barely managed to slap it aside. Jason scrambled to his feet. He feinted with a diagonal slash transitioning into a vertical chop. The Sinskrill warrior tried to dodge and took a deep cut to his shoulder. Jason whipped his sword about and eviscerated the man.

The final two mahavans were cut down shortly after.

Jason scanned the area atop the hill. No more enemies, only blood and corpses littering the ground. The iron-sharp smell turned his stomach. He breathed through his mouth, trying to settle his nausea as he took stock of their situation.

They'd killed four mahavans and five unformed in the assault. He counted his warriors and cursed. Of the ten he'd led up this hill, only five remained and one was gravely injured.

Gravel crunched, and the remains of Tam's group crested the height. Only Tam and one other remained.

Jason pondered his first command. By any measure the mission had been a success, but it was cold comfort, not with all the men and women who had died to achieve it.

"It's the way of war," Tam whispered, standing next to his elbow. His hard eyes softened. "You never get used to it, and you shouldn't want to."

~

Daniel still had trouble believing how much his life had changed. He'd grown up on Arylyn but went to the Far Beyond with his parents, all to test and maybe help a potential magus, William Wilde. Lien had gone with them, pretending to be a foreign exchange student, and they'd gone to high school together, all the way to their senior year. Kohl Obsidian had ended all that, and Daniel and his family had been forced back to Arylyn where he'd taken up his duties as a journeyman magus. Then had come the attacks on Sinskrill and rescuing William and Jake. Now, Daniel was a warrior, a lieutenant in Arylyn's first army. He would command his first combat, and if he survived he'd become a husband to Lien, the girl he'd loved since she'd first arrived on Arylyn a dozen years ago.

He shook off his memories. Twenty-four Irregulars worked alongside him, and they hauled five cannons up a treacherous switchback on the north face of a rugged hill. On the map the climb had looked straightforward and gentle, but reality had bitten them in the ass. The ascension was a hard as hell, never-ending slog. The weather didn't help, either. The Irregulars dripped sweat with no wind to keep them cool.

The only sounds to be heard were those of their crunching boots as the Irregulars slipped and slid on the loose shale and gravel. All to haul the stupid cannons up this God-forsaken hill. Even with five magi per cannon, all of them pulling on the ropes, attached to the weapons, the lug was still a bitch. It would have been a helluva a lot easier if they could have used their *lorethasra* but doing so might give away their positions to the mahavans who hunkered a hundred yards away.

Daniel cursed profanely, scatologically, and sacrilegiously, any one of which would have earned him a scolding from his mom or Lien.

Thinking of them, he prayed again for their safety. Word had it that the Servitor's ships had arrived in the morning and were pounding Lilith with cannon shot. *How the hell did the mahavans figure out how to build cannons anyway?*

Worse, the Sinskrill fleet had some kind of shield, like what Rukh and Jessira could create, that deflected Lilith's own cannon fire. The ships drifted in the bay, inviolate as they lobbed attack after attack, serene since the village's defenders couldn't do anything to stop them. Some of the terraces had already been leveled.

Now the unformed were heading toward Lilith. Daniel didn't want to think about what would happen if the shapeshifting bastards found a way to attack the village while the fifty defenders stationed there were distracted by all the destruction going on around them.

He did his best to set aside his worries. He had a battle of his own to fight. He only hoped he'd have a chance to pay the mahavans back for all that they'd done. A good start would be lugging these fragging cannons to the top of this fragging hill to kill the fragging mahavans.

Rukh's f-bomb had a cool sound to it, and Daniel liked it.

Daniel didn't see the murder of crows in the sky nor their descent. One of the other Irregulars did, though, and she shouted warning.

Daniel's gaze shot upward and fear momentarily froze him. *Unformed. Seven of them.* He snapped out of his panic and began calling orders.

The unformed swept down, gliding the last few feet only a few yards above the ground. When they hit they transformed into burly, heavily-coated cats. Two Irregulars screamed as the unformed tossed them off the steep hill. The cannons they'd been hauling slipped from the grasp of the remaining magi.

Daniel gaped as two more Irregulars were pulled off the hill. "Let go of the cannons!"

The Irregulars carried out his order. The cannons crashed to the ground far below.

Daniel drew his sword and sourced his *lorethasra*. He sent a web of Fire at the unformed. Other braids, of Air that hissed like a hundred cobras, or Water rippling like a monster's tentacles, whipped about. The unformed dodged, twisting and diving. Daniel fired a bolt of Air and clubbed one out of the sky. Two lances of Fire put down two more of them. A shotgun blast of pebbles and rocks took down another pair. The last two unformed fled.

When he could finally pause and collect himself, the world seemed full of thunder. Daniel realized it was only his heart. He slowly calmed and surveyed the scene.

Nine Irregulars had been killed. All their cannons had been shattered and the rest of his troops huddled close to one another in shock. They clustered close, and some spoke quietly with one another. *Shit. What a fubar clusterfrag.*

Daniel reached into his pack for the satellite phone. He'd only finished dialing when something exploded at the top of the hill.

His eyes went toward the sound. His mouth went dry.

A flood of rocks and boulders rumbled toward him and his troop. There was no chance to run. A tide of stones swept toward Daniel and his magi. Pain filled his body, stole his thoughts, leaving only the regret that he'd never again get to kiss Lien.

~

"I ncoming!" Mr. Zeus shouted.

Serena looked skyward and saw a pair of shells descending on their position. They roared, low-pitched like approaching thunder, and trailed yellow fire and smoke. She ducked and readied a weave of Air to thrust the shells away. She didn't have to worry. The shells shifted their flight and shot straight down. They blasted into a terrace. Stone shattered, the sound ripping outward like a thunderclap. Someone's home had been destroyed. Dozens of them had been.

For the past four hours Lilith's terraces had suffered steady bombardment, and the magi hadn't been able to effectively protect them, not with everyone gathered on Clifftop. Many of the structures below had been blasted apart. Yawning holes gaped within the decking of broken bridges, ragged piles of rubble replaced what had once been homes, and debris was all that remained of much of the various Main Stairs.

Thankfully, no structure on Clifftop had met such a fate. Here the buildings had largely escaped unscathed. While the mahavans had launched their shells, their attempts at attacking Clifftop had proven to be futile. The magi, both Irregulars and civilians, had hurled aside any shells launched this high,

Nevertheless, fires raged upon the terraces, and black smoke billowed. It hid the bright sun beneath a blanket of soot and ash.

The Irregulars watched all the destruction in disbelief and anger. They couldn't do anything about it. Their cannons remained impotent, unable to breach whatever protection the Servitor's ships possessed. An hour of lobbing shell after shell at the Sinskrill fleet had taught them the futility of doing so, and Jessira told them to save their ammunition.

Serena ground her teeth as she watched the slow-motion destruction. A gust of wind wafted a sinuous length of smoke into her face, and she coughed and hacked, eyes tearing and blinking as she tried to clear her vision. She didn't need to see in order to hear the chaos all around her or the sobbing of those who knew they'd lost their homes.

Ms. Sioned approached, leaving the safety of wherever she'd taken cover, and Serena eyed her in question. "I'm too old to hide from the bogeyman," the old *raha'asra* explained to Serena's unvoiced query. She moved closer to the escarpment's edge and fury and sorrow warred on her features.

"You shouldn't stand so close to the rim," Serena said, coming to stand by the older woman's elbow.

"If I had Ward Silver's Fire," Ms. Sioned growled, "those boats would be burning."

Serena smiled at the words. Ms. Sioned's voice had been fierce and full of loathing, both of which were at odds with her grandmotherly persona.

"We're about to take the fight to the mahavans," Serena said.

"How?" Ms. Sioned asked. "I saw those warriors who broke ranks and descended the Main Stairs."

"Jessira told them not to go," Serena quickly said.

"I know," Ms. Sioned replied, "and I saw them killed just as Jessira warned would happen." She tilted her head in thought. "What's different this time?"

"Jessira has a plan," Serena explained. "She's sent several crews with cannons to an area south of the village and the bay. They'll swing north from there and haul the cannons overland through the jungle surrounding my cottage. They'll set up in the tree-line and fire at the mahavans' ships from point-blank range. Jessira hopes the closer distance might penetrate the Sinskrill fleet's shields."

In that moment, Jessira, who stood a few yards away, tensed. Serena wondered at it. She searched for whatever had captured the other woman's attention. She saw nothing different. The Sinskrill fleet continued to hold their positions in the bay and fire at Lilith. Nevertheless, worry and concentration remained on Jessira's face and Serena couldn't understand why.

An instant later Jessira called Fiona forward. "Dial the crews I sent down," she ordered. "Tell them to hold off their attack." She addressed Serena. "Get your cannon ready. Send a shot at *Demolition*. I want to see what happens."

Serena didn't know what Jessira had in mind, but she'd long ago learned to trust the other woman's instincts. She quickly gathered her crew: Mr. Zeus, Fiona, and the Logan sisters. They wove their braids, and the air around the cannon warped like in a heat haze. Fiona's Spirit glistened silver, and a second later the *nomasra* exploded from the mouth of the cannon. It soared, glowing red and taking the size and shape of a basketball.

Serena stepped aside and watched the shell's flight

So did Jessira. She held binoculars to her eyes, obviously studying the Servitor's ship. "Send it straight at *Demolition*. Explode it five yards above their main mast. Don't worry about dodging their control. They won't try to push the shell aside. They know we can't hurt them."

Fiona did as instructed. Several yards above the main mast, the shell exploded. Instantly the protective, gray webbing took shape. *Demolition* might have nudged a bit deeper into the water and rocked slightly, but otherwise she showed no damage.

"Another," Jessira called. "No explosion this time."

Serena and her crew obliged.

This time the shell ricocheted off the gray webbing.

Jessira still had her binoculars trained upon the ship. "One more," she said. "Same effect. No explosion, descend it more slowly, though. As slow as you can."

Serena wasn't sure what Jessira had in mind, but she and the others did as instructed. They fired, and Fiona slowed the shell until it hung nearly motionless, suspended above *Demolition*. No defenses emerged until the shell was a few feet above the main mast. Then the webbing formed, this time creeping out slowly rather than shooting around the vessel all at once.

"Explode it," Jessira ordered.

The shell blasted. The webbing snapped into place.

Jessira set aside her binoculars and smiled in pleasure. "The shield disseminates from the prow, from near the figurehead. A gray globe."

Serena didn't know how that information would help them. "Yes, but what can do we do about it?"

Jessira faced her. "We've been using the wrong type of ammunition. What we need are shells with no touch of *asra*."

"Why?" Mr. Zeus asked.

"Because I think their shield reacts to *asra*," Jessira said. "If nothing else, the webbing is the color of all the Elements mixed together."

Fiona protested. "But we'll never be able to maintain control of a shell like that. It's too hard."

"Not from up here we can't," Jessira agreed. "We need to get closer to their ships."

Serena understood what she meant. "We need to take the shells to the cannons already below." She inhaled deeply. "I'll do it."

"We'll both do it," Jessira said.

～

Rukh peered closely at the rocky canyon—a wide ravine really—where the battle would take place. Rugged hills with stony slopes made of gravel, stunted trees, and shrubs, boxed it in. A mournful wind moaned intermittently, like a ghost calling for help. It also blustered, raising a cloud of dirt and debris. Rukh formed a film of Air to protect his eyes. As soon as the wind passed and the dust settled he was able to see again.

Nothing had changed. The canyon remained empty, but according to the scouts, the mahavans had scraped together a low wall fifty yards from where the ravine curved south and narrowed further. A good place to defend against a frontal assault, especially if the Sinskrill commander also positioned his warriors along the flanks to ward off an attacking enemy.

Rukh pursed his mouth and imagined where the enemy troop placements would be. He had a fairly good notion, but the unformed were the wildcards. They hadn't abandoned the mahavans. They'd fought Jason's unit less than an hour ago, and they'd likely fought Daniel's troop as well, but of that Rukh couldn't be certain. He hadn't heard from them yet and the lack of information worried him. Daniel should have checked in by now. The fact that he hadn't caused Rukh to believe that something terrible must have happened. The rumble he'd heard. A rockslide. He'd sent William and another twenty warriors to take the hill originally intended to be held by Daniel's unit, and he wouldn't move his own warriors until the mahavans' cannons were neutralized.

The pause also gave Aia a chance to reach him. He sensed her presence in the back of his mind. She couldn't be more than several miles away and charging fast. He wished he could wait for her arrival, to fight with her at his side as they had on many other occasions in their long, shared past. Other than Jessira, there was no one else he wanted with him.

His satellite phone rang.

William spoke from the other end. "We've got the hill."

Rukh's heart lifted briefly, but it sank an instant later. He had to know the answer to a question he dreaded asking. "Daniel?"

William didn't answer at first. "We found their remains," he said after a short pause. "An avalanche took them. Part of the cliff face sheered off. Must have been the mahavans. They probably got off a lucky shot with their cannons."

Rukh stilled the grief in his heart. *Focus on the Trial at hand.* "What about the unformed?"

"Three of them attacked as we ascended. We killed them all. No losses on our part."

Rukh unconsciously nodded. "Are you in position?"

"We will be in five minutes. We're setting up the cannons now."

"The mahavans?"

"They've sent ranging shots," William answered. "Nothing major. No damage. When they fire on our position, we're able to take control of their shells. They can't hold onto them the entire way to us."

"Good. When you're set up, fire at will. I want those cannons gone."

"Yes, sir," William answered. "One other thing. I didn't see any of our cannons on that hill. The ones they have are of their own design. They must have ours on their wall."

"Which means they'll be that much easier to bring down."

"My thoughts exactly, sir," William said.

Once he hung up, Rukh allowed himself to momentarily acknowledge the pain aching through his heart. *Daniel.* The young man, so happy, carefree, and silly, really. He reminded him of Keemo. A fresh pang of loss took Rukh, and he bowed his head, saying a prayer to Devesh for his long-lost friend—a brother of his heart–as well as for Daniel, a young man who shouldn't have had to die today. In a better world, he would never have known battle.

It occurred to Rukh how many good men and women he'd seen die before their time. He'd lost count of how often those same fine folk had entered into a battle and trusted their fate to his command. But he'd never forgotten their names. Devesh help him, there were so many.

Sometimes—oftentimes—he thought he and Jessira had lived too long.

Say that after you've snatched my chin, a distant voice said to him.

Rukh smiled in relief. *Aia.*

CHAPTER 29: FIND THE FLAW

O ctober 1990

Serena tiptoed along the edge of a gaping hole in Chimera Seed, a blocky bridge that stretched from Cliff Water to Cliff Spirit. Taking this route let her bypass much of the destruction that made travel to the base of Lilith's escarpment all but impossible. In this section, only a two-foot shelf of the bridge remained, and on one side was open space and on the other, a cascade that plunged into a pool fifty feet below. The waterfall hurled spray in a fine mist and made the uncomfortable footing even worse, turning it slick as ice.

Serena moved slowly. She controlled her breathing, inching forward as she clutched the railing. She focused on the placement of her feet. She couldn't afford to slip up here. Not only would she plunge to her death, but Selene and so many others she loved might be the ones to pay the price for her failure.

Jessira had chosen no one else to accompany her on this mission, only the two of them traveling across the bridges and streets of Lilith's abandoned terraces. Everyone else remained at Clifftop. While they could have brought along more magi for the journey to the base of the Cliffs, Jessira feared that more people would simply raise the possibility of one or more magi drifting outside the scope of her Blend, the strange weave only she and Rukh could create and which made them essentially invisible.

Thankfully, the mahavan shelling had slowed over the past hour, which made their journey easier. Serena gritted her teeth at the damage the mahavan had inflicted, promising to repay the Sinskrill fleet for what they'd done to Lilith. She'd sink every one of them. It didn't matter that the mahavans had once been her people. They weren't any more, and they certainly weren't family.

She and Jessira finally reached the end of Chimera Seed and Serena breathed a little easier.

She must have exhaled too heavily because Jessira paused and eyed her in question. "Do you need a break?"

"I'm fine," Serena said, shifting the burden on her back.

Both she and Jessira carried a sack full of white-phosphorous shells encased in iron that Lilith's blacksmiths had created in record time. The munitions were individually wrapped in soft cotton but still managed to shift about, making their travel more difficult. Serena noted that despite the unwieldy weight Jessira still moved with more grace than most women could have managed unencumbered.

"We're going to the Main Stairs now," Jessira said.

"Yes, ma'am." Serena shuffled forward, making sure to remain in the shadow of Jessira's Blend once they set off. They traded Chimera Seed's slick stones for the dry ones of the Main Stairs, where ragged fires and stinging smoke replaced the waterfall's mist. Serena created a braid of Air to protect her eyes from the drifting smoke, and she sensed Jessira copying her weave.

"Much better," Jessira said.

They pressed on until Jessira paused unexpectedly. "Five steps are missing up ahead. We'll have to jump together. Otherwise, you'll leave the Blend. On three?"

"On three," Serena agreed.

Jessira counted, and on three, they leapt. Serena landed well, but the weight of the iron shells on her back threw her off-balance. She threatened to fall and tumble down the steps but Jessira jerked her back.

"Thanks," Serena said. She wiped the sweat from her brow and glowered at the cloudless sky. *Just a little rain.* Anything to replace the oppressive humidity they'd had for the past few weeks.

The rest of the trip down the Main Stairs passed uneventfully, with only a few more obstacles to avoid. They reached the base of Lilith's Cliffs and approached the Guanyin. *Not much farther to go.*

They crossed the silvery bridge, and for once Serena didn't bother looking at the statues carved along the walls of the narrow gorge.

Jessira came to a halt when they reached Lilith Beach. Despite the swirling smoke, the sun beat down, and Serena shaded her eyes with a braid of Air, Earth, and Water. *Sunglasses.* She'd first created them while teaching William to sail, and she wistfully recalled those happier times.

Jessira pointed to the Sinskrill fleet floating in the bay. "Now comes the hard part. We've got to cross the beach and hope no one sees us."

"You think they can see us through the Blend?" Serena asked in surprise.

"I think the unformed can, and the Servitor is supposed to have some of their power."

Serena cursed. She'd forgotten about her father's unformed powers. She shifted her regard to the trees south of their location. The jungle leading to her cottage stood several hundred yards away, and a simple path of white bricks covered by a film of sand led to the tree-line. That's where the Irregulars Jessira had sent down earlier should be, and while Serena couldn't yet see them, she knew they were there. They'd phoned in an hour ago and confirmed their position.

"We'll take it at a run," Jessira said. "Stay on my left hip."

Serena made one final adjustment to the shells on her back. "Ready."

Jessira took a deep inhalation. "Let's roll." She set off at a sprint.

Serena immediately chased after her, keeping her head down as her world shrank to the path directly before her. She barely heard her own panting breaths or the dull clanking of the iron shells she carried knocking against one another. The susurrations of waves sweeping against the shore never entered her thoughts. Instead, she hummed "Gloria" and even managed to lose herself in the rhythm of the sprint. When she lifted her gaze to the jungle, she took heart. Only fifty more yards to cover.

Movement at the corner of her eye caused Serena to glance at the bay. *Demolition* had fired. A shell screamed straight at them. "Incoming!" she shouted.

Jessira had already seen it. She Shielded even as she picked up speed.

Serena tucked her head, pumped her arms, and ran flat out, barely able to keep up with the other woman. Her heart seized as the shell accelerated toward them. An instant prior to impact she threw herself on the ground and covered her head. The shell blasted like a thunderclap. Serena peeked a look.

Despite being braced for impact, the explosion had cast Jessira twenty feet through the air. She slammed into the beach, and an explosion of sand billowed outward. She rolled another ten feet and banged her head hard on the ground.

Serena ran to Jessira, casting a fearful gaze at the Sinskrill fleet. They hadn't fired another shot, but that could change at any second. She reached Jessira right as the other woman sat up with a groan. Blood leaked from a scalp wound, and she explored it with her fingers before cursing and levering herself upright.

"Fragging unholy hells," Jessira growled.

Serena helped her the rest of the way to her feet.

Jessira glared at the Sinskrill fleet. "I'm going to hurt every one of those fraggers." She shook off Serena's help. "Let's go."

They set off once more. Jessira shambled at first, but after a few seconds, she apparently had her legs under her. Serena kept an eye out toward *Demolition*, but no further shells blasted toward them. The last few yards to the jungle's safety passed in a blur.

～

W illiam kept his focus on the mahavans on the distant hillside. Perspiration beaded his forehead and soaked his chest and back. He wiped a drop of sweat threatening to drip into his eyes, and he shot a glare skyward, wishing the humid weather would go away or at least the winds would pick up some.

"Looks like we've wiped them out," said Mink Ware, his second in command. Her brown hair, which she kept cropped, and her equally dark eyes and light-brown skin proclaimed her as native-born to Arylyn. She also resembled the animal for which she'd been named: small, cute, and deadly and had been the one to land the shot that had detonated like a brick of dynamite amongst the mahavans.

William reckoned that Mink's one blast had wiped out half the Sinskrill forces. After that, the rest had swiftly fallen to the Irregulars' shelling. Once he might have lamented the death of the mahavans, but not now. Not after seeing Daniel's mangled form along with the ruined bodies of so many Irregulars, men and women he had come to know and love.

Mink created a braid, a weave of binoculars. "I think one of them is still moving."

William focused in the direction of her gaze. The dust raised by their attack had yet to settle entirely on the mahavans' encampment. *Is anyone still alive over there?* He couldn't tell for certain, and Rukh needed him to be certain.

For you, Daniel. He bared his teeth and quoted one of his friend's favorite lines. "Nuke the entire site from orbit. It's the only way to be sure."

Mink regarded him in confusion.

William shook his head. Except for Daniel and Jason, no one got his nerd references. "One more shell," he said. "Then we destroy those battlements before our forces reach them."

"Yes, sir," Mink said. She carried out his orders.

Seconds later, a *nomasra* launched toward the hillside. The subsequent explosion ripped open a chasm. Some of the mahavans' corpses slipped into the hill's gaping wound, as did all of their cannons.

That did it. William moved his attention to the battlements, which crawled with mahavans. "Bulldoze them, if you please," he ordered.

"Ah . . . bulldoze, sir?"

William hid a sigh. "Just blow the hell out of them."

Mink saluted. "Yes, sir."

William sensed her and the other Irregulars sourcing their *lorethasras* and fusing braids of Fire, Air, Water, Earth, and Spirit to the cannons. Within seconds, disk-shaped shells rocketed skyward, and William watched their flight. Some juked as the mahavans sought to push the munitions away.

The Irregulars maintained control of the shells, and the *nomasras* fell like fiery balls, trailing smoke and heat. They exploded into the mahavan battlements, demolishing the fortifications, blowing off their tops or tearing them apart.

Rocks and dirt shot outward and upward. It took a few seconds for the sound to reach them, a rumble of thunder along with the clamor of stones cracking and being crushed to powder. The noise overwhelmed any screams the mahavans might have made, and William was certain there were screams amongst the din.

"Again," he ordered.

The shelling continued as Rukh's forces advanced unopposed. Suddenly one of the fortifications vaporized. It blew apart as if a giant foot had crushed it. A wide throat opened up and the Irregulars rushed in. The battle began in earnest.

William could only watch. The Irregulars formed a beachhead, one established almost single-handedly by Rukh. He could easily be seen as he held off mahavans, slashing and moving faster than any normal person should.

William noticed movement to the north of the battlements. He focused his attention on it and quickly made out another set of cannons, two or three of them. Mahavan design. *Some latecomers*. He pointed them out to Mink. "Send them our regards."

She stared at where he pointed and called out commands. Their cannons were shifted. Three volleys later, they obliterated the enemy position.

The battle below had also largely ended. A few last mahavans put up a knot of resistance and quickly died beneath a storm of Air and Fire.

William's phone chirped. It was Rukh. "Yes, sir," William answered.

"Get down here," Rukh said. "We captured one of the mahavans. She has something interesting to say. I want to know your thoughts about it."

"What about our cannons?"

"Tell Mink and the rest of your unit to remain with them in case we missed any mahavans."

"Yes, sir."

"Make it fast."

William passed on Rukh's commands to Mink before setting off. He slid down the steep hill and hit the canyon floor at a run, crunching across the pebbled, dusty surface. A shallow rise slowed him a bit, but he made up the time on the other side where the ground dropped-off slightly. He pumped his arms and built up speed. His boots kicked up puffs of dust as his necrosed-enhanced endurance and strength allowed him to sprint the half-mile in a little under two minutes.

He passed through the torn-apart mahavan's fortifications where Rukh met him on the other side. William managed a sloppy salute.

"Catch your breath," Rukh said.

William bent over, hands on knees, and panted.

Rukh silently passed him a canteen of water.

William nodded his 'thanks' and took a deep swig. His pounding heart slowed, and he no longer gulped his breaths.

"You made good time," Rukh noted.

"You told me to," William said.

Rukh grunted. "Come with me."

William followed Rukh to a figure sitting upon the ground, bound with hands tied behind her back and feet secured before her at the ankles. Her blue eyes flashed as she glared at everyone around her. For once, her auburn hair lay flat and disheveled, but William still recognized her. Evelyn Mason.

"She's the only mahavan who survived," Rukh said. "I put a lock on her *lorethasra*." Rukh faced the mahavan. "Tell him what you told me."

Evelyn smirked. "Which part? The fact that you only defeated part of our forces? Or the part where the Servitor will burn your precious Lilith to the ground?"

Rukh blurred forward and clenched Evelyn by the jaw. He squeezed hard enough to leave a bruise. "We don't have time for your games. Speak and live. Waste my time and I'll end you." He shoved her to the ground.

Evelyn's breezy confidence faltered. "Adam left with the rest of his unformed." She spat in disgust. "He's one of them."

William folded his arms. "How many unformed are there?"

Evelyn snarled. "What difference does it make?"

Rukh stepped forward.

"Fifty," Evelyn said quickly.

"How many mahavans remain?" Rukh asked.

"Seventy. Samuel commands them. He's got a long head start on you." She sneered. "You better run if you want to catch them."

William eyed her in revulsion. Evelyn represented the worst aspects of an already ugly people: arrogance married to brutality and with no regard for others. "Why were you left behind?"

Evelyn's smirk remained in place, and William imagined smashing it off her smug face. She must have sensed his anger because her smiled widened. "Little *raha'asra*, you don't scare me."

Rukh tilted his head to the side, and his gaze grew distant, as if in consideration or listening to a conversation only he could hear. A second later, he broke into a grin.

Evelyn's apparent good mood broke. "What?" she asked, her face suspicious.

William's gaze snapped toward the northwest. A dust cloud arose from that direction as something approached, something running faster than he could. A tall form became apparent, along with several less distinct forms.

"Hold," Rukh said, setting the Irregulars at ease. Many had readied weapons.

Moments later, the forms took shape: Travail and two large cats. One had a familiar calico pattern and the other one had the tawny coat of a lion.

Yards away from William and the Irregulars, Travail and the two cats slowed to a walk.

Rukh! a voice shouted in William's mind. The calico cat approached with a flick of her tail and a shiver of her coat. She seemed to bristle with excitement.

Rukh wore a broad grin of sheer joy, happier than at any time William had seen him. *Aia!* He reached the calico cat and hugged her while she rested her head on his shoulder. Her eyes closed, and she purred like rumbling thunder.

Rukh hugged her tighter for an instant more. He leaned back. *I missed you, little girl.*

The cat pressed her forehead against Rukh's. *I missed you, too, little human.*

William did a double-take. *Aia?*

The calico cat lifted her head. *Of course, William Wilde.*

Aia, once a small kitten, now stood as high as William's shoulder, and he couldn't get over the changes in her.

I'm not done growing, she said, sounding smug.

Rukh approached the tawny cat and rubbed the space in front of his ears. *Hello, Shon. Jessira can't wait to see you.*

I can't wait to see her. Shon's eyes closed, and he, too, purred. *That is nice, but not as nice as when Jessira does it.*

Of course, Rukh said with a chuckle. *You'll see her soon enough.*

"Are these Kesarins?" William asked, still confused.

Rukh nodded. "Formal introductions will have to wait, though." He addressed Aia and pointed to Evelyn, who had watched the entire scene with wary fear. *I could use your help. This one knows secrets she won't divulge.*

Aia growled, baring her fangs as she took a menacing step toward Evelyn. *She'll divulge them to me.*

~

Serena wiped the perspiration off her forehead. Though she worked in the shade, she sweated heavily here. Lilith Bay's golden beach stood no more than ten feet away, but the gusting trade wind dissipated as soon as it hit the tree-line. The highest branches shook and a few low-lying fronds and leaves whispered, but otherwise the jungle sweltered in silence. The cannon crews Jessira had sent down waited quietly. No animals cried out. Not even any birds or insects. They seemed to sense the violence being made ready within their home. *Hopefully the violence won't come from me dropping a shell.*

Serena carefully lifted one of the phosphorous-filled iron munitions and braced it on the lip of the cannon's mouth. Each round shot had been welded to one of the *nomasra* shells. The *nomasra* portion would hopefully allow the Spirit master to guide the shot, but the combined construction made handling them awkward.

Serena licked her lips. *Now to seat the shell inside the cannon.* This would be the hard part. She took a set of bracing breaths while readying herself to load the munition the rest of the way. She couldn't let it crack. The white phosphorous would probably kill them all if it did.

Diana Mangold, a stoutly-built magus with short, spiked hair, stepped forward then. "I've got a brace of Air behind the shell. It won't crack. You can let it go."

"Thank you," Serena said. She let the shell slip off her fingers, even as she mentally chided herself. *I should have thought of doing something like that.*

Diana's bracing braid held, and the shell slowly slid down the barrel, dropping softly into place. Serena's heart pounded the entire time. She made her features drone-flat. She didn't want anyone seeing her fear and distantly wondered if she'd ever rid herself of the habit. Or if she wanted to. *A question for another time.*

"All done," Diana said with a grin.

Loading the second cannon took less time. Serena stepped away from the weapon and faced the mahavan ships. The ten-member cannon crew—twelve now with Serena and Jessira—had dragged the two cannons to the edge of the tree-line. From here, they had a clear line of sight at the Sinskrill fleet. After shelling her and Jessira on the beach, the Servitor's ships hadn't fired upon them any further. Serena didn't know why. They had them dead to rights. Instead, the mahavan fleet had resumed their destruction of Lilith's terraces, reducing more and more of it to rubble. The ships floated serenely in the aqua-blue water as they eradicated a place of beauty.

Jessira held motionless but carried the sense of a caged animal. "Stay within the Blend," she ordered the crew. "The Servitor can probably see through it, but hopefully the screen of trees and bushes will keep us hidden until we burn their ships to the waterline."

Serena stood with arms crossed and glared at the Sinskrill fleet. *Burn them to the waterline.* She nodded. That sounded like a great idea.

"Get ready to fire," Jessira said.

Serena retreated from the cannons. She had no further role here.

The two crews of five magi sourced their *lorethasras.* They intended on firing their projectiles at maximum velocity at the Sinskrill fleet, but yards before impacting the mahavans' protective webbing, the *nomasra* portion of the shell would disintegrate. The thinly-cased, white phosphorous would continue on and hopefully smash into the Sinskrill ship. Even better if they exploded close to the gray globes Jessira had noticed.

At least that was the plan.

The cannons slowly reddened, and Serena prayed the white phosphorous wouldn't ignite due to the heat.

She readied the satellite phone. Mr. Zeus answered. "We're about to fire," she told him.

"I hope this works," he answered.

Jessira held binoculars to her eyes and studied the mahavan fleet. "We've got company coming," she announced.

Serena quickly wove binoculars and saw what Jessira meant. Two rowboats, each one filled with five mahavans, had been lowered to the water. They pushed off and accelerated toward the beach. They'd arrive in no more than a few minutes. Worse, the boats were heading for their position.

Jessira set aside her binoculars. "Serena and I will defend against the mahavans approaching us."

Serena passed on the information to Mr. Zeus.

Jessira pointed. "I want the ships that launched those mahavans burning. Fire!"

"Firing," Serena relayed to Mr. Zeus.

Both cannons boomed, and the shells trailed a white plume as they streaked across the sky. The projectiles took on an arrow shape with a round, black tip. Several seconds passed. The shots continued aimed dead-on for each ship's prow.

A dozen yards out from the vessels, the *nomasras* disintegrated. The iron balls shivered in their flight and lost height.

Serena sucked in her breath.

A single iron casing slammed into each ship several feet below the bowsprit and exploded.

Serena cheered along with the rest of the cannon crews. *Yes! Jessira was right. Nomasras couldn't penetrate the Sinskrill shields, but normal metal could.*

The ships caught fire and belched smoke. Wood cracked. Planks splintered and charred. Mahavans shouted and rushed about, weaving braids of Water. The forepeak of one ship split off from the vessel with a sharp report. Both ships lost their gray globes.

Serena whooped in joy, sharing her happiness with the other Irregulars who also cheered.

"Tell Mr. Zeus," Jessira reminded her.

Abashed, Serena quickly told Mr. Zeus what had happened. "Two ships down. Take them out."

"We saw," Mr. Zeus said. "Stay safe."

"Will do." Serena hung up the phone as Jessira snapped out more commands.

A series of booms thundered from Clifftop. *Nomasra* shells streaked across the sky.

"Fire on the rest of the ships," Jessira said. "Kill them all before they have time to figure out we're doing." She addressed Serena and pointed to the mahavans in the boats. "We have to stop them. Keep the mahavans attention on us instead of the cannon crews."

Serena loosened her sword, ready and willing. Her jaw clenched. She'd promised the mahavans some payback, and she had every intention of fulfilling her vow. She followed Jessira onto the sands of Lilith Beach.

CHAPTER 30: KILLING FIELDS

ctober 1990

William ran smooth and easy along a gravel path that wound through a hollow amongst the hills. He traveled with Rukh, Travail, Aia, and Shon, although he still had trouble accepting the size of the two cats, especially Aia. She'd been a tiny kitten when he'd last seen her. Then again, he had never forgotten the lightning-flash afterimage when she'd attacked Kohl Obsidian. In that frozen moment, she'd stood as tall as the necrosed, which meant she still had room to grow. As for her tawny brother, he would eventually overtop Aia.

Kesarins. That's what they're called, Apparently Aia belonged to Rukh, or maybe it was the other way around. William couldn't tell, but their love for one another was as obvious as the vibrant, calico colors of Aia's fur. Shon and Jessira were another matched pair.

The five of them ran on. The gravel crunched beneath William's and Rukh's booted feet, the Kesarins' padded paws, and Travail's leathery soles. Their travel had taken them miles southwest of the destruction of the mahavan forces and the land had transitioned from rugged, rocky mounts to the rolling, swarded hills northeast of Janaki Valley. Copses of spruce, cedar, and aspen intermingled amongst the greenery and a vagrant breeze occasionally carried the scent of pine. Despite the lowering sun and the shade amongst trees and hollows, the stifling humidity remained.

William sweated heavily, and he was pleased to see Rukh do the same. They'd been running hard, and the man was finally showing some of the fatigue that weighed down William's limbs. It was understandable, their tiredness. They had been pushing hard. None of them could afford to give in to weakness.

William smiled to himself when he realized how much his thoughts sounded like something Serena might say. Thinking about her, he once again sent a prayer for those at Clifftop, for their safety and health. He prayed also for the strength to catch the unformed.

Despite Evelyn's attempts at deception, she hadn't been able to lie to Aia or hide her true thoughts and motives. According to the maha-van, the Sinskrill commander, Adam Paradiso, had split his forces into three parts. Evelyn had been left behind with a diversionary unit while a second one raced toward Lilith armed with cannons. Ward would have to stop them. Meanwhile, a third force, this one comprised entirely of unformed, had taken a different, more circuitous route toward the village. However, the unformed had spent themselves too heavily with flying about on scouting missions. They'd worn themselves out, and now they journeyed in the swiftest form they could maintain: horses. Thankfully, they couldn't gallop all the way to Lilith and to the Sinskrill fleet. They'd have to walk part of the way.

William and the others had to catch them. Signs of the unformed herd's passage, droppings and numerous overturned stones, told them that they were gaining on the creatures. They'd reach them within the next few hours, somewhere in Janaki Valley or possibly in the northern areas of Lilith. When that happened, William, Rukh, Travail, Aia, and Shon would have to defeat nearly forty unformed on their own.

William shook his head at the thought.

The Nobeasts, the creatures you misname as unformed, left seven of their own to impede our progress, Aia said.

Where? Rukh asked.

Aia transmitted Rukh's question to William and Travail.

Less than a half-mile ahead, Shon answered. *They plan on rolling rocks onto our heads when we pass through a narrow gorge.*

Are they bunched up? William asked.

Yes, Aia said. *Why?*

William's mouth thinned in a predatory smile. *Jason taught me something a few months ago, how to create and split lightning. I can take out all the unformed with one weave.*

Travail tsked. *Unless one of them is as powerful as a secondus or a prime.*

My guess is that they'll be low- ranking, Rukh said. *From what I've read about the unformed, the powerful ones send the weaker ones out in situations like this. They expect battle to cull those who lack the cunning to survive.*

Travail grunted acknowledgement.

They traveled on, and soon found themselves entering a rocky ravine lined with steep cliffs and loose boulders. A river might have carved the canyon, but its remnants persisted only in a small stream. A herd of goats shuffled atop the cliffs and lazily chewed their cuds as William and the others approached them.

The unformed creatures are a hundred yards ahead, Shon said.

William frowned as he stared about. He didn't see the unformed.

The goats, Aia added helpfully.

Reluctant admiration for the unformed washed over him. *Smart.*

"Smarter for our sakes if they were dead," Travail said, speaking aloud.

William privately agreed, and he sourced his *lorethasra*, linked its component Elements to the corresponding ones found in *lorasra*. He braided a thick weave of Fire and Air and held it at the ready. It crackled across his shoulders and chest like lightning. Seconds later, he had seven more braids—these made of Earth and Spirit—rippling in his hands as well.

Fifty yards, Shon said.

Any time now, Rukh said.

Yes, sir, William said. He thrust out his arms, and the braids of Earth and Spirit arrowed toward the goats, attaching to them in less than a blink of the eye. They'd act as lines of conduction. The weave of Fire and Air blistered down his arms, off his hands, and onto the braids of Earth and Spirit. There, it split into seven white-hot, blazing lances of lightning. A wall of light sparked toward each goat. One of them had time to bleat in fear. A few transformed into falcons.

Too late. Each lance caught an unformed in mid-leap or in mid-flight. It didn't matter. They were all burned to charred husks.

Aia beamed at him as her eyes crinkled. *I knew you had the heart of a predator.*

~

Serena raced alongside Jessira as they burst out of the tree line. Ten mahavans tumbled out of their rowboats as they reached the beach. Serena ran harder, barely keeping up with Jessira.

As they approached the Sinskrill warriors she leaned on her mahavan training to suppress her feelings. She imagined her fears and anger locked away in a thick, impenetrable box until they remained at a distant remove. Serena's heart still raced but she viewed the approaching Sinskrill warriors with resoluteness and determination. *I've fought mahavans before. I battled the Servitor. This can't be any worse than that.*

"We only have to hold them off," Jessira reminded her.

Serena nodded.

Behind them, the magi cannon crews worked frantically to get their weapons ready to fire again. Three more Sinskrill ships still floated undamaged in the harbor. The magi behind her shouted and raced about as they loaded the phosphorous rounds.

"Be careful," Serena heard Diana Mangold call out. "If you drop that round, we'll all burn."

The cannons on Clifftop roared again, and their shells screamed across the sky. Serena traced their path as they arched heavenward. Their rise slowed, halted. They descended then. Serena heard their whistling scream as the *nomasras* picked up speed, moving like shooting stars. They shattered the damaged Sinskrill ships into kindling.

The three remaining vessels of the Servitor's fleet had already altered course and drifted farther into the harbor. Serena sourly noted that one of them was *Demolition*.

"Cover my back," Jessira said.

Serena's attention snapped back to the here and now as Jessira blurred forward, too fast to follow. Serena did her best to remain at her side but quickly fell back. Nevertheless, she ran on. Her focus narrowed to the mahavans on the beach, who had unsheathed their weapons. She could see their faces. She knew them. They weren't her friends.

Serena shouted defiance as she and Jessira closed the distance.

~

Jake pedaled hard and ignored the crick in his side, the pounding of his heart, and the sweat pouring off of him. He gasped for breath but never let up. He kept going. He had to after the word they'd just received.

The mahavans had split their forces. One large group had been held in reserve to delay and distract Rukh's warriors while the rest, roughly seventy, had marched non-stop through the southern foothills of Mount Madhava. Their intention was obvious in hindsight. They meant to use Firedeep Gorge, the narrow trail that winded through the eastern foothills and entered Janaki Valley five miles north of Clifftop. From there, it was only a several-hours hike along Sita's Song, even with the cannons the mahavans were said to possess.

Ward's force had to cut them off, but Jake wasn't sure they could. All this time they'd remained stationed toward the northern end of Janaki Valley waiting on the mahavans, but now, they had to race south and cover twenty twisting miles as quickly as possible.

No one spoke as they sped along. The only sounds were their panting breaths. They knew what awaited them if they delayed. They'd already passed Firedeep Gorge and come across signs of the mahavans passage. Fields burned, and farmers and their families slaughtered.

Jake couldn't get the images of women and children lying in pools of blood out of his mind. They'd tried to run. Some had made it to Sita's Song before the mahavans had cut them down.

Jake clenched his teeth in rage. *I'll see the mahavans dead. Every one of them.*

Pungent smoke clouded the sky. It carried the scents of burnt corn, wheat, and blood. In that moment, some of it drifted across the Irregulars, causing several of them to slow down and cough. As soon as they cleared the smoke, they picked up the pace again. Jake tried to shut his mind off from the sights and smells. He concentrated on Ward, who rode ahead of him.

Minutes later, they reached Sile Troy's farm. His fields burned, but Jake saw no sign of the farmer or his wife. He sent up a quick prayer, hoping Sile and Jennifer were safe. *Two more miles to go.*

The distant sound of thunder reached them, and Jake eyed the sky in confusion. There were no clouds, only a late afternoon sun.

Ward held up a hand, and they coasted to a halt.

Jake shifted about, restless at the delay.

Ward twisted around on his bike to face them. "Watch the skies. The mahavans may have unformed up there," he warned. "When we reach the enrune fields, we should have a sense of where the mahavans are positioned. From now until then, we can't afford to ride flat out into hell and danger. We have to pay attention to what's around us, especially from above." His features became fierce, and he stared about, making everyone meet his gaze. "Remember your training. We've gone over this. A third of you each will follow Jake and Julius and a third will follow me. You already have your assigned commanders. Once we see what we're up against, we'll attack."

With that Ward got going again, and they picked up the pursuit. This time, though, they rode more slowly, not pell-mell, and Jake scanned the skies the entire time. *Nothing.*

A mile later, they crested a rise. Lakshman's Bow arched across River Namaste, less than a hundred yards away. And on the other side of the bridge, planted on the enrune fields like hideous weeds, were the mahavans. They'd managed to haul three cannons with them and were presently obliterating Clifftop.

Jake's heart dropped. Fifteen buildings were already down, crumbled and broken. They could have sheltered dozens of people each. Hundreds might have died. Jake wanted to scream in fury.

Ward kept his head. "Cross the bridge and split into three columns. Ride hard and kill them all."

They set off at a pedaling sprint. Jake pumped hard. They rattled across Lakshman's Bow and separated into three groups of around thirty riders, spread out in a line. Jake and Julius had the wings and Ward took the van. *Two hundred yards.*

The mahavans saw them coming and frantically brought their cannons around. Jake unconsciously sucked in his stomach. *God save us.* He rode straight down the barrel of a cannon. Its mouth yawned. *Seventy yards.*

He reached for his *lorethasra*, formed a thick cord of Spirit, and stretched it into a lock. He desperately hurled it at a clustered crew of mahavans readying the cannon aimed at him and his riders. He managed to place the weave on one of them. Another mahavan rushed to fill the space. *Forty yards.*

A cannon went off, a shotgun blast that annihilated many of Ward's riders.

Thirty yards.

Another cannon went off.

This time Julius' left flank was obliterated.

Twenty yards.

The cannon aimed at Jake's warriors reddened. Jake pumped harder. He scanned ahead, and saw what he needed. *Just a few more seconds to reach it.*

The cannon's color grew richer. Any second now it would go off. *There!*

Jake used a braid of Air and Earth to pull a boulder from the ground. He stuffed it in the barrel of the cannon.

"Halt and shield!" he shouted.

Relief flooded through him when his Irregulars braked hard and created a shieldwall.

Jake sent a thick thread of Spirit into the shell. He hoped the cannon worked the same as their own.

The barrel exploded like shrapnel into the faces of the mahavans. A dozen of them went down, shredded into mincemeat.

Jake's gorge rose, but he didn't let it slow him down. "Attack!" he ordered.

His Irregulars surged forward, crossing the final few yards to the remaining mahavans.

Jake called up all his Elements He sent braids of incinerating Fire, crushing Earth, stabbing Air, and drowning Water, savaging the mahavans who remained upright by the cannons. He leapt off his bicycle and drew his sword. "To me!" he shouted. "Form on me!"

His Irregulars responded, forming a knot of flashing steel and Elements. They advanced.

Jake blocked a lunge, snapped a riposte that bit into a mahavan's face. The man fell back. Jake sent a line of Fire at another mahavan. She cried out in terror and tried to throw herself aside. The Fire followed her, punching through her chest. Another mahavan, a heavily built man, attacked with a blistering set of thrusts and slashes. Jake dove out of the way. He couldn't take on the man with his sword alone. Instead, he hurled a shotgun blast of pebbles at the mahavan, who defended with a shield of Earth. The thick-set man was now open to a different attack. Jake attached a lock on him, not letting him link to Arylyn's *lorasra*. A boulder crushed the man's head.

Jake pushed on, searching for more enemies. He cut and thrust, but mostly continued to lock out the mahavans. As a *raha'asra*, none of them could match him in mastery of Spirit. Nor could they overcome his lock. His Irregulars easily killed those who held steel but not *lorethasra*.

The mahavans fought on. They must have realized that no quarter would be offered. Not after what they'd done to Clifftop.

The killing might have lasted a lifetime. Blood sprayed. Bowels emptied, and men and women cried out in pain. Time froze, but Jake fought on. *These are the murderers who enslaved me and killed my people. I'll see them all dead.*

He stabbed a mahavan through the chest, kicked the man off his sword, and spun around, glaring as he sought out another enemy.

There were none. No mahavan remained alive. All of them had been killed.

Jake did a quick count of the Irregulars. They had taken heavy losses. Of the hundred who had crossed Lakshman's Bow, fewer than forty remained afoot. *So few.*

Fatigue and grief weighed him down like a barrel of water on his back, and his sword drooped. He swayed a moment, struggling to maintain his balance.

A crackling sound mixed with the snapping of wood and stone drew Jake's gaze to Clifftop. Lilith, his home, burned in great gouts of fire, smoke, and ash.

~

Jessira launched out of the tree-line and cut a zigzag course toward the mahavans. Flames rumbled in counterpoint to the cannons blasting from both forces, and smoke roiled skyward from the broken ships. Distantly, she noted that Serena had fallen back, unable to keep up. *Good. At least the girl will remain safe behind me.*

As she raced across the sand, Shon surprised her. *I come,* he said, plainly close enough for them to share their thoughts.

Gladness filled Jessira's heart. She'd missed her Kesarin as much as Rukh had missed Aia, but now wasn't the time for a reunion. *No time to talk,* Jessira said to Shon. *Be safe. A battle beckons.*

Be safe as well, Shon replied, ending their conversation.

Jessira's attention returned to the coming battle. The roar of cannon fire continued. Sand kicked up behind her as she sprinted toward the mahavans. They were forming ranks. One of them, a young man, probably the one in charge, pointed at her and Serena and shouted orders.

Jessira Shielded before putting on a final burst of speed. She hurled a Fireball from no more than ten yards away. It screamed through the air and punched a hole through a mahavan's chest. The Sinskrill woman collapsed, smoke wisping from her corpse.

Jessira distantly realized that her actions today would cause her grief and sorrow, but she set aside those worries. She could mourn later. For now, she'd do whatever was needed.

The rest of the mahavans scattered as Jessira hurtled into their midst. She unsheathed her sword, blocked a thrust, and spun around a lunge. A front kick crumpled a skinny mahavan.

A movement in her periphery. She bent backward at the waist. A blade sliced the air above her Shield. Jessira snapped upright, blocked a wild swing, ducked low, slashed out. A scarred mahavan went down screaming, one leg amputated at the calf. Blood soaked the sand.

She somersaulted over a swinging blade, did a front roll across the beach, and came up with a fistful of sand. She flung it at the skinny mahavan she'd earlier kicked. He clutched at his face. A thrust of her blade into his chest put him down.

Instincts honed by thousands of hours training against Rukh detected a blow coming from behind. She twisted aside, deflecting a sword aimed at the center of her back. An axe-kick sent the mahavan woman stumbling.

Jessira had a momentary respite. She hurled another Fireball at a pair of mahavans who'd foolishly bunched together. One of them tried a braid of Water but it wasn't enough. The Fireball hammered into them, blasting both mahavans through the air. They landed with a thump, rolled a few times, and neither rose. The Fireball had blasted a foot-wide hole through both their torsos and instantly cauterized the wounds.

Jessira used a *lorethasra*-powered leap to carry her over the heads of the final five mahavans. They watched her soar through the air with mouths agape. She landed and resumed her attack.

The female mahavan she'd kicked earlier immediately fell to an overhand swing, which cut her deep from shoulder to chest. The woman tried to scream but her strength left her in a rush. She collapsed, and Jessira tugged her sword free. Blood and sand coated the blade and her hands. She disregarded both and took a moment to assess the remaining mahavans. They'd stepped away and spread out. *A wise decision, one they should have implemented far sooner.*

Serena arrived. She stood a few paces behind. *Good.*

On a gesture from the young mahavan in charge, the Sinskrill warriors charged.

Jessira blocked a slash, spun away from a thrust. Her return took a mahavan in the armpit, her sword sliding into his heart. He snarled once, but then the pain hit him. His face drained of color and his knees buckled.

Jessira leapt away from the remaining three mahavans. She needed distance and a chance to catch her breath. Rukh might be able to fight for hours without rest, but she couldn't. She sensed movement out of the corner of her vision. A white bolt of Fire. It roared toward her from *Demolition*.

Jessira's eyes widened. She'd seen this particular Fire before. It was the Servitor's. She reached deep, draining the last of her *lorethasra* as she called up a Shield and braced her legs, prepared for impact. *Devesh, save me.*

The Servitor's Fire hit with the force of a rockslide. Jessira's Shield brightened. Bolts of electricity crackled off it. Even with its protection, the air around her bloomed hot as an oven. The Fire continued, pitiless as the desert sun, and she found herself pushed back. Her feet slid ten feet. The Fire went on and Jessira barely managed to remain upright.

Hold on! Shon urged in her mind.

Jessira's teeth clenched as she strained to hold off the Fire.

CHAPTER 31: LEARNING DISASTER

October 1990

William breathed heavily as he ran along Sita's Song. In the back of his mind, the red-eyed beast snarled. It hadn't been entirely removed, and a part of him was thankful for the monster's presence. Its fury gave him the strength to keep going. If he could have sprinted more quickly, he would have. He wanted to. He needed to.

They'd reached the southernmost part of Janaki Valley, but William realized they were already too late. In the distance he saw great gouts of smoke clouding the sky and knew what it meant. Lilith burned. So did the part of Janaki Valley through which they ran. Mahavans and unformed had been through here, and the trail of their destruction, unchecked fires and shocking murders, left William red with rage. They hadn't spared the women and children.

Fragging bastards. The angry beast snarled again, and William let it breathe to life. *I'll kill every mahavan I find.*

A surge of adrenaline powered him forward. William gritted his teeth, keeping pace with the others. Rukh ran next to him, breathing hard. He must have finally felt the fatigue of their fifteen-mile run. Sweat coated his shirt and poured down his face.

Even Travail appeared bothered by the long, hard run. His braided hair bounced with every step he took. Rivulets of perspiration dripped into his beard and soaked the short, black fur lining his body. William guessed his coat made it difficult for him to tolerate the muggy weather.

Only the Kesarins remained unaffected. If anything, they seemed to thrive. William could have sworn they'd grown a full hand or more in the past few hours.

This climate is what we were bred for, Aia said to his unspoken thought.

The unformed things are less than a mile ahead, Shon added.

Break, Rukh called. He slowed to a fast walk and pulled out his canteen. "Drain your water. Drink it all. We won't need any more after this final sprint."

William unstoppered his canteen and did as Rukh ordered. Afterward he felt marginally better, but he still gulped deep breaths.

"Control your breathing," Travail said to him. "Deep breaths, in and out."

William remembered his lessons from Sinskrill when Travail had been in charge of their training. He took deep breaths, in through his nose and out through his mouth. *In and out. In and out. Slow and steady. Focus on the heart. Slow it down.*

After a minute it started to work. His heart slowed its rapid rate, and his breathing came more easily.

"Drop all your equipment except your weapons," Rukh said. "Same with any food. Eat what you can, but leave the rest behind."

William dropped his compass, watch, and pack. He didn't need any of it for the last leg of their run. All he required was his sword.

Seconds later, they headed out once more. They ran more swiftly this time, racing past rolling hills where crops had been ripped apart. Farmers, shock and grief on their faces, silently watched them pass. The sun stood unmoving and heat blurred the gray stones of Sita's

Song. William was soon panting again, but he never slowed down. He wouldn't be the weak link.

How much farther? Rukh asked after they'd covered several more miles.

Half a mile, Shon answered.

William did some quick calculations. They had passed Sile Troy's farm a few seconds ago, which meant the unformed were approaching Lakshman's Bow. "What about Ward's group?" he asked aloud.

Rukh slowed to a jog, pulled out his phone, and quickly dialed it. After a few moments of terse conversation, he hung up. *Twenty magi are at the enrune fields. The rest are involved in search and rescue. The mahavans killed . . .* He grimaced. *Let's get this done, and figure the rest out later.*

Minutes later, Shon called out the distance again. *The unformed have slowed.*

Why don't they fly to safety? It would be easiest for them Travail said. *Are they still so fatigued?*

Rukh shrugged. *I don't know, but I'll take whatever blessings come our way,* he said. *Jake's in charge of the remaining Irregulars in the enrune fields. He's heading north. We'll act as the hammer to his anvil.*

They set off again in their ground-chewing jog and quickly crested a rise. *There!* The unformed came into view, still heading south. No more than a hundred yards away, and all in the shape of horses. They had yet to reach Lakshman's Bow, still a half-mile distant.

William drew *lorethasra* and quickly wove binoculars. The unformed leapt into focus. Sweat lathered their sides and caked their frothing mouths. Their breathing came labored, and as he watched, they stumbled to a halt. They shifted about in apparent nervousness as a group of magi—Jake's unit—crossed Lakshman's Bow. The magi rode bikes and advanced straight at the unformed, who turned about and retreated.

Aia growled in anticipation. *Easy meat.* She licked her lips

There are almost thirty of them, Travail reminded her.

Shon shrugged, a roll of his shoulders and a flick of his ears. *So?*

William shook his head at the Kesarin's cockiness. *The unformed are deadly.*

*We *are deadly,** Aia growled in reply. She roared a challenge.

Wait! Rukh called out.

Too late. The Kesarins accelerated as if launched.

William gaped in astonishment.

Travail made a sound of amazement. "My Lord, they run swiftly."

"Too swiftly." Rukh scowled. "Fragging idiots. Let's go." He raced after the Kesarins, picking up speed.

Travail took off, too. William tried to keep up but quickly realized he couldn't. He felt like a slug in comparison. Seconds later, he reached the battle, ironically in the same field where the Irregulars had trained early on.

The Kesarins reached the unformed first and attacked in a buzzsaw of fangs and claws. The screams of horses and the stench of entrails filled the air. The unformed snarled in response, transforming into bears, lions, cape buffalo, elephants, and rhinos as they tried to fight back. None became birds who could simply fly away.

William couldn't understand why. His questions ended when he engaged an unformed boar.

～

Rukh cursed floridly when Aia and Shon took off on their own. *They should have remained close at hand so they could support the rest of us. Those two have too much faith in their speed.*

A moment later, he set aside his irritation. He had a battle to fight. He sourced his *Jivatma*, his *lorethasra*, and imbued his muscles with power. He raced after Aia and Shon, toward the unformed and quickly reached the battle.

Rukh left his sword sheathed and more deeply sourced his *Jivatma*. His hands lit with Fireballs.

Several bears charged his way. Rukh let them come. He flung the Fireballs and they screamed toward the creatures, exploding into their midst. One unformed fell dead with a massive hole in its abdomen. The stench of seared flesh roiled the air.

The other bear seemed to inhale the Fireball, consuming it. Still, it took damage as wisps of smoke drifted off its fur and from its snout.

When the bear stumbled, Rukh at last unsheathed his sword. He blurred forward with the unmatched speed of his Kumma Caste. A single thrust through the creature's throat put it down.

He landed and readied himself as three more unformed came his way, these also bears. *Too close for Fireballs.* Rukh Shielded and took them on. They charged, but he didn't back down. One of the bears lunged, swinging a massive paw. It would have raked him from the crown of his head to the base of his chest but he was no longer there.

He leapt over the creatures. He briefly marked their snarls of confusion as he soared above their heads. He landed and thrust backward without looking. His blade, powered by *lorethasra*, punched deep into one of the bears, taking it through the back and into its heart.

The creature grunted once and stiffened. It crumpled to the ground.

Rukh whipped his sword free and spun around. He readied his sword, facing off against the other two unformed. One of them swiped at him, but Rukh remained in the pocket, willing to take a shot to give one. The blow landed against his Shield, and Rukh rocked backward. Another blow struck, this one from the other unformed. Rukh gave ground. He went with the motion, ducked another swipe, and regained his equilibrium.

He snarled. *Enough.* He taunted the unformed, gesturing them forward. The creatures roared in answer.

Rukh shot toward the bears like a dart. A thrust to the chest knocked one of the unformed off-balance. A follow-up slash to the other unformed removed a paw. Blood sprayed in an arc as the beast roared in pain and withdrew its ruined limb.

Rukh didn't give either of them respite. He launched at them. A snap-kick boot to the jaw stove-in the head of the unformed he'd stabbed in the chest. He landed, crouched beneath a blow from the other bear and sent out a whip-fast slice. It cut the throat of the remaining unformed. The creature clutched its neck as blood spurted.

You've grown slow, Aia noted. She fought several yards away with Shon defending her back.

Rukh smiled at her observation before attacking another group of unformed. Five of them this time, a mix of lions, tigers, and cape buffaloes. A pair of Fireballs took out two of them. He attacked the rest with sword only.

He evaded claws, leaned away from snapping teeth, and pushed aside impaling horns. A spinning back-kick crushed a tiger's jaw. A diagonal slash ended a lion. The cape buffalo charged. Rukh leaped straight up, somersaulted in mid-air, and came down like an arrow, sword-thrust ready. The cape buffalo never saw him coming. He slammed his sword home, punching through hide and bone, landed on the unformed's back, and rode it to the ground where it shivered once before dying.

Perhaps not so slow, Aia said, a smile in her voice.

~

W illiam front-flipped over an unformed boar and evaded its goring tusks. He landed, spun about, and slashed with his sword. A scoring line across the beast's back caused it to roar in pain. The boar sought to rip with its tusks, but again William evaded. This time he had a thick braid of Fire at the ready. A snap of his wrists sent the weave spearing into the unformed, punching diagonally through the creature's chest, penetrating through its flank. The animal grunted, took a hobbling step, and fell dead.

The earth shook. Movement at the corner of his vision spun William about to face a charging rhino. He braided an Earthen shield. The rhino transformed into a clawing eagle. With no time for defense, William could only cover his head with his hands. The eagle gashed his arms, cutting deeply. He wove a braid of Air and blasted the bird away, gaining a momentary respite. The eagle dove at him again but this time he was ready. Another blast of Air knocked the bird to the ground, and a single thrust with his sword ended it.

William took a knee. He gulped deep breaths, needing a breather. His arms burned from the eagle's slashes. His hands went weak. The wounds streamed blood, and he healed them as best he could.

Movement in his peripheral vision caused him to spin about, sword at the ready. An elephant trumpeted and reared above him. He dove to the side, losing his sword in the process as heavy feet crushed the ground inches from where he'd been kneeling. The elephant shifted his head and twisted. William dove again to avoid its tusks. The elephant reared once more. In desperation, William flung a fan of boiling Water at the creature's eyes. The elephant screamed and shook its head.

William took the brief reprieve to gain distance and gather his wits. He couldn't move the unformed with Air or Earth. It was too strong. But maybe he could drown it in Water.

The elephant charged.

William formed a thick weave of Water, a globe the size of a baseball. He hurled it at the charging elephant and struck the beast straight in the head.

He smiled. *Mario Soto couldn't have done better.*

The weave of Water expanded on impact and engulfed the creature's entire head, including its trunk. The unformed stumbled to halt and lurched backward in panic. It transformed into a fox and tried to slip out of the bubble of water. William wouldn't let it go, and within seconds the unformed went limp. He drew a knife. A stab to the creature's throat finished it off.

He breathed in relief as he lurched to where he'd dropped his sword. He bent to retrieve it. Something slammed him to the ground. A weight settled on his back and teeth bit deep. Claws tore into his back. William screamed. Pain burned like fire where he'd been scored. His vision blurred.

William went weightless. Something had flung him through the air. He landed on his back, and his head smacked the ground. Consciousness flickered, but he retained enough awareness to make sense of his peril. A tiger leapt at him.

William drew up a barrier of Earth. The tiger cleared it in a single bound. William shuffled backward and snapped a whip of Fire. It struck the tiger on the snout. The unformed snarled and momentarily retreated. Its tail snapped in fury, and once more it leapt. William prepared a braid of Air.

Aia slammed into the tiger. She was bigger, smarter, faster, and more ferocious. In seconds, her jaws snapped onto the tiger's throat, and she disemboweled the creature. She gave the unformed a final shake before dropping the creature and padding toward William. She licked his forehead with her raspy tongue, leaving a bloody streak behind. *Stay here,* Aia said. *You've done enough.*

William ignored the throbbing pain in his arms, the bone-deep, burning sensation in his back, and levered himself upright. His vision swam, and he had to lean on Aia to remain on his feet. He took a pause to once again form the healing braid Ward had taught him. Blood still seeped from his wounds, but at least it wasn't pouring out like from a faucet.

What about the unformed? he asked.

Aia gestured with her head. *Look for yourself. They're in retreat.*

The unformed had broken. They fled south, still on foot and heading for Lakshman's Bow and Jake's magi. While he watched, their wretched remnants—no more than a dozen of them—collided with Jake's magi. A flash of steel, of lashing Fire, Water, Earth, and Air, and the unformed finally took to the sky. Only eight managed to trans-form into falcons and wing their way to safety.

William snarled. *No chance I'm letting them get away.* He let the raging spirit dwelling within him, the red-eyed beast, surge to life. It allowed him to ignore his pain. He sourced his *lorethasra* and created the lightning weave he'd used earlier. The braids in his hands coiled and hissed like snakes.

William thrust out his arms and the weaves lengthened, streaming into the sky. The braids split into eight lances of lightning. Each one stabbed skyward and pierced a falcon. William smiled in satisfaction when many of the unformed screamed in pain. They transformed into falling pyres. They plunged to the ground, crashing as blackened corpses. All but four. Those had somehow consumed the lightning and raced away to safety.

William watched the birds for a moment. He swayed on his feet and heard both Rukh and Shon shout Jessira's name in terror. They sounded like they were a mile away. Whatever had sparked their alarm, William couldn't help with it. He had nothing left to give. He dropped to the ground.

~

S erena watched the unfolding battle on the beach, unsure of what to do or how to help. The mahavans were entirely focused on Jessira as she decimated their numbers. Seven of them were already down.

A flicker at the corner of Serena's vision caught her attention. She shifted her gaze and her heart seized.

A white-hot lance of fire roared from *Demolition*. *The Servitor and his Spear. It had to be.* The air shimmered in the heat-haze of the Fire's passage.

Serena shouted a warning. "Jessira!"

Jessira must have noticed the oncoming attack at the last moment. She held a hand out as if to stop the Fire. Something like electricity sparked from each of her fingers and encased her in the green webbing of her Shield.

The blast of Fire slammed into her. The webbing brightened and sizzled like meat landing on an overheated pan. Jessira dropped her sword, gritted her teeth, and thrust out both hands. More electricity bled forth. Her feet carved lines into the sand as she was slowly pushed back.

The Fire kept coming. Jessira's protective webbing brightened further. It glowed red. Her face was a rictus of effort and pain.

The mahavans merely watched, seemingly transfixed.

Serena threw off her hesitation and rushed forward. She didn't know if she could help, but she had to try. She called up a wall of water from Lilith Bay. Steam erupted where it contacted the Servitor's Fire. A concussive blast knocked Serena off her feet, but she scrambled upright. She'd ended the Fire, but Jessira had been smashed twenty feet away. She lay unmoving.

The second time today. Serena hoped she still lived but finding out would have to wait. She still had to fight three mahavans. She recognized them, had trained with them, and counted one as an ally at one time. They all glared at her with faces full of hate.

"Traitor," Brandon Thrum spat.

The words didn't touch her. Serena smiled at Brandon. Sword ready, she taunted him, gesturing him toward her.

He surprised, losing his mahavan equilibrium. He shouted inarticulately and sprang forward, outstripping the others. He didn't even bother using his *lorethasra*.

Sloppy to let his anger control him so.

Serena slid to the side and didn't bother parrying. Brandon tried to spin and keep her in front of him. *Too slow.* She snapped off a question-mark kick. It crunched into Brandon's head, and he face-planted, instantly unconscious.

Serena moved on.

Another mahavan, a young man, Quinn Clair, challenged her. He held a weave at the ready. Serena attacked. She feinted a diagonal slash. The mahavan bit and moved to parry. Serena pulled her strike and hit out with an arrow of Air. It whistled until it stabbed into the mahavan's chest. He fell dead as blood fountained from his wound.

The final mahavan, another man, this one older, was Park Alawah.

Serena sent a feint. Park didn't take the bait. He thrust forward. Serena retreated. Park sent a swift slash. Serena, unready for the man's speed, clumsily managed a parry. She shifted, going with the flow of contact. Park, old but crafty, was ready. He cracked her in the head with an elbow. Serena almost dropped her sword. Her vision swam. She stumbled away, barely blocked a lunge, and evaded Park's next attack on instinct alone.

She sensed a weave of Earth and Water beneath her feet and jumped aside. A spear of Air hurtled toward her. She called up Fire to burn it away. Park hurled another spear of Air. She dodged this one. Water softened the ground around her feet. She leapt away and rolled under a powerful overhand strike.

The momentary respite allowed her vision and balance to restore. Serena set herself and waited as Park advanced.

Fire screamed at her, but she snuffed it out with Earth. She doused another lance of Fire.

By silent accord, Serena and Park stepped back, each one measuring the other.

The momentary standoff ended.

Serena sent a questing slash at Park's neck. He blocked it, but Serena saw a possible opening in his defense. His recovery was late. *I hope.* Serena sent another questing slash. Again, Park parried, but as she'd noticed a second ago, he was slow to recover.

Serena sent an upward rising slash that transitioned into a lunge. Park blocked the first but couldn't evade the second. Serena sliced into his bicep.

Park winced, and his sword dipped.

Serena took the opportunity and attacked. Her strikes came hard and fast. A thrust. Parry a return. Diagonal slice leading to a hammer blow with her hilt.

Park reeled away, blood flowing from where she'd bashed him on the forehead. A line of Earth tripped him and he fell with a thud. Serena finished him off with a single thrust to the throat.

Park hissed out his last breath, and Serena paused then, taking stock of her situation. She stood amongst a field of corpses. Her head drooped over how many she'd killed and how little she regretted it.

~

Axel waited impatiently aboard *Demolition* and watched as four falcons winged his way. He recognized them as unformed. *But where are the rest of them?* Where were the hundreds of mahavans he'd sent to destroy the magi? He'd known their losses in today's battle would be extravagant, but only these four? It couldn't be.

And yet . . .

Axel hadn't heard from Adam in hours, not since his brother had called earlier and said his forces were approaching Lilith. He worried now what the lack of further information might foretell.

Axel continued to study the unformed as they flew closer, and the entire time he continued to hope that these four weren't the only survivors of the forces he'd sent ashore. Even outnumbered, his mahavans should have rolled the soft magi like a flood washing away a farmer's crops. Perhaps the unformed speeding toward *Demolition* were the vanguard of his returning, victorious warriors.

Hope bloomed in Axel's heart. He had to believe it was true. Otherwise, events had transitioned from worrisome to dire. His fleet had already been obliterated—only *Demolition* remained afloat. He couldn't afford it if his mahavans had also been extinguished. Axel scowled at the possibility, not bothering to hide his emotions as those weaker than he were forced to do.

The loss of his other ships had been the fault of the female World Killer, Jessira Shektan. Axel had seen her on the beach, and a shallow tingle of pleasure climbed his spine. He'd hurt the woman, possibly killed her—would have killed her if not for Serena's interference. She'd interceded and saved the World Killer. Axel could have still slain Jessira, but the killing blow would have also resulted in Serena's death.

He hadn't been able to do it. Love for his daughters was the one weakness he allowed himself.

Axel threw off his morbid thoughts when he saw that the unformed would arrive in a few minutes. While he waited for them to fly the final half-mile, he returned his attention to Lilith.

The village burned. Fires raged on nearly all of its terraces, dull red to yellow in color, and a continuous, low-pitched, crackling rumble emanated from them. Thick columns of smoke lofted skyward, intermittently concealing the village. The buildings on top of the cliffs hadn't fared much better. They too, burned, overcome by an inferno of flames and a thick pall of soot.

It wasn't enough. Axel could still see hundreds of magi on Clifftop struggling to contain the blazes. Whether they succeeded or not, it didn't matter to him. They lived, and he wouldn't have it. They'd stolen his *raha'asras* and his daughters. They had attacked his home, and he knew they would try to do to Sinskrill what he had done to Arylyn. They would come for him.

But only if they can source lorethasra.

"Ready Executioner," Axel commanded.

Mavahans raced about to carry out his order. It took two of them to lift the shell he had called for. It was a massive, bullet-shaped *nomasra* the length of a short spear and with the heft of a boulder. The mahavans set it within Axel's cannon, but the bore couldn't entirely contain it. The tip of the shell poked past the end of the barrel, glistening with an oily, black sheen.

Axel sourced his ocean-deep *lorethasra* and the scent of burning oil filled his nostrils. He'd long since learned to ignore its acrid scent. He quickly created braids as thick as his thighs. They gurgled, hissed, pulsed, and throbbed across his chest, torso, and abdomen. He sourced deeper. The braids thickened, and he collected them in his hands.

He sent the weaves into the shell, and it sucked them up like a vast desert. He kept pouring more and more of the Elements into Executioner. The shell finally warmed. Its oily blackness eventually built to a white-hot color too painful to stare at. It lit up, brighter than any previous munition he had fired and cast dark shadows all about. The cannon's barrel couldn't entirely contain the heat, and it also glowed dull-red.

Axel shielded his eyes and measured the moment. The shell whined. Its pitch rose higher and higher, became a banshee scream as it continued to shine ever brighter.

Now. Axel thinned his Spirit and released Executioner, which exploded from the barrel with a whoosh. It erupted skyward, trailing a comet tail of light during its ascension. Axel remained tied to it and guided its movement. It soared ever higher.

The magi tried to wrest control of it away from him. They might as well have tried to pry a bone away from a bear. Axel wouldn't let go of the shell. He aimed it like a dagger at Lilith's heart, at the center of the village. Executioner arched above the buildings atop the cliff, and Axel swelled its size. He inflated it until it bloomed as large as a hot air balloon he'd once seen in his time as a bishan in the Far Beyond. *Soon.*

Axel readied himself. Once he unclipped control of the shell, it would explode over the heads of his enemies. Not all the magi would be affected by what he intended, perhaps not even many, but maybe it would be enough.

Now! Axel exploded the shell and watched for a few moments as a nacreous cloud drifted across the buildings above the cliffs. He smiled in satisfaction. *Good.*

He turned away from the horror he had unleashed and called out orders. *Demolition's* sails puffed with air, and they were swiftly underway.

Moments later, the unformed landed and transformed. Adam, Jeek, and two others.

Axel stood impassively as he prepared to receive his brother. He wondered if he'd have to kill his latest Secondus for failing him.

~

Adam did his best to avoid the fighting taking place all around him. He especially held his distance from the giant cats tearing through the unformed like a storm of claws and teeth. He'd never seen anything like them. He also remained at a distance from Travail, who swung a staff the size of a felled tree. The troll clobbered the unformed, braining or smashing them to bloody pieces. He even inched away from William in newfound respect. The young *raha'asra* blazed energy and danger, fighting with all his Elements.

However, nothing concerned Adam as much as Rukh. The man remained every bit as deadly as Adam remembered. He destroyed everything he came across, crushed unformed left and right. Nothing tested him or those strange cats.

Adam edged farther from the battle, eyeing it in alarm. It shouldn't have ended like this. Despite his improvised plan, it still should have worked. He was a Walker. He'd listened in while the magi discussed the dispersal of their warriors. They had held back a large intercepting force north of Janaki Valley and cannon crews to defend Lilith itself. However, both were out of position, one too far north and the other on the wrong side of Clifftop. Adam had strategized accordingly. He'd left a reserve squad—a sacrificial force—to pin down the bulk of the magi forces centered near Mount Madhava. Another unit of cannon crews had been sent racing to Lilith to destroy the village and escape in the chaos. The unformed would have then swooped in and ravaged the survivors.

Given the fires raging over Lilith the cannon crews must have accomplished their part of mission, but Adam didn't believe they'd escaped. He could see their bodies strewn on the other side of the broad bridge crossing River Namaste, along with a force of magi heading toward his position. As for the unformed—

A trumpeting elephant snapped Adam's attention back to the

battle. It was lost. The unformed had been destroyed. There was no point in remaining here.

"Unformed! Take flight and flee!" Adam shouted. He had enough energy remaining to transform into a falcon, and he hoped some of the others did as well.

Less than a ten unformed took flight alongside him. They beat their wings hard, fighting for height and speed. Adam believed they might make it free of the carnage when a light blazed from the ground.

He glanced back. His falcon eyes easily picked out a magus, William, holding a fistful of light that burned as bright as the sun. Adam's eyes widened. Braids leapt into the sky. One touched his chest, sticking to him like a line of spider web. He reached for his *lorethasra* to cut the braid attaching him to William.

Lances of lightning surged up the sticky braids.

Adam had an instant to prepare himself. The lightning hit, burning like a branding iron. He shouted in pain. Panic threatened, but he managed to maintain his senses. He reached past the pain and held onto his *lorethasra*. He channeled the lightning, letting it flow through his body and into a quickly spun weave of Earth.

The lightning snapped off, and Adam breathed in relief. A second later, his relief became anger and fear when he realized that only three other unformed had survived the battle and the lightning. He cursed. *What had William done?* His attention turned to *Demolition*. The ship floated in Lilith Bay. It sailed alone. The rest of the ships burned.

Adam gaped. The fleet was destroyed. All the mahavans were dead. Nearly all the unformed were similarly destroyed. He cursed anew at the disaster that had befallen Sinskrill.

∼

Selene huddled between Mrs. Karllson, Ms. Sioned, and about twenty other people in Mr. Reed's tailor shop on Clifftop. Bolts of fabric lined the walls, and everyone sat on cushioned chairs, sweating in stale air that smelled of mothballs, hemp, and soot.

Lilith burned all around them. Flames engulfed a building across the street, and Selene watched as people ran around trying to control the fire's fury. Thick tendrils of smoke curled upward like a snake. It drifted apart, forming a curtain that wrapped the sky in a black shawl. The world contained the gloom of a perpetual twilight.

Selene tried to close her ears to the screams from outside, forcing herself to remember what it meant to be a drone, how to control her emotions and act like nothing bothered her.

But she was bothered, terrified by the events of the past few days, especially for Serena, William, and Jake . . . for all the people in her life. They were out there fighting her father and his mahavans. *What if they died?*

Selene immediately cut off the line of her thoughts. Her family, all her loved ones, would survive. They had to. *But what if they don't? What if father destroys Lilith?*

Again, Selene sought to cut off the terrifying trend her mind kept taking. She took a deep breath, trying to keep her thoughts from tumbling into disarray like River Namaste over the cataracts. *I'm not afraid of anything.* Another deep breath. *I'm not afraid of anything.*

She repeated the mantra, and her heart settled. It slowed down and began beating more easily.

Selene exhaled in relief, but an instant later, another explosion made her yip in fear.

Mrs. Karllson reached over and gave her hand a supportive squeeze. "It'll be fine. The mahavans won't win."

Selene wished she could believe her, but she didn't.

More explosions blasted into Lilith, and Selene covered her ears and pressed her head against her knees. Fear quickly became rage. She wanted to scream. She wanted all this to be done with. She wanted her father and his mahavans to go away. Selene gritted her teeth. No, she wanted to kill the mahavans, destroy them all like they were trying to destroy Lilith.

Another detonation went off. This one rolled on and on like some terrible hammer of doom. Shouts of abject terror penetrated through Selene's fury and she could see people outside Mr. Reed's store gesturing and pointing, clearly horrified by something in the distance.

An Irregular, someone Selene couldn't recognize through the

smoke and soot covering her from head to foot, popped into the store. "Stay inside," the woman ordered. "We'll evacuate you if we have to."

"Evacuate?" Mrs. Karllson stood. "What happened?"

The Irregular's face went ashen, visible through the soot. "Something terrible. We're still trying to figure it out. Just stay here. Don't move."

Once again, fear for Serena and those she loved filled Selene's chest.

Mrs. Karllson wore a worried expression, and fearful conversations broke out amongst the grownups. Other than Elliot Dare, Selene was the only child here. She wished she had a girlfriend to talk to.

Mrs. Karllson addressed her. "I need to talk to the others." She rose. "Stay here. I'll be back." Without another word, she marched to the rear of the store where a group of grownups huddled.

Selene understood. Mrs. Karllson's son and husband were members of the Irregulars. So was Lien. In a lot of ways, she was like Selene since everyone she loved was outside fighting.

Elliot slid into Mrs. Karllson's seat and pulled out a deck of cards. "Want to see some magic?"

Selene rolled her eyes and made sure Elliot saw it. She wasn't in the mood to smile or be entertained. "We're on an island full of magi," she said, using her best world-weary tone. "Of course I don't want to see magic. I see it every day."

Elliot surprised her by not taking offense. Instead, he smiled. "Then how about an illusion?" He spread out the cards and pestered her to pick one.

With a disgusted sigh, Selene did as Elliot asked. *King of Hearts.*

Elliot handed her a fountain pen, instructed her to write her name across the face of the card, and put it back in the deck. Next, he handed her an envelope and asked her to write her name on it, seal it shut, and leave it on her lap. He did some hand-waving stupidity and shuffling before pulling out a card and setting it face down on his thigh. "Are you ready to be amazed?" he asked.

Selene's interest piqued in spite of her worry.

Elliot flipped over the card.

Eight of Clubs.

Selene smiled. "That's not my card."

He flipped over three more cards in rapid succession. Each one was wrong, and Selene grew smug at his failure.

Elliot scratched his chin, clearly puzzled by his failure. After a few seconds of thought, his face brightened with apparent understanding. "I think I know what I did wrong." He pointed to the envelope. "Open it."

Selene lifted her eyebrows in question.

"Trust me." He smiled, and her heart beat a little faster.

He had a cute smile. She decided to humor him and opened the envelope. She gasped in amazement. Inside was the King of Hearts. "How did you do that?"

Elliot smiled wider, and Selene's insides did another little somersault. "A magician never reveals his secrets." He shuffled the cards. "You want to see another trick?"

Selene smiled. "Sure. Why not?" While the fear for her loved ones remained, it eased off a little, and she silently thanked Elliot for distracting her.

Elliot kept her attention focused on his seemingly endless supply of illusions and away from whatever was going on outside. She was grateful to him.

In the middle of a trick involving rings, Elliot paused. "Do you hear that?"

Selene listened. All she heard was the roar of the fires and people shouting. She said so.

He shook his head. "No. There aren't any more explosions, not even our cannons."

Selene realized that Elliot was right. The mahavans had stopped firing. She lifted her head, gazed out the front door, and dared to hope. *Is it finally over?*

Seconds passed, but nothing more came. Selene's fears eased, and the need to see her family overwhelmed her. She stood, sprinted for the door, and flung it open. For the first time in hours, she stepped outside.

Elliot followed her. "We shouldn't be out here," he warned.

Selene disregarded him, but then came Mrs. Karllson's sharp rebuke to remain inside as well. Other grown-ups shouted at her, too.

Selene hesitated and looked at Mrs. Karllson and the others still inside. She frowned when she noticed her shadow etched on the ground. With all the smoke to cloud the sun, it had been dark as twilight. She puzzled about what her shadow meant.

Something exploded overhead, and Selene's gaze shot skyward. A shimmering, green light blasted out and white flakes fell like snow. They landed on her hair, lashes, and upturned face.

CHAPTER 32: THE WISDOM OF PYRRHUS

"Roll him over."

William couldn't tell who was speaking. He couldn't tell if the words had been said out loud or in his mind. *Maybe one of the Kesarins?*

His arms and legs flopped like wet noodles. He had no control of them. Pain bloomed in his back. He groaned, but even to his ears, it sounded no louder than a puppy whimpering. Fatigue and savage agony sapped all his strength.

The burning sensation faded, and William discovered his head resting on something soft, furry, and muscular. His eyes slowly came into focus, and a blue sky shaded with veils of black met his blinking, confused gaze. An instant later his vision blurred once again. *What happened to me?*

He couldn't recall. His thoughts drifted like an unmoored raft on a slow-moving stream. So did the voices of those around him. They made no sense, and he struggled to piece together his last moments of consciousness. He remembered a battle, and he remembered killing an unformed, a bunch of them. He vaguely realized that maybe he shouldn't have sourced his *lorethasra* so deeply, that he should have let the final eight unformed escape.

William sighed and closed his eyes. He wanted nothing more than to sleep for a few weeks. The voices of those around him kept him awake, though. *What are they saying?*

"An unformed mauled him."

William didn't know who said that.

"What about his arms?" a deep, rumbling voice asked.

William realized it was Travail who had spoken the question, and it was also the troll who held him.

"I'll Heal them later." *That's Rukh.* "His shoulder and back need attention first. We have to stop the bleeding. Now roll him over."

A patch of torn, grassy field came into view.

"Hold him," Rukh said. "He'll jerk, and I need to make sure the Healing goes into his back."

"Will it leave a scar?"

William wanted to smile. *Jake.*

"They'll be thin," Rukh said. "The one on his shoulder will be uglier." He paused. "Ready?"

"Ready," Travail said. His grip tightened, and William grimaced. "He'll not slip from my grasp."

Something nosed him, whuffling his hair. Aia spoke in his mind. *Be brave.*

A moment of silence overcame the group.

William knew pain. The color of healing light blazed through him. It etched his arteries and sank into his bones. The light hurt worse than the mauling of the tiger. It seemed to go on and on, but finally, it faded. The terrible pain from the tiger's claws and teeth no longer burned. Only his arms throbbed where that damn eagle had raked him.

William's earlier lethargy redoubled.

Jake whistled in apparent appreciation. "Hardly a scar at all."

"Look at his shoulder," Travail said.

"Oh." William could imagine Jake's face falling in disappointment. "At least the girls might think the scar there is cool."

Rukh sighed. "I've got others to Heal. Can you take care of his arms?"

Jake muttered something that sounded affirmative, and Rukh moved on, his footfalls retreating.

A moment later, a cool sensation eased the throbbing in William's forearms. The pain abated, and while it wasn't entirely gone, it was much more manageable.

Memories returned. Janaki Valley aflame. Lilith burning. Buildings destroyed. Smoke and ruin.

William shook his head, and willed himself to rouse. His eyes and thoughts cleared, but lethargy still weighed him down like an anchor.

He had to help those in need. He'd rested enough.

"I'm all right," he said. He shifted out of Travail's grasp and tried to lever himself upright, but his knees gave out. He would have fallen if not for Shon, who stood nearby. William leaned heavily against the tawny Kesarin. He went light-headed as his vision swooned. He could hear his heartbeat in his ears. He waited for the dizziness to pass, and the world eventually resolved.

Part of him wished it hadn't.

William found himself upon the enrune fields. Dozens of corpses lay scattered about. Many were animals, but far too many were human. *How many had died here?*

A coil of smoke drifted close by, and William coughed.

Jake handed him a canteen. "Drink."

"What happened?" William asked. His memories remained fragmented.

Jake explained how his unit had tracked down the breakaway group of mahavans. He pointed to Lilith, where smoke continued to pile skyward. Fires burned, the heat extending all the way to the enrune fields.

"The mahavans had cannons," Jake explained. "They got in a lucky shot. It collapsed a building and a bunch more around it." He hesitated. "They also had something like napalm. That's what's burning."

William took in Jake's drone-flat mien. His friend was trying to hide his pain.

"How many died?" William asked.

Travail moved to his elbow. "We don't know." His tone was soft and filled with sorrow. "We're still trying to find out."

It wasn't enough of an answer. William faced Jake. "How many?" he demanded.

"At least three hundred," Jake said. His drone-flatness broke beneath the weight of the number. "And we probably lost more than a hundred Irregulars fighting the mahavans. Ward's gone."

More than four hundred dead. William's light-headedness returned as grief hollowed his heart, and he stared at the ruin of his home.

⁓

Serena stood beside Jessira as the two of them watched *Demolition* slowly exit the bay. The lowering sun etched the lines of the great, black vessel, highlighting it and casting it as a deep, long shadow aimed at Lilith. Serena imagined she could see her father standing in the ship's stern, smiling in pleasure at the carnage he had wrought, at the village glowing orange and red from the many fires burning on terraces and Clifftop.

Serena scowled.

Too many Irregulars had died to repel the mahavan invasion, and too much of Lilith had been destroyed. It would take months, possibly years, to repair all the damage. On top of that, they'd have to train a new group of warriors for the inevitable invasion of Sinskrill.

At least her father's fleet had been mauled. It would be a long time before he could mount another sea-based assault on Arylyn. The mahavan ships lay wrecked in Lilith Bay, broken and burning. Their carcasses were nothing more than charred beams, torn sails, and ruined ropes. Their annihilation carried a revolting stink, a combination of burning wood, oil, and pitch, along with acrid columns of pluming smoke and the iron-sharp tang of blood.

The latter arose from the dead mahavans on the beach and the ones who had leapt overboard when their vessels caught fire. Most of those hadn't made it to shore, and their corpses floated amidst the debris of their ships. A dozen, however, had managed to straggle to Lilith Beach. They should have surrendered, but they hadn't. They'd fought on in a short, vicious battle.

By then, Jessira had recovered enough from her injuries to lead the cannon crews against the mahavans, but even with her help, they'd lost four Irregulars, and several more had been critically injured. None of the mahavans had survived the battle, and the bodies of those killed still lay where they'd fallen. With the blood soaking the sand, the horrific wounds marring their bodies, and the near-identical rictuses of pain upon their features, Serena couldn't tell foe from friend.

Serena sighed. She was tired of thinking of death. She looked away from the beach and her eyes went to Clifftop. Clouds of smoke bloomed and people shouted, their cries audible all the way to the beach. Some shrieked as if in heart-wrenching pain.

A pit of fear opened in Serena's stomach. She couldn't get anyone on the phone. Something bad had happened up there, and that didn't include that last shell from *Demolition*. She only hoped Selene, William, and all those she loved had somehow survived the violence. She closed her eyes. *Let them live*, she silently prayed.

Diana Mangold approached. Dried vomit crusted her chin. Most of the magi had retched after the brief battle on the beach. Until today, none of them had ever killed another person, and Serena figured that today's events would spawn nightmares that they would have to live with for years to come, maybe the rest of their lives. As Serena reckoned matters, it was as it should be. Good people *should* grieve over something as horrible as killing.

Then why don't I feel anything more? She had actually known the mahavans she'd killed. She'd grown up with some of them and been taught by others.

Diana addressed Jessira. "What should we do with all the bodies?"

Jessira had a large bandage wrapped around her forehead and seemed to be holding herself upright by sheer force of will. She closed her lids for a moment, possibly reaching for a last vestige of strength. She exhaled softly and opened her eyes. "Gather the mahavans. When we can, we'll build them a floating pyre and set them out on the water. It's the Sinskrill way."

Serena nodded in agreement. She would have hated to see the magi disrespect, or worse, desecrate, the mahavan corpses. Showing them respect was better, more humane and civilized.

"What about our own?" Diana asked.

"We'll carry our own up the Main Stairs," Jessira said. She swayed, and Serena reached out to steady her. Jessira had stumbled a few times now, a surprisingly ungainly movement for such a graceful woman.

"I think you should let us carry you, too," Serena said.

Jessira smiled wryly. "Please don't tell Rukh what happened here," she said. "He'll think I rushed into danger like *he* always does."

"Don't you think he already knows?" Serena asked.

Jessira blinked in confusion.

"That weird way you two have of always knowing what the other one is thinking."

Jessira grimaced. "I forgot about that," she muttered. "Sometimes it's a blessing, and other times it's an annoyance."

Serena forced a smile. "Well, Rukh won't hear anything from me."

"Too late for secrets," Jessira said with a yawn. "Shon's up there, too. He's probably already told them everything."

Serena's curiosity awoke. "Shon's your Kesarin, right? You told us about him."

Jessira nodded and gestured vaguely toward Clifftop. "He and Aia are with Rukh." Her words slurred, and she slumped again.

Serena reached to catch her, struggling to hold her up. *Mercy, Jessira is heavy.* Serena's knees buckled, and her eyes flitted about as she searched for a place to cushion her fall.

Diana stepped in and took the weight. "I'll carry her." She grunted as she took over. "She's a big girl, isn't she?" She glanced about and called to Josh Cormier, one of the cannon crew. "Help me out, would you?"

Serena stepped out from Jessira's limp form. "Thank you."

As Diana and Josh helped Jessira back toward Lilith, Serena eyed her in fresh concern. *Does she have a simple concussion or is it something worse?*

"What now, ma'am?" Diana asked. "What do we do about him?" She gestured to Brandon Thrum.

It took Serena several seconds to realize that Diana was speaking to her, and the notion surprised her. *Who am I to lead anyone?* Then she recalled Jessira's conversation on that long ago bike ride home to Lilith. *"Everyone believes you can lead. You should believe it, too."*

Brandon had survived the battle, choosing to surrender rather than fight to the bitter end. He sat on his knees, ankles and wrists tied and with a lock on his ability to source *lorethasra*. He glared at her.

"We'll leave three of our own to watch him down here," Serena said. "It's probably where he'll be safest. Our people might kill him if we take him to Clifftop." As she considered matters, it was a reasonable fear. Many magi had been killed today, and they might seek vengeance on their tormenters by killing Brandon.

She chose the three to guard the mahavan and turned to Lilith's ruin, the crumbled stairways, the crushed homes, and the bridges with missing spans that gaped like wounds. She tried to imagine her home restored, Lilith made whole, but in this, her imagination failed her. "As for the rest of us, we go up and hope it's not as bad as it looks."

∼

It took an hour for Serena and the others to make the climb to Clifftop. It was a long, hard ascent made worse, not because they carried their dead with them—they left them at the base of the Cliffs with plans to bring them up for a proper funeral pyre later on. Nor was it because they had to support their injured—Jessira roused during the hike up to Clifftop but still needed assistance the rest of the way. It was because so many stairs and bridges had been destroyed. They frequently had to backtrack and find another way.

They reached Clifftop as the sun set, arriving to find a weary and wary group of Irregulars manning Cliff Fire's Main Stairs.

Serena found herself facing a phalanx of spears and aimed arrows. "Please point your weapons toward someone else," she said in annoyance. *We're the ones who destroyed the Sinskrill fleet.*

The Irregulars relaxed when they heard her voice, and Karla Logan, who was apparently in charge, stepped forward and took in their battered, disheveled garb. She addressed Serena. "You look like you had it rough down there." She gestured to some of the Irregulars alongside her, and they took over the injured, leading Diana and the cannon crews away. "We've set up a triage near Linchpin Knoll. It was the only place the mahavans didn't tear up."

"What happened?" Serena asked, glancing about. The area near the Main Stairs held swatches of destruction. Flames leapt from crumbled buildings while ragged holes pockmarked many of the streets. Everywhere people raced about, many carrying the injured or the dead. Serena's stomach lurched at the latter. It was worse than she had feared.

"We got chewed up," Karla said. Her face, normally happy and friendly, held a bitter cast, and her jaw clenched. "Ward's Irregulars held Sita's Song, but the damn mahavans went cross country. They cut behind Ward and hurt us. They had cannons. None of us were looking back until it was too late."

Serena's head slumped. "How many died?"

"Hundreds," Karla said. "We're still figuring it out." Again, her jaw clenched. "If Rukh had held back more of the Irregulars, this wouldn't have happened."

Serena shot the woman an angry glare, not believing she would actually blame Rukh for this disaster. "Rukh did hold back some Irregulars. Fifty of them. The cannon crews. Didn't you say that no one was looking back?"

Karla scowled. "Sure, but why weren't we defending Sita's Song? Where was Jessira?"

"Killing the Sinskrill fleet," Serena said, "and nearly dying for her trouble. Besides which, remember this. If it wasn't for Rukh and Jessira, the mahavans and unformed would have killed us all." Karla opened her mouth as if to respond but Serena cut her off. She was already tired of this conversation. "Now isn't the time to assign blame. Do you know if William and Selene made it through?"

"William and Jake did," Karla said. "So did Mr. Zeus and Ms. Sioned." She swallowed. "Afa died. I heard it from Daniella."

Serena swore softly. She'd always liked the old *raha'asra*. He'd been among the first to have faith in her. "Who else?" she asked.

"Too many."

"Selene?"

Karla shrugged helplessly. "I don't know. I can ask around."

"Thank you," Serena said, forcing gratitude into her voice although she remained annoyed at Karla's attitude toward Rukh. "I'll be at the triage center. I'll heal whoever I can."

Karla nodded. "Good luck."

Serena pushed past the other woman and made her way alone to Linchpin Knoll. The destruction intensified the farther north she went. People still worked to control the blazes, weaving Water and Earth to douse the fires. Others worked in bubbles of Air hardened with Earth to protect themselves from the heat as they carefully pushed into fallen buildings and tried to free those who remained trapped within them. Braids of all kinds hissed, rustled, rumbled, and flared as the rescue attempts continued. Their sounds and smells mixed with the smoke and ashes of Lilith's desolation.

Serena might have paused to help, but something called her on. An inexplicable need to reach Linchpin Knoll suffused her thoughts. She bypassed wrecked buildings that had collapsed into the street and rushed past the injured being taken to the triage center.

She reached Linchpin Knoll and entered a scene of madness. People screamed in pain. Others shouted for help. The uninjured rushed about, doing their best to bring relief to the suffering. Healing braids for burns. Bandages and compresses for wounds. Puddles of blood all around. The stench of it overwhelmed the smoke and soot.

Serena wanted to find someone in charge, and she slowly panned across the chaos. Mr. Zeus and Mayor Care seemed to be directing aid the injured. Bar Duba, as well. She saw Rukh working feverishly. He crouched next to a man, his hands lit and glowing with the lightning of his Healing. An instant later, he discharged it, and the man's back arched like a bow. He slowly relaxed, and Rukh settled back, fatigue marring his features.

Serena gazed about, wondering how she could help.

She saw a familiar form then, and her heart eased. *William.* He knelt beside a small form, and the easing in Serena's heart became a tightness. William clutched the figure's hands, and Serena knew who she would find lying in front of him. *Selene.*

Terror filled Serena, and she rushed to William's side. He pulled her into his embrace and held her wordlessly. She held in a cry, but frowned in confusion when she beheld the girl with whom he sat. She didn't know this person.

An instant later, her eyes widened in recognition. It *was* Selene. Her sister, normally dark-skinned, dark-haired, and dark-eyed, now had pale features, reddish-blonde hair, and icy-blue eyes. Selene smiled briefly before slumbering again.

Serena pushed down the fear. "What happened to her?"

William shook his head. "She's been stripped."

EPILOGUE

December 1990

William stepped out of the T-bird, flipped the front seat forward, and helped Selene exit the vehicle. She stepped onto the driveway of Jake's family's home in the Far Beyond and glanced at the surroundings. Her face held an impassive, seemingly bored countenance—a teenager's typical world-weariness—somehow mixed with the flat mask of a drone.

William knew Selene too well. He knew how hard she struggled to control her sorrow. He could see the grief and fear lurking behind her clear, sky-blue eyes.

Serena, Jake, and Elliot disembarked the vehicle as well, and they too, gazed about, likely staring at the Christmas decorations adorning most of the large homes on their large lots. Despite it only being late afternoon, some of the ornaments had already been plugged in and lit. Gray clouds scudded across the sky, and an ill wind carried the scent of a wood fire from the neighbor's fireplace across the street. It was all a world away from Arylyn's warmth and golden sunshine, from

Lilith's normal Christmas displays such as the tree covered with ever-changing lights, chiming bells, and scents to remind a person of home.

This place in the Far Beyond would now be Selene and Elliot's home.

The last shell, the Servitor's parting shot, launched from *Demolition*, hadn't done damage to Lilith's buildings, terraces, and streets. Instead, it had done far worse. Rather than rip apart structures, it had ripped apart people. Most who had stood outside when that final shot had burst had been wise enough to form a barrier of Air between themselves and the falling ash. Otherwise, the losses would have been far more horrific.

But nearly fifty people hadn't been as fortunate. They'd remained unprotected from that ashen snowfall, which had tormented them with hours of fiery agony. When it finally ended they had awakened to a worse pain. Their ability to use or even sense *lorethasra* had been erased. It was more horrific than a normal stripping. The Servitor's final shell had torn away their lives, burned them out, and left them as broken shells of who they had once been. They couldn't stay long on Arylyn. The *nomasras* that might have protected them from the island's *lorasra* didn't work on them. Their only choice was exile.

As soon as they realized the extent of their loss, nine of those affected had leapt to their deaths from Clifftop, twenty-six had taken sedatives from which they never awakened, and another eleven had sailed a boat into the ocean and never came back.

Only Selene and Elliot hadn't taken their lives. They'd been moved off-island to stay in an apartment in Cincinnati with Serena until their situation could be figured out. They couldn't return to Arylyn, but they also needed a place to live and grow up. Jake's parents had agreed to take them in.

An icy wind blew, and Selene clutched her coat tightly about herself. Her pale features scrunched in distaste as she shivered. "I'd forgotten what it was like to be cold." Her voice came out husky, another change. Nevertheless, she remained a budding beauty.

"Do you think they'll put up the Christmas tree on Arylyn this year?" Selene asked.

"I doubt it," William replied.

With all the destruction, no celebrations or displays had been readied. Everyone had more important matters to take care of. If it had only been the buildings leveled, the bridges torn down, and the streets ripped apart, maybe people would have still wanted to celebrate. But with a final tally of over seven hundred dead, a full ten percent of the population, no one much felt like ringing in the holidays. Every family had lost someone dear to them.

Selene shivered again. "I hate being cold."

William smiled at her, hoping to lift her mood. "Daniel hated this weather, too."

Jake sighed. "Let's go on in," he said, his voice as dull as Selene's features.

William wanted to kick himself.

Jake hadn't seen Daniel die, but he had been the one to inform Lien and the Karllsons. He'd been the one who'd held Lien while she cried, and he remained haunted by the images of all the death he'd endured.

They all were. William felt it no less than any of them, but he'd forced himself to ignore the pain in his heart, to drown it under layers of work and commitments. He wanted nothing more than to forget it all, and some days his plan worked. He could pretend nothing was wrong. Other times, though—many times—the nightmares found him, day or night, trapping him in visions of blood and terror. He couldn't unsee Daniel's broken body or put away the horror of killing someone.

Elliot shivered. "Does it ever warm up?" He held himself every bit as bravely as Selene, but William could tell that the changes in his life, left him wounded and hurting every bit as much as Selene. He'd also been marked with a lightening of his skin and hair, but not to the same extent as Selene.

William answered, "In the spring."

"When's that?" Elliot asked.

"About four months from now." William forced another smile. "Not too long, and when it comes, it feels so incredible. You'll want to dance in the street."

"I wish my parents could have come," Elliot said.

"I wish they could have, too," William said, "but you know why."

Elliot's parents couldn't survive in the Far Beyond for longer than a few days, even with *nomasras*. Some *asrasins* were like that.

Serena went to Selene. "I'll visit you all the time," she promised.

"We all will," William said. "Nothing's more important than making sure you're happy." Sinskrill and the mahavans could wait. Lilith needed rebuilding, and so did his heart. He would miss the girl he'd come to think of as a little sister.

Serena embraced Selene. "I love you. I always will."

Jake spoke up from the front porch. "Goodbyes are for tomorrow. Let's go inside."

Serena shot him a questioning look. "What about your parents? They said I'm not allowed . . ."

Jake waved aside her worries. "I called them when we stopped for gas. They'll have to let you see Selene. They can't keep you away from her and Elliot." Jake ruffled Selene's hair. "Isn't that right, Tiny?"

Upon hearing Jake's explanation, William exhaled softly in relief. Selene would have it hard enough with all the changes she had to endure. To be denied her sister's presence in her life would have been a blow too much to endure.

He silently studied Elliot and wondered how the boy would get along. He had his parents, who he could only see rarely. They were his only family. Life for him would be much harder.

William made a mental note to try and get to know the boy better. He couldn't replace Elliot's family, but an extra friend was always a good thing.

Selene studied Jake's house and managed a smile. "At least I'll get to live somewhere nice," she said, obviously pretending to see the bright side of things.

"Somewhere nice," Elliot repeated, his voice wistful, "but not home."

His eyes glistened, and Selene slipped her hand into his. Together, they climbed the steps to the front door.

~

D*emolition* limped into Village White Sun's harbor. A ceiling of mournful clouds hung over the hamlet, and mist clung to the buildings and streets. It blurred the images of the distant, rugged foothills and left them vague in shape and structure. Icicles gathered upon the eaves of the various hovels, hanging like spears, Other than smoke rising from several chimneys, Village White Sun could have been deserted.

Adam stared about, wondering what the drones were doing. *Probably huddling next to warm fires.* They certainly couldn't work outside on such a dismal day.

As if to punctuate his thoughts, an icy wind blew the rain sideways and soaked his face. He grimaced but didn't bother pulling his coat more tightly about himself. He had returned home and home had no room for weakness. Besides, the rain and horrible weather greeting them seemed apropos given the disaster they'd endured on Arylyn.

Two hundred warriors had traveled to Lilith but only twenty returned. It was the same with the unformed. Of the roughly fifty who had made the journey to Arylyn, only three had survived. They'd kept to themselves the entire way home to Sinskrill, remaining in their quarters, but as soon as the island hove into view, their Prime, Jeek Voshkov, had asked for permission to leave. Adam's brother had granted it, and before the final syllable had left Axel's mouth, the unformed had flown north.

Adam's eyes narrowed when he noticed a few hardy individuals waiting for them at the frozen docks, a half-dozen drones and five mahavans. He also noticed the consternation on their faces when *Demolition* tied off and the bare score of mahavans disembarked the ship. Some of the mahavans on shore craned their necks as if questing for the rest of the vessels of their proud fleet or the other warriors who had taken part in the attack on Arylyn.

Adam readied to depart.

"Hold a moment," Axel said.

Adam paused, standing at the railing alongside his brother. He faced Village White Sun, waiting until no one else remained aboard ship. He disregarded the biting wind and stinging rain as he waited for his brother to speak.

Axel clutched his Spear as if it were a lifeline. "We did not strike a mortal blow upon the magi."

Adam had no reply. His brother's statement was an obvious fact, something they'd long-since acknowledged.

"The magi will come for us," Axel continued. "After what we did, they'll have to."

Adam nodded in agreement. He recalled the words of a Japanese admiral in a movie he'd seen in the Far Beyond: *I fear we have only wakened a sleeping giant, and filled him with a terrible resolve.* "If they do, we won't have the numbers to defeat them. Whether they attack by land or anchor line—"

Axel's head jerked up. "How would they attack by anchor line? They don't know the key to open it."

Adam shrugged. "A poor choice of words. I was merely pointing out our weakened state, our inability to defeat them no matter the direction from which they come for us."

Axel eyed him, and Adam sensed his brother's mistrust. It was said that the Servitor could peer into a man's heart. Then again it was also said that the Servitor was undefeatable, and yet twice, possibly thrice depending on how one counted such matters, he had been defeated by the magi.

Still, the Servitor was a power, a fearsome one, and Adam knew better than to allow his traitorous thoughts to reveal themselves on his face. Therefore, rather than anger or scorn he held himself still, wearing a composed, mildly curious expression.

Axel continued to stare at him in suspicion, and his eyes narrowed. "How did the unformed die?"

Adam bit back a sigh of impatience. He'd already explained what had happened on that accursed island many times. Nevertheless, he once again recited what he'd seen of the battle's finale. "William can create powerful lightning. Other than your own, it's more pure than anything I've ever seen. It stabbed out and killed the unformed, all of them, the eight who survived Rukh and his damnable cats."

"When you knew the odds were against you, why didn't you fly straight to *Demolition*? Why go overland?"

Adam had also explained this, but he did so again, careful to keep his tone even and smooth. "The unformed were fatigued. I had them take the form of horses. We had to conserve our strength. I thought to raid Lilith and kill as many magi as possible before rejoining the fleet."

Axel grunted when he finished. "I can understand your thinking. It wasn't right or wrong. A bad choice amongst no good ones." He scowled. "You understand how Shet will respond when we tell him of our failure?"

Adam eyes widened in disbelief. *Tell Shet . . . Why?* "Then tell him nothing," he urged. "Don't use the Spear to travel to Seminal. He's coming to Sinskrill no matter what we say or do. Let him find out what happened then."

Axel wore a strange smile. "No. I can't risk his wrath by simply ignoring him. We can still survive this."

"How?" Adam asked, unable to hold back the challenge in his voice.

Axel chose to disregard his disrespectful tone. "I'll tell him that we killed thousands of magi and only lost several hundred mahavan."

Adam frowned. "He'll still see it is a failure."

"Perhaps," Axel said, "but we'll also tell him that once we realized we couldn't entirely destroy the magi with the resources at our disposal, we decided to wait for his aid. We'll kill them all then."

Adam shook his head. "He'll see through the lie."

"What lie?" Axel countered. "Everything I said is the truth. We *did* strike a great blow."

"What about the magi themselves, then?" Adam asked. "You said they would come for us. How will we stop them with our seventy remaining mahavans, eight hundred drones, and fifty unformed?"

"We leveled their village," Axel said. "According to your report and that of Jeek Voshkov, we killed hundreds of them. By the time the magi recover and come after us, we'll be ready. Within a year, those eight hundred drones will become several hundred mahavans, all of them trained to kill." Axel smiled, chill and pleased. "We'll also have an advantage that the magi will never expect."

Adam frowned in confusion. "What advantage?"

"All of Shet's creatures on this world answer to me," Axel said. "They will obey my summons."

Adam couldn't help it. He gaped. His brother meant to call the monsters of the world to Sinskrill, the necrosed, the unaffiliated unformed, and the few remaining vampires. All of them. *Madness.*

Axel chuckled, obviously misinterpreting Adam's gaping shock for amazement.

"It is a bold move, yes," Axel said, clenching a fist, "but it is also the means by which a Servitor rules. Boldness and power. I'll destroy them all." He gave Adam a sharp nod and strode ashore.

Adam stared after his brother in disbelief, watching him march along Village White Sun's pier. He was no longer sure of Axel's sanity. Bring monsters to Sinskrill? *Lunacy.* They'd overrun the island, kill all the drones or enslave them.

As Adam continued to consider Axel's plan, he found himself wondering if the loss of so many mahavans and unformed had truly been a disaster. Perhaps it had actually been a blessing in disguise. After all, the magi weren't Sinskrill's real enemy. That title belonged to Shet and his monsters, the very monsters that Axel intended to call upon. The mahavans would not survive their coming.

Adam had an uncomfortable awareness that the treasonous thoughts he'd so often considered might no longer suffice. Perhaps he'd have to become a traitor in truth.

ARYLYN

ARYLYN: DRAMATIS PERSONAE

Afa (name means 'storm') Simon: He is originally from French Polynesia and came to Arylyn in 1886 when he was 33. By the time William arrives, age has left him stooped and weak, but he somehow still maintains the lush gardens around his home. He is also the most creative *raha'asra* on Arylyn.

Bar Duba: He is native born and possesses features typical of those types with Mediterranean dark skin and hair. In addition, he is the councilor for Cliff Air and is known to enjoy his food and dislike folk who are long-winded.

Break Foliage: A native born magus who is also born politician. He's a small, weaselly man with a nasally voice who represents Cliff Fire on the Village Council. He and Zane Blood generally vote together, and Rukh can't stand either of them.

Daniel Karllson: Native born, but his parents are not. They are Trace and Magnus Karllson, and he is their only child. When William was discovered, Daniel's parents were asked to help evaluate this potentially powerful *asrasin*. In addition, they wanted Daniel to experience life in the world beyond Arylyn's shores. He was initially hesitant to go. At the time, he had no belief that the Far Beyond could teach him anything. It took Jason Jacobs, his best friend, weeks of hounding to convince him to temporarily leave Arylyn. Then Daniel saw *Star Wars*, and his world changed. He became a proud participant in all things nerdy. He also became a good friend to William Wilde and later on, he fell in love with Lien, who also accompanied the Karllsons to the Far Beyond.

Daniella Logan: Native born, but like her older sister, Karla, she has blue eyes. She doesn't like enrune and tends to be quiet until people get to know her.

Emma Lake: A young native born girl, and one of Selene's earliest friends on Arylyn.

Fiona Applefield: She was originally from England and kidnapped to Sinskrill when her *lorethasra* flowered to life. For decades, she was the only *raha'asra* on the island (other than the Servitor), and consequently, for the past sixty years, she has functioned as a battery for the rest of the mahavans. She is also Serena and Selene's grandmother.

Jake Ridley: He was originally a rich snob, athletic, good-looking, and smart, but life hasn't been kind to him. Growing up, he and William disliked one another. Much of it is because Jake is a bully, and yet he can also be quite charitable and loving, especially to his brother, Johnny. His rivalry and distaste for William continued through high school. However, they have to set aside their differences when they're both kidnapped to Sinskrill. There, the two of them forge a tight bond and become the best of friends. Eventually, Jake escapes to Arylyn where he continues his training as a *raha'asra*. His parents are Steven and Helen Ridley.

Janine Dale: A native born blacksmith.

Jason Jacobs: He was born in New Orleans to Randall and Amelia Jacobs but entered a *saha'asra* at age nine. In that moment, his *lorethasra* came to life. He would have died, but his great-great grandfather, Odysseus Louis Crane III (Mr. Zeus), discovered him. Jason moved to Arylyn, and that was also the last time he saw his parents or the rest of his family. He doesn't speak of why that occurred. He and William are close friends.

(An interesting historical note: Jason' great-grandmother, Layla, was the only daughter of Odysseus and Edith Crane. Layla was half-black and married a white Cuban Hispanic. They had seven children, including a son, Sonny who married Julia, a member of the Cherokee tribe. Sonny and Julia had three sons and one daughter, Amelia—Jason's mother. She married Randall Jacobs, whose family hails from Scotland and Germany.)

Jean-Paul Bernard: A flamboyant, somewhat obnoxious Frenchman. He was once a pot-smoking hippie from Paris, France before emigrating to Arylyn. He loves to surf and taught Serena how to do so. She considers him one of her only friends on Arylyn. He is married to ThuDuc Thu.

Jeff Coats: A farmer murdered by the mahavan, Evelyn Mason, during her scouting mission to Arylyn.

Jimmy Webster: A native born restauranteur. He owns and operates *Jimmy Webster's Restaurant.*

Julius O'Brien: He is originally from Montserrat, British West Indies, but his parents moved to Jamaica when he was young. He was a bit of a black sheep, falling into the Rastafarian life, of which his parents disapproved. However, he eventually pursued civil engineering at Purdue University, but on a trip home to visit family in Jamaica, he came in contact with a *saha'asra* and emigrated to Arylyn. He helps rescue William and Jake from Sinskrill and later takes part in the battle to free Travail and Fiona.

Karla Logan: Native born, but like her younger sister, Daniella, she has blue eyes and wears glasses. Her grandfather was a rector in the

Episcopal Church in the United States. She loves enrune and often plays the sport with Serena and Lien.

Lien Sun: She is originally from China, but as a teenager, she found herself on the wrong side of the Communist Party. She fled and ended up in a *saha'asra* in Beijing. Luckily, Peter Magnus Karllson was visiting the city at the time and saved her by bringing her to Arylyn. She originally stayed with Mr. Zeus for the first three years of her life on Arylyn, but when he moved to the Far Beyond to determine William's eligibility for Arylyn, she moved in with the Karllsons and pretended to be their foreign exchange student. She loves to sing but is a terrible singer. She also prides herself on not being a nerd, although she is one.

Lilian Care: Originally for England, she moved to Arylyn in the 1940s, shortly after the end of WWII. She once worked as a governess and has been Lilith's mayor for the past five years.

Lucas Shaw: He is originally from Charleston, South Carolina and retains the accent of his blue-blood forebears. He emigrated to Arylyn in the 1920s. He is a member of the Village Council and represents Cliff Water.

Maxine Knight: She is originally from a small town in Indiana. She runs *Ms. Maxine's*, the best place for ice cream in all of Arylyn.

Mink Ware: Native to Arylyn. A member of the Ashokan Irregulars and good with cannons.

Odysseus Louis Crane III aka Mr. Zeus: At the time of the events of William Wilde and the Necrosed, he is 134 years old, but he only appears to be in his sixties. He has a a deep, soothing voice, a long white beard, and looks like a wizard. He emigrated to Arylyn in 1878 and married another emigrant to Arylyn, a black woman named Edith Naomi Merle. However, when their only child, Layla, proved to be a normal—a person without *asra*—they took her to the Far Beyond and raised her there. Edith never returned to Arylyn, though. She died somewhere in Mississippi, and Mr. Zeus has never explained how she passed away, although he's let slip that she died at the hands of a necrosed.

A more detailed biography of Mr. Zeus:

Mr. Zeus's great-grandfather, Lucius George Crane, emigrated to the American Colonies in the mid 1700's. He settled in Savannah, a young town in what later became the state of Georgia. Lucius worked as a fisherman, but when the Revolutionary War erupted, Lucius joined the Continental Army. Later, after the war's conclusion, Lucius bought land near Augusta and became a farmer, founding the plantation Aria. By the time Mr. Zeus' father, Odysseus Louis Crane II, inherited the plantation, it had a thousand acres of land and almost 35 slaves.

Decades later, the Civil War broke out, and Mr. Zeus's father joined the Confederate Army, serving in the 6th Regiment, the first unit mustered from the state of Georgia and commanded by a good friend of the family, Colonel Arthur Colquitt, whom his father had met while the two men were studying at Princeton. Mr. Zeus' two brothers, both much older than him, joined the Confederate Army as well, but they were assigned to the 19th Regiment. His eldest brother, Joshua, was killed at Cedar Mountain, while Jeb died at Second Manassas. His father learned that they had expired when the 19th and the 6th both fought at Antietam. He wrote home to Mr. Zeus' mother (Miriam Francis Crane) that his heart was empty. All he had seen was death and suffering, and soon after, he died at the battle of Fredricksburg. Later, General Sherman burned Aria to the ground, leaving Mr. Zeus' family destitute.

After the surrender of the Confederacy, Miriam married Zachary Thomas, a local plantation owner whose entire family had also perished during the war. Mr. Thomas adopted Zeus and his sister, Ruth Esther, and moved the family to California in 1866. He wanted a fresh start and no memories of a way of life that had died in a flood of fire and blood. They moved to Santa Barbara, where Mr. Thomas, took his remaining savings and bought land. He grew oranges and established an orchard. Within 12 years, the family was living prosperously. Mr. Zeus' mother had several more children, a girl, Susan and a boy, James. Ruth Esther married a local lawyer;

the son of a well-to-do family that had been in Santa Barbara for many years.

As for Mr. Zeus, at twenty-six he was sent east to take a tour of Europe, but he never arrived. Instead, he came across a saha'asra in New York City, in a swampy field that would eventually become Central Park. His lorethasra *came alive, and Afa Simon brought him to Arylyn.*

Peter Magnus Karllson (aka Magnus): He is from Sweden and looks like his Viking forebears. When his *lorethasra* came to life, it broke his heart to have to leave his family. He spent years hating what had happened to him, but eventually Trace arrived, and his life changed. He married her within nine months of their meeting, and they have a son, Daniel. When William is discovered, they accompanied Mr. Zeus to Cincinnati in order to expose Daniel to the wider world beyond Arylyn's borders. In addition, Magnus discovered Lien in China and brought her to Arylyn prior to the events of *William Wilde and the Necrosed*.

Rail Forsyth: A scout in the Ashoka Irregulars.

Robert Weeks: A native born blacksmith who helps build Arylyn's cannons.

Seema Choudary: She is a small, quiet Indian woman originally from what became the Krishna District in Andhra Pradesh after the end of the British Raj. Her caste is Kamma, which Rukh and Jessira find interesting. She emigrated to Arylyn in the early 1900s when she was still in her teens and is the councilor for Cliff Earth.

Selene Paradiso: Serena's younger sister, and they share the same parents. She is aware of this shared lineage—the fact that they're true sisters and that the Servitor is their true father. Until escaping to Arylyn, she didn't know about her grandmother, Fiona Applefield. William and Jake have semi-formally adopted her as their little sister.

Serena Paradiso: She was born on Sinskrill to Axel Paradiso and

Cinnamon Bliss. However, at age 11, when she passed her Tempering, she was taken from Cinnamon and given to Axel's wife, Alaina, to become her daughter. She eventually became a bishan, but not until after she saw her birth mother, a woman she loved with all her heart, whipped to death in front of her eyes. This event is the main reason why Serena became so hard and ruthless. The terrible lesson is also why she became a consummate liar.

Sioned O'Sullivan: She is originally from Ireland and came to Arylyn when she was twenty-three. She is a *raha'asra*, and William's and Jake's originally instructor in *Jayenasra*, the Beautiful Art. By the time William arrives on Arylyn, she is over 140 years old.

Sile Troy: Native born to Arylyn. He works as a farmer with a plot of land in Janaki Valley. His wife is Jennifer Troy, a singer and baker, and his grandmother is Sioned O'Sullivan. Sile agrees to take on Serena as an apprentice farmer, acting as her master.

Stacey Cloud: A scout in the Ashokan Irregulars.

ThuDuc Thu: Originally from Saigon, Vietnam, he emigrated to the United States as part of the Vietnamese boat people in 1978. Shortly thereafter, he emigrated to Arylyn. He is married to Jean-Paul Bernard.

Trase Karllson: Born in Ethiopia, and her birth name is Hanan Malak Abdullah ('merciful angel' in Arabic). She was engaged to a family friend at age fifteen, but after she was attacked by her fiancé's older brother, she had to flee, fearing an honor killing. She entered a *saha'asra*, and its glory calmed her pain. She stayed there, preferring to die, but Mr. Zeus saved her. As a result, she has a deep and abiding gratitude for him. On Arylyn, she eventually met Peter Magnus Karllson. They have a son, Daniel.

Travail Fine: He is a young troll, only about 200 years old. He was tricked into coming to Sinskrill by a prior Servitor, and with his fear of open water, he was trapped there. As a result, he has a deep and abiding hatred for Sinskrill and all mahavans. Like all trolls, he is massively built, quiet and solitary, and a Justice. In addition, he was William's and Jake's protector and teacher during their time on Sinskrill, and they love him for his friendship. Fiona Applefield was once his bishan and has always acted in his best interests, although they kept their friendship secret.

Ward Silver: He is a native to Arylyn and master of multiple Elements: Fire, Earth, and Water and Spirit. He is young and is the one who eventually teaches William how to properly braid his Elements.

William Wilde: Born in the mountains of North Carolina but moved to Cincinnati, Ohio when he was ten. As a result, his mountain accent sometimes still comes through. His parents, Kevin and Jane Wilde, were killed by the necrosed, Kohl Obsidian. It was assumed that his brother, Landon, was similarly murdered. These events started William on the long road to becoming an *asrasin*. He is also a *raha'asra*.

Zane Blood: A native-born man who has a large sense of self-worth, much of it undeserved. He is the councilor for Cliff Spirit, and he and Break Foliage are allies on the Village Council.

HISTORY

The island was discovered in 7545 B.C. At the time, it was volcanic and uninhabitable, but in 6257 B.C., a small colony of *asrasins* was eventually established there. Most were followers of Shokan—magavanes--and fleeing the *Nusrael*, the catastrophic war amongst the *asrasins*. At the time, the island was a relative backwater given its active volcanism, tortured landscape of flowing lava and erupting sulfur vents, and its meager *lorasra*. As a result, it was largely ignored during the worldwide war. However, as the battles raged on, some of the *asrasins* who had once scorned the island chose to settle there.

The *Nusrael* eventually settled down to a low-level conflict, and the island was once again largely forgotten as many of its inhabitants rejoined the larger world. However, as the millennia passed, more and more *saha'asras* were slowly bereft of *lorasra*, and Arylyn was found to be one of the few places in the world that could sustain the life of those with *lorethasra*. It was permanently settled in 2039 B.C. with the founding of the village of Lilith. The volcano at the island's heart was put to sleep through the magic of the dwarves, and a *sithe* of elves made the place more pleasant when they planted forests and jungles on the once barren hills and valleys of Arylyn.

In the centuries that followed, with the ongoing failure of all the world's *saha'asras*, the island was conceived as the final home of the magi. A *sithe* of elves and *creche* of dwarves—the descendants of those who had helped tame the island—was allowed to live there as well. The three races built defenses into the heart of their new home since the war with the mahavans never fully ended. The three races remained ever vigilant, and by 533 AD, no other community of magi existed in the world.

Still, the passage of time did not leave Arylyn untouched. The *saha'asra* dwindled, the *lorasra* faded, and the elves and dwarves living there died out. They became nothing more than Memories. The island's magi population shrank as well, and but the time William Wilde enters the island, it has become a shadow of its former self, although its inhabitants don't seem to realize it. Nevertheless, it remains a place of peace, beauty, and grace.

GOVERNMENT

Lilith is governed by an elected council with one councilor representing each of the five Cliffs upon which the village is built. The councilors serve for three years. In addition, the mayor who oversees the government, is chosen in a village-wide election. Lilith, though, basically governs itself without much input from the Village Council. This was actually the intention of Lilith's founders.

The current Village Council:
   Mayor: Lilian Care.
   Cliff Air: Bar Duba
   Cliff Fire: Break Foliage
   Cliff Water: Luke Shaw
   Cliff Earth: Seema Choudary
   Cliff Spirit: Zane Blood

GEOGRAPHY

Charybdis Pass: A narrow gorge that cuts across the northern slopes of Mount Madhava. It branches off the Jaipurana Pass and rejoins the Riven Road far to the south.

Chimera Seed: A blocky bridge that connects Cliff Spirit with Cliff Water. Carved into the posts of the bridge are figures of fantastical creatures, who Rukh and Jessira recognize as Chimeras from their home world of Arisa. No one knows how such carvings came to be.

Elven Tor: A large, rocky hill where the Elven Memory comes to collect those who are on their pilgrimage to examine Arylyn's history.

Guanyin Bridge: A reflective, silvery bridge made of an unknown material. It traverses River Namaste at the base of Cliff Spirit where the river recollects after plunging down Lilith's cataracts.

Jaipurana Pass: A mountain pass skirting the northern shoulders of Mount Madhava. The Scylla leads to it, and Riven Road passes through both passes.

Janaki Valley: The name means 'mother' in Hindi, and it is a mystical valley of fertile fields and lush orchards. It is where the bulk of Lilith's crops are grown, and all magi hold the valley in reverence.

Lakshman Bridge: A stone bridge that traverses River Namaste near the enrune fields. The name may be derived from that of

Rama's brother, Lakshmana, in the ancient Indian epic poem, the *Ramayana*.

Lilith: The only village in Arylyn. It is built upon and along terraces carved into five cliffs that overlook the Pacific Ocean. The five Cliffs are **Cliff Air**, **Cliff Fire**, **Cliff Water**, **Cliff Earth**, and **Cliff Spirit**, and each one is bifurcated by a set of Main Stairs. They also all contain a number of smaller stairs and bridges to connect the various terraces of each Cliff.

    Clifftop: The area atop the Cliffs. It's Lilith's industrial heart.

    The Village Green: The heart of Lilith. It sits at the point where Clifftop eventually runs into the Main Stairs of Cliff Spirit and that portion is shaped like a ship's prow.

Linchpin Knoll: A small hill near Clifftop where all the known anchor lines that connect Arylyn to the rest of the world are located.

Mount Madhava: It is the only true mountain on Arylyn, visible from nearly every vantage point on the island. It had once been an active volcano until the dwarves calmed it. The descendants of those dwarves would go on to live in a set of villages they built within the mountain's broad shoulders.

Riven Road: A rugged road that branches off Sita's Song north of Janaki Valley. From there, it extends past Mount Madhava, through Scylla Pass and Jaipurana Pass, and eventually to Arylyn's northern beaches and watchtowers.

River Namaste: The river that feeds Janaki Valley. The waters collect from the foothills that surround Mount Madhava. From there, the river flows through Janaki Valley and tumbles over the cataracts, spreading like a fine mist throughout Lilith before recollecting at the base of Cliff Spirit. The waters then sweep north through a narrow canyon lined with statues of great figures from Arylyn's past.

Scylla Pass: A mountain pass on the northern slopes of Mount

Madhava. It eventually leads to Jaipurana Pass, and Riven Road passes through it. The Scylla sits south of the Charybdis Pass.

Sita's Song: A long road that runs through Janaki Valley and all the way to the southern base of Mount Madhava.

Village of Meldencreche: It was the last, living dwarven village on Arylyn before the dwarves became a Memory. It sits within the bulk of Mount Madhava and the Dwarven Memory resides there.

MISCELLANEOUS

On Arylyn, those who wish to progress in a profession start out as apprentices. From there, they become journeymen. Finally, they become adepts, or masters.

Enrune: The national game of Arylyn. It utilizes speed, physicality, and skill with *asra*. The latter is actually the most important attribute for success in enrune.

Treatises on Travel—A Translation: A translated book about anchor lines.

The Intervention: A very boring book about the *Nusrael*. William discovers it in the library. The librarian advised him to never open the book's pages, but William didn't listen. He wishes he had.

SINSKRILL

SINSKRILL DRAMATIS PERSONAE

Adam Carpenter(went by the name Adam Paradiso in the Far Beyond): The powerful Secondus to his true brother, Axel. He was also Serena's Isha during her pilgrimage as a bishan in the Far Beyond.

Axel Carpenter: Raised to the status of Servitor over twenty years ago when he successfully maintained his position on the Servitor's Seat. He is the unopposed leader of the mahavans.

Brandon Thrum: Born to two nameless drones. He is a Walker and was once Serena's fiercest supporter when he thought she might become a Village Prime.

Darren Pyre: Fire Prime. An old mahavan. He served as Adam's Isha.

Devon Carpenter: Prime of Village Bliss.

Evelyn Mason: An intense, young Rider with auburn hair that billows about her head when her passions run away with her. She was also once Serena's supporter on Sinskrill, but she now wants to do nothing more than kill Serena, who she believes a traitor.

Gold Imbue: Tender Prime. Like all mahavans, he can be casually cruel.

Hannah Yearn: Captain of the *Deathbringer*. Competent but risk-averse and Brandon replaces her command of *Deathbringer* before the battle at Lilith.

Josiah Danks: The foreman who replaced Justin Finch upon his demotion.

Justin Finch: A Sinskrill foreman who disliked William and Jake enough to fight them. He was broken to the rank of peasant for striking those considered of higher rank than him.

Mary Commons: Justin Finch's fiancé before he was broken to the rank of peasant for fighting William and Jake.

Rail Swift: Rider Prime. He is a known coward who hides during conflict.

Sherlock Carpenter: Prime of Village Paradiso on Sinskrill. He died shortly after lashing Jake.

Thomas White: A Tender occasionally in charge of William and Jake during their time on Sinskrill.

Trina Batter: Walker Prime. She often works with Darren Pyre, the Fire Prime. They have a true son, Aaron Batter, who is a Spirit Master, which is an embarrassment to both of them.

Tristan Winegate: A young Tender who had initially supported Serena in her bid to become a Village Prime. He died at the teeth and claws of a small tribe of unformed.

HISTORY

The island was founded as a refuge for the mahavans in 3659 BC but not permanently settled until 1943 BC. Originally Sinskrill was a barren land with a climate similar to the Faroe Islands. As a result, the first inhabitants had to import much of the fauna and flora. They planted tough grass and heather to hold the soil of the lowlands and forested the hills with lodge pole pines, spruce pines, feltleaf willows, black cottonwoods, green alders, beech, caneloes, and hard log marten. The work might have gone easier with the aide of a *sithe* of elves. However, since mahavans tend to enslave any woven race they encounter, that proved impossible.

Nevertheless, the island flowered. It is known that at one time, tens of thousands of mahavans once called Sinskrill home. This included Amethyst, a smaller island off the coast of Sinskrill. However, a combination of the fading of the world's *lorasra* and the foolish importation of several tribes of unformed led to the devastation of the mahavan population.

By modern times, all of Sinskrill's northern villages have been abandoned, and so, too, was Amethyst. The only remaining places of habitation exist along the island's southern coast. The rest of Sinskrill has been given over to wilderness. In essence, the island has returned to its roots as a rocky place full of rugged mountains. It has once more become a hard place for a hard people, a fact in which the mahavans take great pride.

Of note, there are no rats, mice, frogs, gnats, or mosquitoes on Sinskrill. The early settlers wisely chose against allowing pests onto the island.

GOVERNMENT AND SOCIAL STRUCTURE

The government is fairly simple in that the Servitor is the island's unquestioned sovereign. This unchallenged rule is felt to be ordained through the will of Sinskrill's god, Shet, who supposedly chooses the island's next rule upon the death of the prior Servitor. This happens when a mahavan manages to sit upon the Servitor's Chair for a full minute, thus earning Shet's blessing. Any mahavan can make the attempt but lack of success can be painful and earn the enmity of the new Servitor. As a result, it is generally only the Secondus who tries for the Chair, and from that point on, the newly raised Servitor—regardless of whether they are male or female—is referred to as 'liege', and they take the surname 'Carpenter'.

Of interesting note, Servitors tend not live as long as other mahavans, and no one knows why. Some have speculated that it might be due to the fact that upon their elevation, a newly made Servitor is transformed into both a *thera'asra* and a *raha'asra*, a truth not widely known.

An even less known secret—one known only by Servitors and the Secondus'—is that, in addition to their abilities as *asrasins*, all Servitors and some of the Secondus' have the power of an unformed.

Of course, like all places, Sinskrill contains politics and a wise Servitor plays each faction off another. In this case, the wise Servitor plays each *collegium*—around which mahavan society is structured—and their respective Primes, against one another.

Every mahavan belongs to a single *collegium*, and there is one for each Element. In addition, the various *collegia* have different levels of respect amongst the overall mahavan population.

Those belonging to the Fire Master *collegium* are known as Seres, and they the finest warriors on Sinskrill, with training in unarmed and armed combat. The Air Masters are called Walkers, and they are the Servitor's spies. They are also in a constant conflict with the Seres for dominance in Sinskrill. Those from the Water Master *collegium* are known as Riders. They cleanse the water of impurities, such as heavy metals that seep down from the northern mountains as well as *lorasra* that flows from Shet to Sinskrill. The lowest ranking *collegium* belongs to the Earth Masters, who are known as Tenders. They are essentially farmers.

As for the Primes, they are mahavans of note who are given command over a *collegium* or one of Sinskrill's villages. In this case, Paradiso or Bliss since the Servitor rules Village White Sun directly. The village Primes are also adopted by the Servitor into his/her family and take on the surname 'Carpenter'.

In addition, there is a fifth group of mahavans, Spirit Master, or Spiritualists. However, they are of quite limited power and prestige and are not afforded an independent *collegium*.

*It should be noted that mahavans believe themselves to be superior to all magi, especially when it comes to physical conflict. Recent events have not borne out this viewpoint.

SINSKRILL MISCELLANEOUS

Bishans: Shills who have progressed deep into their training. They are tested a final time at age eighteen after their pilgrimage, and those who pass are made mahavans. However, just as important as completion of the pilgrimage is *how* such an accomplishment was managed. It is the latter that often determines into which *collegium* a newly minted mahavan is accepted.

Demolition: The Servitor's ship.

Drones: This is the status of all children at birth, including those born to mahavan parents. Their status remains unchanged until the age of ten when they are given three attempts to pass a Tempering. Failure on all three occasions leads to stripping where they still have some of their *lorethasra* but can no longer link to *lorasra* in any meaningful fashion.

From that point on, their life path is forged and they work as peasant farmers, largely under the regulation and control of the Tenders.

*All drones take the surname of the village in which they were born. In addition, boys are eventually sent to a different village from their birth.

Lord Shet: The god of Sinskrill. He is also the lord of *raha'asras* and master of all Elements. His compiled wisdom is found in *Shet's Council*. Most *asrasins* believe him to be a myth.

Isha: One who trains a shill or a bishan.

Mahavans: the elite *asrasins* of Sinskrill. It takes years of forging to create one. Once a bishan is accepted as a mahavan, they can exchange their village surname for that of their parents, or even that of the *collegium* into which they were accepted. Most choose family.

Shill: A drone who has passed their Tempering. At age fifteen, shills are retested and those who pass become bishans. They have two chances to pass and failure leads to stripping

THE FAR BEYOND

DRAMATIS PERSONAE IN THE FAR BEYOND

WIZARD BILL'S WANDERING WONDERS

The circus that William, Jason, and Serena join in order to temporarily escape Kohl Obsidian.

Bill Londoner: Portly, co-owner of *Wizard Bill's Wandering Wonders*. He gave William, Jason, and Serena a job when they were on the run from Kohl Obsidian. He's married to Nancy Londoner, and he enjoys his beer.

Dubrovic Family of Tumblers, the: A supposedly famous family of tumblers from Croatia. In reality, all of them are American gymnasts who are unrelated to one another and thrown together by the manic madness of Mr. Bill for his circus.

Elaina Sinith: a beautiful, mysterious woman who claims to be a witch from a village called Sand. This inevitably leads to the joke that Elaina is a 'sand witch'. She worked at *Wizard Bill's Wandering Wonders* as a fortune teller.

Jane Smith: Seamstress at the circus, *Wizard Bill's Wandering Wonders*.

Jimmy Hanson: The cook at *Wizard Bill's Wandering Wonders*. He's not too bright but very loyal to Bill and Nancy.

Luc Dubrovic: A gymnast who is supposedly the head of the famous Dubrovic Family of Tumblers from Croatia. In reality, his name is Stanley Wilson.

Nancy Londoner: The tall, slender co-owner *Wizard Bill's Wandering Wonders*. She was the one who pushed her husband, Bill, to give William, Jason, and Serena a chance to join their circus.

ST. FRANCIS HIGH SCHOOL

The high school that William, Jason, Jake, Daniel, and Lien attended. Serena joins them at the beginning of their senior year.

Principal Alfred Walter: School principal.

Mrs. Gertrude Nelson: Biology teacher. She has a pet boa and William is terrified of the animal.

Jeff Setter: Defensive captain of the St. Francis High School football team.

Mrs. Jennifer Clancy: English teacher. She is later put on bedrest during her pregnancy.

Mrs. Katherine Wilkerson: William and Serena's homeroom teacher. She has a yearly winter sweater contest that she holds right after the Christmas holidays.

Lance Owens: Wide receiver on the high school football team. Jason dusts him in a sprint, which earned the interest of Coach Rasskins.

Mr. Mike Farther: Jason's homeroom teacher.

Father Richard Jameson: Religion teacher who takes them to a church in Over-the-Rhine in downtown Cincinnati.

Mr. Robin Cleating: Substitute English teacher when Mrs. Clancy is put on bedrest.

Vice-Principal Roger Meron: A bulldog of a vice-principal who's more clever than most realize.

Sonya Bowyer: Jake Ridley's longtime girlfriend in high school. William had a crush on her until Serena walked into his life.

Coach Steve Rasskins: Head football coach at St. Francis.

Steven Aldo: Part of Jake's group of friends at St. Francis. As such, he's not expected to show much in the way of friendship toward William, but he subtly does so anyway.

Mr. Thomas Callahan: American History teacher and speaks like it's still the 1950s.

Aia: Once a small kitten who helped kill Kohl Obsidian. A Kesarin. She is bonded to Rukh.

Helen Ridley: Mother to Jake and John Ridley. Married to Steven Ridley.

John Aaron Ridley: Jake's little brother, and he used to go by

'Johnny'. He was born with a neurodegenerative condition that's slowly limited his mobility. Jake loves him fiercely.

Shon: A Kesarin. He is bonded to Jessira.

Steven Ridley: Father to Jake and John Ridley. Married to Helen Ridley.

THE WOVEN

*All beings who are created through the work of *lorethasra* and *lorasra* are collectively known as 'woven'. In addition, most woven have an instinctual understanding of the Elements that *asrasins* lack. However, once a task is identified, it is often the *asrasins* that accomplish the deed. For instance, in the founding of Arylyn, once the dwarves and elves showed what was needed, it was the magi who performed the deeds.

Antalagore the Black: The greatest of all dragons. He betrayed Shet and was eventually killed by Sapient Dormant for his treason.

Dwarves: Mountain dwelling woven. They live in large matrilineal villages, which they name a *creche*. Their ability to bring calm and peace—a skill they call to those around them extends to the dragons, who often share a mountain range with them. Shet has a special hate for dwarves.

Elves: Live in large groups they call *sithes*. Generally smaller than humans but swifter. Arrogance is often an adjective associated with them.

Holders: Assassins meant to kill *asrasins*. Their greatest weapon is the Wildness, an ability to impart energy into their weapons and render them capable of cutting through anything.

Landon Vent: He is the merged consciousness of Landon Wilde, William's older brother, and Pilot Vent, the holder who became Kohl Obsidian.

Necrosed: Monstrous woven created thousands of years ago by Shet at his fortress, Clarity Pain. They were meant to be the antithesis of dwarves, bringing fear rather than calm and death rather than peace. Since holders were assassins meant to kill *asrasins*—specifically mahavans—Shet wished to turn their power on the magavanes. Thus, he captured a large group of holders and tortured them until he created the first necrosed, **Grave Invidious**. Shokan, though, placed a curse upon the necrosed, such that they are in a continual state of decay and rot.

Necrosed can enter long periods of catatonia, measured in decades, before cycling to awareness, and when they do, an insatiable hunger for flesh and *lorethasra* fills them.

The exact number of necrosed is unknown but it is likely small. Nevertheless, all woven and *asrasins* fear the necrosed, and it is believed that no one except a holder can kill one of the undying monsters.

KNOWN NECROSED:

Grave Invidious: The first necrosed and the keeper the Shet's temple, Clarity Pain. He is also the protector of Shet's sword, Undefiled Locus

Kohl Obsidian: He was once a holder named Pilot Vent but was transformed into a necrosed by Sapient Dormant, the Overward of the Necrosed. Kohl would go on to kill William's family, thus setting him on the road to becoming an *asrasin*.

Manifold Fulsom: A large, powerful necrosed.

Sapient Dormant: Overward of the necrosed. Created by Overlord Shet. He was born in Clarity Pain, and one of his first act is to slay the dragon, Antalagore the Black.

Scourskin: Extinct on Earth, but their species still lives on in Seminal. They are a short, blue skinned race of woven with heads that look like catfish. They live off of *therasra* and are among the stupidest and weakest of all woven.

Trolls: Powerful, intelligent woven. They are universally massive and have horned heads. Throughout history, they have served as Justices, possessing an ability to see to the heart of the matter and render a judgment that can never be unknown. It is a power all *asrasins* respect. Of interesting note, they procreate by parthenogenesis.

Unformed: Shape-changing woven. They can take on the form of nearly any animal, regardless of size. They generally live in small tribes of 40-50, which are led by a Prime—either male or female. Each

Prime is supported by a Secondus, a powerful ally who can later become a threat.

They have a first and last name, which is that of their tribe.

However, their surnames frequently change since unformed move about quite often. Their allegiances shift from tribe to tribe, whose territories also tend to rapidly change. As a result, unformed don't bother remembering their lineage. It is unimportant. For unformed, nothing is truly fixed.

One bite from a Prime will transform nearly any woven into an unformed. Only *asrasins*, holders, and necrosed are immune.

KNOWN PRIMES (BOTH IN SINSKRILL):

Jeek Voshkov

Arcus Elder

*An interesting aside:

Most of the dangerous animals on Sinskrill, such as wolves, are actually unformed. In addition, the bears who come over from Amethyst, are also unformed. The unformed were brought to Sinskrill long ago by a Servitor whose name was intentionally forgotten.

DEFINITION OF TERMS

*Brief history of *asrasins*: It is thought that many of the gods and goddesses of the ancient pantheons, such as those from Sumeria, Babylon, Egypt, and China were actually *asrasins* of some sort. Those ancient warlords waged horrific wars of conquest, dominance, and enslavement upon the rest of the world, especially normals, those without *lorethasra*. But when Shokan inspired the magavane servants of the mahavans to overthrow the rule of Overlord Shet, an event known as the *Nusrael*—the Catastrophe—the *asrasin* control of the world began to crumble.

Asra: Magic or more specifically, enchantment.

Asrasin: General name of the ancient magic practitioners. In ancient, *all* children of a single *asrasin* parent became an *asrasin*. In modern times, this certainty has been lost. Nevertheless, there are still several ways to become an *asrasin*. Most commonly, they are born within a *saha'asra* to *asrasin* parents. There are also those who have the potential to become *asrasins* but are born outside *saha'asra*. These individuals generally lead normal, unremarkable lives, although many mention that experience frequent bouts of ennui, as if they are perpetually unfilled. However, if such an individual is exposed to a *saha'asra*, their *lorethasra* stirs to life, and they have to go to a *saha'asra* that contains a sufficient amount of *lorasra* to sustain their life. The only two such places today are Arylyn and Sinskrill.

Braid: A magical spell or creation. Also called a weave.

Clarity Pain: Overlord Shet's temple stronghold and place where he created the necrosed.

Council of Magavane: The *asrasins* who fought to free humanity. They were inspired by Shokan and Sira and later on, became the progenitors of the magi of Arylyn. Interestingly, prior to Shokan's and Sira's arrival, most who called themselves magavanes were servants of the mahavans. An unsubstantiated rumor states that the magavanes also enacted a plan to slowly drain the world's *saha'asras* of power to further erode mahavan dominance.

Five Elements, the:

Fire: crackles and smells like sulfur.

Air: hisses and pulses as it distorts the air.

Earth: rustles like ivy.

Water: possesses a rushing sound, like a breaking wave.

Spirit: White but with flecks of color that are reflective of an *asrasin's* natural moral tendencies.

Far Beyond, the: the world outside the borders of a *saha'asra*.

Great Dying, the: The one hundred and eighty-five year period of time in the Middle Ages when most of the magical races perished. Most historians date the Great Dying to approximately 1209-1394 AD. The cause is unknown but likely due to the ongoing fading of the various *saha'asras* throughout the world.

Jaycik Kornavel: Author of the *Lore of Itihasthas*. He is reputed to have been a magavane and personal friend of Shokan and Sira.

Jayenasra: The Beautiful Art. An ancient word to describe the use of *asra*. The term has fallen out of use.

Ley lines: Arterial or root like systems that extend from primal nodes and spread *lorasra* throughout a *saha'asra*. They can become corroded or corrupted over time and are maintained through the work of adepts in the Elements of Water, Fire, and Spirit. However, proper repair or installations of new ley lines can only be done by a *raha'asra.*

Lorasra: The *asra* contained within a place. It is a phenomenon that *asrasins* use to create their braids and weaves. When it is polluted, it is called *therasra.*

Lore of Itihasthas, the: Author Jaycik Kornavel. A book written sometime between 6200-5000 BC about the *Nusrael* and ancient *asrasins.*

Lorethasra: The *asra* or magic contained within a person. *Lorethasra* rests upon five primeval Elements: Earth, Air, Water, Fire, and most importantly, Spirit. In essence, these are the five Elements of classical Buddhist thought, but what the Buddhists thought of as 'void', *asrasins* recognize as Spirit. All *asrasins* can bend these Elements to their will, although they are usually adept at two or perhaps three of these forces.

Magavane: *Asrasins* who were inspired by Shokan and Sira and came to believe that mundane humanity deserved more than enslavement. They formed the Council of the Magavanes and fought the lords of the Mahavana Axis.

Magus: Name for those *asrasins* from Arylyn. They descend from the magavanes.

Mahavan: The ancient *asrasins* who ruled the Earth. The greatest of them was Shet. In their view, all lesser *asrasins* and woven are fit for nothing but servitude. As for normal humans, those without *lorethasra*, they were meant for nothing more than slavery. The mahavans eventually formed the Mahavana Axis as a counter to the Council of the Magavanes.

Mahavana Axis: The enemy of the magavanes.

Nomasra: Any object imbued with *lorasra.*

Nusrael: "The Catastrophe". The ancient war among the *asrasins*, whose beginning was heralded when Shokan inspired the magavanes to fight for freedom.

Overlord Shet: Set as Egyptians called him. The greatest mahavan of all time and at one point, the acknowledged, unchallenged ruler of the world. For now, he resides on Seminal and is still the god of the mahavans of Sinskrill.

Primal Nodes: *Nomasras* that are repositories of *lorasra*. From a primal node, *lorasra* extends into a *saha'asra* through ley lines, which can variously be likened to an arterial or root system. Primal nodes can only be created by a *raha'asra* or a skilled adept in Spirit.

Raha'asra: A type of *asrasin* who can create *lorasra*. Such an individual is often quite powerful.

Saha'asra: Places of magic.

Seminal: A mythical world where Shet is said to have fled following his defeat at the hands of Shokan and Sira. Little is known about the world except that *lorasra* is said to be unconstrained there. Somehow, it is perpetually made, and the plants and creatures of this world have adapted to it in their own fashion. However, the *lorasra* is so potent that it can be too much for even an *asrasin* to safely use. There are said to be lakes of *lorasra* in Seminal that are deadly to all creatures.

Shokan: The great enemy of Shet. The Lord of the Sword. Husband to Sira, the Lady of Fire.

Sira: The great enemy of Shet. The Lady of Fire. Wife to Shokan, the Lord of the Sword.

Thera'asras: Asrasins who are masters of all Elements. However, their control of Spirit isn't at the same level as a *raha'asra's*.

Theranom: Special *nomasra* vessels specifically designed to contain *therasra*, which would otherwise pollute the environment.

Therasra: *Lorasra* that has become polluted from use, which can then destroy the environment by utterly distorting trees, bushes, plants and even animals and people.

Undefiled Locus: Overlord Shet's sword. The weapon was somehow turned against during his final battle with Shokan and Sira, leading to his defeat. Shet left Undefiled Locus within the heart of Clarity Pain, guarded by Grave Invidious, the greatest of his necrosed, until the god's return.

Woven, the: Magical races created by *asrasins*.

SHEVASRA

The ancient mother tongue of the asrasins. *This is a partial list of some of the surviving words from that language.*

Asra: Enchantment.

Asrasin: General name of practitioners of *Jayenasra*.

Bishan: Young master. The term has fallen out of favor in Arylyn but is still used in Sinskrill.

Hastha: The past.

Iti: That

Itihasthas: That which has happened.

Isha: Masterful instructor, meant to convey teacher in the ways of life. The term has fallen out of favor on Arylyn, but it is still used in Sinskrill.

Jayen: Beauty made alive.

Lor: Secret. Hidden.

Loreth: Within.

Maga: Servant of greatness.

Maha: One who wields greatness.

Mayna: Someone of interest.

Nome: That which is malleable.

Nusrael: Catastrophe.

Raha'asra: Builder/creator

Rashasra: Most High. God.

Saha'asra: Place of magic.

Sahar: Place.

Shev: To submit.

Shevasra: The language spoken in ancient times. Translated as submission to *asra*.

Shevela: Submission.

Shill: Incompetent person with potential. The term has fallen out of favor on Arylyn, but it is still used in Sinskrill.

Thera: One who wields power.

ABOUT THE AUTHOR

Davis Ashura resides in North Carolina and shares a house with his wonderful wife who somehow overlooked Davis' eccentricities and married him anyway. As proper recompense for her sacrifice, Davis unwittingly turned his wonderful wife into a nerd-girl. To her sad and utter humiliation, she knows exactly what is meant by 'Kronos'. Living with them are their two rambunctious boys, both of whom have at various times helped turn Davis' once lustrous, raven-black hair prematurely white. And of course, there are the obligatory strange, strays cats (all authors have cats—it's required by the union). They are fluffy and black with terribly bad breath. When not working—nay laboring—in the creation of his grand works of fiction, Davis practices medicine, but only when the insurance companies tell him he can. Visit him at www.DavisAshura.com and be appalled by the banality of a writer's life.